PRAISE FOR MARY ROSENBLUM AND THE DRYLANDS:

"THE DRYLANDS is a powerful vision of an all-too-likely future America, compelling and compulsively readable. The writing is supple and vivid, the characters complex and human and achingly real. Rosenblum is one of the best new writers of the nineties."

Gardner Dozois, Editor,
Asimov's Science Fiction

"An exciting and vivid novel by a fine new writer."

Greg Bear

"Far more than a cautionary tale, THE DRYLANDS marks one of the strongest debuts in recent science-fiction history. Clearly the work of a major new talent."

Lucius Shepard

"The kind of book that makes me remember why I love to read sf. Mary Rosenblum is a terrific new writer, and I can't wait to see what she does next."

Joan D. Vinge, Author of
The Snow Queen and *The Summer Queen*

Look for these Del Rey Discoveries . . .
Because something new is always worth the risk!

THE
DRYLANDS

Mary Rosenblum

A Del Rey Book
BALLANTINE BOOKS • NEW YORK

A Del Rey Book
Published by Ballantine Books

Copyright © 1993 by Mary Rosenblum

Library of Congress Catalog Card Number: 92-97250

ISBN 0-345-38038-X

Manufactured in the United States of America

First Edition: April 1993

To Nate and Jake,
who read over my shoulder

I'd like to thank the many people who contributed to this effort: Virginia, John, Michaelene, Gregg, Bill, Jane, Diane, Tony, and Thea, who critiqued this. A special thanks goes to Mike Moscoe for his patient advice on military details.

CHAPTER ONE ☆

The crowd was bigger this afternoon. It grew every day, spreading like a dark cancer across Michigan's dry lakeshore. Waiting. For them. In the lead transport truck, Major Carter Voltaire clutched the side for balance, eyeing the crowd through the view-slit cut into the protective siding. They hated him, that mob. They hated the tired men and women riding with him. Because they were Corps, because they wore uniforms. Cold anger twisted into a knot in Carter's guts. Every day they gathered on the strip of dusty ground between Lakeshore Drive and the sudden dropoff that had been the shore of Lake Michigan once but wasn't anymore—not by five miles or so. When the troop trucks got closer, the fuckers would start throwing stones.

"Heads up." Carter's dust mask blurred the order. "Get ready for rocks." Gray lakebed mud caked their suncloth coveralls, cracking off in ugly scales as they moved. The salt in the dust burned the eyes, burned the lungs. Breathe enough dust out here and your lungs would never be the same, mask or no mask.

Just so those stone-throwing assholes on the lakeshore could drink. Rumor blamed the latest ration reduction on the Corps. Carter's lips tightened. What did it take to get it through their thick skulls that there *wasn't* any more water? Sure it wasn't enough, but there wasn't *enough* water anywhere anymore. At least there was *something* in the damn pipes. After the bastards got done throwing the day's quota of rocks and insults, they could slip back into the damn refugee camp, or hit the welfare taps, and get a nice drink of water. Courtesy of us, Carter thought sullenly. Courtesy of the Corps. Because the Corps had built most of the Rocky Mountain Trench Reservoir and the Great Lakes Canal system. Without the water it brought down from

1

the blessed wetness of the arctic tundra, Michigan would be a lot farther from its old lakeshore than it was.

He could hear them now, not chanting, just growling. Like animals. Carter's teeth snapped together as the truck dropped into a rutted, dried-out sinkhole. "Get ready to hit the deck," he yelled. High sides had been added to the flatbed trucks the Corps used as crew transport. It protected them from the worst of the thrown shit. But it was only medium-weight plastic board, and it wouldn't stop a bullet. Carter touched the Beretta at his hip, reassured by its weight. All officers went armed. An armed guard went out with every crew, carrying one of the new laser-sighted M20s. Carter shaded his eyes, stomach churning.

You were always nervous, coming in. Running the damn gauntlet. His crew braced themselves against the lurch and sway of the truck, watching through the slits or staring at each other, waiting for the rocks. They used to joke about it—toss a little black humor around. No one was joking today. It was getting to all of them. Working conditions were bad enough on the lakebed, and this shift had been hell. They'd slid around in sticky mud—had mired a dozer to the seat in a sinkhole trying to get that purification intake in on schedule. The CO was going to be pissed.

In the five years he'd been posted here, he'd built how many new intakes? Lake Michigan's sullen, scummy beach receded farther every year. On the old lakeshore, a young black man danced out from the edge of the crowd, waving his arms, yelling something; giving them the finger.

Yeah, we get the drift.

The level beams of the setting sun turned the dust haze to gold. Carter shaded his eyes, but the dust had blurred individuals into a dark, faceless mass. It got into your soul, the dust. Ate it away, the way it ate your lungs. The setting sun reflected back from the glass of the Chicago towers, blinding him, making the black panels of the solar arrays stand out like the wings of crouching demons.

"Shit, look at 'em." Lieutenant Garr spat over the side of the truck. He had been responsible for miring the dozer, and he was still touchy. "I kinda wish one of those bastards would try something big." He jerked his head at the corporal with the M20. "Let Murphy blow a few away."

"Cool it, Lieutenant." Carter rubbed a hand over his face, knowing exactly how Garr felt. The Beretta hung like a lead weight on his belt. "We could lose."

"Me, I'd go for grenades." Garr grunted, made as if to spit again and didn't. "Even with bone grafts, Abado's never gonna be happy with what he sees in the mirror."

Corporal Abado had driven the dozer—until he stopped a brick. The protective sides didn't deflect everything, and brick did a lot of damage if it hit in the right place. Like your face.

"If I was doin' it, I'd just shut off all the welfare taps," Garr said harshly. "If they can't pay for it, let 'em die. Who the hell do they think keeps the water running? If it wasn't for us, they'd have died a long time ago. Turn off the fucking water, I say."

"Ease off," Carter snapped. Yeah, he understood, but this kind of talk didn't help morale at all. Hell, how could you help but share Garr's feelings? They hated you—the civilians—and you hated them back. Every time a new water cut came down, the Corps took the blame. Keepers of the water? Yeah, sure. Scapegoat, Carter thought bitterly. Maybe you had to hate *something*, just to stay sane. And here we are. Yahoo. Grab a brick and take your best shot.

The truck slowed. Willy, their driver, had had a lot of practice running brick alley. He took it in slow enough so the trouble-makers had time to get out from under the wheels if they hustled, but fast enough that not too many rocks got over the sides. They could see the faces now; black faces, Hispanic, and white. The cheap masks hid gender and the lakebed dust turned them all the same grayish color. It was as if the drought had done what laws had never quite achieved; it had blurred color and gender lines, blending individuals into one gray, sexless race of thirst and rage.

Carter took a deep breath, a hot bubble of anger swelling in his chest. He was tired of living in a damn cage. He was tired of getting screamed at and ducking rocks. You couldn't wear a uniform off base; you'd get knifed. The bubble of anger was expanding, pressing against his lungs, making it hard to breathe. *We didn't make it stop raining,* he wanted to scream at them.

The first chunk of concrete clanged against the truck's fender and Willy sped up slightly. "Incoming!" Clutching the bed wall, Carter squinted through his window. The other two trucks were right behind, practically on their bumper. More rocks. He ducked as something *whammed* into the plastic board. Almost home. A few dozen meters and they'd be through the gate, safe once more inside the chain-link and razor-wire fence around the Corps base. Safe inside their cage.

Eyes stared at him—holes into a vacuum above public-issue

masks. The masks muffled the shouts, turning them into the ugly unintelligible barking of animals. A bottle arched over the side of the truck and smashed against the wall. Glass fragments and wetness stung the exposed skin of Carter's face and his heart skipped a beat. No smell of gasoline or organics. No feel of a chemical burn. The puddle on the warped floorboards was yellow. Piss? A security detail was opening the gate. "Everyone clear the area immediately," a burly captain bellowed through a loudspeaker. "This area is off-limits to civilians. Clear it immediately. I repeat . . ."

Now the crowd would back off, closing in behind the trucks to chase them through the gates, hooting and howling, throwing the last barrage of stones and garbage. It had turned into a warped dance, almost a ritual . . . The crowd stirred suddenly, bunching into thick knots. The wall of faces and bodies parted and a battered van charged through, raising a plume of dust behind it.

It was heading straight for them.

"What the hell?" someone yelled from behind Carter. "Watch it, Willy!"

He was trying. The truck veered, but it was like an elephant trying to dodge. The right front wheel slammed into another sinkhole with a crash. Bodies went flying, slamming into the walls, bouncing around like so many balls. Carter clutched his view-slit, muscles screaming as the truck tried to shake him loose. The van was almost on them . . . Murphy was down and God knew where his rifle was. No help there . . . The van was aiming for the rear of the cab. Trying to blow the fuel tank? It could be loaded with plastic . . . a kamikaze run . . . Carter grabbed for his Beretta and drew it smoothly, just like on the range. Line up the sights . . . don't miss . . . The truck swerved again, slamming him against the plastic board. Damn, *damn*, he couldn't see the driver . . . sun on the windshield . . . He squinted down the barrel. *Now!* The gun roared, bucking in his hands. He fired again as the windshield dissolved in a glittering shower of glass. Got you, Carter thought, and the anger in his chest blossomed, sweet in his throat. Got you, you fucking bastard, you hating son of a bitch. The van swerved wildly, sideswiping the truck with a groan of crumpling metal. For a moment the two vehicles locked, and Carter looked down, through the smashed windshield, into wide, surprised eyes in a small face, a blue shirt splotched with dark blood. Then the big truck seemed to shake itself free and they were past, roaring for the gate and safety. Behind them, the van rolled slowly over. It exploded with a *whomp* of burning fuel and the dark mob surged forward, screaming, hands reaching for Carter, reaching to tear him apart . . .

"Carter? Hey, Carter."

Carter bolted upright, fighting them off—

"Hey, wake up, it's me. Johnny."

Johnny? The room came suddenly into focus—his bedroom, on the base—not the lakebed. Bedspread, nightstand. Johnny's face bending over him, worried in the pale light that seeped in through the window. "I-I'm awake." Carter ran a shaking hand through his hair. "It's all right."

"Like hell it's all right." The mattress dipped as Johnny sat down. "That was some nightmare from the sound of it. You okay?"

"Yeah." Carter looked at the bedside clock. Six A.M., and just getting light. The Chicago riot was weeks over. No trace of the gutted van remained. The burned-out rubble of the camps and the looted stores had been bulldozed into trucks and dumped out on the lakebed. The unclaimed bodies—so damn many bodies—had been cremated.

A kid. Carter shoved his hands under the blanket so that Johnny wouldn't notice they were shaking. *I shot a kid.* He'd looked ten, maybe twelve. It had felt so *good* to pull that trigger.

He remembered that feeling. He had felt the same way when he'd gone for old man Warrington, all those years ago. He had wanted to kill the old bastard—truly meant to end his life right there, and never mind what he'd told Johnny's father or the judge.

He had never expected to feel that way again. But he had. He'd *wanted* to kill that kid. No. Carter closed his eyes briefly. Not the kid. He'd wanted to kill the driver of the van—because he stood for all the bastards who threw rocks, and spit, and called you filthy names just because you wore a Corps insignia and a uniform.

And that driver had been a kid.

"It was just a bad dream," he said out loud.

"Yeah, I guess. Carter, what's bugging you?" Johnny reached for the bedside lamp. "The inquiry? They cleared you, remember? You got a commendation for protecting your crew."

"Yeah. Hey, relax." Carter winced as the fluorescent bulb flickered to life. "I just had a bad dream." He kept his voice light. "Probably from all the beer last night."

"You're shitting me." Johnny's blue eyes narrowed. "Something's eating you. I'm not so wrapped up in Committee business that I can't see. Spill it!''

''Oh, hell, I don't know.'' Carter threw the sheet aside, reluctant, and angry at himself for it. He'd always been able to tell Johnny anything. Even about his mother, and her pills, and old man Warrington. This unexpected reluctance was a sign . . . of what? That he had changed? That the lakebed was changing him? ''I guess it got to me. So many people *died*.'' He avoided Johnny's eyes. ''And I . . . started it.'' The words shook him. *I started it.* He hadn't been able to say that before—not out loud, not even to himself.

Johnny was shaking his head. ''You are a *case*, you know?'' He laughed harshly and clapped Carter on the shoulder. ''You're responsible for the drought, aren't you? I forgot. You stopped the rain, didn't you? You dried up all the farmland and lost all these nice, kind folks their jobs, right? Damn, you are some kind of bastard.''

''Cut it out.'' Carter shrugged, but Johnny's mock-serious teasing helped. ''Okay, so I'm wallowing,'' he said. ''I'll stop.''

''You're not wallowing.'' Johnny's face had gone serious again. ''It looked like Chicago was burning to the ground on the news. I figured all you guys were dead. You didn't start it, and you can't end it, and you know it,'' Johnny said softly. ''The water's running out. People are ending up in the refugee camps, and they're coming unglued. The economy's shot to hell, they've lost everything, and they're going to take it out on *you*. The Corps.'' He stabbed a forefinger in Carter's direction. ''So you get out the guns. You did what you had to do.''

Maybe. Carter prowled across the room to stand in front of the huge north window. It had taken two brigades of the 82nd Airborne, and the 75th Rangers, to deal with Chicago. And they had dealt with it, in spades. The South Side and the camps looked like the aftermath of a war: burned-out buildings, scorched piles of rubble. He looked beyond the vicious thorns of the wire perimeter fence, out to where water shimmered in the lakebed. Scummy, salty, precious water—the dying lake seemed to exert some kind of strange magnetic power. The Chicago refugee camps had been the biggest in the country, as if the lake had attracted all the rootless people for a hundred miles in any direction, had drawn them into the shadow of Chicago's soaring towers and arcologies. It had attracted darkness with them—pulled in the frustration, the despair, and the rage that made people want to lash out, to break something, anything.

"Funny, how we both ended up serving water." Carter kept his eyes on that distant shimmer. "Priests of the new religion?" His voice was sour.

"Speak for yourself." Johnny grimaced as he buttoned his shirt. "I'm divorced, *not* celibate. Just ask Amber. I think my ex is keeping count."

"You know what I mean."

"If you mean water is power, you're a tad slow figuring that one out." Johnny heaved a theatrical sigh. "You know, you're not much fun, Lieutenant Colonel Voltaire. I came here to celebrate your promotion and transfer, and you're not doing a very good job of celebrating. You've got a hangover." He picked up Carter's robe from the end of the bed and tossed it at him. "Go take a hot shower and let's get some breakfast. That's an order." Johnny yawned and stretched. "As a member of the Water Policy Committee, I'm your boss, remember? Hell, I'm a *god*. Hop to it."

"Yes, sir." Carter gave him a mock salute and went into the bathroom.

Johnny was almost right—about his being a god. This had been a fancy hotel once, and the officers had their own showers. Carter shivered as he stepped under the feeble spray of tepid water. Too early for the solar panels to have warmed up the tanks. Yeah, Water Policy decided who got the water, and how much. But it was up to the Corps to get it there, keep it running, and defend it. In the old days, the Corps had been a bunch of engineers. They had built levees and designed dams, and were mostly civilian employees. Carter wondered if any of them had ever gone armed. Probably not. He banged the soap into its tray and turned the spray back on to rinse off the lather.

It had taken presidential emergency powers to condemn private water rights in the first place, and *that* much had nearly triggered a revolution. Afterward, no one could agree on who should administer the water, so . . . they had redefined the Corps. Water Policy might not be a bunch of gods, but they answered only to God, and the Corps answered only to Water Policy. Which made Johnny a member of the most powerful body politic in the United States. No, that was no surprise at all—not if you knew Johnny. A few people made the mistake of not taking him seriously, writing him off as nothing more than a rich man's spoiled son. That was a serious mistake. When

Johnny wanted something, he didn't kid around. It was no accident that he was the youngest member of Water Policy. When they were kids, Johnny had said he was going to be president. When he got older, he'd realized that Water Policy had more power.

And he'd done it, young as he was.

Shaking his head, Carter hit the dryer and raised his arms to let the stream of warm air evaporate the moisture from his skin. Beneath his feet, the last of the water gurgled into the recycle filter for tomorrow's shower—you tried not to think about that too much. "So you make the decisions and everyone gets pissed at *us*," he said in the direction of the other room. He reached for his uniform coverall as he stepped out of the shower. "Want to explain that to me?"

"You turn off the taps, not us." Johnny stuck his head through the doorway and grinned. "We keep our hands clean. What's the beef? Somebody tell you life was fair, or something?"

"I'm just griping." Carter sighed, haunted by that damn dream. The Corps could call in whatever force was deemed necessary to maintain and protect waterflow; regular Army, Marines, the Air Force if they wanted it. "We could probably nuke Washington," Carter said. "If we really needed to."

"Only if we told you to do it."

Johnny sounded like he thought he was kidding. Carter sealed the front of his coverall. "We've walked all over the Constitution and the Bill of Rights," he said bitterly. "You know, it bothers me sometimes. It bothers me a lot, but the numbers work, Johnny. We *make* them work." If he had said this to the mob on the lakeshore, would any of them have listened? He shook his head, still damp with recycled, reused water. "Hell, all I want is to get the job done and to keep my people from getting hurt while we do it."

"Which you will, of course, do with flying colors," Johnny said softly. "You're just the type of officer the Army loves, Carter."

A hint of needling in Johnny's voice? Carter looked up, but Johnny was smiling, his expression casual. "I don't know about that," Carter said slowly. "But I'll do my best. This transfer was a surprise. It's not the normal rotation." He shrugged. "I've heard that the Columbia Riverbed has its own share of troubles."

"Hey, it's not bad out there." Johnny slapped him lightly on the back. "That's my district, remember? The locals around The

Dalles are mostly soaker-hose farmers. You get tough with them, and they'll fall into line.'' He grinned. ''Of course, I'll have to keep a close eye on you.''

''It's a long way from San Francisco.''

''Hey, we're supposed to be mobile. Besides, I can do what I damn well please.'' Johnny squinted into the mirror, running a hand over his carefully cut sandy hair. ''How can anyone with your black hair burn and peel like you do?''

''Wrong genes, I guess.'' Carter shrugged. ''All the melanin ended up in the hair and not the skin. Let's go get breakfast.'' He ushered Johnny out into the hall.

The original carpeting had been left in place when the building had been renovated as a Corps base. Its rich magenta pile was worn in the middle, faded to a dull red. Along the edges, however, the rich color glowed, clashing with the drab pastel yellow that had been used on the walls. Some Army shrink had probably decided pale yellow was an uplifting color. Carter thumbed the elevator button. It was working this morning. The elevator was a privilege of rank—when it worked. Even with the solar arrays, you didn't waste power. The car dropped fast enough to leave Carter's stomach somewhere behind.

He *had* drunk a little too much beer last night. It had been awhile since he and Johnny had hung out together. Oh, they'd talked on the phone, or exchanged letters. But they hadn't really spent any time together, not for a lot of years now. Then, all of a sudden, Johnny had showed up—stranded by some canceled meeting and the iffy airline schedules—and they'd had a long weekend to catch up.

It hadn't been the same.

Which wasn't too unexpected, considering that they'd been pursuing their own lives for the past several years. But somehow . . . it *had* been unexpected. And uncomfortable. Something had changed between them, and Carter wasn't sure what it was, or when it had happened. So he had drunk more beer than he should have, to hide from it. Carter swallowed a sigh as the doors whispered open. Maybe he'd get to see more of Johnny out in Oregon. Maybe they could recover whatever it was they had lost. He felt bad about that change, as if it were his fault. ''You were pissed at me,'' he said as they stepped out into the old hotel lobby. He hadn't been able to say this last night. Or maybe Johnny hadn't wanted to hear it. ''You were pretty upset when I wouldn't quit the Corps and come work for you and

Water Policy," he went on. "I never understood why you were angry."

"Didn't you?" Johnny paused in the middle of the lobby, ignoring a trio of privates who saluted Carter and hurried past. "I needed you," he said in a low voice. "I was a compromise appointee, and I know it, Carter. I was Trevor Seldon's bright young son, the hotshot rising-star economist, picked to satisfy the young movers and shakers with all the money. I'm not too popular on the Committee. If I fuck up, I'm screwed. You always kept me out of trouble, when we were kids." His eyes held Carter's, gray and flat as a cloudy sky. "You were always right there, behind me. I can trust my back to you. I needed someone behind me that I could trust."

"I didn't exactly back you up when we were kids," Carter said. This sudden change in tone made him uncomfortable. "You mostly dragged me along kicking and screaming. I was always scared shitless we'd get busted."

"Maybe that's why I needed you." Johnny looked away. "You kept me from fucking up too badly. It was Dad's money that got me off when I got in trouble—and I don't have that to fall back on anymore."

"You never fuck up. I do that." In spades. And it had been Johnny's money and his dad that had saved Carter's ass, too. Maybe it *had* been him who hadn't wanted to bring this up last night. "I'm sorry," he said awkwardly. "I didn't understand . . . what was going on with you. I don't think I'd be much help working for you. I'm not the political type."

"Hell, let's drop it. It's water under the bridge." Johnny shrugged and gave him a crooked smile. "I'm where I want to be, and you're happy with your Corps."

Yeah, maybe. Carter looked away. And maybe it wasn't all under the bridge. Johnny acted as if Carter had let him down— that much came through. And I didn't *know*, Carter thought. I didn't know what he was asking. He still wasn't sure he did. A captain with MP insignia was walking toward them across the lobby. Security. Carter returned his salute irritably. "What's up, Captain?"

"Were you planning on going outside, sir?" The captain nodded at the gasketed revolving door that led out into the main compound.

"No. We're on our way to breakfast."

"Fine, sir." The man nodded. "Just stay inside, please, until we give the all-clear. We got a possible sniper up in the old tower across the drive.''

Not another one. "I thought the city was going to let us drop that thing," Carter growled.

"There's some kind of hangup on the demolition permit." The captain's thick blond brows drew into a single line above his scowl.

"What's up?" Johnny was looking from the captain to Carter.

"Snipers." Carter jerked his head. "You get a clear shot into the compound from that old office building across Lakeshore. We've been trying to get permission to tear it down, but the city's dragging its feet. I think the mayor's son-in-law owns it. Anyone hurt?" he asked the captain.

"Negative, sir." The man shook his head. "No shots, just a report of movement. We've got a sweep team over there now."

It hadn't ended, the rage that had erupted into the riot. It had simply gone underground, smoldering like a fire beneath the surface. No mob along Lakeshore anymore. Now they were dealing with snipers and homemade bombs. You checked with the sentries before you walked out into the compound, and you didn't stand too close to your window after dark. Every piece of equipment on the lakebed required an armed guard at night. "I'll be glad to get out of here," Carter said softly.

A small commotion erupted behind them. Carter turned. Medics were pushing a stretcher down the hallway that led from the underground parking, moving fast. A uniformed figure lay on it, an IV bag swinging from the pole. Carter hurried over, recognizing the major who trailed the medics. It was Renkin, who had taken over his crew.

"Someone planted a bomb." Major Renkin's lips were pale and there was a smear of blood on his cheek. "They got in past the guard last night. It was wired to the number-two dozer."

It was Lieutenant Garr on the stretcher. His face looked white beneath his tan, and the front of his uniform was soaked with blood. "What about Rogers?" Carter asked softly. She drove number two. He swallowed and looked away from Renkin's headshake. "Didn't you check out the equipment?" His voice came out husky, harsh. "Didn't you have them *look*?"

"Hell, yes, of course I did." Renkin's face darkened. "My God, we've got a guard posted twenty-four hours a day. He's up for court-martial, as far as I'm concerned." Renkin slapped salty lakebed dust from his coverall. "He must have been asleep. He let that bastard walk right past him."

Renkin didn't like to waste time running equipment checks. He was too worried about maintaining his unit efficiency record. And it took a lot of time to check every piece of equipment for sabotage. It slowed you down, if you were thorough. Rogers was always in too much of a hurry. Carter had had to lean on her before about her equipment checks.

"Don't look at me like that, Voltaire." Renkin was breathing hard. "You wouldn't have done any better. You think that promotion means something, don't you? You're a little display for the media, because the media thought we came down too heavy on these animals. So the Corps promotes a few extra people— just to show that we're pleased with ourselves—that we didn't do anything we're ashamed of. And you get tapped, *Lieutenant Colonel* Voltaire. But I'm no floor show. I'm still out there in the dust, so don't give me shit, you got it?" He stomped away.

"Whoa." Johnny came up behind Carter and whistled softly. "What's eating him?"

"It was his fault," Carter said flatly. He looked down the hall, but the medics had disappeared into the infirmary. Garr had looked bad.

Wheels creaked, and another stretcher followed the first. The team pushing it wasn't hurrying. Carter looked away from the covered form, throat tightening. Rogers? He smelled burned flesh and his stomach twisted. She talked to that damn dozer as if it were alive, and she could make it dance. She never mired it, no matter what kind of shit she got sent into.

If he'd been out there this morning, would this have happened?

"Hey, it's not *your* fault." Johnny touched his shoulder. "That jerk was in charge, not you."

"He was right, you know. About my promotion." Carter watched the second stretcher follow the first down the hall. "It was a media message."

"Christ." Johnny snorted explosively. "That still doesn't make it your fault. Cut yourself some slack, Carter. You aren't responsible for the entire world. I hate to break the news to you."

"Excuse me, sir." The captain was back. "It's all clear. You can go out any time."

"Good." Johnny nodded. "You got the guy, huh?"

"We got him." The captain saluted Carter, pivoted, and went back to his post at the lobby desk.

We got him. He was dead, whoever he had been. No question

about that. Carter turned away as the stretcher bearing Rogers's body vanished around the corner. There had been a grim tone of satisfaction in the captain's voice, and he felt it, too. Revenge. Who cared whether the guy in the tower had a rifle, or if he was just some battered drifter with the poor sense to camp out there? An eye for an eye . . .

It was in all of them, that cold, deep rage. Carter could feel it, surging through his veins with every beat of his heart, part of his flesh. You could see it in every pair of eyes around you. It's fear, he thought, and felt a small chill. The world was drying up, and they were all scared of dying. So you hit out at anyone, anything. You had to hurt someone, break something, or the fear would eat you alive. They'd started it with the riot—and maybe it wouldn't stop. Killing. No one needed a reason anymore. They'd all go on killing each other forever, because the fear was inside them all. They were like animals caught in a trap, chewing at their own limbs. We've let the genie out of this bottle, he thought bleakly. An ugly one, with the face of death. Maybe there's no way to put it back. Rogers had been what . . . twenty? Something like that. "I've got to go check on Garr," he said to Johnny. "You go ahead and get breakfast. I'll catch up with you."

"Want me to come along?"

"No. Thanks." Carter shrugged off Johnny's hand. "I'm going to be CO at The Dalles," he said softly. "I am not going to let this happen out there."

"You won't," Johnny said, and his eyes glittered. "I have faith in you. You'll do exactly what you need to do."

For a moment, Carter hesitated, a little uneasy, a little taken aback by Johnny's intensity. Then he shrugged and hurried down the hall to the infirmary to find out how badly Garr was hurt. He could ask Johnny what he meant later. It would keep.

CHAPTER TWO ☆

The ride was a bad one. Nita Montoya sat stiff and straight in the seat of the decrepit Winnebago as it groaned around another bend in the road. Twilight was falling, and the air reeked of cheap perfume. A bottle must be leaking somewhere in the jumble of black-market items that filled the rear of the RV. Beside her, clutching the wheel, the man reeked of lust. Rachel squirmed on Nita's lap, fussing, her face screwed up, fists waving.

"Easy, love." She bounced her daughter gently on one knee, watching the dark, bearded driver from the corner of her eye. Andy, he had said his name was. He was a trader, doing the little town markets, selling black-market clothes, electronics, pharmacy-labeled medicines and cosmetics. He had offered her a ride this afternoon and she had accepted, because she was tired, and there was a long way yet to go. He had felt all right then.

"You sure you want to chase after this old man of yours?" His grin turned into a grimace as the old RV tried once more to lumber off the narrow, broken road. "Anyone who'd walk away from a sweet thing like you ain't worth it. I make a pretty good living, doin' the markets. These Dryland hicks can't trade for squat. You wouldn't believe what I can twist 'em out of."

Asshole. "I think I'll get out pretty soon." Nita hugged the fussing Rachel to her chest. "She's going to cry like this for a long time."

"No problem." His smile revealed his yellowed, uneven teeth. "I don't mind kids."

He was lying. A darkness had been building inside him for the last hour—a gathering storm charged with lust and threaded with the red lightning of violence.

14

She felt it. Since she could remember, Nita had felt it all: Mama's pain, Ignacio's anger at the dusty world, and Alberto's terrible resignation. Joy, lust, fear, anger. The world around her shrieked with the noise of humanity. It had driven her into herself as a child, the more frightening because the adults in her life hadn't understood. It wasn't until much later that she had learned why, that she was unique. A freak. *A mutation,* David had said, trying to be kind. *That's how the species evolves.*

Unique was another word for alone.

The Winnebago was slowing. The dark storm inside this man was about to break. Nita sucked in a quick breath, stifled by the stuffy air, struggling with the urge to fling the door open, leap out with her daughter, and run, run, forever, get away . . .

She could die without her pack and her water jugs. Rachel could die. Rachel was screaming now, back arched, feet kicking. "Easy, love. Rachel, it's all right." Feeble words—they didn't touch the fierce brilliance of her daughter's distress. But they covered the motion as she tucked her struggling daughter into the sling she wore across her chest and slid her hand into her pocket. The switchblade clicked open. He was thinking about fucking her, hurting her, his erection a hot ache in his pants. This close to him, she felt it, too, couldn't help but feel it. The RV was edging off the road. Nita swallowed and leaned toward him, her throat dry with his storm. "We're getting out now."

He started to laugh, then flinched as the blade pricked through his shirt. The RV swerved and the muscles in his arms bulged, corded tight with fury. Rachel shrieked. Teeth clenched against the black and crimson deluge of his rage, Nita tried to keep her hand from shaking. I will kill him, she told herself. If he moves. The decision made, her hand steadied. He made a small sound in his throat as she edged the blade deeper, his anger collapsing.

"Stop now and turn off the engine. Keep your hands on the wheel."

He did, and sat very still as she reached behind herself to open the door. He was afraid now, afraid that she would stick the knife into him anyway, hurt him. He could understand hurting, Nita thought, and disgust clenched her belly. She groped behind the seat, awkward with the weight of Rachel in the sling, and swung her pack one-handed out the door. It thudded onto the dusty asphalt, the tied-on water jugs bouncing. Carefully she backed out of the door. "If you come near me, I will kill you," she said between her teeth.

"You fucking bitch." His lips trembled. "I'll get you, you little tramp."

She slammed the door and stepped back, clutching Rachel to her. If he wanted to, he could shoot her. He must have a gun in there and who would know, out here? Who would care? He could run her down with the RV. There were only fields beside the road; neat lines of sugar beets, with nowhere to hide. Stupid! She should have tied him up, locked him in somehow—but his dark violence had battered at her, drowned rational thought in a primitive urge to get away. Nita shoved the now-useless knife into her pocket, slung her pack onto her shoulder, and ran. Behind her, she heard the Winnebago's engine growl and then catch. Rachel hiccoughed and cried as Nita pounded through the drifted dust at the verge of the road.

A house! Preoccupied with escape and emotion, she hadn't noticed it. Old and weathered, sprouting the black wings of solar arrays, it would belong to the beet farmer. It might save her, if this guy was afraid of witnesses. Yes! The Winnebago roared past her on the far side of the road, raising a cloud of dust that stung her eyes and coated her throat. Panting, *safe*, she staggered to a stop.

"Are you all right?" A figure limped out of the deepening dusk, an old man with wispy white hair. "That was Andy Belden's rig, wasn't it? The trader?" He stopped in front of her, weathered and stooped, his worry clouding the darkness. "He's a slimy bastard—gonna get himself hung one of these days. Or shot. Did he . . . hurt you?"

"No. No, he didn't." Nita tried to laugh, but it wanted to turn into a sob. "I just decided to walk."

"It's too dark for walkin'. You come on inside now. My name's Seth." His smile crinkled his face into a thousand folds. "I got an extra bed for you and the baby, and I'd love the company."

His worry was soft against her mind, like gentle winter sun. "Thank you," Nita said, and let her knees begin to tremble. "I would be very pleased to stay."

The house was pleasant inside. There was a kitchen–dining room with a table and cupboards. A shirt hung on the back of a chair and a worn Bible lay on the tabletop, beside a small clutter of odds and ends. He ushered her into a small adjoining living room. It was crowded with upholstered chairs, a table, a china cupboard, and a sideboard of dark wood. Curtains hung at the window, striped with darker fabric at the edges where the sun hadn't bleached out the blue-flowered print.

"You sit," Seth told her. "Stew's almost done. I'll bring you a glass of water."

Nita sat down gratefully in one of the oversized chairs. Rachel was hungry, groping at her. She looked around the small room as she lifted her shirt and tucked her daughter's small warmth against her. It was neat and very clean, but it had an unused feel to it, as if Seth didn't come in here very often. The glass shelves in the corner cupboard were filled with small china animals: dogs, horses, ducks, even a white goat with curly horns and a golden bell around its neck. A memorial, she thought. They had belonged to the woman who must have lived here once. Her picture stood on a shelf. It had to be her—there was a respectful space around it that made it the focus of this clean, unused room. Nita studied her as Rachel nursed. She had a wide smile, but there was a subtle sadness to her eyes. In the picture she was young, with only a few gray hairs in her dark curls.

"Here we are." Seth appeared in the doorway, a tray in his hands. A blue ceramic pitcher stood on the tray, flanked by two matched glasses. "I thought we'd do it formal." He set the tray down on the table. "How's the young one?"

"She's fine." Nita watched him pour a silver stream of water into the glass, her throat tightening. You were always thirsty out here in the Drylands. You put it away in the back of your mind, ignored it, until someone offered you a glass of water. And then, suddenly, you were dying of thirst. She picked up the glass, forcing herself to drink slowly. It tasted so sweet, water. No, not really sweet—honey was sweet. Maybe it was *life* that she tasted. That's what water was. "Thank you," Nita said. "For the water, and for letting us stay."

"Like I said. I get lonely. Leah was always proud of this room." He gave the picture a quick smile, as if she were listening to him. "I don't use it much, and that would make her sad. She'd be pleased to see me use the pitcher, too. I gave that to her for our twentieth wedding anniversary. Got it in Portland."

"It's lovely," Nita said. His grief was new and sharp, but the love beneath it had a timeless feel to it. Nita felt the last of her tension draining away, leaving her tired. Secure.

Seth was watching her over the rim of his glass, legs crossed, eyes sharp and dry as the land outside. "You on your way somewhere?" He leaned forward to tickle Rachel's belly. "She's kind o' young for wandering around, ain't she?"

Curiosity gleamed through his words. He wanted her story. News was the coin of the Oregon Drylands—personal or general—payment for water and hospitality. Nita stifled a sigh. "We're on our way to The Dalles." She settled the sleepy Rachel more comfortably on her lap. "David—my husband—heard of a job there," she said reluctantly.

"The Dalles, huh? What kind of job?" Seth leaned forward to refill their glasses.

"Working for the Corps. Pipeline work."

"Yeah?" His sparse white eyebrows rose. "I heard there's trouble up that way. Trouble about the Pipe. Hope he got his job. Where you from, anyway?"

"The Willamette Valley, west of Salem." Nita stirred uneasily. She knew the questions that were coming—knew them too well. She didn't want to hear them from this man's lips, but Rachel had fallen asleep, and her sleeping weight pinned Nita to the chair.

"All the way from the Valley? That's some hike." Seth whistled. "How come you got stuck on your own? Seems like this David of yours'd be worried sick if he knew. There's not a whole lot o' law outside the big towns like The Dalles and La Grande. Lot can happen out here."

He was referring to Andy and his stinking RV. Nita's lips tightened. "I haven't heard from David." She said the words because they had to be said out loud, had to be faced every morning with the silent, rising sun. "I couldn't go when he got the word about the job. Rachel was too little, and it was honeyflow season. We were bee-hunters," she said. "We'd have missed the harvest if we'd both left. So I stayed until it was over."

He was supposed to have sent word when he got settled. He had planned to come back for her, if he could. For four months, she had waited. Nita stroked Rachel's sleeping face, listening to the murmur of her daughter's dreams. "We hunted bees way up in the coast range," she said, and heard the defensiveness in her tone. "Messages get lost all the time."

He heard it, too, and his sympathy was like the soft hum of bees on the still air. "Yeah, messages do get lost." He picked up the tray and got stiffly to his feet. He didn't tell her that people get lost, too. He didn't have to.

"I'll go dish up the stew," he said, and put out a hand as she started to rise. "You stay put. When I got the table ready, you can put her down on the bed."

Nita blinked back tears as he shuffled out of the room. A lot of dusty miles lay between their tent in the mountains and The Dalles. Andy and his stormy violence wasn't the worst she could meet out here. It was easy to die in this dry land. But it wasn't his death that haunted her dreams. Nita stroked a wisp of hair back from Rachel's face. *She looks like you,* David had said, and he had been afraid. He had always been afraid of her, deep down inside. Ever since he had understood what she was—that she would always know what he felt. *It's all right,* he had told her. *I don't mind.* And part of him didn't. Part of him was happy when she translated the bees' soft song for him, told him how the hive was content or nervous or happy. Part of him liked it that she knew when he needed a touch, or a little private space.

And part of him was afraid.

He wouldn't look into that shadow, wouldn't face it. But it had always been there. After Rachel's birth, it had grown darker. He had been full of a nervous restlessness, like the bees before they swarmed.

She looks like you. He had said it so many times. It was easy to die here. It was easy to walk away, too. You could disappear down the road, vanish into a horizon of dust and sun and never look back. The Drylands ate yesterday. They buried it in dust, dried it up, and blew it away.

"Think you can put the little one down?" Seth stuck his head through the door.

"I think so." Nita scooped Rachel gently into her arms and carried her into the tiny back bedroom. Seth didn't seem to have noticed her tears. Nita laid her sleeping daughter on the bed and wiped her face on her sleeve. "You're not like me," she murmured. "You're normal." *Normal.* The word hurt her. "You can't hear him. He doesn't have to be afraid of you."

Rachel whimpered softly in her sleep—she would look like Nita, yes, and like David, too. "I love you," Nita whispered. She tucked the spread around her daughter and tiptoed out of the room.

Seth had cleared off the table and spread a flowered tablecloth across it. He had set out thick white china and a cut-glass bud vase full of golden grass stems. "You get sloppy living alone," he said as he ladled bean and vegetable stew into a bowl. "I'm glad I got an excuse to set a proper table."

She took the filled bowl with a smile, but something was wrong. There was a stiff uncomfortableness to him that hadn't been there a few minutes ago.

"This is great," she said as she tasted the stew. "You're a wonderful cook."

"Thanks. It's garlic does it. You can't never get too much garlic in a dish." He put the pot back on the small electric ring on the counter and sat down. "You know, if you want to hang around until tomorrow afternoon, I can give you a ride on into Tygh Valley. You could likely find someone heading north on 197, who could get you closer to The Dalles."

He was lying to her. Why? Nita's earlier sense of safety began to leak away. "We're close to 197, then." Nita made her voice light. "I wasn't sure."

"Yeah, you're close." Seth put his spoon down, eyes fixed on his stew, as if a fish had suddenly jumped in the middle of his bowl. "We got a good weekly market there. Folk come in from all around. Few weeks back we had some excitement." He poked fork tines into a thick cube of squash. "Some guy come through doing magic tricks. Cards and stuff, but more than that." He looked up suddenly, frowning. "He made stuff . . . appear. Frogs and butterflies and such. Out of the air, like. It was a gadget, he said. Little black box." He reached for his water glass, took a long swallow. "Good thing for him. Couple of us kind of got him aside, eased him on out of town. He got the message real quick, and beat it."

"What kind of message?"

"That folk around here don't have no sense of humor when it comes to that kind of thing. You know, a lot of weird stuff happens in the Dry." He held his glass up, stared into its crystal depths. "Kids get born strange. Some folks say it's the water, or the dust." He shrugged. "The Reverend, he says it's the devil. Rev says we've killed the land with our wickedness and now its ghost is raising up, looking for vengeance. It's taking over our children, right in the womb, turning 'em evil. You got to stop it 'fore it gets out of hand."

There was something hot and hard running through the softness that she had felt before—a shining thread, like a thin stream of molten metal. It frightened her, that hot thinness. It was aimed at Rachel. He had overheard her in the bedroom. Nita put down her spoon. "You're wrong," she said, and her voice caught in her throat.

For a moment, he looked her in the face, his eyes dry and pitiless as the sky. The hot-metal feel of him burned her so that she clutched the tabletop to keep herself from leaping to her feet. She felt the weight of the knife in her pocket, but it didn't reassure her. Not this time.

Seth looked down suddenly, and the hot glare faded. "I don't know," he said, and his voice was unsteady. "Leah and I, we had three kids. They all died. She said it was the will of the Lord, Leah did. That it was God's way. Maybe, but a little bit of her died with each of 'em." He looked at her, looked away. "I believe in the Rev," he said slowly. "He's a pure man. I believe God speaks through him. When he holds out his hand, the dust storm ceases. But . . . I don't know. The Robinson boy was a good kid—but when he touched someone, they . . . glowed. Like colors in the air—all around. He said you could see sickness that way. Leah tried to stop 'em when they started to throw stones. He got away—the Robinson boy. The Rev said she was a weak vessel, that God would punish her. She died a month later." He picked up his fork again and ate the cube of squash. "It was my fault," he said, and guilt beat in him like a second pulse. "I should've taken her home."

"I'm sorry," Nita whispered. The stew tasted like dust, but she ate it, spoonful at a time, afraid to reject the food, afraid, period.

They had stoned a child. Because he was . . . different.

She helped Seth with the dishes, hiding her fear. He told her that he got up early to soak the beets before it got hot. The scary part of him was watching her, waiting for her to go to bed first. Nita smiled for him and shut the bedroom door tightly behind her. There was no lock, but she jammed the back of a chair beneath the doorknob. *Don't tell people what you can hear.* David had told her that years ago, when he had first understood. *"Different" scares people,* he had said. *Scared people can hurt you.*

Oh, yes. David had known about being scared. Rachel's diaper was wet, and Nita changed it, wrapping the wet one in the plastic bag from her pack. No time to let it dry now. She sat down on the edge of the bed with the switchblade in her hand. Listening.

Part of Seth grieved for that boy, and for his own dead children. But another part of him was forged from that hot, molten ugliness. She heard his footsteps in the hall, soft and careful. Nita held on to her knife, fear a stone in her chest. The doorknob turned gently. The chair creaked a little and skidded an inch or two across the wood floor. Silence. Nita held her breath, hearing only the rush of blood in her ears. She watched the single window, waiting for a face to appear, for the glass to smash in.

Silence.

Perhaps . . . just perhaps, the grieving part of him had coaxed his body to sleep. She didn't dare hope, but . . . perhaps.

Silence.

After a long time, when the house had creaked and groaned itself to sleep, she gathered up her daughter, her pack, and her water jugs. Heart pounding, she climbed through the window. No Seth. The moon was up high enough that she could see to walk along the cracked asphalt of the county road. She fished the map from her pocket and spread its creased folds out on the moonlit asphalt. Yes. If she took this road, it would bring her to 197 well north of Tygh Valley. Nita refolded the map, slid her arms through the pack straps, and tucked Rachel into her sling. An owl screeched thinly as she started walking, and fear lurked in the darkness behind her, nipping at her heels.

CHAPTER THREE ☆

Carter fought the wheel of the little car he'd drawn from the Corps' Portland motor pool. It was a new model, and light enough that the wind kept pushing it off the highway. The Columbia gorge would make a great wind tunnel, he thought sourly. Sheer vertical walls of black rock rose on his right. The dry Columbia bed yawned on his left, like an ugly wound in the earth's crust. Wind towers stood in silver ranks, their long blades turning briskly, scouring energy from the wind. Those were Corps towers. They powered the pumps that pushed water through the Pipeline. You couldn't see the Pipeline itself—the six immense pipes were buried like veins beneath the riverbed. Another truck convoy thundered past him on the left—triple trailer rigs doing about eighty—and the car tried once more for the ditch.

A ramp was coming up. Arms aching, sweating in spite of the laboring air-conditioning, Carter fought the car off the highway. REST AREA, a blue highway sign proclaimed. The ramp curved gently toward the towering cliff wall, ending in a small roadside parking lot. It wasn't much of a rest area, but at least the wind wasn't so bad down here. Carter slammed the car door, his sweat springing out in earnest in the dry heat. The asphalt lot was empty except for a big semi rig parked at the far end and a lanky man with a tail of blond hair sitting in the narrow strip of shade cast by a bank of vending machines. Carter headed for one of the three pay-toilet units beside the machines, very conscious of his uniform.

He had a new CO to meet and no time to change, or he would have been in civvies. You didn't wear a uniform off base, not if you could help it. Even out here, civilians tended to do antisocial things—like spit on you. The blond guy didn't seem to notice,

23

or he didn't care, anyway. Carter pulled the door shut after himself. The plastic box was an oven in spite of its reflective coating,
and Carter held his breath as he unzipped his fly. These new
composters were supposed to be odorless, but something was
wrong with this one.

Yeah, this was about typical for the week. He had come in
three days ago, expecting to meet up with Johnny. But Johnny
wasn't here—he had been called back down to the regional office
in San Francisco for some kind of emergency meeting. So he
had kicked around Portland on his own, seeing what sights there
were to see. The refugee camp didn't do much for the atmo-
sphere. It reminded him too much of the big one outside of
Chicago.

He glowered at the vending machine. It offered water, pop,
and a few snack items. Carter stuck his debit card into the slot.
A plastic pack of water thunked into the tray at the bottom of
the machine, blood-warm. Grimacing, he poked the attached
straw through the plastic and took a swallow.

Beyond the parking lot, the sheer cliffwall of the gorge towered over the ruins of a wooden building. The stone was grooved
with the traces of a long-dead waterfall. This must have been a
park once. Someone had tacked a laminated postcard to the
splintered remains of an old signpost. The colors had bleached
to yellows and greens in the sun, but you could just make out a
waterfall. Carter squinted at it. This waterfall? He lifted the card
carefully. MULTNOMAH FALLS. The brittle cardboard cracked as
he read the upside-down caption and the card came away in his
hand. Carter stared at it, not sure what to do with it. *Someone*
had put it there—as a reminder? He finally managed to wedge
it under a thick splinter of wood. Johnny would laugh at him,
Carter thought, and felt a new stab of disappointment.

He had looked forward to a few days with Johnny. Golden-
boy Johnny. Carter shook his head, smiling, remembering.
Johnny had been king of the private school they'd both attended,
and Carter—forever on the outside—had watched him operate
with a resigned envy. It had turned his universe upside down
when this star picked him to hang out with. At eleven, he already
knew how the world worked. It didn't work like this, except in
fairy tales. So he'd been wary. Surly. He knew how elaborate
the crueler jokes could get. But it had been for real. Never mind
that his mother was a housekeeper—that everyone knew old man
Warrington paid Carter's tuition because he was screwing his
mother. Johnny had wanted Carter for a friend. He had dragged

Carter with him into every inside clique. *That* had turned the school's closed little universe upside down—which was probably the joke that Johnny had intended in the first place.

But by then they had become real friends. Carter blinked, sighed, found himself staring at the crumpled water pack in his hand. He spiked it into a trash can. There would be other times, now that he was out here on Johnny's turf. Carter started to turn, and froze. In front of his eyes, the cliff face wavered and changed. A silver tail of water fell down that cliff face, exploding into white mist in a rocky basin. Ferns sprouted from the rocks and emerald grass covered the shady ground beneath the trees.

The postcard—this was it—only this was *real*. For the space of three heartbeats, Carter stared at that green vision. Then—it vanished. Only dust and waterworn rock remained, above the dry hollow that had once been a pool. "Mother of God," Carter said out loud. The falls stayed dead and he looked around, half embarrassed by his exclamation. The lot was still empty. The blond man was leaning on the rail that edged the parking lot. He was staring at the falls, ignoring Carter.

Fatigue, Carter told himself. Stress. Better watch the driving. He started for the car, uneasy, more disturbed by his momentary vision than he wanted to admit. He had never hallucinated in his life. And there had been a strange feeling of . . . reality to that brief vision. As if it wasn't a vision at all, as if, for an instant, he had stepped back through time into the green, unbelievable past. He unlocked the car door.

"Hey, soldier? Hang on a minute."

Carter stiffened, turned, saw the blond man limping toward him. He leaned on a stick and his legs looked crooked, as if they didn't bend quite right. He was wearing a faded shirt and worn jeans, and his long, sunbleached hair was tied back into a thin tail. He looked as if he might be about Carter's age—in his thirties, but it was hard to tell. His tanned face had the lined, sundried look of someone who had spent most of his life outside.

"You heading east?" the man asked as he got closer.

"To Bonneville."

"Could I get a ride? I was hitching in the truck, but the guy sleeps afternoons and I'm not sleepy." He gave Carter a crooked grin.

He didn't look like much of a threat. He was a head shorter than Carter, slender and wiry. People hitched a lot. Who could afford a private car with the price of alcofuel these days? A lot of people couldn't afford to pay for any kind of transportation at all. "Sure." Carter reached inside and popped the car's hatchback. "Put your pack and your stick in back. This thing's got as much room as a tuna can."

"Thanks." The stranger stuck out a hand. "My name's Jeremy. Jeremy Barlow. I appreciate the ride."

"I'm going there anyway." Carter returned Jeremy's firm grip. His hands were misshapen, the joints thick and ugly, and he handled his pack clumsily.

"You coming from Portland?" Carter asked as he headed the car back up the ramp and onto the interstate.

"Yeah." Jeremy shrugged. "Looking for a job, but jobs are tight and there are a lot of things I can't do too well." He held his hands up briefly. "Rawlings keeps saying that the depression is over, but I think he's talking for the next election. So, I guess I'm hitting the road again."

"The president has been saying that things are looking up since the last election. The line still seems to work, don't ask me why." Although if Johnny was right about the Alliance breaking up, that might not be enough to get him through the next election. Carter and the car ducked as a single triple-trailer rig roared past. "What do you do? On the road?"

"I'm a magician. I do a few card tricks and stuff." He looked at Carter, a hint of a smile at the corner of his mouth. "Don't run off the road, okay?"

A tiny dragon appeared on the dashboard in front of Carter. Its green scales glittered in the sun and it glared at Carter with ruby eyes. Abruptly it reared back, snorted a tiny tongue of flame, and vanished.

"Good thing you warned me." Carter stared at the spot where the dragon had stood. "How the hell did you do that? Holo projector?"

"Yeah." Jeremy held out a small gray box. It resembled an electronic noteboard except for the lens at one end. "It fools people."

"I'm impressed. That's a damn sophisticated piece of equipment. You're some electronics whiz."

"Not me," Jeremy said a shade too quickly. "I got it from this old guy. *He* was the whiz."

He sounded nervous. Maybe he'd stolen the gadget, or maybe he was afraid Carter would steal it. It would be something to worry about—*someone* had done something pretty marvelous.

"This seems to be my day for visions," Carter said to change the subject. "I was looking at that old waterfall beside the rest area and, for a moment, I could see it like it must have been. Full of water. Green." He shook his head, pierced by unexpected longing. "It was a beautiful world," he said.

"It was." Jeremy was looking at him, his expression enigmatic. "You're not from around here, are you?"

"I just flew in from back east." Carter let his breath out in a sigh. "It was something, seeing the country from the air. The Pipeline feeds tundra water into the Missouri, so the Mississippi drainage isn't too bad. They do a lot of agriculture still. Biomass crops, mostly. But then you cross the Missouri, fly on into Colorado, Wyoming . . . and all of a sudden, it's dead. You look down from the airplane and you see desert."

"The Drylands," Jeremy said softly. "That's where I was born—way out in the eastern part of Oregon. You can live there, but you got to live by the rules. There's only so much water. Out there they take the extra babies, and the ones who aren't perfect, and they leave 'em out somewhere. Out in the dust."

"You're kidding."

"No, I'm not kidding." Jeremy was staring through the windshield, rubbing his crooked hands gently on his thighs. "If you don't do it, maybe your family doesn't make it through next summer. It's another world out there. Sometimes you got to make ugly choices."

Carter looked sideways at this slight man with his crippled hands and bad knees, wondering if he'd been born this way, wondering if someone had made that kind of choice about *him*.

"It makes it worse that you can see the way it used to be," Jeremy said softly. "You catch it out here—a flash of yesterday once in a while." He looked over at Carter, the faint grin quirking the corner of his mouth again. "No, you weren't going crazy."

"Glad to hear it." That vision had been so damn *real*. BONNEVILLE, a green sign proclaimed. NEXT THREE EXITS. "We're here," he said.

The highway curved out and around, and now he could see the dam. Bonneville Dam. It stretched across the dry riverbed like a gray wall, broken by the silver arches of a pumping station. Solar arrays sprouted like wings from the top, aimed at the setting sun. "You want to come to the base?" Carter asked Jeremy. "They might be hiring civilians."

"Maybe later." Jeremy nodded. "It's been awhile since I've

hit the big Bonneville market. I'll do that first. You can drop me at the next exit, if you would. You stationed here?"

"No. I'm . . . on my way to The Dalles." The dam was so *big*. This close, it loomed like a vast cliff. Carter pulled off at the exit ramp and went around to get Jeremy's pack from the hatch. "Come by the base, if you get up there. Maybe you could do some shows for the personnel."

"Maybe I'll do that." Jeremy slung his pack over his shoulder and picked up his stick. "I'll be along. I stick to the highway towns out here."

"I imagine the little rural communities are pretty slim pickings."

"It's not that." For a moment Jeremy's face was grim. "They don't like magic out in the Drylands. Thanks for the lift. Good luck in The Dalles." He raised one crooked hand in a salute and walked down the ramp.

Carter pulled back onto the highway, puzzled. Why didn't they like magic out there? Local traffic cluttered the lanes here in town; pickups and little propane-electrics, converted gas-burners. Below the highway, new silocrete buildings and hap-hazard shacks cluttered the shelving slope of the old riverbed. Solar arrays sprouted from every rooftop and the ubiquitous wind towers lined the riverbed. Up ahead, a ramp exited left, to curve down behind the dam itself. The turreted castle of the Corps gleamed in the level beams of the setting sun. This was it. Carter slid the little car in behind a rickety truck with a goat in the back and turned off onto the ramp. The buildings of the Corps' headquarters huddled on the south side of the Pipe, up against the inner wall of the old dam. Rec or mess halls, apart-ments for enlisted and officers, a playground with a pair of bas-ketball hoops—so normal—but Carter felt a sense of foreboding as the shadow of the dam swallowed him.

He had to slow to a crawl as he zigzagged through the anti-sabotage barriers. The Green Beret on the gate ran his ID through the computer and didn't crack a smile until after Carter's thumb-print had cleared. By then, a corporal had appeared to escort him to General Hastings's office.

Tight security. All security had to be tight these days, but it didn't do anything for Carter's mood as he followed the corporal's brisk pace. Administration was inside the dam itself, in the space that had once been taken up by the huge turbines and generators. Carter's sweaty uniform dried quickly in the cool, conditioned air as he followed his guide through a set of gasketed doors and down a long corridor. He looked up at the pastel yellow ceiling, imagining that vast bulk of concrete squatting above his head. It gave him an uncomfortable twinge of claustrophobia. Uniformed men and women wearing the Corps insignia passed them. They saluted as they hurried by, but Carter caught their quick surmising looks. New kid in town. He wondered what rumors had gone around.

"In here, sir." The corporal opened a door marked GENERAL HASTINGS.

Inside, a cluttered desk, a computer terminal, and two plastic chairs stood on a nondescript magenta carpet. A large framed photograph hung on the wall above the desk. It looked like an old photograph of the dam. White water poured through the spillway and the cliffs of the Columbia Gorge glowed with greenery beneath a gray sky.

"Hard to imagine, isn't it, sir? All that water, running right over our heads?" The corporal grinned.

He couldn't really imagine it, but it didn't help his claustrophia to try. Carter suppressed a shudder as the corporal ushered him into the inner office. "Lieutenant Colonel Carter Voltaire reporting for duty, sir." He saluted, stood at attention.

The thickset man with the square face and general's star didn't even look up from his terminal. Carter waited, listening to his own breathing. Nice welcome. The small office looked as shabby as the corporal's cubby. The carpeting was worn and the furniture looked like refugees from a second-rate school. The Chicago base was luxurious by comparison. A large vid screen covered one entire wall. Pictures stood on Hastings's cluttered desk: a flat photo of a smiling young man in dress greens, holo cubes of a woman holding a baby and a blond boy leaning on the handlebars of a new bike. Carter stared at the man in the dress greens. I know him, he thought, but the name eluded him.

"At ease, Colonel." Hastings looked up at last, extending a stiff hand. "Welcome to the Columbia."

He didn't sound very welcoming. "Thank you, sir." Carter returned the general's strong grip. "My orders, sir."

"I already looked at the electronic copy." Hastings took the hardcopy, tossed it onto his desk, and crossed his arms. "Tell me what you're going to be doing up in The Dalles."

This felt like a test. "My unit is responsible for maintaining the Pipeline in our sector, including the diversion complex where the Klamath Shunt splits off to the south, sir." Carter could feel blood seeping into his face. "I've reviewed the flow reports for the last year, along with maintenance records and the tech manuals for the Pipeline and the Shunt complex. I understand the requirements of the system and the mechanics of its operation, sir." I did my homework, General. Screw you, too.

"I *hope* you understand the mechanics." Hastings's expression didn't thaw. "I hope you also understand the importance of maintaining the Pipeline flow. The Ogalalla aquifer has been pumped out, and the Columbia aquifer will be too low for cost-effective pumping in less than a year. That means the Pipeline *is* the water source for most of two states."

"Yes, sir."

"I wanted someone with more years," Hastings said coldly. "The Dalles isn't the place for an inexperienced CO, no matter how much of a hotshot you were in the riot."

Carter flushed. There had been rumors about the extra promotions after Chicago. And he *had* been deep-selected. Five years in grade was the minimum to make lieutenant colonel. The bare minimum. "My name was added to the promotions list very recently, sir," he said stiffly.

"I didn't ask you, Colonel." Hastings's tone was cold. "I just hope you can handle the situation. Because of the Shunt valves, The Dalles sector is particularly critical to the function of the Pipeline. There has been some local unrest there lately, including acts of sabotage against the Pipe. The integrity of the Pipe must be protected, no matter what the cost. Do you understand me, Colonel?"

"Yes, sir."

"Good." Hastings nodded. "Your predecessor, Colonel Watanabe, was murdered. Did you know that?"

"Yes, sir." Hell, everyone knew it, just like everyone knew who'd fired the first shot in Chicago. "Has anyone been charged yet, sir?"

"No, but we know who was behind it. The same terrorists who are sabotaging the Pipe." Hastings was watching him closely, his blue eyes sharp and wary. "They call themselves the Columbia Coalition. A man named Dan Greely heads it. Watch out for him."

"Yes, sir."

"You can get whatever else you need to know from your second in command, Major Delgado." Hastings waved a dismissive hand. "Sandusky can drive you up there. Report in to me when you're settled."

"Yes, sir." Carter saluted smartly and marched out of the room. Great. This was about as bad a start as you could imagine.

Corporal Sandusky was waiting in the outer office, his expression carefully neutral. "If you'll come with me, sir." He cleared his throat. "I'll drive you to The Dalles."

"Fine." Carter let his breath out in a rush. "I've got a Portland car."

"You can give me the keys." Sandusky held out a hand. "Is your luggage in the car?"

"Just a carryall and a duffel bag." He'd shipped the books and the few items too heavy to carry.

He followed the corporal back outside. It was already getting cold, as the daytime heat radiated away into the dry air. The corporal didn't say much as he transferred Carter's bags into a motor-pool Chevy. It was dark beyond the yellow glare of the base lights. Scattered lights gleamed like a small galaxy across the black gulf of the riverbed. In the old days, the cities had blazed with light. People had squandered it the way they had squandered water—had decorated with it, put up displays of color and dazzle. Not anymore. Electricity cost, and the national power curfew cut all power at 10:00 P.M. local time.

The small galaxy of Bonneville disappeared behind them as Sandusky turned onto the highway and stepped on the gas. "Tell me about Colonel Watanabe." Carter spoke into the humming silence.

"A routine patrol found him by the Pipe. Shot in the head at close range, sir. They figure it was a setup." Carter nodded. "Rumor was that the colonel got too close to the Coalition, sir."

"You think they did it? This Coalition?"

"Who else?" Sandusky shrugged. "They're the movers and shakers around here, and they don't like the Corps much. It's just gotten bad these last few months. A couple of our guys got shot while they were out on patch jobs. Hicks picked 'em off with a thirty-ought-six. Bastards.'Scuse me, sir." Sandusky threw Carter a quick, nervous glance over his shoulder.

"Yeah, they were bastards." Carter looked out the window. Darkness filled the gorge, so thick that it threatened to stifle him. You could feel the high walls on either side of you, holding in the darkness, squeezing it down around you. Violence. Maybe you found it anywhere you found water. Maybe you couldn't separate one from the other anymore. Carter shook himself and took a deep breath of the cool, conditioned air. "What about this Dan Greely person?"

"Don't know much about him, sir," Sandusky said briskly.
"He bosses the Coalition, and I heard he's an ex-con. Guess it
tells you something about the hicks around here—who they pick
to run the show." He snorted. "The general won't let him on
base, so he doesn't bother us."

Being an ex-con didn't necessarily mean much. He'd come
damn close to earning that label himself. Carter struggled against
a growing depression. Hastings wanted to hate his guts and he was
walking into what sounded more and more like another Chicago.

"Sir?" Sandusky whipped the Chevy around another car. "I
heard you were in the Chicago riot. We sure kicked ass, sir."

"Yeah, we kicked ass." Carter stared out into darkness, images forming and re-forming on his retina.

"Those campies are real scum. The hicks are about as bad.
Sometimes I think we ought to just go down the whole damn
riverbed, run the troublemakers out into the Dry." Sandusky
slapped the steering wheel for emphasis. "Let 'em make trouble
out there."

He had felt that way . . . Carter closed his hand slowly, remembering the weight of the gun, the sweet feel of his hatred
as he pulled the trigger. "It wasn't just the camps," he said. It
was as if all the darkness and despair generated by the shriveling, dying land had trickled slowly down to the lakeshore, had
gathered like a dark, ugly oil spill around the feet of the towers.
Until finally a single spark had set it off.

He'd been the spark, no matter what the investigators had
decided. "It was all of us." Carter sat forward, peering at Sandusky's young face in the rearview mirror. "It was the towers
and the base and the camp. We were all ready to start killing
each other. So we did it, and the Corps came out on top, because
we had the guns and the organization. Everyone else was just
out there going crazy. It was hell, and it just happened. Let's
drop it, Corporal."

"Yes, sir."

Sandusky shut up after that. He didn't understand. He probably saw the world in black and white, Carter thought. That was
how you had to look at it, sometimes. Them and Us. Because
you had a job to do, and shades of gray could make it hell.

He must have drowsed for a while, because the next thing he
knew, they were at The Dalles gate. If anything, this one was better
defended than Bonneville. Which said a lot about the situation,
Carter thought sourly. The guards positively gleamed—they'd been
expecting him. Wearily Carter returned the razor-sharp salutes.

He was the Old Man now, and everybody had to show for him. He stifled a yawn as Sandusky finally pulled the car up in front of a residence block. Security lights shed a yellow glow on the apartments. They were ugly boxes, defended from the heat by reflective composite and tinted windows.

Sandusky led him to the front door of the second unit from the end. A gusty wind pushed dust and trash down the concrete street, whirled grit into Carter's face. Beyond the apartments, he could make out a bulking wall of deeper darkness. The Dalles dam? Like Bonneville, the Corps base seemed to have been built at its foot.

Sandusky was fumbling with the door. A dying geranium sulked in a pot on the narrow, concrete porch. A door opened somewhere and Carter heard a woman's laughter before it slammed shut again. The wind buffeted the geranium, yanked at his uniform.

"Is it always like this?" Carter shielded his face against the windblown grit.

"Windy, you mean? Yes, sir. It either blows up or down the gorge. Down is usually worse, sir." Sandusky picked up Carter's carryall and pushed the door open. "Here you are, sir."

Carter stumbled over the threshold, blinking in the sudden glare of the fluorescent ceiling lights. The door was tightly gasketed to keep dust out and cool air in. Sandusky grunted as he yanked it closed behind them.

"Anything else, sir?" He flicked on a small air conditioner set into the wall and saluted without meeting Carter's eyes.

"No, I guess not. Thanks for the ride."

He shouldn't have been so short with the kid. You couldn't blame him for being curious about Chicago. Carter looked over the two-room suite—it was smaller than what he'd had on the lakebed. The main room held a wide sofa bed, two upholstered chairs, and a big-screen video. A refrigerator–single-burner stove combo and a sink had been fenced off into a kitchen by a Formica-topped breakfast bar. Doors led to the bedroom and a tiny bathroom, which was equipped with a digester toilet and a self-contained shower cabinet.

It looked impersonal without his books and his stereo equipment, like a cheap motel room. Carter took his carryall into the bedroom, trying not to wonder if this had been Colonel Watanabe's quarters. The warm, dry air smelled of disinfectant. The clock said ten o'clock—which meant that his body thought it was midnight. Carter flopped onto the double bed that nearly filled the small room, still bleary from his nap in the car. What he needed right now was a beer, a shower, and about eight hours of uninterrupted sleep. He'd settle for sleep.

Someone knocked at the door.

Now what? Carter stomped across the floor and jerked the door open. Whoever it was had better have a damn good reason . . . he blinked. A civilian stood on the threshold, dressed in jeans and a faded denim shirt.

"Welcome to The Dalles, Colonel." The stranger walked past him as if Carter had invited him in. "I know it's late, but I thought I'd better drop by and introduce myself." He waited while Carter closed the door, smiling wryly. "I'm Dan Greely," he said. "I'm afraid I don't know your name."

"Voltaire," Carter said slowly. "Carter Voltaire." He looked the tall, lanky man over, wide awake now. Greely had weathered brown skin, dark eyes, and brown hair streaked with gray. Carter placed him in his forties. No sign of a weapon. "You're the leader of this sabotage ring," Carter said deliberately. "What the hell are you doing here? Who gave you a pass?"

"If you mean the Coalition, we aren't behind the sabotage," Greely said. "I think we're on the same side, Colonel."

"That's not what General Hastings told me."

"No, it wouldn't be." Greely smiled wryly. "That's why I wanted to introduce myself in person. There isn't much . . . official communication between the Corps and the Coalition. Hastings hates my guts, to put it bluntly."

That was probably an accurate assessment. Carter crossed his arms, a little impressed in spite of himself. If this guy was the enemy, he was a cool one. "Tell me why I shouldn't call the MPs."

"You could do that. You could even make a trespass charge stick, because I *am* trespassing. I didn't come in through the gate." A grin flashed and faded on his face. "That's it, though. If you could get away with anything else, Hastings would have locked me up a long time ago."

He sounded matter-of-fact. Carter tugged at his lip. "Why risk it? Why sneak in here like this? You showing off for me, or what?"

Greely's expression sobered. "I'm here because *we* want to find out who's sabotaging the Pipe, too. We don't want to take on the Corps, or stop the water. We're a bunch of farmers who're trying to keep crops alive long enough to make harvest. Someone's sabotaging the Pipe, yes, but it's not us. Colonel Watanabe knew that—he finally listened to us.''

"Colonel Watanabe's dead," Carter said softly.

"Exactly." Greely held his eyes. "Think about that, okay? Think about this, too: What the hell do we gain by cutting off our own water? Don't let Hastings sic you on us. It's the wrong trail.''

"I guess that's for me to decide," Carter said. Yeah, this guy had guts. Carter lifted the phone and called base Security. "I have an unauthorized civilian in my quarters," he said coldly. "I want an escort for him." He cradled the phone and faced Greely's wary stare. "I'll tell you this much," he said slowly. "I'm the CO here, which means my people and the Pipeline come first. But I make up my own mind about things. If you want to cooperate, show me. I'll listen to you."

Knuckles rapped briskly at the door. "Base Security, sir." The grizzled sergeant's face was expressionless as Carter opened the door. "You have an unauthorized civilian, sir?"

A retreaded Green Beret? They made up the bulk of the MPs these days, and this soldier had the look. "Escort this man off base, Sergeant," Carter said coldly. "I want him to go through the gate in exactly the same condition he is in now. And then you tell your CO that I expect to see him here in ten minutes."

"Yes, sir." The sergeant's salute was precise. "This way," he said to Greely, and his tone was absolutely neutral.

"Fair enough." Greely nodded as he started for the door. "I'm glad I got to meet you, Colonel. If you need to contact me, leave a message at the government store in town. I don't have a phone."

"Greely?" Carter waited until the man met his eyes. "This all sounds very positive, but any more killings will screw everything up.''

"I'd like to be able to guarantee that there won't be any more deaths." Greely paused in the doorway, his expression grim. "We're trying to stop it, too. You think about Watanabe."

Yes, he was thinking very hard about Watanabe, thank you. Carter watched the clock, frowning. The sergeant's commanding officer—a young captain—arrived in exactly five minutes. He left ten minutes later, his back ramrod straight. No one in Security was going to sleep tonight, Carter thought grimly. Not until they'd found the fucking hole Dan Greely had walked through. Whether Greely was friend or foe, security mattered.

"Sir?" This time, the man at the door was a major, dark-haired, with a long face that gave him a saturnine air. "Major Delgado reporting, sir," he said. "I understand you had some trouble here tonight, sir."

Aha. It hadn't taken the man long to get dressed and get over here. "A trespasser," Carter said. "At ease, Major. Come in." He stood aside, tired and twitching with tension now. God, what a beginning. "Security's dealing with it."

"Security had standing orders to arrest Greely any time he turned up on Corps property," Delgado said tightly.

Delgado's order. Carter eyed the major. "On what charge?" Delgado was pissed, and it showed. Because Greely had walked? "Trespass?"

"Yes, sir." Delgado's eyes glittered.

Carter shook his head, too tired to deal with any more of this tonight. "We'll talk about it tomorrow," he said. "In my office at oh-nine-hundred. I don't want to be disturbed any more tonight, unless it's a major emergency."

"Yes, sir." Delgado saluted, the anger still visible in the set of his shoulders. "Tomorrow, sir." He marched out of the apartment, his stride as stiff as if he'd been on the parade ground.

No one else knocked. Frowning, Carter stripped out of his clothes. Dan Greely had sounded sincere—which might make him nothing better than a damn good actor. Or maybe Hastings was letting personal feelings get in the way of objectivity. Carter could believe *that*. But Delgado was no fan of Greely's, either. He tossed his dirty clothes into the corner and flopped naked on the bed. Two votes against Greely, and the situation felt more and more like another Chicago. The bottom line was that he didn't know squat about what was going on here, and he'd better start fixing that first thing in the morning. Carter grabbed for the sheet—way too wired to sleep—and was out before he had pulled it all the way up.

CHAPTER FOUR ☆

The shrill beep of the alarm jerked Carter out of sleep just as he took aim at the sun-bright windshield of the van. Groggy, he reached for the clock . . . and nearly fell out of bed as his hand missed the nightstand that wasn't there. The adrenaline rush woke him up fast.

He was in The Dalles, not Chicago. The nightstand was on *that* side of the bed. He slapped off the alarm. Four-thirty. He blinked at the glowing red digits. Five hours of sleep should have been enough, but it felt more like ten minutes. Carter threw back the sheet and stumbled to the bathroom. Day one as Old Man on this base—time to start getting a feel for what the hell was going on here, and from the sound of things, he'd better do it fast.

He wasn't sleepy anymore. He turned on the shower, gasping as the cold water hit his skin. Lousy insulation on the storage tanks; Carter made a mental note to get on Building Mainte-nance's ass. No one needed a cold shower to start the day.

It was still dark as he left the apartment and walked quickly through the yellow-lit streets. According to the map in his apart-ment, HQ was down this street. He turned right, feet crunching in gravel. The blocks of buildings on his right showed only a few lights. Enlisted personnel housing, according to the map. Toys cluttered the grass-carpeted front yards—bikes and three-wheelers, a battered doll lying spread-eagled beside the side-walk. The base was closed here, as in Chicago; you lived on post. Inside the cage. It was hard on the families.

Headquarters was a long, low concrete building, ugly and functional. The duty sergeant showed Carter to his office and gave him a quick tour of the layout. His office was about as shabby as Hastings's, Carter decided. Flow reports in hardcopy lay neatly on his desk, waiting for his signature. Carter leafed

37

through them quickly. No problems, but he would know if there'd
been any problems. A map of the Pipeline covered one wall and
a blowup of The Dalles sector covered another. Veins, Carter
thought as he studied the blue tracery, and those veins made him
uneasy. *I wanted someone with more experience,* Hastings had
said. Hastings could go take a flying leap . . . but those veins
carried the lifeblood of this damn dusty here-and-now. Cut them,
and a lot of people would suffer. How close to a war *were* they
out here?

Carter turned around at the sound of a cleared throat. "Sir."
A gray-haired sergeant with the wiry build of a jockey saluted.
"Sergeant Willis, sir. Anything you need?"

This would be the topkick—the senior NCO. The duty ser-
geant had called him, and probably Delgado, as well. The new
CO was up and roaming around. "Everything's fine, Sergeant."
Carter looked around at his cramped office. Time to get rolling.
"Notify all the COs that there will be a staff meeting at seven-
thirty," he told Willis. "Right now I need some breakfast."

"I'll take you over there, sir," Willis said.

"Ten minutes." Carter turned back to his desk to take the
pulse of the Columbia riverbed. It was interesting that Delgado
hadn't arrived. Perhaps the duty sergeant hadn't called him after
all. Or had Willis ordered him not to? Carter frowned at the
numbers on the screen in front of him. What did Willis have to
say that he didn't want Delgado to hear? He would listen during
his tour. He'd listen very carefully.

The sun was well up as Willis showed him around the base.
A light wind flicked Carter's hair back from his face, but it was
going to be hot later. Half asleep this morning, he'd forgotten
sunscreen. Bad move. He had dark hair, but his fair skin never
tanned. The dusty street ended at the vast wall of the dam. "This
was a power-company dam." Carter looked up in awe at the
enormous intakes that yawned like cave mouths in the stained
concrete. "It never stored an acre-foot of water."

"I guess they had plenty of water back then, sir." Willis
shrugged. "We wouldn't be so tight now if the Trench Reservoir
had been built sooner."

True. Carter remembered his momentary vision of the waterfall. How could you worry about water when you looked at that
every day? By the time federal condemnation of private water
rights had finally made it through the courts, it had been almost
too late. Not that it could have kept the climate from changing,

or kept the glaciers from growing, but it would have helped. If they'd started sooner, the Trench might be full clear to capacity. Now—if Johnny was right, and Canada shorted them on the tundra water—it might never be full.

"The O club's down there." Willis nodded. "We use it as the officer's mess. Enlisted mess is the oh-one-oh building—that green monster down there. The exchange and the drill hall are across the street. This is Main. The MEQ is down there." He pointed south, down the street Carter had walked up in the darkness.

"How tight is it on base?" Carter watched Willis's face as he asked.

"It's tight." Willis's eyes flicked toward him and away.

"How tight?" Carter asked. Morale mattered. These were his people, and he needed to know how they lived.

Willis frowned, as if he were picking his words. "The kids've gone, so my wife and I took a single-bedroom unit."

"You're entitled to more."

"Yes, sir." Willis nodded. "There's two families sharing the three-bedroom unit we had." Willis cleared his throat. "Colonel Watanabe authorized extra air conditioners, sir. For some of the units."

He was waiting to see how Carter would react, or maybe Delgado had pulled the extra units. "Good move," Carter said, and watched Willis not show his relief. Friends in one of those crowded units? Carter shaded his eyes, squinting into the harsh sunlight. The gray wall of the dam zigzagged across the dusty gouge of the riverbed. The Corps buildings and residences clustered on the Oregon side, sheltered by the concrete wing of the dam. Firs and a few thirsty maples shaded the dusty streets. An old spillway had been converted into a tunnel that led to the west gate. Beyond the dam, the spidery span of a highway bridge arched over the riverbed. People still used it.

He watched a bright-blue semi pull a triple trailer across the bridge. Beyond it he could see The Dalles. Metal-sided warehouses and a couple of ancient wooden grain elevators baked in the sun. Fruit, Carter remembered. And wheat. That was what people had grown around here, back when the river was full of water. Now they grew drought-tolerant soybeans and sugar beets, all dependent on those blue veins full of water. Wind vanes turned slowly, ranked along the shelving riverbanks like strange metallic trees. Parallel strands of bright-orange wire fenced the compound on all sides, strung four inches apart on six-foot poles. Carter approached it cautiously.

"Don't touch it, sir. It'll knock you cold." Willis stepped up beside him. "It could kill you if you got tangled in it. A cut strand activates an alarm."

It hadn't stopped Greely, Carter thought sourly. Security better have found that hole. He stared at the orange wire, tired with a weariness that went beyond the physical. Why couldn't the people on the other side of that fence understand that there was only so much water? "Where do you keep the coffee?" Carter asked.

"This way."

"Not today." Carter shook his head. He needed to know how his people ate, too. That counted. "We'll hit the enlisted mess," he said.

The noise level dropped by an order of magnitude as Carter walked through the door. The CO. It didn't quite get silent, but he felt the eyes as he picked up a tray at the end of the serving line. The mess was open, he noticed. Families could pay and eat here. Which meant that the food situation locally wasn't good—or it wasn't a good idea to shop locally. The families sat on one side of the hall, the active duty personnel on the other. Not many families this early. A very young woman with an infant in her lap was trying to hush a complaining three-year-old girl.

"The colonel opened the mess, sir. You got to go to Bonneville to buy a lot of stuff, these days." Willis held out a plate for scrambled eggs. "Gas costs ten bucks a gallon."

Which most of the lower grades couldn't afford. "Why can't you shop in The Dalles?" Carter filled a mug with coffee—or what passed for coffee these days. "Local attitude?"

"It's not bad, sir." Willis stressed the words slightly. "The colonel opened the mess before we closed the base. You don't have much choice outside of the local market or the government store. The locals don't live so good, either."

This man didn't hate the locals, anyway. Delgado did. Carter picked up a glass of orange juice. Maybe that was why Willis hadn't included him this morning. Carter had a feeling that Willis was doing a little subtle propagandizing: *The situation doesn't have to be this bad. How about it, boss?*

They were all asking, every man and woman on the base. How about it, boss? How are *you* going to handle things? Carter felt the weight of their silent questions as he picked up his tray and turned away from the line. Then the child threw a bowl onto the floor with a clatter and launched herself into a screaming temper tantrum. The whole room went silent. The woman's face was red as she tried desperately to silence her daughter, and now the baby was crying. Carter looked away, straight into the agonized face of a corporal on the other side of the room. Dad, Carter realized suddenly. Scared shitless that Carter might just get pissed and close the mess, that his daughter might have blown it for his family and every other family on the base.

It was tough for the enlisted personnel.

Carter waited until the woman looked up, then caught her eye. ''Kids,'' he said, and smiled for her.

The food wasn't bad. Soy eggs and bacon, but what else did you get when it took half the water to raise a pound of hi-pro soybeans that it took to produce one egg? Just *forget* real meat. There was real orange juice—tank-grown stuff, but that was real. Time was breathing down his neck now. The staff meeting was coming up. Carter ate fast and pretended that he wasn't aware of the inaudible and collective sigh of relief as he left the mess.

Delgado and Captain Arris, Security's CO from last night, were waiting in his office.

''There is no breach in the perimeter of this base, sir.'' Arris's eyes were locked on Carter's left shoulder. ''Sir.''

''How did a civilian get in here?'' Carter asked. From the corner of his eye, he could see Delgado's scowl.

''I don't know, sir.'' Arris's face was stone. ''No excuse, sir.''

Shit on that. Families lived on this base, and this could end up a war zone any day. ''Go find it,'' Carter said gently.

''Yes, sir.'' The captain saluted, departed.

''I could have found out, sir,'' Delgado said. ''If we'd arrested Greely.''

That glitter was back in his eyes. Hatred? ''We don't play that way, Major,'' Carter snapped. Easy, he told himself. You need this man, whether you like him or not. ''I'm going to be feeling my way for a while,'' he said, making his voice warmer. ''The general warned me about Greely, and I'll keep my eyes open. If he's behind this, we'll get him.''

''Yeah.'' Delgado didn't sound convinced. ''Just watch yourself, sir. They shot Colonel Watanabe in cold blood.''

Everybody wanted to use some variation of that line: Think

about Watanabe. Carter thought about pursuing the subject, but
the clock on his desk glared at him. "We've got a staff meeting
in five minutes," he said. "Afterward, you can give me a tour."
And tell me about Greely, Watanabe, and what you think is
going on here, he didn't say.

The staff meeting was everybody's chance to size up the CO,
and Carter's chance to take their measure. Operations, Communications, Pipeline Maintenance, Base Support, MPs, and
even Battalion Aid; they all gave Carter a brief evaluation of
their situation. It wasn't as bad as he had expected, and he felt
a cautious relief as he listened. There was tension here, yes, and
hostility toward the locals, but morale seemed to be solid. Sabotage—aside from the two sniping incidents—had been limited
to shooting out the guts of the wind turbines or busting the solar
arrays that powered the pumps. The chief surgeon reported that
stress levels on the base were within normal parameters for a
low-threat combat zone. This wasn't a war—yet.

That feeling was borne out as Carter toured the rest of the
base. The comments he overheard were that the locals weren't
too bad as a whole, but there was open hatred for the few terrorists who had been doing the shooting. No, it wasn't a war
yet—and with luck, it wouldn't end up as one.

It was midafternoon before he got a chance to tour Operations
with Delgado. This was the nexus of the job—the air-conditioned
heartbeat of their sector of the Pipeline. Carefully protected
from dust by a double set of doors and an autonomous air-
filtration system, the room was a maze of electronics. Inset ter-
minals lined the four walls and the long stations that ran down
the center of the room. Screens glowed with multicolor offerings
of curves, numbers and graphs, monitoring water flow, turbulence, temperature, and pipewall stress. One entire wall was
covered with a detailed topographical map of The Dalles sector
of the Pipeline. Uniformed men and women bent over their
screens, faces intent.

"This is the readout on the main flow." Major Carron, who
had been conducting the tour, stopped beside a bank of four
monitor screens.

"Everything is within normal parameters, sir." A small, redheaded lieutenant saluted, his eyes sweeping Carter with one
quick, appraising glance.

"Tell me what you're doing." Carter leaned over his shoulder.

"I'm monitoring flow turbulence, sir. These screens give us a view of the Pipe's interior wall via optical fibers. Those screens give a readout from the flow sensors. An increase in turbulence means a leak. A sudden decrease indicates a failed pump, sir. The water backs up into the sumps."

"You see a lot of pump problems?"

"Yes, sir," The lieutenant's face was expressionless.

Courtesy of the locals. He wasn't going to say it. "When I have some time, I'd like to go over this with you in more detail. I would like some more input on flow dynamics, and you're the expert."

"Yes, sir," the lieutenant saluted. "Any time."

It paid to understand what your people were doing—at all levels. You made better decisions, and they knew it.

Apart from the main line, The Dalles sector was responsible for the first miles of the Klamath Shunt, a major diversion that led down the old Deschutes bed, down through Bend to Klamath Lake, and on through the Klamath Aqueduct to augment the output of California's vast desalinization plants, watering the fertile Sacramento Valley. Turbulence and wear on the Pipeline was intense at the enormous valve complex of the Shunt. The Corps also monitored every local diversion line, every branch, and every individual tap line. Consumption was recorded by individual ration meters, but the Corps kept flow data on every line, no matter how small. If piracy was suspected, the flow rates could be retrieved and reviewed for evidence of a tampered meter or an illegal tap.

Diversion and branch lines were big enough to require leak monitoring. Carter prowled the Operations room, checking line codes against the big map, getting a feel for what water went where and how much. To his casual eye, it seemed like the local farmers used a lot of water. Carter resolved to look up some of the production stats for the high farmland above the gorge, then compare it to what was coming out of the Willamette Valley, say. You didn't have the right to be wasteful. Not anymore.

Carter jumped as a beeper went off. It snapped heads up from monitors, stiffened shoulders.

"Leak," the redhead, Carson, called from his monitor bank.

First crisis. "How bad?" Carter leaned over the lieutenant's shoulder.

"Flow turbulence in the ninety-second subsector indicates a

third-stage leak, sir, with a priority rating of twenty-three point four percent.''

The weary hours spent with the manuals and briefs were paying off. A rate of 23 percent meant a small leak—possibly too small for a spotting crew even to find on a visual sweep, possibly a waste of their time when they might be needed elsewhere. Carter scowled at the numbers, aware that Delgado and the lieutenant were waiting for some kind of decision. The question was whether to send out a crew or not. Wasted crew hours would reflect poorly on the efficiency rating of the sector, but the leak could get worse if it went unpatched. Eventually it might graduate to a second-stage leak with some measurable loss of flow in the pipe. That would be bad for the farmers downflow, and bad for his records.

''Do we go?'' Delgado asked.

Carter glanced involuntarily at the map. Damn. Subsector 92 was clear out at the far end of their territory, near the west edge of the John Day sector. ''Right away,'' he said. ''Draw an APC from the motor pool.'' The teams had been using the standard 4×4s for patrol, but after Chicago, he was damned if he'd send people out in soft-skinned vehicles.

''With a gunner?'' The glitter was back in Delgado's eyes, and the silence around them was almost palpable.

Carter drew a deep breath. ''Only self-defense.'' He raised his voice slightly. ''I don't want any accidents.''

''Yes, sir.'' Delgado saluted, his face expressionless again.

This had been some kind of issue. Carter wondered what the orders had been under Delgado's command. His hand twitched with the memory of the Beretta's smooth butt, the sweet hot feel of his rage as he lifted it . . . Carter looked around the room, registering both positive and negative reactions to his order. ''Keep me posted.'' He turned back to Lieutenant Carson. ''Page me when that leak is patched.''

''Yes, sir.''

There had been relief on Carson's face. What had he expected Carter to do? Oh, hell. Carter looked at his watch. It was late. He sighed, smelling his own sweat, wishing for a shower and a few peaceful hours to relax and assimilate the day. Those hours would be better spent going over reports. There wasn't any time to relax, not yet. The wind tugged at the loose fabric of his coverall as Carter left the building, and the level beams of the setting sun edged the rim of the dam with gold. A crumpled candy wrapper skidded along the concrete sidewalk, bounced

over the low curb and into the street. Three lanky young enlisteds in khaki shorts crossed at the end of the street, laughing and
talking loudly. The tall black kid in the middle carried a bas-
ketball, spinning it lightly on his fingertips. Showing off. Carter
smiled as the kid flipped the ball easily to his buddy. It was cool
enough for a pickup game now. Carter felt a little wistful.

He wouldn't have much time for basketball for a while. He
turned down the narrow alley between two storage buildings.
This was a natural shortcut to his quarters, and the buildings cut
off the infernal wind. It was quiet, already dark with evening
shadow. He passed a door and heard it open. Turning, he caught
a glimpse of fast motion behind him, then someone slammed
into his back and sent him stumbling forward. A hard forearm
clamped across his throat, choking off his cry of surprise.
Stunned by the unexpected attack, fighting for breath, Carter
stabbed backward with his elbow, felt it connect. His attacker
grunted hoarsely and clutched at Carter's arm.

Choking . . . Carter twisted violently, but black spots were
wavering in front of his eyes. Someone grabbed his hair, yanked
his head back and sideways. Carter caught a glimpse of red hair,
a face. He gasped as the choking arm relaxed beneath his chin,
sucked in a desperate lungful of air and something else, a cold
stinging nothing that numbed his lips and throat, numbed his
chest, soaked upward into his brain and downward into his
knees, numbing them, too.

Floating, weightless, Carter watched the pale wall of the shed
slide past him, moving upward as if the ground were sinking
under him, sinking like an elevator down into some dark, cool
basement . . .

CHAPTER FIVE ☆

Heat woke him; searing heat that glared red through his closed eyelids. Thirst. He opened his eyes, squeezed them shut as light and pain lanced through his skull. Stones grated beneath his cheek. He was lying facedown in the dust. The alley . . . vague memory of a choking arm . . . darkness. Where was he? Carter got his knees under him, got halfway to his feet. Dun land and *light*. It began to revolve slowly and he lurched onto hands and knees again, retching bile onto the sunbaked clay between his palms.

The spasms eased finally, leaving him sweaty and shivering. Memory was coming back, slowly and in pieces. Someone had jumped him and used some kind of gas. Cautiously he eased himself back into a sitting position; this time, the land stayed still. Empty hills stretched away on all sides, streaked with afternoon shadows. No road, no buildings—just dirt, sun, and rock. The shivering had stopped, and Carter wiped vomit from his chin, trying to think through the fierce ache in his skull. Someone had grabbed him right off the base and had dumped him out here. Nice going, he thought bitterly. Great security. He was naked except for his shorts. He touched his arm and winced. From the look of his sunburn, he'd been out here for a long time.

Here. Fear tightened his stomach and dewed his face with sweat. Where the hell was *here*? The dun, dead land marched away on all sides of him, broken by tilted bands of rock and gray clumps of sage. Empty. He swallowed, his mouth dry as the ground. The riverbed and the highway could be a thousand miles away, or in another universe.

That pitiless space squeezed in on him from all sides, threatening to crush him. Carter slumped beneath its weight, panting, shuddering with the immensity of it. He could die; right here, right now, and nothing would change. Nothing. He was helpless, and it was the most terrible feeling he had ever had. *Just lie down,* the wind whispered to him. *Lie down and die.*

And he *would* die if he sat here and waited for it. The wind rasped across his sunburned shoulders and slowly his flare of panic began to ease. No, he wasn't helpless. Not quite. He straightened, thinking again, examining the horizon. The sun was setting beyond the shoulder of a mountain peak. West. So that was probably Mount Hood, unless the people who had jumped him had hauled him an awfully long way to dump him. Which they could've done—don't think about that. You are not that far from the riverbed. It's north. That way. Walk that way and sooner or later you'll hit a road, or a house, or something.

Or he'd collapse and die.

No way. Carter clenched his teeth. He owed someone for this. He made it to his feet, wavering as the world revolved briefly again. All right—he had a couple of hours of daylight yet. People lived out here, even if it didn't look like it. Carter picked out a thumb-shape lump of rock to the north, fixed his eyes on it to shut out the emptiness, and began limping toward it.

His confidence—what there was of it—kept trying to dissolve. His head didn't hurt so much now, but thirst tortured him. He tried to chew some of the dusty grass, but the tough stems merely cut his mouth and made him feel thirstier than before. His back hurt with every movement. When he touched his shoulder, blisters burst beneath his fingers, spilling sticky fluid. He must have been unconscious in the sun for hours. Goddamn bastards. Twilight was a blessing when it came. An early moon rose, three-quarters full, shedding enough light to get by. But the pleasant coolness turned cold quickly. Before long Carter was shivering. And the landscape didn't change. It didn't fucking change. He could have been walking in place. Going in circles. He wasn't getting anywhere, wasn't going to make it.

Somewhere, they were laughing at him, safe and secure, sitting around drinking beer, maybe. Carter clutched at that thought, squeezing new rage from it. They were going to pay for this. In spades. He hung on to that anger, and for a while it kept the cold and the darkness at bay. Then a sharp piece of obsidian sliced his foot, tripped him onto his knees. He clutched at a rocky outcrop and dragged himself to his feet. His arm hurt, and he touched the bend in his elbow gingerly. In the colorless moonlight, he could just make out the dark bruise. Someone had shot him up with something. To ask him questions? For a moment, the ache in his head intensified, and he had a vague memory of a voice whispering, whispering in his ear.

They thought he knew something. Whoever "they" were. Carter forced himself to his feet again, burned shoulders screaming, mouth too dry to even swallow. What had they been after? He took a limping step, then another. He'd ask them. Oh yeah, he'd ask them. Step by painful step, he limped northward, leaving spots of blood in his faint footprints. He was fuzzing in and out of consciousness now, but still moving, more or less. He saw Johnny, but his mouth was too dry to talk. Then Johnny turned into the kid in the van. Carter was trying to ask him why he'd done it when a thin cry banished his ghost, bringing back the night and the cold and the pain.

The sound came again, like a baby crying. Coyotes? Wild dogs? Carter looked around, barely able to stay on his feet, trying to make his eyes focus. The moon had been so bright, earlier. It was dimmer now, or maybe the darkness was thicker. The coyote or dog baby-cried again. Close. Something moved in the darkness behind him and Carter broke into a stumbling run, adrenaline wringing the last whisper of energy from his muscles.

It was chasing him, right behind him. Big coyote . . . wolf . . . Carter's feet slapped down on a hard surface, snapping his teeth together, nearly bringing him down. A road. Finally a road, but it was too damn late. He staggered to a halt, out of breath, out of strength, turning to face whatever was after him, only he couldn't *see* anything. The road tilted under him suddenly, slamming up against his hip and shoulder. It surprised him a little that it didn't hurt. It should have hurt.

Hands were touching him. He remembered hands holding him down and a face bending close, asking questions that hurt his head, hurt him even when he answered, until he cried with the pain . . . Carter swung his fist up blindly.

"Hey!" A high-pitched voice said, and the hands grabbed his wrist. "Cut it out. I'm trying to help you, okay? Just take it easy."

It wasn't *the* voice. Carter stopped fighting as his vision cleared. He was lying on his back on a road. The moon was still up, still casting pale light.

"What are you *doing* out here?" A woman was kneeling beside him, the thick braid of her hair dangling forward over one shoulder. "What happened to you?"

His tongue wouldn't work right. "Water?" he whispered. "Hang on."

She walked away, and Carter struggled to his elbow, terrified suddenly that she would vanish into the darkness and not return. But she was back in a second, a plastic jug and a cup in one hand, a small solar lantern shedding wonderful light in the other. She set the lantern down, and water gurgled as she tilted the jug. The sound made him tremble.

"Here." She slid an arm beneath his shoulders. "Take it slow, okay? This is all I've got until we get to The Dalles."

He forced himself to drink slowly, wanting desperately to gulp it down, letting the incredible sweetness of the water run across his tongue and down his throat. She refilled the cup for him and he emptied it again. "Thanks." The words could come now. "Thanks a lot," he gasped.

"I'm sorry if I scared you." She tilted her head and the lantern pooled shadow beneath her high cheekbones. "I called, but you didn't hear me."

"I thought you were a coyote," Carter said. She was young, twenty maybe, dressed in faded jeans and a jacket. Hispanic, with a wide face and tilted, dark eyes. "I'm glad you weren't."

"Me, too. I'm Nita Montoya," she said gravely. "How did you end up out here? Who did this to you?"

"My name's Carter Voltaire." He started to add that he was with the Corps, but caught the words in time. Perhaps it would be safer to leave that part out. "I don't know who dumped me out here." He pushed himself into a sitting position. "But I'm going to find out."

"Not tonight." She touched his arm lightly, then got to her feet. "I'll bring my stuff here. I've got some extra clothes that might fit you."

Blessedly, she left him the light. He listened to the reassuring sound of her footsteps, the crackle of dry sage. In a few minutes she reappeared, lugging a frame pack and carrying a bundle in her arms. "You don't have to be afraid of the dark," she said as she laid the bundle on the ground. "Don't blame the land. It isn't evil."

"I'm not afraid—" he began, then stopped. "Yes, I am." He looked past her into the darkness that had tried to eat him. "It's so damn big out there. I don't know. I guess I've always lived in cities, around people. You could die out here and no one would even know."

"That's true." She sat down beside him and reached for the

pack. "But you can die anywhere. I know what lives out here—what can hurt me and what can't. I know how to deal with it. Towns scare me," she said softly. "People can be so full of ugliness."

Ugliness? Yeah. Carter remembered the bodies in Chicago, stiff and grotesque in the streets. Some had looked surprised, as if death had sneaked up on them. Others had looked resigned, as if they had been waiting for Death for a long time. "It still bothers me. All this dead emptiness."

"Empty, yes, but not dead." She pulled a roll of blue fabric out of her pack and shook it out. "There's life in the cracks, even if you don't see it; mice, the tough weeds, even flowers. This shirt should fit, and maybe the jeans. They're David's. My husband's." She handed them to him.

He reached for the clothes and groaned. His sunburned back had stiffened while he sat, and it felt as if the skin were splitting open.

Nita hissed softly between her teeth and knelt behind him, reaching for the light. "I didn't realize how bad it was."

Carter winced at the light touch of her fingers. "I was out in the sun for a while."

"No kidding." She fumbled again in her pack and took out a small plastic tub. "This will help. You're bad all over, but your back is the worst."

"No kidding," he said dryly. Even the cool touch of the salve hurt. "What are *you* doing out here in the middle of nowhere?" he said through tight lips.

"This isn't the middle of nowhere." A smile warmed her voice. "We're not too far south of The Dalles. I hope." She capped the tub and tucked it back into the pack. "I'm on my way there. To meet David. He works for the Army." She reached for the shirt. "I'll help you."

Her husband worked for the Corps? "What's his name?" Carter gritted his teeth as he eased his arm through the shirt-sleeve. "Maybe I know him."

"David Ascher." Hope leaped in her voice. "He's in his forties, with curly brown hair. It's just going gray. Do you know him?"

"I'm sorry." Carter buttoned the shirt, grateful for its warmth. This David was bigger than he. He'd have to use something for a belt. "Is he a civilian?" he asked as he tugged the jeans on.

"Yes." Her shoulders slumped. "You're really shivering. I've got a sleeping bag you can wrap around you."

He *was* shivering, and it was a strange sensation, because he didn't really feel cold, although he must be. Drug hangover? He zipped the too-large jeans, teeth chattering again, wondering what they'd used on him. They. The enemy—whoever they were.

Nita had unrolled a patched sleeping bag from her pack and draped it over his shoulders. "David has to be in The Dalles." She spoke softly, as if she were talking to herself. "I'm sure he's there."

Carter looked at her more closely, seeing tears in her eyes. She wasn't sure at all. "Where are you from?" he asked gently.

"West of Salem." She lifted her chin. "We hunted bees in the mountains."

A thin cry made Carter jump. A baby? That's what he'd heard, and not a coyote? Incredulous, he watched her lift an infant from the bundled cloth. "You walked all the way from Salem with him?"

"Her." Nita sounded amused. "This is Rachel. I hitched a lot and yes, I walked. How do you get around where you come from, anyway? Go back to sleep, love." She rocked the baby gently in her arms. "You're not really hungry."

She had walked all this way, looking for a David who might not even be in The Dalles. Carter felt a small, brief anger for this man who had left her behind.

She raised her head suddenly to look at him, her expression defensive, as if she'd felt his anger. "The bees were dying," she said sharply. "We couldn't make it trading honey anymore, and we had to do something. A friend told him about this job."

"Listen, I'm with the Corps, in The Dalles. I'm the new CO." Carter watched her face, half expecting hostility. "I can check on David Ascher for you. If he ever worked for us, I can find the records."

"Could you do that?"

"Yes," Carter said. She was almost beautiful when she smiled like this. "I owe you a lot more than that."

"No, you don't," she said gravely. "Out here, you don't walk away from people who need help. You could be there tomorrow. Remember that, okay? Pay me back that way."

"I will. I promise." His words had the feel of a promise made not only to her, but to some god whose nature he hadn't discovered yet. "I don't understand this world," Carter said. "And I need to."

"Why?" She tilted her head, eyes on his face. "Why is it so very important?"

"Because I'm one of the people who has to make decisions about water, and I don't know what water means here. I knew what it meant in Chicago—I knew what the lake meant, and the dust, and the salt. But I've walked into something, and I don't know what's going on. I don't know this land. I don't know its soul, and I could make the wrong decision. I've seen what the price of wrong decisions can be, and . . . I'm fucking scared." His hands were trembling. He clasped them together, feeling light-headed, drunk, and more than a little embarrassed. The words had tumbled out on their own, unstoppable. From the drugs, maybe, or dehydration, or maybe just because he had thought for a while that he was going to die, and he wasn't going to after all.

"It's all right." Nita took his hand in hers, fingers closing firm and cool around his. "You'll understand, because it matters to you. You'll make the right decisions."

"I hope so." He looked restlessly northward, into the darkness beyond the lantern's yellow pool. "People have to be out looking for me. If we could get to a phone, I could call."

"A phone?" She was amused again. "I think we'll wait until morning. I don't have any extra shoes, and your feet are a mess."

"What about water?" The specter of thirst haunted him. "I drank it all, didn't I?"

"Not quite. Relax." She squeezed his hand. "Even if I'm wrong about where we are *exactly*, we're pretty close to The Dalles. People still drive on this road; it's nice and clean. We'll catch a ride tomorrow."

As if her words had conjured it, the distant sound of an engine broke the silence. Someone. Help. Carter staggered to his feet, wincing at the pain.

"Wait." Nita clicked off the lantern. "Get down." She pulled him off the asphalt, into the sparse sage. "Lie flat," she whispered fiercely. "Out here you want to see before you get seen. Sometimes it matters, Carter." She tucked her sleeping daughter against her side.

He crouched beside her, nervous now, feeling utterly visible. The engine growled suddenly louder. Twin cones of yellow light splashed across the landscape, picking out rocks and sage, casting stark shadows. Carter blinked, momentarily blinded by the light. The car was a 4×4, going slowly, as if the driver were scanning the sides of the road.

Nita's hand closed tight on his arm and Carter pressed himself against the rocky ground, infected by her caution. The car cruised by. The turreted castle was visible on the door, illuminated by the backsplash of the headlights. A Corps vehicle! With a whoop, Carter staggered to his feet. Terror gripped him—that the car would drive on down the road, disappear into the darkness. "Here!" he yelled. "I'm here!"

It was stopping, thank God. Backup lights flashed whitely and, with a growl from the transmission, the car backed toward him. It stopped and a uniformed man sprang out. "Colonel? Is that you?"

Delgado's voice? Yes! "Major!" Carter limped forward. "Am I ever glad to see you."

"My God, we all thought you were dead, sir." Delgado grabbed him by the shoulders, eyebrows rising as he took in Carter's clothes. "I was looking for a body. What happened?"

"Somebody jumped me in the alley." Carter leaned against the car, his knees shaky again.

"Are you hurt?" Delgado caught his arm and opened the door. "Sit down, sir."

"I'm just dehydrated. And sunburned." Carter sagged gratefully onto the car's front seat and grimaced. "I don't do so well, hiking barefoot."

"Greely screwed up this time." Delgado's tone had gone cold. "He didn't figure on us finding you in time. You out there—hold it!" He dropped into a half crouch, yanking his pistol from his unsnapped holster.

"Don't," Carter yelled. "She's with me." God. He ran a shaking hand across his face as Delgado holstered his weapon. "She helped me. Nita? It's all right. We'll give you a ride back to town."

"I don't mind walking." Nita stepped cautiously into the light. She was clutching Rachel tightly, and her dark eyes were ringed with white. "I expected to walk."

"I'm sorry, Nita." Carter held out a hand. "Listen, a ride's the least I can do. You're out of water, remember? Major, put her stuff in the back."

"Civilians don't ride in government rigs," Delgado said—but he said it under his breath, bending to lift the Chevy's rear gate as he did.

Reluctantly Nita handed him her pack. Rachel had waked and was fussing, waving tiny fists. "I don't know," Nita said, and her eyes followed Delgado.

"Come on." Carter tried to ease her nervousness. "Get in. I'll worry about you out here by yourself."

"I get along better out here than you do," she said, but she gave him a faint smile.

Delgado was calling in to the base to let them know that he'd found Carter. "I want to get you into the infirmary pronto." He cradled the phone and put the car into gear.

"What makes you think Greely was behind this?" Carter clung to the dash, trying to keep his blistered back off the seat.

"Who else, sir?" Delgado glowered at Nita in the rearview mirror. "There's a car missing. I figure Greely wanted to make it look like you'd walked away from a breakdown and got lost. Quite a coincidence that she ran into you."

"Yeah, it *was* a coincidence." Not a setup, no matter what you want to think. "I can almost remember one of them . . . maybe the face will come back to me."

"It'll be Greely. I *know* that guy."

In the backseat, Rachel was crying in short, breathy bursts of noise. "Is she all right?" Carter twisted painfully to peer over the back of the seat.

"She's just upset." Nita looked pale and tense in the glow of the panel light.

"Are *you* all right?" he asked. Poor kid. Delgado had scared the shit out of her.

Nita shook her head impatiently. "I'm fine," she said. "Will you let me out on the edge of town, please?"

"I owe you some more water, at least." They were speeding down a long hill now, and Carter could see the twinkle of curfew-exempt lights in The Dalles, although the base was still invisible. A few lights had never looked so good. "We'll take you to the motel. I'll pay for a few nights. That'll give me some time to check on your husband."

"No." She held her daughter close, eyes on Delgado's back. "I appreciate it, but no thank you. You can let me out here," she said as they reached the bottom of the hill.

Delgado pulled over to the side of the road with a screech of brakes. He jumped out and went around to the rear of the car, dumping Nita's pack unceremoniously out onto the ground.

"Wait a minute." Carter flung the door open and struggled to his feet.

She had tucked Rachel into a cloth sling across her chest. The baby was quieter now, whimpering softly. With a deft twist, she shrugged the pack onto her shoulders.

"Don't just walk away," Carter said. He had a terrible feeling that he would never see her again, that she would vanish into the darkness and never reappear. "How do I get in touch with you when I've checked on David?" David—his name was a talisman, a magic charm that brought the smile back into her eyes. "I've got to give you your clothes back, too," he said desperately.

"I'll come to the base, okay?" She touched his hand lightly. "I'll ask for you."

He watched her walk away into the dark, light-headed and dizzy with exhaustion. He had been naked in front of this woman—naked in a way that had nothing to do with clothing. And somehow she had made it all right. He wondered who David Ascher was, and why he had left her, and found himself hoping that he didn't find that name in the Corps personnel files.

"Come on, Colonel." Delgado put a firm hand under his elbow. "You look like you're going to pass out."

CHAPTER SIX ☆

"You're damn lucky Delgado found you in time." General Hastings's face filled the screen on Carter's office terminal. "I'd file charges against Greely's bunch tomorrow, but that damned judge Lindstrom won't issue a warrant. He's been on the side of the Coalition since day one."

"There's no hard evidence that the Coalition was behind it." Carter kept his tone as neutral as possible. "Someone got onto the base with a forged pass. The guard went through our file of local troublemakers, but he couldn't make a positive ID. It wasn't Greely."

"He wouldn't be at the wheel." Hastings's snort was contemptuous. "He's not stupid."

Carter shut up. No point in continuing this discussion—and he didn't have any evidence that it *hadn't* been Greely. Greely had called Carter the day after Delgado had brought him in. He'd been upset—worried that Carter was going to blame the Coalition. And he'd been ignorant of the circumstances of the kidnap incident, enough to be believable. Maybe. Carter sighed. The hostility of the locals was a real quantity, but it was different here from Chicago. It was more focused. Personal. It made it a little harder to believe in Greely's absolute good faith.

"I *saw* one of them," Carter said out loud. "I wish I could remember him clearly enough for an ID."

"Me, too." Hastings's face enlarged, as if he had leaned closer to his terminal pickup. "I wish I knew what they were after. It'd give me a better idea of what we can expect around here."

Carter had a feeling that Hastings wouldn't have grieved much if they'd ODed him in the process. Tough luck, getting stuck with this bastard, but he'd survived Hastings's type before. Do your job well, keep a low profile, and pray you got transferred out before you collected too many poor evaluations.

"I assume you've dealt with your security problem?"

"Yes, sir." Which was a lie. Arris still couldn't find Greely's Goddamned hole. Carter's back was itching again and the need to scratch made him sweat. His skin was peeling off in sheets and the bloody itching never stopped. "That kidnap bothers me," he said slowly. "They must have guessed that the broken-down car bit would put someone on my track the minute you put a 'copter into the air." Delgado had been right about that stunt. Carter shook his head. "They also had to figure that I'd walk north, heading for the riverbed. If I did, I was bound to cross that road. People use it all the time. It was a better than even chance that someone would find me." Carter scowled at the fading bruise of the injection site. "I don't think they meant to kill me."

Hastings grunted.

"We had another sabotage attempt last night," Carter continued doggedly. He reached for the hardcopy report of last night's incident. The skin between his shoulder blades itched, and he willed it to stop. It didn't stop. "One of the patrols scared them off. The shaped charge they left behind would have punched a decent-size hole in the Pipe." The sabotage was escalating. "I need more people," he said bluntly. "I've got everyone putting in extra duty hours already. We can't keep this up."

"I can't give you any more." Hastings looked down at his desk. "Anything else to report, Colonel?"

"General, morale is going downhill fast. These doubled patrols might stop the sabotage, but I'm running everyone ragged." He had hired civilians to help with mess and housekeeping, but attrition was high. Working for the uniforms didn't make you very popular in town.

Hastings was scowling. "I sent in a request for more troops and got turned down. Water Policy is soft-pedaling. Probably because of Chicago." His stare was accusing. "A lot of people thought we overreacted there—thanks to the damn media." His lips twitched as if he wanted to spit. "If you start a war in The Dalles, you're on your own, Colonel."

Thanks for nothing. Carter clenched his teeth, struggling with the burning need to scratch. Johnny was going to be in town tomorrow. He'd ask him if this Water Policy line was on the level. You started laying heavy blame when you were spending your sleep time doing guard duty. You started thinking that you

were already in a war, that everybody on the other side of that
hot fence were gooks, hicks—not farmers or shopkeepers whose
names you knew yesterday. That same ugly darkness he'd felt in
Chicago was creeping in here, coloring the conversations in the
mess and the rec halls. Carter discovered he was scratching his
shoulder and yanked his hand away. "Sir?" He drew a deep
breath. "I've talked to Dan Greely," he said. "I'm going to
meet with the Coalition leaders this afternoon."

"Are you crazy?"

Hastings wasn't reacting any better than Delgado had. "No,
sir," Carter said wearily. "If we're going to keep a lid on things,
there has to be some talking. Or we *will* have a war on our
hands." He hesitated, gauging Hastings's frown. "I might pick
up some critical details, sir."

"You might get yourself killed this time. You're underestimating Greely. He *is* the Coalition."

"Believe me, I'm not underestimating him."

"Aren't you? Did you know that he's an old-time con man?"
Hastings's expression was hard. "He worked for the Corps as a
civilian employee, back when he was a scruffy kid. It was my
first year here in Bonneville. He's bright, all right. He worked
up to surveyor's assistant, then he ran off with some pretty
expensive equipment. He played a scam all over the state—
pretending to be a Corps surveyor. He ripped people off; paid
them in fake Corps scrip. This is the kind of man you're dealing
with, Carter. Don't let yourself be fooled by that golden tongue.
He's given it a lot of practice."

Huh. Carter frowned down at the hardcopy scattered across
his desk. This might put a new twist on things. "I still need to
go," he said stubbornly.

"It's too dangerous."

Maybe. And if he just sat here and plugged leaks, would he
end up in another Chicago? This time it *would* be his fault, and
Hastings wasn't about to back him up. He'd made that fucking
clear. He raised his head, met Hastings's eyes. "Are you order-
ing me not to attend this meeting, sir?"

For a moment they scowled at each other. "Hell, no." Hastings's face receded, as if he had leaned back in his chair. "It's
your sector. You're the CO. You get to screw up on your own,
but you'd better keep Watanabe in mind."

"I do, sir." Carter saluted, his teeth clenched. "Thank
you, sir." And go to hell.

The screen blanked, and Carter leaned back in his chair,

sweaty in spite of the air-conditioning. Hastings had made it *quite* clear: Fuck up, and it was Carter's ass on the line. He picked up the report of last night's sabotage attempt, tossed it back onto his desk. It wasn't that hard to punch a hole in the Pipe, and the pumping stations were easy targets. These bastards could wear them out playing hit and run. Things were tense between Corps and locals, but not impossible. Not yet. But it was only a matter of time before some tired, edgy trooper shot an innocent local by mistake. That could blow it good.

His back was driving him nuts. Carter unzipped his coverall and reached for the analgesic cream the doctor had given him. It didn't work as well as Nita's salve, he thought sourly. She had never come to the base, but no David Ascher had ever worked for the Corps. She must have found him somewhere else, or had found out that he wasn't here and had moved on. Carter tossed the bottle back into his drawer, slammed it shut. He'd meant to ask around for her in town to return the clothes, but he hadn't had the time. No, he hadn't made the time. He hadn't wanted to hear that she'd found her husband. It was almost time to leave for the Coalition meeting. Carter pushed her face out of his mind and put in a call for Delgado. It would be good to see Johnny tomorrow. Maybe he could put this mess into some kind of perspective.

The meeting was held in a house. It stood back from the two-lane highway that wound up the side of the gorge on its way toward Dufur and on southward, and had once been one of several suburban residences built close together on the steep hillside. A satellite dish gleamed on the roof. The houses on either side were dark, although Carter thought he caught the glimmer of a dim light in one upstairs room. Candle or lantern? It was half an hour past the power curfew. As they drove up, Carter made out the remains of a flagstoned patio beside the house. Skeletons of yard furniture rusted beneath the eaves, their plastic webbing shredded to colorless fringe.

"I don't like this place." Delgado set the brake hard.

"You'd rather we were meeting in a church?" Carter said easily. "If they're going to shoot us, they could do it there just as easily."

"Not funny," Delgado said, and frowned. "I know this crowd, remember?"

"Yeah, I remember." Carter sighed, wondering if he'd made a bad decision in letting Delgado come along; his hostility to the locals could be a major liability tonight. But Delgado was his second in command, and needed to be in on this. "I think we're safe enough," he said. "If the Coalition is behind the sabotage, they're being too careful about covering their tracks to blow it so openly. It's on record where we are and who we're meeting." Carter hoped he sounded confident. Neither of them was armed, and Delgado hadn't liked that much. "Wait a minute." Carter put a hand on Delgado's arm as the major started to get out of the car. "My job is to keep the water running, and I don't want to spill any more Army blood to do it. The Coalition may not like us and vice versa, but if they're not behind the sabotage, we need them. We need some local support. You will keep your opinions to yourself. Am I understood?"

"Yes, sir." Delgado's face was stiffly neutral.

"But I want you to listen to every word anyone says. I might miss something."

"*I* won't miss anything," Delgado said grimly.

They gingerly climbed the sagging porch steps. Light seeped through the thick curtains at the window. The house faced west, so the curtains were heavy enough to shut out the afternoon sun. You thought about the sun, and where its light would fall and what the heat would do. Not so long ago, people had been able to ignore the sun—they could ignore weather altogether. Not anymore.

The warped boards of the porch creaked loudly beneath Carter's feet and the door opened. "Colonel Voltaire." Dan Greely stood in the doorway, silhouetted by the light. "I'm glad you came." He held out his hand.

"This is Major Delgado," Carter said as he returned Greely's brief, firm grip.

"We've met." Greely withdrew his hand smoothly when Delgado ignored it. "Everyone else is here," he said, stepping aside. "Come in."

A wooden table occupied one end of the long room, opposite an old sofa and two upholstered chairs. A cluttered desk stood against the wall, topped by the blank eye of a computer terminal. Faded wallpaper boasted a ghostly memory of flowers, and the carpet was worn but clean. Three women and three men sat at the table, their faces stark and shadowed in the light of two solar lanterns that hung from an overhead chandelier. They were all in their forties at least. One woman looked older, her face lined and etched by wind and sun. Her wispy hair was gray and she alone smiled. The others looked wary or downright hostile.

Carter tried to file names with faces as Dan introduced the four soaker-hose farmers and two town merchants who made up the decision-making core of the Coalition. The air in the room felt stuffy, charged with tension. Carter sat down, and after the briefest hesitation Delgado took a seat, too.

"Water?" Greely carried a plastic pitcher to the table.

The words had a ritual sound. Without waiting for a response, he began to fill glasses, handing them around the table. Only Delgado shook his head when Greely offered him a glass. Everyone drank, or at least sipped a little of the water, faces formal, almost reverent. It *was* a ritual, consciously done or not, Carter thought. Sharing water. Nita had been right—he was beginning to understand this world and its values. He drank some of the cool water and lifted the glass slightly in a kind of salute. Greely gave him a faint smile.

"So how come you're here?" One of the farmers sat forward, thick arms bulging under the tight sleeves of his T-shirt. "You Army people don't give a shit about us."

Nice start. "We do give a shit, or I wouldn't be here." Carter set his glass down. Harold Ransom; he dredged the name from Greely's introductions. A beet and soy farmer. "We need to talk. This sabotage is hurting everyone and it's not going to bring one more drop of water down the Pipeline, or make it one cent cheaper."

Silence settled over the table as Ransom's face reddened. "You really think we're doing this? Cutting our own throats?" He half rose, muscles cording in his thick forearms. "You Army asshole. *We're* the ones going thirsty—not you. You bastards keep cutting our ration and I've seen *flowers* growing on that damn base. You think we're that dumb, don't you?"

"I don't know if you're dumb or not." Carter kept his voice level. "If you're not, then help us catch the people who *are* sabotaging the Pipe."

"Screw you," Ransom snarled. "You ain't really looking. You've already decided it's us."

"*I* haven't decided anything. Yet."

Ransom made a rude noise.

The gray-haired woman cleared her throat. "I've got three rose bushes in my garden, Harold. I'm willing to spend water money on them. I don't see why Army people can't grow flowers, too," she said gently. "It doesn't mean they're stealing water."

Ransom grunted.

"Colonel Voltaire's willing to talk to us." Greely leaned forward. "That's a start. How long do you think our crops are going to last if someone wrecks the Pipe and all the water stops tomorrow?"

"That's not what's bothering me," Ransom growled. "Down in the Valley, they arrested those folks who wouldn't pay the new water tax, remember? Sent 'em to prison and took their land. We're gettin' set up for that, and you bet the Army'll get their cut. You're awfully damn hot to be buddies with the uniforms." He glared at Greely. "You gonna get a cut, too? For keeping us quiet?"

"Knock it off, Harold." The gray-haired woman leaned forward. "Try thinking for a change."

Sandy Corbett. That was her name, Carter remembered.

"Dan's stood out in front around here for longer than you've been growing weeds," she went on. "He's paid a stiff price for doing it, too, which is more than I can say for you, Harold Ransom. You listen to him. We've all got an interest in stopping this sabotage stuff before it gets worse. Yes, we've been blamed for this—what do you expect? We've been giving Bonneville trouble for years." She ran an impatient hand through her hair. "Damn it, Harold, this time people have gotten killed, and so what if they're Army? It could be one of us next time. Maybe we can work together and maybe not, but we won't get anywhere if you've got to pick a new fight every time the colonel opens his mouth."

Ransom went red, white, and red again. "Okay," He shoved his clenched fists into his pockets. "I'll shut up. Let's see you do better."

Carter cleared his throat, watching the eyes shift his way. "Water's tight," he said. "Mexico's screaming about its water share falling off. The media doesn't have the story yet, but there's a possibility that Canada may pull out of the Alliance. If that happens, we're going to face a major shortfall. All of us. That's why agricultural rations have been cut lately—to keep the Alliance in one piece." Bless you, Johnny, Carter thought. The men and women around the table were listening to him at last. Carter met the eyes that didn't shift away from his—everyone but Ransom and a merchant whose name had slipped past him. "I know you folks are tight," he said slowly. "There's nothing the Corps can do about that."

"I don't know." Sandy Corbett looked troubled. "I keep

hearing that the valleys aren't getting cut—that they're getting the water you're taking away from us.''

Carter had been waiting for this accusation. ''They aren't getting cut as badly,'' he said. ''I called up the numbers. A lot of water goes down the Klamath and Willamette shunts, but that's where the production is.'' He opened the folder he'd brought and took out the sheaf of hardcopy he'd printed up that afternoon. ''Take a look for yourselves.'' He handed around the pages. ''We're pulling our maximum share out of the Trench. Per acre-foot of water, the Sacramento and Willamette valleys are leading you in production by a factor of fifteen percent.'' He paused, listening to the dry rustle as they turned pages. ''Those numbers count,'' he said flatly. ''A lot of people have to eat.''

''So do we.'' Ransom tossed his copy down. The white pages spilled off the table, fluttered to the floor. ''The valleys are all big ag-plexes, growing biomass bushes.'' His lips twisted. ''They're growing salt-tolerant test-tube shit for the tanks and I'll bet you ain't counting the seawater they use for irrigating, either.''

''I figured in the seawater. They *still* get fifteen percent more production for every gallon of sweet water that they use. Why don't you put in biomass shrubs up here?''

The silence slapped him in the face, hard and hostile again. Even the Corbett woman looked angry, and Greely was staring bleakly down at the tabletop.

''You uniforms really don't give a shit.'' Ransom pushed his chair back with a harsh scrape. ''Just do biomass, huh? I'm through wasting my time.'' He spat.

The glob of spittle landed on the toe of Carter's shoe. From the corner of his eye, Carter saw Delgado stiffen. ''Hold it,'' he barked.

For a moment they all froze. ''I'm sorry,'' he said, his eyes on Ransom's face. ''I'm new to this part of the country and I don't know enough about how and what you farm. If there's a reason why biomass crops won't work for you, I'd like to hear it.'' He was speaking to Ransom, no one else. This was the man to reach.

The heavyset farmer hesitated, chewing his lip, scowling at Carter. He glared at the door, hunched his shoulders. ''Takes three years to get a decent first crop,'' he said harshly. ''You gonna feed my kids for three years while I wait? We don't have no savings. Not after we pay your damn water bill. Yeah, I can buy a start on credit from Pacific Bio. Then they own me *and* my land. You think I'll ever get free of that debt?'' His lips worked. ''That's how they got to own the whole fucking Valley.''

So that was it. ''What about government loans, or a subsidy?'' Carter asked.

Ransom's laugh was bitter.

Hell, it had been a stupid question. Carter rubbed his face wearily. The welfare camps ate it all. There *wasn't* any extra money.

''It's not just the wait.'' Sandy Corbett spoke up. ''They're using seawater to irrigate down in the valleys because the bushes can take it. That's how you make them pay. It's cheap enough to pump it in from the coast, but the salt builds up in the soil. You go look at that land,'' she said softly. ''Nothing grows there but the bushes. The salt kills everything else. Once you start growing bushes, you can't stop. Once you start growing them, the land dies.''

''Amen,'' someone murmured.

Amen sounded right. Her words had the feel of a prayer. He'd been down in the Valley. He'd noticed the salt crusts, but after Michigan's bed, it had seemed normal. He hadn't really looked at the land. ''I'll do what I can to keep your water from getting cut any further.'' Carter looked at the wary, sundried faces one by one. ''That's all I can promise, and you're going to have to help me stop this sabotage. I can't argue for more water if we're losing it to leaks.''

''We've been trying to catch the suckers.'' Another of the farmers spoke up. ''Dan's organized some patrols, but there's a lot of Pipe out there.''

''And your soldiers are shooting at us,'' Sandy Corbett put in with a frown. ''It's dangerous to go anywhere near the Pipeline anymore.''

''They're under orders to return fire only.''

''You'd better check on that,'' she said tartly.

''I will. We have to work together on this.'' Carter ignored Delgado's restless movement of protest. ''I'd like to use civilian and Corps patrols on the line. My people are wearing out. It would take some of the pressure off them if we could coordinate our efforts.''

''It's a funny thing.'' Sandy Corbett frowned into her glass. ''In a town as small as The Dalles, you hear everything. You know who's in bed with whom and who's out sneaking around where they shouldn't be." She turned the glass slowly between her fingers. "No one knows who's behind the sabotage," she said. "We should know."

Carter frowned. "So you think it's outsiders?"

"Yes," she said. "I do. But whoever they are, they know this part of the country awfully well."

"And why are they doing it?" Carter frowned down at the papers stacked in front of him, listening to their silence. "I'll do what I can." He shuffled the papers back into his folder. "I hope we can work together on this thing."

"I think we've made a good start," Greely said.

"We have, indeed." Sandy Corbett stood up, pushing hair back from her square face. "I figured Bonneville was going to stick us with a real bastard after Mike got murdered." She gave Carter a smile and stuck out her hand. "I'm glad we pulled you," she said.

Her smile was warm and genuine, and Carter returned her firm grip. These people might be telling the truth. *Might* be. He was offered more hands, shook, and was given murmured farewells from everyone except Ransom, who had left the room silently and by himself. Greely waited for Carter on the porch. It was dark now, and the wind was picking up. "I'm impressed." Greely grinned crookedly. "You handled Harold, and Harold isn't an easy man to handle."

"You didn't help me much," Carter said shortly.

"You're right, I didn't." Greely sighed. "You heard Harold. He thinks I've sold out, and he's probably not the only one. You didn't really need me." His grin flashed briefly. "You were doing fine on your own."

In spite of his light tone, Ransom's accusation had hurt. You could see it in Greely's face. Carter wondered about the price he had paid—the one the Corbett woman had mentioned. It didn't fit with what Hastings had told him. "I was serious about running some Coalition patrols," Carter said slowly. "They'd have to operate under Corps NCOs, though. Do you think you can organize it?"

"I'll try." Greely frowned. "There have been some ugly incidents around here. Uniforms aren't too popular."

"Neither are locals, on my side of the fence," Carter said dryly. He frowned. "I'll have my officers pick levelheaded people for the mixed patrols."

"I can tap some people who'll behave themselves. I think it's worth trying." Greely sighed. "You have to understand the situation here. We fight every day just to stay alive. We fight drought, dust storms, debt, and bad crop prices. We don't know how to stop fighting anymore." He ran a hand through his graying hair. "Me, I'm tired," he said. "I'd like to get through this without any more bloodshed."

"Amen," Carter said, and once again the word had the feel of a prayer.

He looked down the hill, toward the riverbed. It was invisible in the darkness. He remembered his vision of the waterfall and the blond hitchhiker. "Do you ever see yesterday?" he asked. "A glimpse of how it used to be?"

"No." Greely sounded puzzled. "That would be a hell of a vision." He was silent for a moment, his eyes too on the distant, invisible riverbed. "I don't know if I'd want that kind of vision," he said slowly. "I don't think I'd want to really know what we've lost."

Yes, it could hurt. "Hastings told me you worked for the Corps," Carter said harshly. "He told me you ran a scam out in the Dry—pretending you were a Corps surveyor."

Greely didn't answer, and Carter found himself holding his breath, eyes on the man's weary profile.

At last he sighed and faced Carter. "Yeah, I did that. I was twenty." He looked down at his hands, turning them slowly palm up. "I stole uniforms, gear. I went around pretending that I was surveying for a drilling project. I'd been begging for most of my life, and I was tired of begging. I hurt a lot of people." He closed his hands slowly, let them drop to his sides. "I gave people hope and then I left it to die." He looked up to meet Carter's gaze, his dark eyes steady and sad. "I went to prison for it, finally. Courtesy of General Hastings. I spent three years behind bars, and while I was there, a good friend of mine got shot. We'd been organizing a water strike here in The Dalles. He had a wife and three kids. If I hadn't been in prison, Sam might not have died." He shrugged heavily. "Or maybe they would have killed both of us. I guess I'll never know."

Carter could believe this man. He wanted to, but he was CO, and a lot of people depended on him not to screw up. "Pick your teams," he said. "And we'll set up a schedule. You can reach me at the base any time. I'll leave word at both gates."

"Thanks." Greely held out his hand and Carter clasped it.

Delgado was waiting for him beside the stairs, just out of their sight. Eavesdropping? Carter clicked on his flash as he went down the steps, lips tight.

"What's your opinion?" he asked as he reached the car.

"They're stringing you along." Delgado sounded sullen. "They're setting you up, like they did Watanabe." He spat. "That dude is slick."

"Hold it," Carter said as Delgado opened the car door. "How come you hate these people so much?"

"I don't hate them." Delgado didn't quite meet his eyes.

"I don't want to request your transfer," Carter said slowly. "But your attitude's going to cause problems. If we don't clear this up right now, it goes in tomorrow."

"You want to clear things up?" Delgado's eyes gleamed in the light from Carter's flash. "I'll clear it up for you. My brother was a corporal here at The Dalles." His voice was soft. "He was out chasing a leak last fall—on his own, because we were only running two to a spotter crew back then and his teammate had gotten sick. Some hick picked him off with a thirty-ought-six. He crawled a half mile through dust and rock to reach the highway, almost made it before he bled to death. Sonny was twenty. He was the first one the hicks got."

So that was it. "I didn't see his name on the report," Carter said.

"Mom remarried. Sonny was my half brother. Sonny Malone. He went into the Corps because I was in it. He was a kid, Colonel. Just a Goddamned kid."

"I'm sorry."

"You think these are decent folk, just because they talk nice to you. You want to believe Greely 'cause he spins a sweet line. They'll kill you in a second if it gets 'em more water. That's all that counts, for them. Water." Delgado slid onto the front seat. "Why don't you worry about our people instead of the hicks?"

"That's enough, Major." Carter flushed. "I'm doing this *because* I care about my people. Go on back to the base. I'm going to walk."

"You sure you want to walk, sir?" Delgado's face was cold. "If you meet any hicks, they may change your mind for you about how nice they are. You better ride. Sir."

"Drive back to the base, Major." He stepped back as Delgado gunned the engine. Easy, he told himself as the car's taillights vanished around the corner. Delgado's attitude was understandable, even if it was out of line. It was the crack about taking care of his own people—I *am*, he thought bitterly. This was the only way.

It wouldn't have bothered him if he were sure.

Fuck it.

Carter started down the hill, walking fast. The major was going to get a transfer. Immediately. He had reasons for his feelings, but cooperation was their only hope, and he had no business being here. If the Coalition wasn't behind the sabotage, who was? Bitter locals, Carter guessed, no matter what the Corbett woman thought. Revenge was the most likely motive. Carter made a mental note to check on local bankruptcy and foreclosure records. Maybe something would click. *Do you believe Dan Greely?* A little voice whispered in the back of his brain, and Carter let his breath out in a slow sigh. *I gave people hope and then I left it to die,* he had said. There had been shame behind those words.

Debris skittered dryly across the asphalt. To the west, the town was almost completely dark. Electricity came from the few operating nuclear plants, from wind or solar batteries, and it cost a lot. Without energy, Carter thought bitterly, civilization rolls back a thousand years or so. Technology had ground to a crawl and the economy had tottered into the Crash.

The moon was up now, low enough on the horizon to be blocked by the rim of the gorge. Carter could just make out the gray mass of the concrete ramp that led to the highway bridge. He walked slowly, paying attention to the night noises, using his flash as little as possible. Delgado had probably been right about the risk. He'd been trying to prove something to Delgado—or to himself? Carter grimaced. He should be safe enough. Most of the trouble had come from soldiers and locals mixing at local bars. His route bypassed town, and the truck plaza was no danger. Truckers stayed out of politics.

Delgado had let Nita off somewhere around here. He wondered if she was still in The Dalles. Six semi rigs bulked darkly in the plaza lot and lights gleamed in the windows of the old motel where the truckers stayed. The riverbed yawned beyond the motel, a vast trench of deeper darkness. In the old days they had shipped wheat down the river on barges. Weird image, a river as highway.

A small noise brought Carter to attention. Footsteps? He slowed. Yes. More than one person, and they weren't trying to be quiet anymore. Carter put his head down and walked faster, listening hard. He might make it to the gate if they thought he hadn't noticed them.

The footsteps broke into a run. "Get him," someone yelled.

Carter ran. The gate wasn't impossibly far away, but he was

panting after only a few yards, his salt-damaged lungs burning with each labored breath. He risked a quick glance over his shoulder. Three of them, and they were catching up. Too late to try for the truck plaza. Carter veered off the asphalt, running down into the rocky scrub that flanked the road. His only hope was to lose them, but the rising moon flooded the ground with light. Gasping, Carter stumbled into the dark mouth of a huge culvert that ran beneath the high bank of the interstate. No hope of losing them; they must have seen him.

Black darkness filled the culvert. Carter crouched against the concrete wall. A figure skidded around the corner and Carter swung hard, catching his attacker square in the belly. He was small and he went down easily, retching and gasping as he rolled in the dust. The other two were right behind him. They skidded to a halt, spreading out to flank him. Kids. Carter's throat tightened. They were just kids. For a second, the kid in the van stared at him from the darkness. Shit. Carter backed warily, keeping them both in view. One of them—a skinny boy with a ponytail of dark hair—edged into the mouth of the culvert, a baseball bat cocked in his hands. Carter dropped into a crouch, his belly full of ice, glad of the wall behind him. The other kid had a knife. If these two knew what they were doing, he was trapped and dead.

"Fuckin' uniform. You lookin' for action, huh? We'll show you action." The skinny kid rushed him.

Carter ducked the bat's swing with an inch to spare and heard a dull crack as it hit the wall. The impact jarred the bat out of the kid's hands. As he grabbed for it, Carter chopped him hard at the base of the neck. The other kid was on him, knife flashing as he slashed at Carter's face. Carter chopped his wrist aside, grabbed it, and pivoted fast. The knife clattered somewhere in the darkness. Carter let himself move with the momentum of the kid's body, dropped to one knee, and felt him come loose. The kid hit the ground flat on his back.

Panting, eyes stinging with sweat, Carter picked up the baseball bat. Cautiously he bent over the ponytailed kid he'd chopped. The boy's eyelids were fluttering and his fingers twitched as Carter touched him. He looked about fourteen. Carter tapped the cracked bat lightly against his palm. The third kid had vanished, but the one he'd tossed was picking himself up out of the dust. Tangled blond hair hung down across his face and he kept his eyes on the bat in Carter's hands. A trapped animal would look like that. Not scared, just desperate. He didn't doubt that

Carter was going to swing at him. "Next time, lay off," Carter
said. "You hear me?"

The kid tore his eyes reluctantly from the bat, looked at Carter.

"Take care of your friend." Carter jerked his head at the
ponytailed kid, who was up on his hands and knees. He backed
toward the culvert mouth, a wary eye on the pair behind him.
Another shadow moved and moonlight glinted on a knife blade.
Carter took a fast step forward, swinging the bat up.

"Don't! It's only me." The shadow darted back into moonlight and became a woman with one hand raised against the
threat.

"Nita?" Carter lowered the bat, hands shaking with the
knowledge of how close he'd come to hitting her. "What are
you doing here?"

She looked down at the switchblade in her hand. "They were
going to kill you."

"I know." Carter glanced quickly back over his shoulder.

"It's all right. They took off the other way."

Carter listened, hearing only wind and a tiny, rodent scuffle.
"You're still here? I thought you'd found your husband when I
didn't hear from you."

"David wasn't in your files, was he?" She hung her head,
her face hidden by loose hair.

"You didn't find him?" he asked gently.

"He's not here. I don't think he ever got here." She closed
the knife and slid it into her pocket. "I think I've asked everyone
in town. No one remembers him."

"I'm sorry," he said, hearing the inadequacy of the words.
He looked beyond her and saw a rumpled sleeping bag spread
out in a small hollow. "You're not camping here, are you?"

"The kids don't bother *me*. I don't wear a uniform." Nita
squatted beside the sleeping bag as Rachel stirred and whimpered. "It's free," she said, picking up the baby. "It's as good
a place as any."

Her face looked thinner than he remembered. The pale light
accentuated her high cheekbones, filling her dark eyes with
shadow. Something had changed in her face. There had been
strength there before, a confidence that was missing now. Her
loosened hair clung to her face in dark wisps as she bent over
her daughter. She looked . . . defeated.

"I still owe you," Carter said softly. "And I need to return
the clothes you lent me. Why don't you stay with me for a day
or two? I've got an extra bed. You can have a shower and catch

your breath. It's a genuine offer, okay? No price tag. No strings attached.''

She looked up at him finally, frowning as if she were going to refuse. Then Rachel whimpered again and she sighed. ''Thank you.'' Her shoulders drooped. ''I think I'll take you up on it. Just for a night or two, all right? Until I decide where to go from here?''

''You can stay as long as you need to.''

Carter helped her gather her belongings, keeping an eye out for the kids. He kept seeing the blond boy's feral, hopeless eyes against the darkness. He'd seen eyes like that on the lakeshore. And now here. He picked up Nita's pack as she tucked Rachel into her sling. ''I'll feel a lot better when we're inside the gates,'' he said, but he wondered if it was any safer in there.

CHAPTER SEVEN ☆

Waiting outside the base's ugly wire gate, Nita wondered if she was making a mistake. She had meant to move on, go down the riverbed to Bonneville; maybe David had gone there. But she was tired. Rachel whimpered and Nita hugged her. It was a weariness of the spirit more than of the body. Carter was talking to a uniformed soldier just inside the gate. The man held an ugly rifle and he didn't like her. The gate itself scared her. There were two gates, actually, all steel mesh and razor wire, one on either side of the small, square building where the soldier was now tapping keys on a terminal. The soldier was like the gate, all razor-sharp barbs of hostility.

Nita looked away from the glinting, thorny gate. Razor wire had fenced the ag-plex where she had grown up. A drifter had tried to climb it one night, drunk or just desperate. Nita remembered the blood that had soaked his clothes and darkened the dust beneath his tangled, slashed corpse. She shook herself, angry at her own weakness. The past week had left her fragile, full of darkness and childish fears. Carter had offered her a clean place to sleep, and this was just a wire gate, nothing more. He was waiting for her. Nita tossed her head, picked up her water jugs, and marched past the razor-wire soldier.

"You'll have to carry this when you go in and out." Carter offered her a small plastic card. "You can't get past the gate without it. Are you all right?"

He was concerned. "I'm just tired." Nita reached inside the neck of her shirt, fished up the small bag that held her few remaining pieces of scrip, and tucked the card into it. "Thank you," she said. He was also nervous. His feelings radiated strongly, unmistakably, at this close range. She looked around, jumpy in this strange place, reacting a little to his nervousness.

Houses lined the dusty street, bathed in yellow light from lamps on tall poles. So much light! "It looks like a city," she said.

"It's like a town—a very small one," Carter said. "The base where I was stationed in Chicago was a lot bigger. This way." He turned abruptly onto a narrow walk that led up to one of the buildings.

It wasn't too bad. There were fewer people here than in The Dalles, and it wasn't as noisy. Carter had unlocked the door and Nita followed him inside, blinking in the sudden light. The luxury of the room took her breath away. There were curtains at the windows, carpet on the floor. She touched the padded arm of a sofa, feeling a little dizzy. "The foreman at the ag-plex lived like this," she said out loud. "We used to peek through his windows. It looked like heaven to us kids."

"It's just a basic Corps apartment. No frills."

She'd embarrassed him for some reason. Nita bit her lip. The last of her self-assurance was evaporating in the face of this luxury. She was lost here, out of her depth. No, it was David who was lost. Carter was speaking and Nita forced herself to pay attention to his words.

"You and Rachel can sleep in the bedroom," he was saying. "That'll give you some privacy. The shower's in there. I'll get you a towel." Carter was bustling around as he talked, covering his discomfort with motion.

Nita put Rachel down on the soft, wide bed, hoping she'd stay asleep for a little while longer. The shower was in a small white room along with a toilet and a sink. Incredible luxury. Nita peered through the glass doors, feeling as if she were sleep-walking or trapped in a dream. "How do you work this?" she asked.

"Haven't you ever used a shower before?"

He was so *surprised*. Shocked, almost. "We used a pail," she said. "When the water got too muddy, we poured it on the squash or the bean plants. Where did you grow up, anyway?"

"Western Pennsylvania. Outside of Pittsburgh." Carter looked away.

"Carter, it's all right." Puzzled, Nita groped for the source of his discomfort. "There was a shower house on the ag-plex, but it cost too much for us kids to use it. Then I went to live with David. We hunted bees, so we lived in a tent, up in the hills. Does that bother you?"

"No, no. It's not that." Carter laughed awkwardly. "I guess I took some things for granted. I mean, water's tight, but even in the suburbs, even on a welfare card, you get time in a public shower. The water gets recycled," he said hastily. "It doesn't get wasted."

"I've never lived in a city, that's all." Nita gave him a tentative smile. "You do things differently in the Dry, I guess. What do I push, or turn, or whatever?"

He showed her the lever that turned the water on and told her that it was on a timer and would go off by itself after a few minutes. Then he retreated, closing the door tightly behind him. Nita stripped off her shirt and jeans and stepped into the cabinet. Water fell down on her like rain, but gentle and warm. It ran sensuously across her skin, funneled down between her milk-heavy breasts, over the flat curve of her stomach, and into the dark hair between her legs. Nita shook her head and smiled when water spattered the cabinet walls. She unbraided her hair, let the water wash through it, and combed the squeaky wet strands with her fingers.

It was wonderful. She wanted to stay in there forever.

The water shut off all too soon. Regretfully Nita dried herself, careful not to drip any of the precious water onto the floor where it would be wasted. In the bedroom, Rachel was beginning to fuss. Nita pulled on her clothes hastily and opened the door. Carter was hovering in the doorway to the bedroom, eyeing Rachel, his indecision humming in the air. He wasn't used to babies. Nita slipped past him and scooped Rachel into her arms. "I'm sorry." She lifted her shirt, letting Rachel find a nipple. "She really is a quiet baby, most of the time."

"That's all right." Carter was carefully not looking at her breast. "Do you need anything else?"

Aha. "We're fine." Nita smiled for him, trying to make him feel easier. "Thank you for letting us stay here," she told him.

His eyelids flickered. "Good night," he said, and closed the door softly behind him.

That was it. He had offered her a sanctuary, but now he wanted her, and he was angry at himself for it. Nita sighed and shifted Rachel to the other breast. He was honest, this man. He had been honest about his fear, out in the darkness. She liked him for that. Lying down, she curled around her daughter, pulling the quilt over them both. She was tired, but sleep brought its own dangers. It brought dreams of David, ugly scenes of injury and thirst. She dreamed of David hit by a truck on the highway, killed by some faceless human predator, or shot by a Drylander as he tried to beg for help.

She dreamed of David walking away from her, walking away from the daughter who might be too much like her.

Rachel whimpered.

"It's all right, love. It's all right," Nita murmured. It wasn't all right. She closed her eyes against the stinging tears and concentrated on her daughter's primitive, hunger-satisfied comfort.

Nita woke suddenly, wondering when she had fallen asleep. She had dreamed, but she couldn't remember it. David again? Throat aching with dream-tears, Nita eased herself off the bed, tucking the quilt and pillow around Rachel. It was dark in the room, but light from the tall lamps outside seeped in through the windows. Nita peered out. The world looked dead, colorless and gray. She tried to swallow the lump in her throat, but it wouldn't go down. It was so easy to die in this dry land.

David had loved her. She had felt his love for her, warm as his body against hers at night. She had felt the dark shadow of his fear, too; she had had no choice but to feel it. The darkness and the silence pressed around Nita, closing on her like a fist. It made her feel more alone than she had ever felt before—even on that long-ago day when she had run away from Mama and Alberto forever.

David had come after her then. He had searched for her and found her, alone in the Dry. And she had told him why she had run, because she had understood at last that he loved her.

The first faint shadow of his fear had been born then, on that day. Nita leaned her forehead against the thick, cool glass of the window. The dream-tears made a hard lump in her throat and that emptiness outside threatened to drown her, suck the life out of her and leave her a shriveled husk. Slowly Nita became aware of Carter. He was awake, too, silent in the other room. He wanted her and, beneath his desire, he felt sorry for her. Because he thought David was dead. Strange man; honest enough to admit that he was afraid, upset because she had never used a shower, angry at himself for his own feelings. He cared about her. In this dark moment of loneliness, Nita clutched at that caring.

The emptiness beat at the window like a dark wing, trying to get in. Nita edged away, reaching for the bedroom door. It creaked a little as she pushed it open. Carter heard it and knew she was there. Nita took a single step into the room, her heart beating fast, his desire flickering through her like heat lightning. He lay on the sofa bed watching her, just visible in the light that seeped in through the windows. He wasn't sure yet why she was there. The darkness crouched at Nita's heels, and she closed the door against it. She had noticed condoms in the bathroom. Nita groped her way to the sink and opened the small cabinet above it. There, on the bottom shelf.

He didn't say anything as she came to stand beside the sofa bed. She took off her shirt and dropped it onto the floor, hearing the soft hiss of his indrawn breath, aware of his gaze on her skin, hot as sunlight.

"I told you there weren't any strings," he said at last, and his voice was husky.

"I heard you."

David had never come to this town. He had been afraid of her, afraid of what Rachel might be. Darkness lurked on the other side of the flimsy walls, vast and empty. Nita closed her eyes briefly and touched the smooth skin of Carter's shoulder. He shivered, propped on one elbow, face turned up to her. Nita ran her fingers lightly across the dense curl of his hair, traced the jut of his cheekbones beneath his pale skin. She touched his lips lightly with her fingertips, heart beating faster now. When he reached up to tangle his fingers in her loose hair, she slid onto the bed beside him, losing herself in the quick hot passion of his lips and tongue, twining her legs with his.

His hands cupped her heavy breasts, then slid down across her belly, gentle and sensuous as the shower water, urgent at the same time, making her shudder with pleasure. He caught his breath as she took his penis in her hand, his erection hardening as she unrolled the condom over it. Nita arched her back, guiding him, breathless and aching with her desire and his, too. He rolled onto her with a soft moan and she locked her legs around his narrow hips, moving with the rhythm of his body, riding the tight, soaring spiral of their mingled passion. The bright nova of his coming burst inside Nita, and she cried his name out loud as he swept her along with him.

His small twitch of reaction told her what she had done— called David's name, not his. She twisted away from him, burying her face in the pillow. The tears came at last, unstoppable. Because she had hurt him, because he wasn't David.

"Nita, it's all right." He pulled her gently against him, cradling her head against his chest, stroking her damp hair back from her face. "I understand," he said, and there was no anger inside him, only warmth and a little sadness. "I'm sorry you didn't find him." He traced the curve of her cheek with a gentle fingertip. "Part of me isn't sorry," he said, and the sadness showed in his smile. "I was afraid I was never going to see you again." He kissed her gently, and Nita tasted the salt of her own tears on his lips. Then he looked down, startled and a little puzzled.

"I'm sorry." Nita wiped at the trickle of milk between her breasts.

Surprised, Carter touched one dark nipple, watching beads of white swell, combine, and trickle slowly down the curve of her breast. "Does that always happen?" he asked, fascinated.

"Usually." Nita smiled through her tears. "Sometimes it's worse. Be glad that Rachel was hungry tonight."

"I didn't know that." Carter met her eyes, his own face serious. "Tell me about yourself," he said. "Anything. Everything—who you are, where you grew up—about David, if you want to."

Tell him about David? She wanted to talk about David; she wanted to tell Carter how much she loved him, how he had been a sanctuary of safety and comfort after a childhood of confusion and hurting silence. She needed to tell him so that they would both know, so that he would understand. Nita drew a shaky breath. To tell him that, she would have to tell him why David had been afraid. She closed her eyes briefly, remembering Seth, remembering the hot, molten feel of him. No. "I was born right here in The Dalles," she said slowly. "We had a soy farm. My father . . . was killed when I was little. After that, we went to live with my brother Alberto on a bush farm in the Willamette Valley. I didn't want to come back here."

"I'm sorry."

"About my father?" He was sad again. "Don't be." Nita turned Carter's hand over and traced the lines in his palm. "An old woman I knew claimed she could read your future in your hand. I never knew my father." Nita laid his hand down and covered it with her own. "He got shot in some kind of water war. Mama never forgave him for getting killed and leaving her. When I was little, I thought it was my fault, her anger. I thought she was angry at me." Nita blinked as long-buried memories stirred again. There were ghosts in this town. Hurtful ghosts. "She was angry at him—because she loved him and he died. I didn't understand until it was too late," Nita said. "I think I could have loved Mama if I'd understood."

Carter's hand closed tight on hers. "I don't remember my father at all. He died when I was a baby. My mother never remarried.'' He lifted one shoulder in a jerky shrug, restless suddenly, his hazel eyes as dark as copper in the dim light.

There was a wound there—something he didn't want to talk about or remember. Nita lifted his hand, kissing his fingers gently.

"I met a woman who reminded me of you earlier tonight." Carter changed the subject abruptly. "She talked about the land as if it were alive, as if we could kill it. The land mattered to her. I can't feel that," he said. "It just looks like dirt and rock to me."

"You have to know how to look."

"Will you show me?" he asked softly. "I think it would help me understand the farmers."

He meant it—that he wanted to understand. "Yes," she said. "We'll go up into the hills, and I'll show you."

He pulled her close again, his breath warm against her face. "You did a crazy thing, you know, coming into that culvert tonight. You could've gotten hurt."

He wasn't angry. He was asking her a question, and she wasn't sure what he was asking. "They meant to kill you." She shut her lips tightly, afraid that he would ask her how she knew, and that her tongue would betray her.

In the bedroom, Rachel whimpered. Relieved at the distraction, Nita got up quickly. She couldn't tell him. She didn't want to feel it again: that gathering shadow, the darkness behind the smile and the reassurances that it was all right. Not again. Not ever again.

Rachel wasn't really hungry. Nita tucked her between them and she smiled, eyes fixed on Carter's face as she nursed. She wasn't sleepy, either. "Sometimes she just likes to play," Nita said, resigned. "Maybe because it's cooler at night."

He didn't mind. He smiled at Rachel's smile and poked a finger into her palm so that she could grab it. He was shy—pleased when she grinned and drooled at him.

Nita wasn't sleepy, either. It was as if Rachel had infected them with her wakefulness. So they talked. She told him about the big ag-plex where she had grown up—about weeding the neat rows of tamarisk while the grown-ups pruned off branches for the digester. She told him about the dust and the cool mud around the soaker hoses, about the white crusts of salt that formed on the bush stems, stinging the cuts on your hands and enticingly prickly on your tongue. She didn't tell him about how the foreman had felt as he had put his hands on her breasts out behind the shed. She didn't tell him about Mama's bitterness, Ignacio's anger, or Alberto's resignation, because she couldn't.

He told her about growing up in the walled suburban enclave outside of Pittsburgh. Son of a housekeeper in the world of the rich. The darkness lay there—a wound that was deep and old and ugly. He tiptoed around it, not close enough to give it away, and she didn't pry. He told her about his friend Johnny, who had given him entrance into this luxurious world that she couldn't even begin to imagine. He worshipped this friend, or owed him a debt that went as deep as the wound . . . or maybe was part of the wound.

She wasn't sure that she liked this friend.

Night was fading into dawn, brightening to morning. Rachel was asleep, finally: head turned to the side, fist by her mouth, drowned in a murmur of dreams. I love you, Nita thought, and felt her heart contract. I love you, daughter. Outside, voices. Army people walking by. On their way to tend the Pipeline? "Why did you go into the Army?" she asked Carter.

"Hm?" His eyelids fluttered—he had been almost asleep. "Oh." He yawned. "Because the Corps was looking for officers at the time, so they paid me to go to school." He frowned, not sleepy anymore. "I liked it," he said. "You know where you stand in the Corps. Your status is very carefully and precisely defined. You don't have any questions about who you are."

He had had a lot of questions as a housekeeper's son in a rich world. She had read that much between the lines.

"I don't know," he went on, and he didn't meet her eyes. "I hope they got the officer they wanted."

Nita winced at the doubt behind his words. "They did," she said, and touched his face. "They got more than they paid for."

He shook his head, frowning. Then he shrugged and smiled for her. "I've got to go to a reception this afternoon. Johnny—the friend I told you about—invited me." His smile grew warmer. "I'm not going to be at my best."

His smile didn't hide those doubts. "You don't have to be at your best. You can be tired today." Nita rolled lightly off the mattress, came around to his side of the bed, and leaned down to kiss him. He reached up for her and she slid onto him, drowning doubts and the past in the vivid here-and-now of flesh against flesh.

CHAPTER EIGHT ☆

The reception was for Johnny—some kind of private party. It was the first time they'd gotten together since their near miss in Portland, but this wasn't Carter's first choice of situation. He grimaced as he parked his car, wishing that they could be hanging out somewhere over a couple of beers. He wanted to tell Johnny about Nita. Maybe he just wanted to listen to himself try to explain to Johnny how he felt.

Then maybe he'd have a clue.

He slammed the door and locked it. The house was on a narrow street that overlooked the public market and the main streets of The Dalles. It was big, with a fresh new coat of paint. Carter stifled a yawn. He had gotten about two hours of sleep— not nearly enough—too much, if you wanted to look at it that way. Nita and Rachel had been asleep when he had left to review the night's flow reports and the morning's business.

Nita . . . He paused on the wide, railed porch, staring blindly at the old warehouses that lined the riverbed's edge far below. Her black hair had veiled the pillow and she had smiled a little in her sleep when he had kissed her. He had felt . . . Carter shook his head impatiently, not at all sure *how* he felt, damn it.

The door opened. "You going to stand out here all day?" Johnny grinned at him, casually elegant in a loose shirt and linen pants. "So I'm sorry I missed you in Portland already. Stop sulking out there and come on in."

"I'm not sulking. I'm asleep." Carter let Johnny sweep him through the door, glad to see him, willing to be distracted from thoughts of Nita for the moment. "I was sorry to miss you, too."

"We'll connect one of these days." Johnny slapped him on the shoulder, but there was a thin quality to his grin. Strain?

80

"Better yet, we'll go down to San Francisco and do that."
Johnny held out his hand to a tall dark-haired woman. "Meet
Gwynn. She's giving this party. She owns the government fuel
franchise for The Dalles."

"It's a living." She held out a hand to Carter, smiling. "Although I'd rather live in San Francisco." She gave Johnny a
quick smile. " Glad to meet you, Colonel."

"I'm glad to meet you. Thanks for letting Johnny drag me
along."

"Oh, I would have invited you anyway." A dimple showed
at the corner of her mouth when she smiled. "Let me get you a
glass of wine?"

"Thanks." Carter watched her walk gracefully away. Johnny's current lover?

She was the kind of woman who attracted him—tall and
elegant. They always reminded Carter of Amber, Johnny's ex-
wife—although he was never going to say *that* out loud. Twenty-
five or thirty men and women milled in the long, well-furnished
living–dining room. A few of them browsed the laden table set
up in front of the windows. The rest clustered at the far corner
of the room, watching some kind of performance. A burst of
clapping and laughter greeted Carter.

"A magician. The guy's pretty good." Johnny jerked his head
at the crowd. "Gwynn hired him off a streetcorner down in
Bonneville. "Here's your wine." He took the glass from
Gwynn's hand and kissed her lightly on the cheek. "When
the show's over Gwynn can introduce you around."

"So what brings you to The Dalles?" Carter asked as he
wandered over to the buffet table with Johnny. "Gwynn?" He
gave Johnny a sideways look. "Or business?"

"Actually, I dropped in to see you. Gwynn and I are old
news." Johnny shrugged and smiled, but there was a serious
undercurrent to his words. "I thought I'd get the lowdown from
you on what's going on here. General Hastings has been putting
in some heavy troop requests. I want to hear your side of it."
He took Carter by the elbow, steering him toward the far corner
of the room.

"Nothing, yet." Carter sipped his wine. It tasted like real
stuff—not a cheap synthetic. Gwynn must make good money on
her fuel franchise. "The troop request is a real thing, Johnny. I
was planning to lean on you. We've got a sabotage situation
that's escalating fast, and not enough people to deal with it. We
need more bodies."

"That's bad." Johnny frowned into his own glass. "Like I told you—Mexico is getting restless. That means there's no extra water to play with. If someone blows the Pipeline, the valleys dry up."

"And we get the blame. So give us more people." Carter watched Johnny's face, struggling with rising frustration. Johnny wasn't hearing him. This was Johnny Seldon, member of Water Policy. The friend you could reach. Not this guy. "Hastings said he got turned down."

"He did. I can't do it, Carter." Johnny smiled, a smooth, seamless smile. "Chicago scared a lot more people than you. Military force to protect water flow was a hot issue, and the media would love to raise it again."

"You think I don't know that?" Carter drained his glass, trying to hold on to his anger. How could he do this? Johnny had to know the stakes here. "Damn it, Johnny, we're going to have trouble if we *don't* get extra people."

"I don't think you understand." Johnny lowered his voice. "No one has more power than we do—not even the president— but it's not a sure thing." His eyes glittered in the light from the window. "You better believe we all know it, even if we pretend to be so civic-minded and above it all. The country amended the Constitution once to create Water Policy. They could do it again and take it all away."

"So the Committee's going to play to the media?" Carter set his empty glass down on the windowsill very gently. "And we can go to hell?"

"Come off it, Carter. You're talking like I'm the enemy." Johnny sighed and sipped at his own wine. "Look, I've got a little leverage, even if the old boys think I'm still in diapers. I'll try, okay? Now I've got to go socialize. I'm Gwynn's major attraction this afternoon—and I need to feel some people out about things." He rolled his eyes. "This job is twenty-four hours a day."

"Thanks, Johnny." Carter touched his shoulder lightly.

He wanted to feel pleased, but instead he felt depressed. He'd known Johnny ever since sixth grade. He'd gone in on the crazy projects—like rewriting the history exam in the school database, stealing the basketball coach's old NBA jersey, a hundred other crazy stunts—and he knew Johnny's tone when he was sweet-talking his way out of trouble. Oh, Johnny had that act down pat.

And he'd just used it, promising to look into Hastings's troop request.

So, Hastings wasn't going to get his troops and Carter was on his own. Dan Greely's volunteers looked better and better. Carter retrieved his glass from the window, wanting more wine, wanting suddenly and intensely to get a little drunk, to go back and get into bed with Nita and pretend this all wasn't happening. It hurt that Johnny had used that voice on him. He could have said no, up front. Too bad, buddy, I've got my own row to hoe. He could've understood that. Carter shook his head. What really bothered him was the look in Johnny's eyes—that bright, hungry glitter when he talked about Water Policy being the most powerful position in the country, bar none.

A waiter offered a tray of full glasses and whisked away Carter's empty one. He wandered back to the buffet table, looking for Johnny and not finding him, scanning the absorbed crowd. He knew some of them—or knew who they were, anyway. They were the upper crust of The Dalles: the professionals, the business owners, the owner of a small trucking firm. Only a couple of farmers, as far as he could tell. No one from the Coalition meeting.

"Colonel Voltaire." A very tall, dark-haired woman in a suit wandered up. "How nice to meet you. I'm Amanda Morrisy." She offered him a long-fingered hand. "I'm with Pacific BioSystems."

"Nice to meet you." Carter wondered how she had known his name. Johnny? "I didn't know Pacific BioSystems had an office in The Dalles."

"We don't." Her smile was cool. "I'm in town looking for contract business." She made a face. "Without much success, so far. There's a lot of resistance to biomass crops along the riverbed."

"So I've heard." Carter returned her firm grip. He had to look up to meet her gaze. "Why do you think that is?" he asked innocently.

"These marginal farmers are a closed-minded bunch." She shrugged. "You have to ram every change down their throats. It doesn't matter if it will benefit them or not; if it's new, it's bad."

Carter kept his expression neutral, remembering the Corbett woman's face at the meeting. "I hear that the salt-water irrigation does a lot of damage down in the Willamette Valley."

"It would be wasteland if we weren't irrigating it with salt-mix water. U.S. food reserves are down to about thirty-six hours' worth.'' She was still smiling and her tone was polite, but her eyes had gone cold and sharp. ''I don't see how you can seriously criticize a system that produces a good yearly crop yield.''

''I wasn't criticizing.'' She was touchy. Carter smiled politely and edged toward the table.

''I want you to know how much we appreciate Corps support.'' She followed him. ''We depend on the water that comes down both the Klamath and the Willamette shunts. We don't waste a gallon of our water allotment, believe me. Yes, we certainly support the Corps. You folks do a fine job.''

''We do our best.'' There was an intensity about this woman that bothered him. She was after something. ''Excuse me,'' Carter said, and reached for a plate. The magic show was over, and people were heading for the table. He wasn't really hungry, but it gave him an excuse to put bodies between them.

''They're feeling you out. They'd like to have you in their pocket, too.'' The low voice at his elbow was familiar. Carter turned, looked down at the small man with the blond tail of hair.

''Jeremy Barlow? So you're the magician from Bonneville! I should have guessed.''

''That's me.'' Jeremy gave Carter one of his crooked grins. A small green frog appeared on the tablecloth beside a bowl of mixed nuts. It stared up at them for a moment, throat pulsing, then leaped onto a cheese plate and vanished. Behind them, someone choked off a squeak of surprise.

''That is some gadget.'' Carter shook his head as Jeremy surreptitiously pocketed his projector. The frog seemed to have bought them some space at the table, and from the look of innocence on Jeremy's face, Carter suspected that that had been his intention. ''What did you mean?'' He lowered his voice. ''About me and Pacific Bio's pocket?''

''What I said.'' Jeremy reached for a small sandwich, picking it up carefully with his clumsy fingers. ''They own a lot of politicians—they pretty much run California, and I guess they weren't too ethical about how they got the job. Now they're after Oregon—or the Valley, at any rate. That's what I hear, anyway.'' He bit into the sandwich.

''Where did you hear this?'' Frowning, Carter balanced his plate lightly on his fingers. This could have bearing on what was happening in The Dalles. Or it could be a purely local matter. The latter was the more likely, he thought. ''I haven't heard it.''

''Maybe you don't talk to the right people.'' Jeremy picked

up another sandwich, then frowned at it. "I ride with truckers a lot."

"Truckers stay out of politics."

"Yeah, but they don't miss much. You can't stay out of something unless you know where and what it is, and they make sure they know it all." His lopsided grin came and went again. "I believe them," he said, and all trace of a smile vanished from his eyes. "I move around a lot. I've been down in California, and back east. Pacific Bio owns a lot of ag land. They own the people who work it." He looked at the half-eaten sandwich in his hand, put it down. A shiny black fly appeared on it, large as Carter's thumb. It took off, zoomed in a tight, silent circle above the sandwich, and then popped like a soap bubble. "It's tough trying to fight the Dry," Jeremy said softly. "You plow your soul into the land, because it's the only way you can keep yourself hanging on, keep watering and weeding and praying that you make another harvest, survive another year." He looked up, his eyes as dry and blue as the sky. "When you lose that land, when you walk away from it, you leave your soul behind."

"Poetic, but hardly true." Morrisy leaned over Carter's shoulder, smiling. "If we contract to grow biomass on someone's land, we don't buy the land. We don't need the taxes. We simply offer a contract that covers our investment in cloned bush-starts and equipment. The farmer still owns the land. He sells to us, and we pay him. Period."

"Except that they owe you for the bushes. And they owe those taxes." He shrugged. "Debt can be a pretty heavy chain to drag." A glowing insect popped into the air between them, then vanished abruptly.

Morrisy flinched. "Did you contract some land to us and then regret it?" Her smile had gone tight. "Is that what's bothering you?"

"No." Jeremy picked up his plate. "My father never contracted our land. It died, and so did he. It wasn't your fault." He gave the Pacific BioSystems executive a slight bow. "Maybe I'll see you in The Dalles," he said to Carter. "Take it easy."

"They have to blame someone." Morrisy gave Carter a wry, conspiratorial smile. "You must catch a lot of it, too. You'd think we'd engineered the climate change just so we could make a buck."

"Yes." Carter looked after Jeremy. "We catch a lot of it." Maybe that was all it was—a sourceless anger and darkness, like in Chicago. Blame for no reason. Because you had to blame someone, as the Pacific Bio woman had said.

Dan Greely had made the anger feel personal. So had Sandy Corbett. And Nita, who had never stood in a shower. *When you walk away, you leave your soul behind,* Jeremy had said.

Had one of them shot Delgado's brother and Mike Watanabe? Harold Ransom, or Sandy, or even Dan? It seemed pretty damn likely. Where the hell could you stand in this mess?

It had all seemed so fucking simple, once upon a time.

Carter felt a tiny click as the stem of his wineglass snapped. He stared numbly at the small blossom of crimson on his palm.

"Hello." Gwynn paused on her way across the room, two full wineglasses in her hand. "What did you *do*?"

"I cut myself." Embarrassed, he grabbed for a napkin. "I'm sorry about the glass."

"Never mind the glass. Come on." She took him firmly by the elbow, smiling over his shoulder at Morissy. "I've got a first-aid kit in the kitchen."

Carter followed her through a swinging door and into a large, bright kitchen. A big sink was set into a center island with a butcher-block top. Stainless steel and copper pots and pans hung from wrought-iron hooks overhead. This woman did not lack for money.

"Wash your hand." She pushed him toward the sink. "I'll get something for it. You know, I was about to rescue you from Pacific Bio's clutches. You didn't have to get so dramatic." She smiled at him over her shoulder as she rummaged in a cupboard.

"I didn't . . ." He stopped, at a loss for a snappy comeback. He was tired, and the wine had gone straight to his head after his sleepless night.

Gwynn reached for his hand and blotted it dry. "I suspect she's feeling you out for a deal. You're the new water lord in town. The only reason she came was to meet you."

Carter stared at her, feeling stupid. "I don't have the authority to make any flow changes."

"You might have the general's ear. If you don't, she won't bother you much longer." Gwynn laughed, reached up, and touched his cheek lightly. "What island did you grow up on? The Corps controls the *water*, remember? These little deals . . . get done."

Carter flushed and leaned slightly away from her touch. Yeah, these deals probably did get done. By Corps people. There were rumors. "I've never paid much attention to politics," he said stiffly, and she laughed at him again. This was too much, today. "I should be getting back," he said as she smoothed a strip of tape over the shallow cut on his palm.

"So soon?" She made a face at him. "Just because my wine-glasses bite?"

Because there's too much going on here, he thought but didn't say. "I've got things to do," he said instead. "Thanks for having me."

"Any time," she said, her eyes making it an invitation.

The waiter saved Carter from a reply by coming in to ask about more wine. Gwynn had to go down into the basement to show him, and Carter used the opportunity to escape the kitchen. The crowd had thinned out in the main room; people were leaving. He didn't see Johnny anywhere, and felt a pang of disappointment. He had probably assumed that Carter had already left, and had left himself. And he didn't even know where Johnny was staying. Damn it.

A set of French doors that opened onto a small side patio stood ajar and Carter went out that way. The car was parked on that side of the house, and all of a sudden, he wanted out. He had seen that same glitter in Gwynn's eyes when she talked about how the Corps controlled the water. What was it? A hunger for power? Water was power, if you controlled it. That's why Water Policy had been created—to keep that power out of the wrong hands.

Carter closed the French doors behind him and stopped. Johnny was out here, standing in the shadow of the eaves with Morissy. The Pacific BioSystems suit was tapping her index finger lightly on her palm. Carter couldn't see her expression, but she reminded him of their sixth-grade teacher, who had done that when she laid down the law in class. Johnny's posture was stiff, angry. Carter's toe caught a loose stone, and at the sound, they both turned.

"Carter." Johnny's laugh was too bright. "You startled me. Are you taking off?"

"I am." Morissy gave Carter a cool smile. "Nice meeting you, Colonel, however briefly. Perhaps we can get together another time." She walked briskly around the corner of the house and disappeared.

She was pissed, too. Carter caught Johnny's arm as he started for the doors. "Wait a minute." He felt Johnny's twitch of irritation and ignored it. "What was that all about? She looked like she was out for blood."

"Just sex." Johnny shrugged and raised his eyebrows. "They're always fishing for a price, but this ain't it. She wasn't happy about my reaction. I saw you in the kitchen with Gwynn." Johnny's smile carried the faintest trace of a leer. "She has the hots for you, my friend. I can tell."

Trying to change the subject? "Are they leaning on you?" Carter asked softly. "Pacific BioSystems?" The Water Policy committee was supposed to be above bribery—with a life term and no permissible private business connections, they were just about pristine, but water *was* power. Gwynn was right. "Johnny, I get the feeling that something's bothering you."

"It's not." Johnny took a deep breath, shook his head. "Look, Carter . . . I try. Do you have any idea of the *responsibility* we have?" His voice was hushed, his face pale, except for twin spots of color on his cheeks. "I was the boy genius economist— the bright and shining new star in the world of water and money— so now I have the real stuff. The real power. But you know me." There was a desperate look in his eyes, and his grin was feeble, a stretching of the lips only. "Sometimes I get . . . carried away."

"You can say that again." Carter gripped his arm hard. "What are you telling me, Johnny? That you're in trouble?"

"No." Johnny closed his eyes, opened them again. His face firmed and he smiled—a real smile this time, rueful, but no longer desperate. "I got a little drunk at a party and . . . said some things that might have been misinterpreted by Morissy. She misinterpreted them, in spades. I'm not for sale." He met Carter's eyes. "Not now, or ever, Carter. But she's being . . . awkward."

"Blackmail?"

"No, no, nothing like that." Johnny laughed, half angry. "I don't put stuff like that into writing, give me a break." He started down the graveled yard, toward the street and the parked cars. "No, it's a nuisance, is all. The media could pick it up and throw rocks, but they won't break any bones. I wasn't kidding about Gwynn, you know." He looked back over his shoulder. "She and I parted friends a long time ago. She's a very sweet lady."

"She seemed like it." Carter tried to keep his voice noncommittal.

"You've got someone already?" Johnny's eyebrows rose. "You never could play poker for shit. When did this happen?"

When had it happened? Last night? Out in the Dry? He could

have told Johnny about it a few hours ago, but now, here, he couldn't summon the words. "I met her here," he said as they reached the cracked sidewalk. "Her name is Nita Montoya."

"Hispanic?" Johnny's eyebrows rose fractionally higher. "Well . . . congratulations, I guess. Is this long term?"

Was it? "God, I don't know, Johnny. You tell me." Carter heard the irritation in his voice, couldn't help it. "Listen, I've got to get back to the base. Can I drop you somewhere, or do you have a car?"

"You can drop me at my motel." Johnny followed him to his car. "Tell me more about this Nita."

He didn't tell Johnny much—just where he'd met her and how. What she looked like. The swirling undercurrents of the party had left him uneasy, full of misgivings. With water came power. Whether you wanted it or not. You could be tempted; anyone could be tempted. He wondered how hard Morissy was leaning on Johnny. When the time was right, he'd ask. But this wasn't the time, and Johnny was vague about when they could get together again. Maybe tomorrow, he told Carter. If he didn't have to bolt out of town suddenly.

It was late afternoon as he drove back to the base. The slanting beams of the sun touched the dusty land with gold and reflected from the random window in bursts of fire. He had checked in on the car phone earlier, and everything was fine at the base. No trouble on the Pipeline. No one had even yelled at him as he drove the Corps car through town. Maybe he *could* keep this situation under control. Carter returned the guards' salute as they waved him through the gate, anticipation stirring in his belly and groin.

He wanted to tell Nita about the party, hear her reaction. She had such a different perspective on this world. He wanted to tell her about Jeremy and his frog on the table. She might laugh. He had never seen her laugh, and he wanted to do that, suddenly—make her laugh. He parked in front of his apartment and hurried up the walk. Whatever would or wouldn't work itself out between them, he wanted to see her *now*, to put his arms around her, bury his face in her hair and breathe the soft musky scent of her skin. The door was locked. He unlocked it and pushed it open. "Nita?"

Her name echoed through the apartment. He knew even as he shut the door. The sofa had been closed and the dirty sheets lay neatly folded on the cushion. He knew, but he looked into the bedroom and bathroom anyway, as if she might be hiding there, playing a silly game with him.

She wasn't there. She was gone.

No note. No pack. Not a single trace that a woman and child had spent the night here last night. Except the folded sheets, and the towel she had used. He picked it up, a stony lump heavy in his gut. Her scent rose faintly from the thick folds.

He threw the towel into the laundry hamper and tossed the sheets in after it. So he had been wrong about last night. It had been a pleasant tumble, nothing more. He had offered her a bed. She had accepted it and moved on. No strings attached, remember? Part of him refused to believe it. She had a pass. She could walk through the door any minute—and she wasn't going to. He knew it as surely as if she'd left him a note. She *had* left him a note—in the folded sheets and the empty apartment.

He wished now that he'd stayed at the fancy, freshly painted house. There was a yawning hole inside him and he needed to fill it up with something. He wanted to get drunk with Johnny, the way they'd done in their twenties, when he had just gone into the Army and Johnny had been bitching and moaning his way through college. He could tell Johnny about Chicago and Johnny could tell him about how Pacific Bio wanted to own him, and they could laugh and maybe cry, like a couple of teenagers who couldn't hold their liquor. They wouldn't talk about love or lovers at all.

He didn't call Johnny. He wasn't a teenager anymore. He needed to go down to Operations and look over the flow reports himself, never mind that Delgado had already done it. He needed to review the day, check things out. He needed to think about the party gossip, and Dan Greely, and how the hell he was going to keep people from dying around here. He walked through the apartment once more, checking to see if she'd left anything behind.

She hadn't.

He didn't slam the door on the way out. He closed it very, very gently.

CHAPTER NINE ☆

Nita looked around Carter's apartment as she braided her hair. In the bright light everything looked too sharp, too vivid. It made her head ache. She tied off the end of her braid with the thin silk ribbon that David had given her.

Last night, alone in the darkness, it had been so easy to believe that he had walked away.

In the harsh light of day, she wasn't so sure. There were no certainties here. Anything could happen. A man could break his leg and spend weeks healing in a farmhouse somewhere. He could run away and then change his mind. "I don't know," Nita whispered. The words sounded as loud as a shout in the silent apartment. She bent and yanked the sheets from the sofa bed. The faint scent of their lovemaking rose from the cloth as she folded them, and she bent her head, pierced by the memory of last night. I came in here because I was lonely, she told herself. That's all it had been—a midnight need for comfort.

If that had been true yesterday, it was a lie now. She bent double over the armful of folded sheets, a stone of pain in her belly. "I love you, David," she cried. "I do."

On the bed, Rachel woke with a hungry cry. "Damn it!" Nita threw the folded sheets onto the floor as Rachel began to wail. "Not your fault, love." Nita calmed herself as she went to pick up her daughter. "I'm angry at me, not you. Have your breakfast and then we'll go."

David might be dead, or he might still be on his way here, delayed by some accident. This was where he would come to find her, so she would wait for him for a while. But not here. Nita stared at the wall as her daughter nursed. She couldn't stay here; she didn't dare. When Rachel had finished, she repacked her pack, filled her water jugs, and tucked Rachel into her sling. Standing

in the doorway, hand on the knob, she looked around at the empty
rooms. She had spent one night here; less than twenty-four hours.

It felt familiar—as if she had lived here for days. Weeks. Nita
thought about leaving him a note, but what could she say that
wouldn't be a lie, or be misunderstood? She bit her lip. Silence
was best; he would understand that message. It was a message
that she had to give him.

And herself.

Nita yanked the door open and walked through it, out into
the hot, dusty wind. A different guard was at the gate, a woman
about Nita's age. She eyed Nita suspiciously, but without the
razor-wire hatred of the man yesterday. She despised Nita a
little, and Nita wondered why. She lifted her head, holding out
the pass that Carter had given her. It wasn't until she had walked
halfway down that dusty road that led to the truck plaza and the
highway that she realized she still had the pass; the guard hadn't
asked for it. Nita held it on her palm, half tempted to toss it into
the dusty weeds that lined the road. But a part of her wanted to
keep it, and she tucked it carefully into the pouch around her
neck, trying to ignore the small prick of her guilt.

If she was going to stay in The Dalles for a while, she would
have to find a job. She was running out of scrip. Hitching the pack
higher on her shoulders, tickling Rachel's belly until she smiled
and gurgled, Nita plodded through the afternoon sun toward town
and the stores there. Maybe one of them had a job open.

"I'm sorry." The round-faced, balding manager of the government store was genuinely apologetic. "I wish I could give
you some kind of job." He leaned on the counter, surrounded
by aisles of controlled items: liquor, beer and wine, cigarettes,
candy, and the other small, water-expensive luxuries that the
government had loaded with restrictive taxes. "Have you tried
Laurel, the manager down at the market? She might have a job
for you, cleaning out the booths or something."

"I tried her." Tired to the bone, discouraged, Nita shifted
Rachel's sling higher on her shoulder. There were no jobs in this
town. She had been up and down the main street, asking at every
store and fuel station, not just the market. "She's got a kid
working for her," she said.

"Oh, yeah, her nephew." The manager frowned, scratching
at the brown spots that speckled his bare scalp. "Things are real
tight in town, what with the water cuts these past two years. The
district supervisor's been making noises about closing this store.

Crazy, I say, because the nearest government store'll be Bonneville, but hell, no one's got scrip to spend except the truckers. All they buy is booze, and they're mobile anyway. I had the news on this morning. Italy and Greece are blowing up the refugee boats coming over from Africa—just sinking 'em; women, kids, and all. Can you believe it?'' He shook his head. "Hell, what's *happening* to us? You'd think our humanity's drying up with the water. Look, I got about an hour before closing.'' He scowled at the clock on the wall. "You can polish the front windows for me and sweep out the back room. I've been meaning to get around to that for a week now. I can pay something for it.''

It was a handout—because the news story had upset him? "Thank you,'' Nita said. She'd take a handout. She didn't have a lot of choice.

"You're looking for a job?'' A man had come in from the street, tall and lanky with dark, graying hair.

"Hi, Dan.'' The manager lifted a hand. "Nita here's been trying to find something, but you know how it is. Dan Greely knows everyone,'' he confided to Nita. "If anyone can find you a job, he can.''

He was already regretting his offer of the sweeping job. Nita was too discouraged to be angry.

"I heard a woman was in town, looking for her husband. Is that you?'' The newcomer leaned against the counter beside her.

"David Ascher. He was supposed to have a job here. He's about your height.'' She looked up, frowning. "He has curly black hair, only it's going gray.'' The faint flicker of her hope died easily at the man's headshake.

"I'm sorry. I haven't heard of him. I might be able to help you out with a job, though,'' he said thoughtfully. "I had a man working out at my farm. He left about three months ago, and I need some help. It's field work, but I have an extra room in the house. All I can offer you is board and a share of the profit—if there *is* any profit this year.''

Nita frowned, watching the man from beneath her lashes, wondering if the offer was genuine. It *felt* genuine, but the ride to Tygh Valley had made her wary. The man's graying hair and his lined, sundried face put him in his forties, maybe more. About David's age. He was staring at her, examining her face with a searching intensity that made Nita uncomfortable.

"Don't I know you?'' he said, and he sounded uncertain. "What's your name again?''

"Nita. Nita Montoya.''

His eyes narrowed. "You're not . . . Sam Montoya's daughter, are you?"

His sudden tension brought her head up. "Yes." Nita eyed him warily. "He died a long time ago."

"I know." The man's voice was hushed, muted by his surprise . . . and pain. "I knew Sam. I even remember you. You must have been four, last time I saw you."

She had been five and a half on the day the men had killed her father. Nita took a step backward as Rachel began to whimper.

"Well, I'll be." The manager leaned over the counter, clucking with delight. "Sam's youngest. I heard the name, even, but it didn't click. He was a good man, your dad." He nodded, light glancing off his spotted scalp. "We miss him, eh, Dan?"

"Where did you go?" The man named Dan spoke as if he hadn't heard the manager; as if he and Nita were the only people in the store, or the world.

She took another step backward, suddenly wanting to run, to put distance between herself and this stranger's frightening intensity. "Mama . . . took us to live with my brother Alberto. Down in the Willamette Valley." The door was right behind her. "Thank you for offering to let me sweep," she told the manager. "I think I'll check one or two other places first." She escaped—door banging shut behind her—out into the hot, dusty safety of the street.

He followed her, stretching his long legs to catch up, his determination like a hot breath on her neck, making her want to flee. It wasn't darkness—it wasn't like the trader in his RV—but it scared her anyway.

"I'm sorry if I upset you. Nita? Want to slow down for a minute, before we both get heat stroke?" He sounded plaintive. "I won't bite, I promise."

"You didn't upset me. Oh, all right, you did." Nita stopped suddenly. She couldn't outrun him, and it was too hot even to try. "I hadn't really thought about it . . ." She wiped her sweaty face on her sleeve, groping for words. "That people here would have known my father, I mean." This town and the dusty yesterday that she remembered were two different worlds. "It just . . . took me by surprise."

"I'm sorry."

He was. "Don't be. It was a long time ago." Dan Greely was his name, Nita remembered. "Mama never mentioned you," she said, hearing the accusation in her tone.

"I'm not surprised." He sighed and pushed hair that needed

cutting out of his eyes. "Maria never liked me much. She blamed me for Sam's death."

Grief? It struck Nita like a blow.

"How is your mother?" he asked.

"She died three years ago." Rachel's sling was rubbing her shoulder and Nita tugged at the knot, uneasy again. This man remembered her father better than she did. After twenty years, he still mourned him. "A spray plane crashed into the residence compound at the ag-plex. Alberto died too," she said. "Ignacio took off. I don't know where he went."

"I'm sorry," Dan said softly. "Poor Maria. She never made peace with Sam's choice. I don't think she ever understood how much that choice cost him."

Nita sneaked a look at his face, studying his weathered profile. "I don't really know what you mean," she said. "Mama never talked much about The Dalles." Except to blame her husband for dying, and Nita for living.

"I was serious about needing a hand in the fields," Dan said slowly. "I've been spending too much time with politics lately, and the beans are suffering. I can't guarantee that you'll get much more than a place to live out of it, but you and your baby are welcome, if that suits."

She wanted to say no and walk away from this man and the ghosts he raised, but she was tired. If she and Rachel were going to eat, she had to find a job. Nita sighed, liking the quiet feel of this man, ghosts or no ghosts. There was no darkness in him, no threat. The ghosts would be everywhere, now that people knew who she was. "I guess I'll take it," she said. "I've never worked beans, but I've worked bushes. I know how to pull weeds and run a soaker-hose grid."

"Great." His smile was warm as sunlight. "I'm glad to share with you. I'll put the word out about your husband. I *do* know a lot of people around here. Your son?" He tickled Rachel lightly under the chin, smiled with her smile.

"This is Rachel. Thank you," Nita said. She had the feeling that she had made a good choice, had found a sanctuary. A place to hide from Carter? She shook her head to banish that thought. "I appreciate the job," she said.

"I appreciate the help." He held out a hand. "Why don't you give me your pack? Rachel looks like quite a load on her own. My truck's parked at the market. I was just on my way home."

CHAPTER TEN ☆

Stomach tight, Carter marched down the long hall that led to Hastings's office. He hadn't been back here since his first day on the riverbed, and the vast bulk of the dam still oppressed him, making him sweat in the cool air. He had received a peremptory summons from the general this morning. No explanation, just an order to report in person.

Either he had fucked up in a big way or something was coming down, something too big to risk to electronic eavesdroppers on the net or the phone lines. Corporal Sandusky wasn't in his cubicle. Carter paused outside the general's door to straighten his uniform and run a hand through his hair. He wasn't sure which possibility worried him more.

"Enter." The general's voice answered his knock. "You made good time," he growled as Carter entered. He was frowning at his big wall map of the Pipeline, tapping impatiently on his desk with a pen. "We've got trouble."

Carter braced himself. Johnny had called him the morning after the party, in a rush to leave for Washington. He'd hinted as much—that something big was coming down. That had been three days ago, two days after Nita had left. Nita . . . he couldn't stop thinking about her. "What kind of trouble, sir?" he asked briskly.

"Orders from the top. We have to increase the flow in the Colorado Diversion line by three percent. Mexico filed a fucking petition with the UN—whining about its share again." Hastings grunted. "Personally, I'd tell them to shut up and be glad we let them in on any of this at all. Greedy Mex bastards."

Carter didn't remind him that Mexico had contributed one-third of the monumental construction cost for the Pipeline system. He frowned, doing the numbers fast in his head. The increase would come from the Trench, because Mexico got its share of tundra water via the Colorado and Rio Grande aqueducts, and they had their origins in the Rocky Mountain Trench Reservoir. The Trench was already supporting its maximum outflow. "Where is the water going to come from?" Carter asked, knowing the answer even before the general spoke.

"It's going to come out of the Columbia's share, every drop of it."

Carter whistled a low, resigned note. "That means a major cut in everyone's water share."

"Not everyone," Hastings said grimly. "We can't reduce the volume going into the Klamath and Willamette shunts without causing crop losses. I've been ordered to keep their flow at current levels."

Carter stared at his commander, not wanting to believe what he had just heard. If they maintained the Shunt flow, the residents between the Deschutes bed and the Willamette bed were going to get hit with an even greater shortfall. Local water use was already cut to the bone. He'd spent hours going over the numbers, looking for answers to give the Coalition. This was going to hit the soaker-hose farmers hard. What had Jeremy said at the reception—that these farmers plowed their souls into the land? The Corps was about to dry some of them up. Carter drew a slow breath, remembering his assurances to Greely and the Coalition. So much worthless shit. Ransom was going to love him.

"I see you understand what we're likely to encounter," Hastings said dryly.

At least he'd said *we* this time. "It's not going to help the local situation." Understatement of the week. The timing couldn't be worse if someone was out to sabotage the situation.

"The locals are going to raise hell." Hastings tossed his pen onto his desk. "I've filed a demand for support troops. Combat units. Maybe this time we'll get some action out of those whipped dogs in Water Policy." He gave Carter a cold, evaluating look. "I hear one of them's your buddy."

"John Seldon's an old friend," Carter said stiffly. "I told him why we needed more personnel, but he said no way."

"We're going to need tanks when this news breaks."

That could be. Carter stared at the wall map, thinking fast. "I'd have to look at the numbers again, but we should be able to divert flow from the Great Lakes canal into the Trench to pick up some of this shortfall." He frowned, struggling to recall the use equations. "The Missouri and Mississippi systems were operating on a comfortable margin when I left Chicago. They could trim it."

"That's for Water Policy to decide." Hastings shrugged. "Give me the numbers and I'll look at them. If you haven't missed something, I'll pass them along upstairs." He looked sharply at Carter. "Don't waste time grieving for the farmers along here, Colonel. They're a damned inefficient bunch."

That had been Morrisy's attitude. And it was true. Biomass crops would dramatically increase the final per-acre food yield along the riverbed. But he couldn't get Sandy Corbett's face out of his mind—the way she had looked as she talked about the dying Valley. Or Jeremy, with eyes full of dry memories. Carter swallowed a sigh. "When is this reduction scheduled to go into effect, sir? I need time."

"You don't have any time. We got a forty-eight-hour notice." Hastings got to his feet and paced restlessly across the room. "Water Policy is trying to impress the media. Save the Alliance. Your buddy's looking for hero status, Colonel. Who cares if we get shit on, as long as the media's happy?" He glared at Carter. "Any protest we make is going to come after the fact."

Carter had said almost the same thing to Johnny. Forty-eight hours? He groaned and rubbed his face, thinking hard. "We'll have to change the flow rates gradually or the turbulence will tear any weak spots wide open. Even so, people are going to see their water flow cut before we have a chance to notify them." Then the shit would *really* hit the fan. "Isn't there any way to stall on this?"

"Nope." Hastings picked up a sheet of hardcopy. "It's our baby."

Carter scowled at the wall map of the Columbia system. The blue lines still looked like veins running across the wrinkled brown skin of the land. They *were* veins, carrying life to the dry land. If they were cut, the land would die. "Sir?" Carter cleared his throat. "Why did you deny my request for Major Delgado's transfer?"

Hastings's eyes narrowed. "Why did you request it?"

"His brother's death has affected his judgment where locals are concerned." Carter chose his words carefully. "He's an excellent officer otherwise, but I think he needs to be stationed somewhere else." With this cut coming down, Delgado's inflammatory attitude could be the spark that started something.

Hastings was scowling at him. "I know about the major's

brother. Yes, he's bitter, but he's been here for a long time. He's had a lot of experience with local politics, and *he* came up the hard way. You need his judgment.''

Because his wasn't adequate? Carter felt himself flushing. "Sir . . . ?"

"That's my final decision."

"Yes, sir." Carter said stiffly. *Goddamn it.* "I'd better go get my people working on this."

The flat photo of the man in dress greens had been moved. It stood beside Hastings's terminal screen, as if he had been looking at it. It clicked suddenly—who he was. "Captain Hastings," Carter said in surprise. "I knew Doug Hastings at O.C.S. We all liked him—he was a good man." And a general's son? That had been a well-kept secret. "Where's he stationed now?"

"He's dead." Hastings picked up the photo. "A retaining wall came down and took out his whole crew. A bad design, approved by an officer who didn't know his ass from a hole in the ground."

Carter stiffened. "I realize that I'm short on experience, sir. I keep it very clearly in mind."

"A pretty speech." Hastings's expression didn't thaw. He put the photo down and straightened it carefully. "Doug should've gotten a Purple Heart. We're in a fucking war: fighting drought and the hicks, all over the damn country. He should have gotten a medal. You'd better get going before all hell breaks loose." He didn't return Carter's salute.

So that was where the hostility came from? Carter walked slowly back to his car, relieved to escape the looming weight of the dam. He was sure as hell on his own—and it occurred to him to wonder if Delgado wasn't reporting back directly to the general.

As he left the complex, he called Delgado on his car phone and told him to pull all the programmers back on duty. He didn't explain why. Hastings was right to worry about eavesdroppers. All he needed was to have someone spread the word that the Corps was about to cut off the water. He'd need those combat troops then. He might need them anyway. The wind had started up again, blowing hard from the east, hazing the air with dust. Dust devils twisted along the floor of the riverbed. The Chevy's seals were shot and dust seeped into the car. Carter pulled on his goggles and touched another number.

"Deshutes government store," a cracked voice said. "Bob, here."

"Hello." Carter raised his voice to be heard over the roar of the engine. "I'm trying to reach Dan Greely. He gave me this number."

"Probably. He don't have a phone." There was a pause and Carter heard distant voices, as if the man were talking to someone else with his hand over the receiver. "Who is this?" he asked.

"Colonel Voltaire. Dan asked me to get in touch with him."

"He's around." The voice had gone flat and cautious. "If I see him, I'll give him your message."

"Listen it's important." Carter kept a tight rein on his rising anger. Maybe he should use a code name, like kids playing spy games. "Please ask him to come to the main gate at the base, will you? I need to talk to him right away."

"If I see him, I'll tell him."

"Could you send someone to look for him?" Carter asked, but the line had gone dead. "Damn." He tossed the phone onto the seat. The suspicious old fart. If Greely didn't show, he'd have to send a detail out to look for him, and that could be misunderstood. Carter clutched the wheel and concentrated on driving. Chicago leaned over his shoulder, and he wished suddenly and intensely that he could talk to Johnny. There *had* to be another way to handle this water shuffle. He felt as if he were tiptoeing across a mine field—one misstep and it would blow up in his face. It was not a pleasant feeling.

When he reached the lower gate at The Dalles, the corporal on gate duty came out to the car instead of waving him through.

"Colonel?" He saluted. "I have a call from the east gate. There's visitor waiting for you, sir. Civilian—a Mr. Greely."

That had been fast. The old fart had given Greely the message after all. "Thanks. Have someone escort him to my office." Carter drove through the gate, worry knotting his gut.

He stopped by his apartment—to get the mask he'd forgotten this morning, he told himself, but it was a lie. The empty rooms mocked him as he retrieved his dust mask from the kitchen counter. She hadn't come back. Part of him kept hoping, coming up with reasons for her disappearance, refusing to believe that it had just been a one-night stand. He had looked for her at the weekend market, but hadn't seen her. He could ask Greely. Dan might have heard of her. He slammed the door behind him and headed for Operations.

Greely was waiting in Carter's office, examining the big wall map of the riverbed. An alert young private watched his every move.

"We locals aren't very welcome here," Greely said as Carter walked in.

"We uniforms aren't very welcome in town. You can go," he told the private, and switched on the office air conditioner.

"I heard you had some trouble out near the truck plaza last week." Greely looked concerned. "I'm glad you didn't get hurt."

"They were just kids," Carter said, remembering the blond boy's feral eyes.

"I also heard that you didn't do any more than you had to." Greely leaned against the wall beside the cool breath of the air-conditioner vent, his expression thoughtful. "Those kids could have hurt you. Killed you, even. You might have been justified in beating the shit out of them, at least."

Carter reached for the insulated carafe on the end of his desk, remembering how damn good it had felt to pull that trigger out in the lakebed. "I guess I don't feel so justified anymore," he said slowly. "I kind of got the feeling that they were settling a score. Water?"

"Thanks." Greely watched Carter fill two glasses. "Those were highway kids. They stick to the convoy routes, come and go with the truckers. Sometimes their parents are dead, some of them come from the camps outside Portland or from families that broke up drifting. They sell ass to the truckers," he said. "You can get any action you want, as young as you want it, for the price of a little water and a ride down the road."

He took the glass Carter handed him and drank the water down in sharp, quick swallows, as if thirst were something that he couldn't quite control, as if he'd never really gotten enough water to drink in his life. Jeremy drank like that, Carter remembered. He had noticed at the party. "Were you born in the Drylands?" he asked.

"L.A." Dan put the glass down. "I spent a lot of time out in the Dry, though. Too much time."

Begging, he had said at the Coalition meeting. Carter took Dan's empty glass, filled it again, and handed it back.

"Yeah, your kids were out to settle a score. A rough customer beat one of the boys to death a couple of weeks ago." Dan stared into the depths of his glass. "A uniform, the rumor goes. Bob said you needed to talk to me right away."

Carter set his empty glass down very carefully. "There's trouble coming. We have to reduce the Columbia flow by nearly four percent in a little less than forty-eight hours. I didn't know about this until this morning."

Dan frowned, his face lined and tired. "I could say that you were stringing us along the other night. I could say that any promises you make are worth so much dust." He lifted a hand. "I believe you." He met Carter's eyes. "I think you're as much on our side as you can be. But I'm not going to be in the majority. Why this reduction?"

He listened without interruption as Carter repeated what Hastings had told him. "So the valleys get the water." Dan let his breath out in a slow sigh. "I'd get strung up for saying it, but you're right about their production rate being better than ours." His lips tightened. "They can do it because they're all big ag-plexes down there. They grow those damn bushes and irrigate with salt-mix water. You heard all this the other night. So." He faced Carter, his eyes narrowing thoughtfully. "You and I have to make some fast plans if we want to keep a lid on this riverbed."

"What if the Coalition backs the cut?"

"Can't happen." Dan shook his head. "Yeah, Sandy and I kind of organize things, but we don't run the show. The Coalition has a lot of members, and Ransom is pretty close to your average soaker-hose farmer as far as attitude goes."

"Great." Carter rubbed his eyes, a headache building at the back of his brain. "Got any other ideas?"

"Maybe." Dan frowned. "Sandy and I might just yell about this, whip everyone into a nice united frenzy, and head out to the Shunt for a big, noisy demonstration."

"Are you crazy? That's just what we want to avoid."

"What we need to avoid is bloodshed." Dan's expression was grim. "There's no way the folks here are going to accept what you're doing. They're going to scream, and they need to scream. I want the media to come hear them scream. It's their families who are going to suffer from that reduction, not their credit balance. This isn't a chess game, Carter." His voice had gone low and hard. "People are going to lose their land, they're so close to the edge now. Do you know what happens if federal ag credit forecloses on you? If you're lucky, you get a job hoeing bushes in the Valley—but bushes don't take much labor. If you aren't lucky, your kids grow up as campies, or hit the highway. Some kind of protest is going to happen. We've got cool heads in the Coalition. They aren't all Ransoms, and they'll help me and Sandy maintain some kind of order. If you help, too, maybe we can at least keep anyone from getting killed."

"I hear what you're saying, Dan," Carter said quietly. "I know it's not a game. I think I know what's at stake—for all of us."

"Yeah." Dan held his eyes for a moment. "Maybe you do, at that." He looked up at the wall map. "It's got to happen at the Shunt. The media won't show unless we give them something tasty. A threat against the Klamath Shunt is a threat against the Sacramento Valley. That'll bring them running. Besides." Dan gave Carter a lopsided grin. "The Shunt is a long way from town. Some folks won't be able to get there, and others will use that as an excuse not to show."

"I can't risk the Shunt."

"I told you, it's not a game." Dan looked down at his hands, his face etched with weariness and years of sun. "We'll do this with or without you. The only way you can stop it is to throw barricades across every access road and try to block the river-bed. You'll be dealing with small groups then, at a lot of different sites. We won't have any kind of control, and a lot of those groups are going to be following the hotheads. There's going to be shooting. If we organize this thing, the Coalition has at least a chance of keeping it under control."

If he let this happen and the Shunt itself took damage, he was dead. "I could call the MPs right now." Carter hung on to his temper with an effort. "Even if we can't make anything stick, we could hold on to you for a day or two."

"What are you after?" Dan met his glare without flinching. "When you cut the water, there's going to be trouble. It might not happen out at the Shunt, but it'll be bad. I thought that's what you wanted to stop? This protest will give folks a chance to scream and yell, blow off some steam." Dan's shoulders slumped and he ran a hand across his weathered face. "You've got no real reason to trust me, Carter. I know it." He sighed again. "We can do this together, or we can do it from opposite sides. You chose."

Stubborn bastard. Carter frowned. If he trusted this man, if he was *sure*, he would risk it. Because the plan made sense. But he couldn't afford to trust Dan; he wasn't on Dan Greely's side. He was in the middle, trying to keep another Chicago from happening, no matter who got hurt in the process. Carter stared through his window, seeing sunbaked dust, remembering how the sun had flayed his naked back. It could be Dan who had dumped him out there. He had no evidence either way.

"All right." Carter laid his palms flat on the desktop. "We're going to have riot gas up there. If *anyone* breaks through our line or makes a serious try for the Shunt bunker, we're going to use it and come down hard on the crowd. That's the best I can do, Dan. You'd better keep your people under control, because I cannot risk the Shunt.''

"Sandy and I know some dependable folk. They're good at keeping a crowd peaceful without making it obvious. I'll see if I can keep some of the hotheads out of this. What about the uniforms?''

"My people won't start anything. I'll put in extra officers to make sure they stay in line.'' Carter shrugged at Dan's dubious expression. "It better work,'' he said. "Or you'll be dealing with a new CO out here.''

"Thanks, Carter. For taking the risk and meeting me halfway on this. They're good people, the ones who are going to go under.'' Dan got to his feet, his eyes full of shadows. "I'd better get going, if I'm going to set up a reasonable demonstration in forty-eight hours.''

"I'll look into that kid's death,'' Carter said as Dan started for the door. "And I'll make it clear that any violence against civilians in town or elsewhere is going to mean serious trouble.''

"Thanks.'' Dan turned back and held out his hand.

Carter returned his grip, saying a small prayer that he was reading this man accurately. "Good luck. To both of us.''

"You're letting Greely set you up,'' Delgado growled when Carter informed him of the plan.

"He's right. This water cut is going to mean some kind of confrontation.'' Carter stared at the quiet bustle of Operations, seeing that blue tracery of life in his mind. "Even you agree with him on that. What do you want to do? Trade shots with the locals from the riverbed?'' Yeah, he probably did. Every local killed would be a notch on his gun—a scalp collected for his brother's ghost. Never mind how many more Corps people would die to pay for that collection. "Dan thinks that this protest will act as some kind of safety valve, and I think he might be right. I don't think we have a lot of choice, anyway.''

"You do it his way, sir, and they'll tear the Shunt apart. I say we arm everyone, wait until they show up, and round up the lot of them.''

"That'll get the shooting started,'' Carter said grimly. "I didn't say we were going to do it Dan's way.'' Trust was a luxury he couldn't afford. He was responsible for too many lives.

"We're going to have armed troops inside that Shunt bunker. If we're lucky, we won't even need the gas. If there's a serious threat to the Shunt, we open fire." And that would end any chance of peace between the Corps and The Dalles.

Delgado's eyes glittered. "That's a good plan, sir."

How many lives would it take to satisfy Delgado's hungry ghost? "We are going to shoot *only* as a last resort," Carter snapped. "There will be no provocative actions taken by any enlisteds or officers during the protest. None. I am holding *you* personally responsible for their behavior." Carter held Delgado's eyes. "Do I make myself clear, Major?"

"Yes, sir." The major saluted.

Delgado was too sure that the locals were going to start the riot he wanted. Carter stalked out of Operations, worry churning in his gut, wishing he was equally sure that Delgado was wrong. Outside, the wind scoured the riverbed beneath the velvet blue of the dry, twilight sky. Carter looked eastward, finding the faint glitter of the first star low on the horizon. It was a planet, not a star. Saturn? Mars? He couldn't remember. He had forgotten to ask Dan about Nita. Wearily he headed toward the mess hall, hoping Dan knew what he was doing, praying that they really were on the same side and he hadn't just fallen for a major con.

The dry eye of the planet winked at him and, in the distance, a coyote howled sorrowfully.

CHAPTER ELEVEN ☆

Dan and the Coalition had managed to come up with an impressive number of people on short notice. Carter leaned against the hood of the parked truck, watching the crowd mill in the blazing sunshine. The afternoon was windless for once, and dust hung in the air.

HANDS OFF OUR WATER. The crude signs had been lettered in bloodred paint. UNIFORMS GET OUT! THIS LAND IS OUR LAND. He couldn't see their expressions from this distance. Here at its mouth, the Deschutes bed was wide and rocky. The crowd had spilled over from the highway, but so far they had stayed behind the tape barricade that the Corps had erected. But he didn't have to see their expressions to know what their mood was like. A man and a couple of women were leading chants: *Army out. It's our water*, and *Water, water everywhere, how come the Valleys get our share?* In between the chants, the crowd murmured with the sound of a big animal growling low in its throat.

They were angry. Primed for violence? Carter hoped not. In Chicago, the violence had built up like a gas pocket in a mine—odorless, invisible. The explosion had come suddenly and violently. Maybe Dan was right, and the yelling would bleed off some of that deadly power. Maybe.

They were chanting again. The media was here, just as Dan had wanted. Reporters with vid-cams stalked the fringes of the mob, angling for dramatic shots. Carter's lips tightened as he walked the line they had set up, clapping shoulders, speaking to his officers and NCOs. They were all nervous. This wasn't what they had signed on with the Corps to do. They were water people, trained to maintain the Pipeline, keep that blue tracery open and the country's watery heart beating. They weren't combat troops. They were welders and flow specialists, dozer drivers and surveyors. "Let them yell," he said to one of his sergeants. The man was wire-tight, and Carter put a hand on his shoulder. "Barking dogs aren't as likely to bite."

"Yes, sir," the sergeant said, but he didn't sound convinced.

They were wearing the new-issue riot gear—helmets, rockshields, and stun wands like thick-handled tuning forks. Riot gear must be a growth industry, Carter thought bitterly. Gas masks dangled from every belt. He had parked the convoy of government vehicles in a rough line about twenty yards in front of the silocrete dome that housed the complex Shunt valves. Inside the Shunt bunker, a carefully selected detail crouched, armed with laser-sighted M20s. If civilians got past the trucks, they had orders to open fire. And it would all go to hell after that. Carter shaded his eyes against the glare, feeling hollow, light and empty, as if he were nothing more than a fragile shell surrounding an aching vacuum of waiting.

Lava rock, eroded by ages of wind and water, stuck up out of the riverbed clay in long ridges. They reminded Carter of dirty molars jutting out of a bare jawbone, like the horse's skull he and Johnny had unearthed in an abandoned field one childhood afternoon. The sun was still well above the horizon and the riverbed held the heat and dust like a bowl. Here and there, umbrellas stuck up above the crowd among the signs, casting tiny pools of shade.

On the slopes above the rocky sides of the gorge, green leaves shimmered in the sun—sugar beets. It wasn't just those beets that had brought these people down here. He'd leaned on that as he briefed his officers this morning. It was damned easy to look at a crowd and see gooks, hicks. It was hard to see anything else. Carter took a hand-held amplifier from the back of a truck. *They're desperate*, he had told his officers. *They're scared for their kids and their homes.*

It was hard to keep that in mind as the crowd chanted and growled.

"Tell us," the florid-faced Ransom bawled from the front rank of the crowd. "Tell us why you bastards decided to cut off our water."

"We're not cutting off your water." Carter kept his voice calm and reasonable, but his hand amp boomed it out over the riverbed, harsh and loud. He winced, intensely aware of the vidcams. "We have to send more water down to Mexico or the Alliance goes down the drain. If that happens, Canada can legally short us. Then you'll really see water cuts."

"Screw Mexico," Ransom bawled. "Don't feed us this Mexico shit. You're taking our water to feed to those damn bush farmers. It was on the fucking *news*. You cut us four and a half percent. You know what those numbers mean? They mean that our kids are gonna go hungry. Or do you care?"

Damn the media. It *had* been on the evening newscasts, and he would give a lot to know who'd leaked it to them. Carter unclenched his teeth with an effort. "This cut means that you're all going to have a hard time," he said. "Some of you are going to lose your farms. I wish that there was something that the Corps could do, but there isn't. If the water doesn't go down the Shunts, a lot more people are going to have a hard time— the people who depend on the valleys for their food. If the bushes die, *they* go hungry. *Their* kids go hungry. We've got to get the maximum use out of every gallon of water. Numbers count. It's damned tough, but they do."

"At least he's not shitting us," a man yelled from the crowd. "He's telling it like it is."

"Sounds like shit to me," a sarcastic voice responded. "Feels like it and smells like it, too." A ripple of muttering and nervous laughter ran through the crowd.

The laughter didn't relieve any tension. If anything, that sarcastic voice had cranked it tighter. "You've got real complaints." Carter raised his voice. "But you're picking on the wrong people. Yeah, we carry out the orders. We reprogrammed the valves that reduced your water, but we didn't make the distribution decisions. Water Policy did that. We don't decide when to foreclose or extend more credit. Federal Credit does that. Going after us won't get you one gallon more water, or one buck's worth of loan money."

"Oh yeah?" the sarcastic voice yelled again. "You gonna send us to Washington to talk to the Committee? You think any of them gives a shit? They don't care about *us* as long as *they* eat. So I say we *do* something about that!"

The crowd roared approval, drawing together like an animal crouching for the attack.

There he was—the voice—a ginger-haired man with a square, calculating face. Carter tensed. He *knew* that face, had a sudden, cloudy memory of an arm beneath his chin, choking him . . . "Violence gets you nothing," Carter yelled into his amp. "If you wind up in jail, who the hell is going to water your crops?"

"Won't matter if there isn't any water." Red-hair faced the

crowd, arms raised stiffly, fists clenched. His voice was like a whiplash, charged with energy, crackling with power and anger. "Yeah, go ahead and listen to the uniforms," he yelled. "Let's shuffle on home like good little citizens. We can sit in our houses, watch our crops wilt and our kids die. Or we can *make* those fat cats in Washington listen. We can hurt 'em where they're hurting us, right? If they're hungry enough, they'll listen. Let's do it!" He spun back to face Carter. "Smash those fucking valves. Let the *bushes* wilt for a change!"

A rock clanged off the fender of a truck. Another starred the windshield of Carter's Chevy. The crowd surged forward, individual voices lost in the mob roar. Dan's people were trying. You could see them, like rocks in a flood: men and women grabbing at people, shouting, forming little whirlpools in the slow forward surge of the crowd. He spotted Dan near the center. He was holding his own, slowing people down, but it wasn't enough. It fucking wasn't enough.

"Spread out," Carter ordered. "Hold the line. Don't break."

They had to stop the crowd well in front of the trucks. His people were moving forward, protected from the scatter of falling rocks by their shields. Out in the crowd, the redheaded man swung a fist and one of the dissenters went down. The first people were hitting the line. Screams sounded—those stun wands *hurt*. You blew it, Dan, Carter thought. Chicago was replaying in his head: flames, bodies in the street. Time to stop this. *Now*. Carter headed for the truck where they had set up the gas launchers. A windshield shattered, spraying him with bits of glass. Carter ducked, searching for Dan again in the milling chaos. He'd disappeared. Dust drifted up in choking clouds, obscuring the struggling bodies. The line was being forced back, pushed toward him and the trucks. His orders had been to launch the gas if the line gave. Carter grabbed the comm link from his belt. "Wilson? Captain?" Nothing but static. What the hell had *happened*? Shit, there was no time!

They were on him: a struggling line of swinging riot sticks and stun wands, still backing. The locals were using fists mostly. A couple of them had gotten hold of riot sticks. Dust blinded Carter, filling his eyes with tears. A corporal staggered backward and collided with him, half stunned, clutching his face where a stone had hit. There was blood on his fingers. Carter got an arm around him and stumbled for the launcher, fear cold in his gut. If they got past the trucks . . . A stone hit him in the back and he tripped, pulled off-balance by the corporal's weight.

A bearded man loomed suddenly out of the dust, a riot stick swinging for Carter's face.

No time to duck . . . Carter flung up his arm, bracing for the blow.

A uniformed shoulder slammed him aside as the soldier pivoted into a high, straight-legged kick. The local took the blow ·in his belly, grunted, and went to his knees. ''Are you all right, sir?'' The soldier grabbed his arm, hauled Carter to his feet.

She was a short, stocky woman. ''Thanks Private—Wasson.'' He read the name from her uniform pocket. ''Take him and follow me,'' he gasped, shoving the dazed corporal at her.

''Yes, sir.'' The square-faced woman grinned, but her eyes looked scared.

He ran for the truck with Wasson right behind him.

''Permission to fire, sir.'' Delgado emerged from the dust. ''They're through the line, sir.''

''Why the hell didn't they launch the gas?''

''Wilson said you called on the link . . . told him to hold off.''

Carter chopped off his words with a savage gesture. ''Do it now.''

''Sir, they're too close.'' Delgado's eyes burned with suppressed triumph. ''It's too late to stop them.''

'*Now!*'' They could do it—just. ''Help them,'' Carter snapped at the private. ''Drop the canisters along the Deschutes edge of the crowd.'' What little wind there was would carry it back over them.

The Corps people who didn't get their masks on in time were going to get a dose, too. No help for it. The *whump* of the gas launcher echoed across the riverbed, and Carter heard the first panicked yells as the white clouds billowed up. People staggered drunkenly as the gas hit them, going down onto hands and knees, sprawling sideways as they tried to stand. The stuff knocked out your sense of balance, left you flat on the ground retching with dizziness. It wasn't much fun. Some of the gagging figures on the ground wore Corps suncloth, but things were starting to break up. A media vid-cammer was down on the ground with the locals. Carter felt a sour satisfaction as the man retched.

''Get our people up here and then start picking up the locals,'' Carter ordered. ''I want to talk to Wilson.'' If Delgado was lying—if he'd interfered with the launch order—he'd face a court-martial and to hell with Hastings. ''We'll pick up only the locals

who were doing the actual fighting. Let the rest go. No rough
stuff, Major.'' They'd salvage what they could out of this fiasco.

"Yes, sir.'' Delgado saluted and vanished into the dust, his
expression carefully neutral.

Carter went looking for Dan Greely, angry and hurting from
the stone bruise on his shoulder blade. It had been close. The
crowd had blown up fast. Dan had underestimated them, or had
overestimated the Coalition's power. Or it had been a subtle
setup, never mind that Dan Greely had been out there visibly
trying to stop things.

Carter scanned the scattered bodies still retching into the dust.
Dan wasn't on the ground. He wasn't among the sullen locals
being loaded onto a truck. The medical team was already on the
scene, and Carter went to get a report on injuries.

He kept an eye out for Dan as he secured the bunker and made
sure that the soldiers didn't get too zealous or too rough about
rounding people up. He did see Sandy Corbett; she was helping
some of the gas-struck. Ironically, the gas had hit the people in
the rear of the demonstration hardest—the people who had hung
back from the fighting. At least Harold Ransom had breathed
gas. If anyone deserved it, he did, Carter thought sourly.

It could have worked. It might have worked, if that redheaded
bastard hadn't started everything going sour. He had been
damned good at getting the crowd hot. Too good, maybe. A
media copter lifted, and Carter groaned inwardly. Ratings ought
to be high tonight. His were pretty damn low. He kept an eye
out for the redheaded agitator, but he had also vanished.

The whole fucking afternoon had been a disaster for everyone
except the media. Carter fought a rising sense of discouragement
as the sun set and darkness crept down the riverbed. They had
arrested twelve locals. Besides an assortment of minor injuries,
a private had gotten his jaw badly broken when he was hit in the
face by a rock. Carter's people were sullen, angry that they
hadn't been able to settle the score. Half a dozen had breathed
gas, and Delgado radiated righteous vindication. Wilson had
cleared him. Someone had played electronic games with his
comm link. That was sophisticated sabotage, not the stuff of dirt
farmers—Carter had to think about that.

Was it inside the Corps? Delgado himself?

At least none of the locals had started shooting, or pulled a
knife. Dan had managed that much, at least. Carter detailed
extra security for the Shunt dome. They'd have to keep a twenty-
four-hour armed guard here, he thought wearily. He didn't dare

trust electronic security anymore. That meant more duty hours
and less sleep for everyone. And the plan to use locals on patrol
was laughable now. The trucks were pulling out, heading back
for the dam. Where the *hell* had Dan Greely got to? Carter's
shoulder twinged as he backed the Chevy around and followed
the last truck up the access road to the highway. He should have
tapped someone to drive.

He drove one-handed, taking it slow. Back at the base, he'd
have to report in to Hastings. He was not looking forward to
that conversation. Carter eased the car around a bulge in the
gorge wall. He wanted Dan Greely to tell him why it hadn't
fucking worked, and he wanted that explanation to be a good
one.

The moon was up. It turned the riverbed into a wasteland of
gray shadow, sterile and alien in the cold light. A blot of darkness bulked at the edge of the bed. Carter took his foot off the
accelerator, letting the car slow even more. A side road took off
from the main highway here, a narrow dirt track that meandered
down into the riverbed from a gap broken though the rusting
guard rail of the interstate. He could just make out a car parked
close against the bank, almost invisible from the highway. It
looked like a Corps vehicle.

If it was, it shouldn't be there.

Carter reached for his car phone, then put it down. If something was going on down there, they could be listening in, and
might hear him call the base. This might be nothing more than
a black-market deal with a local. Or it could be something much
bigger. Carter drove on around the curve of the gorge wall and
pulled over to the side of the highway. This was the kind of
reckless stunt that Johnny had always dragged him into, but
tonight he was feeling angry enough to be reckless. He killed
the headlights and climbed out. It was quiet and already cold.
Carter walked back along the highway, skin tightening into
goosebumps. His footsteps rasped on the gritty asphalt, loud in
the silence. He unsnapped his holster, drew his Beretta. After
climbing over the guardrail, he worked his way cautiously down
the slope, testing every foothold on the steep bank.

Four figures stood in a tight cluster behind the concealed vehicle. Three of them wore Corps coveralls; the fourth was a
civilian. Carter crept closer, hugging the deep shadow cast by
the bank, placing his feet carefully on the eroded soil. Two of
the soldiers held the civilian by the arms. The third soldier stood
in front of him. He hunched forward suddenly and Carter heard

the soft *thud* of the blows. The civilian reeled, coughed, and sagged to his knees. They hauled him upright again and the third man drew his arm back.

"That's enough." Carter thumbed off the Beretta's safety and straightened. "This is Colonel Voltaire. Attention!"

The uniformed trio froze, faces turning in his direction.

Delgado? Carter squinted in the moonlight. "Major! What the hell is going on here, mister?"

"We were on our way back with this prisoner, sir." Delgado kept his eyes fixed on a point to the left of Carter's shoulder as Carter approached. "He tried to escape, sir."

"Did he?" Carter kept his pistol in his hand as he turned to the two men holding the civilian.

The man's hands were cuffed behind him. Dan. "Sit him down and get the cuffs off him," Carter said through tight lips. "You two—you're confined to quarters until further notice." He faced Delgado, anger a hot fist in his chest. "Get these men back to the base. I want you in my office tomorrow morning at oh-nine-hundred sharp."

"Yes, sir." Delgado's face was stony.

The two enlisteds had eased Dan to the ground. Delgado bent and unlocked the cuffs. Stiffly and silently the three men climbed into the car. The engine roared to life and the headlights came on, washing the rocky ground with yellow light, making the blood on Dan's face shine wet and crimson. Carter squatted beside him, keeping an eye on the car as it backed up the slope toward the highway. "Are you badly hurt?" Dan's face was swollen, smeared with blood from a badly cut lip and bloody nose.

"I'll live." Dan touched his mouth tentatively, then wiped his bloody fingers on his jeans. "I'm glad you happened along."

"Those three are going to regret this," Carter said flatly. "What happened?"

"I was trying to break things up and someone hit me from behind." Dan touched the back of his head and grimaced. "I woke up on the floor of the car. What happened at the Shunt?"

"We used the gas. I don't think anyone got killed. The situation went flat to hell. Dan?" Carter drew a deep breath. "Did you set me up?"

"No." Dan met Carter's eyes. "I didn't." His shoulders sagged. "I thought we had things under control. People were mad, but it was the media they wanted to reach."

"They sure got the media's attention."

"As a bunch of crazy hotheads. That doesn't do us any good. I'm sorry, Carter." Dan leaned his forehead against his raised knees. "I thought it would work—guess I'm slipping."

"Too late to cry about it now," Carter said bitterly. "Who is that redheaded bastard, anyway? The one who started things going to hell?"

"I don't know him," Dan mumbled. "He sounded like a pro to me. I was on my way to shut him down when I got hit."

"He sure did a professional job. I don't think he was working alone, either. Sit still." Carter got to his feet. "I'll bring the car down here for you."

Professional agitators in the crowd? Sandy Corbett had guessed that the saboteurs were outsiders. Carter thought about that as he eased the car down the narrow track. Working for the Coalition? Possibly. Working for someone else? Who? Good question. Time to lever the Coalition hard for an answer—while they still had time to use it. Carter pulled up beside Dan and set the brake. "Do you know this redhead's name?" Carter asked as he helped Dan to his feet.

"No." Dan slumped into the front seat.

Carter remembered that face. From the abduction? He wasn't sure, and the more he tried to remember, the less certain he was. "Will you find out who he is?" Carter asked as he climbed into the car.

"I'll . . . try." Dan was leaning back in the seat, eyes closed.

More blood matted his hair, and he looked bad. Both eyes were swollen nearly shut and his face was pale beneath the blood and the darkening bruises. Carter whistled softly. "We need to find you a doctor."

"Could you give me a ride home?" Dan mumbled. "I'll be all right."

"You could have a concussion."

"Don't think so." Dan tried a laugh, coughed, and grimaced. "I've been here before. Nothing's broken."

He directed Carter up a winding road that led east from the Dufur highway. A narrow track took them to the rim of the gorge, then led them back toward the Deschutes bed and the site of the day's disaster. To their left was the gorge, a yawning space of empty air. The eroded hills on the Washington side were a landscape of darkness beneath the starry sky.

"Old Celilo Falls is down there," Dan said as they bounced along the rim. "It's a good place for ghosts." He caught his breath as a bad stretch jolted him. "Turn here."

The headlights splashed back from rows of low-growing bean plants—one of the high-protein soys, probably. The faint track they were on ended in front of a decrepit old house. The weathered siding showed a few traces of white paint and the porch sagged drunkenly. Carter helped Dan up the warped steps, supporting most of his weight.

The inside was sparsely furnished. Carter clicked on the solar lantern that hung from a wire above a rickety table. Its yellow glow revealed an ancient woodstove, the table, a couple of battered chairs, and not much else. The poverty depressed him, and he wondered suddenly how those men and women on the lakeshore had lived—where they had slept. Two doors opened from the main room. One was closed. Through the other, Carter saw a bed and caught a glimpse of colorful pictures on the walls.

"Thanks for the ride." Dan sank onto a chair, breathing harshly. "We had a good plan. I sure thought it would work."

Carter had wanted it to work. You could want a lot of things in life. You didn't always get them. He found a clean rag hanging on a hook beside the sink and wet it under the tap. "Here." He wrung it out and handed it to Dan. "I want to believe you," he said slowly. "That this wasn't a setup."

"It wasn't." Dan folded the cloth and held it against the back of his head, his face tight with pain. "I swear it."

"I'm going to have trouble with General Hastings." Carter looked around, frowning. "I may not be able to deal with the Coalition after this. You're not living here alone, are you? You sure you're going to be all right?"

The closed door opened suddenly. "Dan?" The woman in the doorway yawned as she combed her tangled hair back from her face.

Nita. Carter stared at her, his stomach knotting. So that was how Dan had known about his encounter with the kids. "I guess you'll be just fine," he said. Yeah, he should have asked Dan Greely where she was. "Hello, Nita." He turned on his heel, starting for the door.

"Wait a minute!" She caught up with him on the porch and grabbed his arm.

"I don't have time." He shook her off, numb inside. "I've got to get back to the base."

"Carter, stop it." She leaped down the steps and blocked his path to the car, illuminated by the light from the open door. "Tell me what happened to Dan. Why are you so angry?"

She had been right there, out in the Dry, with her water and her comfort. Pretty sweet coincidence, Delgado had said. Oh, yes. It hadn't even been a casual tumble. What had she been trying to find out for Greely? He wanted to ask her, but he couldn't make the words come. They stuck in his throat. Fists clenched, Carter stared at her, wanting to hit her, to despise her. Instead, he felt a deep, aching hurt.

"You're wrong." Her face had gone white. "It's not what you think."

"You don't know *what* I think."

"You think I betrayed you—that I'm an enemy. I didn't," she whispered. "I'm not. How can you *think* that?"

"Weren't you hunting for this husband of yours? You don't seem to be looking very hard," he said savagely.

"I *am* looking. Dan offered me a job working his beans, and that's what I'm doing here. I have to live somewhere, Carter. I . . . couldn't stay with you. I should have told you before I left, but I was . . . afraid."

He looked away from the anguish in her face. He had offered something of himself to her—and she *had* betrayed him. He shoved past her.

"Carter, wait!" she cried. "Please?"

A part of him believed her. That hurt most of all.

The headlights caught her as Carter backed the car around. She was standing on the porch steps, stiff and still, her hands clasped tightly together. It was a con after all, he told himself bitterly. Delgado had been right. Fuck him. Fuck them all. He drove fast back along the gravel road, bouncing and bucking over the ruts and stones, but he couldn't outrun the hard fist of pain closed up in his belly.

CHAPTER TWELVE ☆

Dan was holding a towel to his face when Nita came back into the house. "Trouble?" he dabbed at his lip.

"I don't know." Carter was so *wounded*. She hadn't meant this to happen. "Here, give me that." She took the bloodstained cloth from Dan's hand, teeth on edge. He *hurt*. "Who did this?"

"Uniforms." Dan groaned as she began to clean the blood from the cut on the back of his head. "The protest got violent after all. It's a good thing that you weren't there."

He hadn't been pleased when she had refused to go. He'd been disappointed. *We need people who will keep their heads*, he had told her. *The more the better*. It was because she was Sam Montoya's daughter, Nita thought resentfully. Sam had done this kind of thing with him, so he wanted her to be part of it, too. She wasn't part of it, didn't belong here. Now Carter was pissed. Damn them both.

"Hold still," Nita said as Dan flinched. She frowned at the reddened towel. "The cut on your scalp doesn't look too bad. Do you have anything I can put on it?"

"There's some stuff in the cabinet over the sink." Dan leaned his head in his hands. "I don't know if I can go through this again."

"Go through what? Getting beaten up?" She couldn't help but share his pain. Nita jerked open the cabinet door and picked up a tube of antibiotic ointment. That stuff cost on the black market. In fact, Dan had quite a supply of very expensive and hard-to-get medical supplies on the shelf. Interesting. She took down a pair of surgical scissors. "This ought to do it. Try real hard to hold still, okay?"

"This is a repeat of twenty years ago." Dan hissed softly between his teeth as she snipped hair from around the lips of the ugly gash. "Back then the Columbia Association was squeezing the water, trying to run the farmers off so they could repossess their land. The Corps was on our side back then. We beat the Association, but barely." He sighed. "People got killed in the process. I don't want to do it all over again with the Corps. I'm too damned old for this."

"Then let someone else do it."

"That's what I told your father last time." Dan looked at her, squinting through the eye that wasn't swollen completely shut. "He was the reason we won. Sam kept everyone together, even when it was tough, even when people were getting beaten up and shot. Folks believed in Sam. If it hadn't been for him, everything would have fallen apart. We'd all be in the camps."

"Why are you telling me this?" Nita filled a bowl from the tap and began to rinse out the towel.

"Sam was my friend," Dan said softly. "I want you to know."

So he had to tell her right now—because he might have died tonight? Because he knew that he might die soon? As her father had died? It was too much, on top of Carter's wounded anger. "Do you want to know what I remember about my father?" Nita twisted the towel, wringing red water into the bowl. "I remember when the men came. He could have run, but I was right there in the yard. So he didn't run. He grabbed me and he threw me behind our old truck. So I'd be safe, I guess." The gunshots had hurt her ears, loud as thunder. "His blood got on my dress when he fell." She looked Dan in the face. "Mama never forgave me," she said deliberately. "Because he hadn't run. Because I was alive and he was dead. Because she loved him, and he loved this damn town more than he loved her. She blamed *me*. Here." She shoved the cloth at Dan. "Hold this on your face. It'll help the swelling."

"I'm sorry." Dan took the cloth, all muddy inside. "I was in prison when it happened. By the time I got out, Maria had left The Dalles. I'm so damn sorry, Nita."

Nita turned her back on him, trembling suddenly. She had never told anyone about that day, not even David. This man *remembered* Sam Montoya. "I am not my father. Don't ask me to be." She fled to the darkness of her room to bury herself in the vivid, wordless immediacy of her daughter's dreams.

Rachel woke Nita with the sun, insistently hungry. Nita nursed her, then stripped off her wet diaper and laid her on the floor on her back. Rachel laboriously rolled herself onto her stomach, face wrinkled with effort. Nita smiled as her daughter rocked herself onto her hands and knees. "You're so determined," she murmured and smiled. Rachel flopped onto her chest, protesting. "Soon enough," Nita soothed. "You'll be crawling all over the place." She stroked her daughter's dark, wispy hair and went to get the rest of the diapers.

They had dried stiff, stained yellow, too soiled to use again without washing. Nita sighed and peered at the brownish water left from rinsing the bloody towel. Ugh. She dumped it into the big plastic pail by the door. She would have to use fresh water, and take it all out to the beans afterward. Carter had been so *shocked* when she had told him about washing in a pail. It hurt to think about Carter, so she thought about diapers some more. At least there was enough water for some washing here. The price for sleeping in a bed was diapers. Out in the fields, Rachel went naked.

Dan was waking up. Nita pressed her lips together as his pain seeped into her thoughts. Why me? she thought bitterly, wishing for the umpteenth time that she had been born normal.

Like Rachel?

Yes, like Rachel. Normal. Nita filled a plastic mug from the tap, her throat dry with Dan's thirst. Mug in hand, she hesitated in the doorway of the bedroom. Pictures hung on the walls, glowing with color in the bright morning light.

"You're a mind reader," Dan said, and didn't notice her small flinch. He tried to sit up, but eased himself back down with a groan. "The first day is hell," he said.

The sheet had bunched around his waist. His stomach and chest were purple and green with bruises, his face swollen and ugly. It looked worse than it felt, and it felt bad enough.

"Nothing's broken." Dan had noticed her expression. "I bet I look like shit, but I'll be all right in a couple of days."

This had happened to him before. Nita put the mug down on the table beside him, wondering if her father had been beaten up like this and how Mama had felt when it had happened. "I'm sorry," she said stiffly. "About last night. I was . . . in a bad mood."

"You were right." Dan sighed. "I've been levering you. I *did* want you to be your father. I guess it scares me that I might be too old to handle this all over again." His smile turned into a grimace of pain as he propped himself on one elbow. "It's ironic. I was pissed when Sam started trying to drag me into things. I'd been wandering all my life, and this place didn't seem

any different from any other town I'd been through. It isn't, I
guess. But Sam made a place for me here, and I've been here
ever since.'' He met her eyes. ''I'll quit levering you. If you
want to take off, I've got a little scrip put by. I can pay you some
wages, at least.''

And go where? ''I'll . . . stay,'' Nita said.

''I'm glad.'' Dan reached for the mug. ''I'm glad you're here.
I'm not sure I could handle a trip to the sink yet.''

''Ignacio was always getting into fights,'' Nita said. ''But
never this bad.'' Her older brother had translated Mama's bitter
anger into violence. Nita took the empty mug from him, frowning. She had never asked Ignacio if he felt people the way she
did. By the time she had understood it enough to ask, Ignacio
was gone, driven down the road by his angry darkness.

Rachel had worked her way to the edge of the quilt and had
started to complain. Nita went to scoop up her daughter, de-
touring into her room. ''This will help,'' she told Dan when she
came back. After plopping Rachel onto the floor again, she
opened the small plastic jug she had brought. ''I'll have to find
another nest before I can make any more,'' she said as she
poured golden liquid into Dan's mug.

''What's this?'' Dan's eyebrows rose as he sipped.

''It's honey water. I ferment it, so it's got some alcohol in it.
It helps, if you're hurting.''

''Maybe you could hunt bees around here.''

''There aren't very many. They've been dying. David said it
must be some kind of disease. That's why he . . . had to go find
a job.'' A hard lump clogged her throat and she looked away,
fixing her eyes on the pictures. Most of them showed a river,
full of water and edged with green, like pictures Nita had seen
in old books and videos. ''Is that the Columbia?'' Nita asked.

''Uh-huh. Jesse—the woman who used to own this farm—
painted those pictures. She could remember water in the riverbed, back before they finished the Trench Reservoir and built
the Pipeline.''

''She must have been old,'' Nita said, her eyes on the blues
and grays and greens.

''I thought so, the first time I saw her.''

Nita felt Dan's smile, and realized suddenly that Jesse had
been his lover. He was remembering her and the echoes of their
lovemaking tickled Nita, softened with his sadness. She had
thought David was old when she had first met him. He had been

nearly forty, ancient to her young eyes. "I'm sorry," she said, knowing without his telling her that Jesse was dead.

"Me, too." Dan sighed. "She was part of the reason I stayed." He was staring at the ceiling, speaking softly as if he had forgotten Nita's presence. "Sometimes I think Sam dropped me on Jesse's doorstep on purpose—that he figured we needed each other. He had a lot of insight about people—he cared, and he cared about keeping the community alive. When he died, there wasn't anyone to take his place. I discovered . . . that I couldn't walk away from that caring. I couldn't let it go for nothing. I guess I still can't." He turned his head to give Nita a lopsided smile. "I'm levering you again," he said. "Or maybe it's this business with the Corps. It makes me ask myself why the hell I'm still involved. Anyway, I'm sorry, Nita."

"It's all right," Nita said. "My father lived here. He was who he was, and I guess I'd better get used to it." Rachel whimpered and Nita picked her up. "The Valley's an ugly place," she said softly. "Salt from the water creeps up out of the ground and coats the bushes with a white crust. The dust stings your eyes and makes you cough. Nothing grows except the bushes. You have to go way up into the mountains to find any flowers."

"We're making things worse," Dan murmured. "We're running so hard to keep ahead of this damned drought that we can't stop. We'll never be able to go back to the way it was, even if the rains start tomorrow."

David had said the same thing. The bushes didn't need bees and the salty Valley had scared him. We scared him, too, Nita thought and settled her fussing daughter onto her hip. "The soaker hoses in the south end of the field are clogged," she said. "If I don't get them cleared, the beans are going to wilt."

"Could I ask you to do me a favor?" Dan asked. "You can drive, right? Would you take the truck and go over to Sandy Corbett's place later? I need to talk to her, but I think she'll have to come here." He grimaced. "I'll draw you a map. The Coalition needs to start dealing with yesterday's mess."

"Sure," Nita said, picking up the mug. The honey water had blurred away some of his pain and he was sinking into sleep. She needed to get out of this house. Her father had sat at the table in the kitchen, had looked out the window at the dry riverbed. Maybe I *will* leave, Nita thought, but there was nowhere else to go. "I'll go give Sandy your message as soon as I get the hoses clear," she said.

* * *

The Corbett farm lay west of The Dalles, on a bench of level land above the riverbed. Nita found the gray-haired, stocky woman out weeding beets, shaded from the afternoon sun by a handwoven grass hat.

"What got into that fool colonel?" Dirt-stained hands on her hips, Sandy glared when Nita told her about Dan's beating. "Dan's the best ally that idiot has. Is he trying to cut his own throat?"

"Carter didn't do it. He brought Dan home." Nita caught the speculative flicker of Sandy's curiosity, heard the defensive note in her voice. "That's what Dan told me," she said in a calmer tone.

"Dan's too quick to forgive. Of course, that's not a bad trait, considering that he's usually smack in the middle of things." Sandy wiped her hands on her dirty jeans. "The man just can't say no to folks' needs. Your father was like that, too."

Not this again. Nita pressed her lips together, pretending to adjust Rachel's sling.

"Anyway, I'm glad you're staying out there. I worry about Dan. He takes too much on himself."

"He says that you need to meet, that you'll know who to tell," Nita passed on Dan's message.

"Oh, I'll round 'em up, although there's a couple I'd like to leave out of it," she grumbled. "I'm afraid we're in for trouble, no matter what miracle Dan thinks he can pull off." Her weathered face crinkled into a sudden smile and she stuck out a finger for Rachel to grab. "Come sit and have a drink. I've got some scones left over from breakfast, too. No sense in going back there hungry."

The house turned out to be three battered mobile homes parked in an open-sided square around an ancient maple tree. A decrepit wooden barn sagged out back. The trailers squatted on their concrete-block foundations, scabby and settled, as if they'd been there a long, long time. A thick layer of old leaves carpeted the space beneath the tree.

"Sit down, I'll bring stuff out. The place is a mess, as usual." She waved vaguely at a few old yard chairs. New fabric had been stretched over the battered frames. Nita spread Rachel's quilt on the crackly leaves, put her daughter down on her belly, and gave her a string of wooden beads to play with.

"Here you are." The gray-haired woman reappeared with a pitcher and two glasses clutched in one hand, a plate of thick golden cakes in the other. "The boys are down in Bonneville, buying some new hose for the east field, and Cathy's teaching at the co-op school this week. She's got the whole brood with her,'' she said as she handed Nita a glass and sat down. ''I've got the place to myself today.''

Nita nodded, not sure what to say, and covered her confusion with a bite of the crumbly, biscuitlike cake. An upright piano was visible through the open door of the trailer. ''Do you play?'' Nita asked.

''Some.'' Sandy sighed. ''My hands aren't as nimble as they used to be. When I was a kid, I was going to be a concert pianist. I had it all figured out—I was going to get a scholarship, be another Van Cliburn or Horowitz. Oh yes, I *did* have dreams.'' She shook her head and laughed gently. ''I taught your mom to play, you know.''

''My mother?''

''Uh-huh. Back before she and your dad were even married. Maria loved music. She had a beautiful voice, too.''

''I didn't know that.'' Nita looked down at the glass in her hand, trying to imagine her mother singing.

''She quit taking lessons when Alberto was born. She said she was too tired, and I guess she was, with the farm to work and all.'' Sandy shook her head. ''You don't hear music so much anymore—not even in church. Art, music, poetry—what's happened to it? I asked Sam that one time. He said we'd had it too easy. We thought we could fix anything, that we had it all under control with our science and such. When we couldn't fix this drought, it broke something in us—our spirits, maybe. I don't know. Sometimes I think our souls are drying up.'' Sandy shook her head, forced a smile. ''You look like your dad,'' she said. ''Did anyone ever tell you that?''

''Yes.'' Nita crumbled the last of her scone between her fingers. There had been no music in her mother, only darkness and twisted anger. ''Look, I don't remember . . . my father.'' How many times was she going to have to say this? Nita met the older woman's eyes. ''Life was hard for us after he died. That's all I know.'' And Mama had remembered his dying every time she had looked at Nita's face.

''You sound a little like Maria.''

''I don't blame him, if that's what you mean.'' Nita pressed her lips together. ''Everyone wants to tell me about him. They all expect me to think of him as some kind of hero, and I don't.''

''Maria was right in a way.'' Sandy sighed. ''Sam did put the community ahead of his own life, ahead of his family. He used to say that we wouldn't make it—any of us—unless we stuck together." She poured more water into Nita's glass. "He wasn't a hero," she said. "He was just a quiet man who saw what needed to be done. He was perceptive, Sam Montoya. Sometimes you could swear he knew what you were thinking."

Dan had said that he had . . . insight. Nita's cheeks went hot, then cold. "I have to go." She got quickly to her feet. "I have to get back. Thank you for the water and the scones."

She drove back through The Dalles automatically, her eyes registering the road, her brain churning. Rachel fussed irritably on the seat beside her. *You could swear he knew what you were thinking.* Sandy Corbett had said it so casually. Nita had inherited his face. And what else? "Did you do this to me?" she whispered. A mutation, David had said. What if he'd been wrong? What if Sam Montoya had passed it on to her? Nita touched her squirming daughter lightly. Father to daughter to granddaughter? "No," she whispered, but the word sounded so feeble.

When she reached the turnoff to the Corps base, Nita swung the truck suddenly onto the road. The guard at the ugly gate watched her as she parked the truck. He carried a rifle and his hostility pricked at her.

"I don't see your name on the list," he said when she asked for Carter. "I'll see if I can contact the colonel."

Rachel started to cry. Teething? Or reacting to the guard? She was teething, Nita told herself. She hadn't been fussy like this until lately.

They had been out in the hills before that. By themselves. They hadn't been living in a town full of angry people. Nita squatted in the shadow of the truck, holding her daughter tightly. "I don't want you to be like me," Nita whispered. She pulled out Rachel's string of wooden beads and dangled it above her daughter's groping fists. She would feel the anger, and the lust, and the broken bones. One day she would look into a lover's eyes and feel his fear. She looked like David—more like him every day. Nita blinked back tears, jumped at the clang of the gate. Carter. Nita got slowly to her feet.

"What do you want?"

"You can be angry at me." Nita straightened her shoulders. "But you're angry at Dan, and you shouldn't be."

"You don't know how I feel."

There was a thread of hurt beneath his anger. "Will you come for a walk with me?'' She spoke to that hurting. ''Please, Carter? I need to tell you . . . about why I left.''

''I can give you a few minutes.'' He was struggling inside, wanting to hear her, wanting to wall her off with his anger at the same time.

Nita tilted her head, hearing a hum of contentment on the hot breeze. Bees! ''Here.'' She shoved Rachel suddenly into Carter's arms and walked away from him, following the gentle note of the nest.

It was in a rock outcrop, back in a crevice. Nita hummed the comfort-song to the swarm as the bees swirled up around her head. She could just get her hand into the space. Carefully she broke off a chunk of sticky comb.

''Nita! What are you doing?''

Carter's voice, and there was fear in it. Fear for her, in spite of his anger? Pain clenched in her chest and the bees felt it, their song rising and sharpening. *Gently.* She hummed it to them as she got to her feet. Calmed by her song, they trailed away as she walked back to the road. By the time she reached Carter and Rachel, only a few stragglers clung to her shirt and hair. Absently she brushed them away.

''Are you all right?'' Carter jumped as a confused worker circled his head. ''My God, they could have been killers, Nita.''

''I can tell killers from honeybees. Here.'' She broke off a piece of golden comb, handed it to Carter. ''I only took a little. It's not a very big nest. Chew it.'' She lifted Rachel from his arms. ''Spit out the wax when the honey's gone.''

Hesitantly, still angry, Carter bit into the dense, sticky chunk.

''I miss the bees.'' Nita dabbed a bit of honey on her daughter's lips, smiling sadly at Rachel's chuckle of surprise and pleasure. ''When the rains come, everything blooms in the hills. You have to look for the flowers, but they're there—down in the crevices where the rocks protect them, at the bottom of the old streambeds. I was like the flowers.'' She looked up at Carter. ''I hid down in the cracks, wounded, afraid of the world. I was fourteen when I met David. I hadn't talked since I was five, and my family thought I was retarded. It was David who found me,'' she said softly. ''He gave me space and time to grow up, to find myself. He sheltered me and . . . he loved me. It wouldn't matter, if I didn't care about you.'' Her voice trembled, and she shook her head, angry at the emotion that threatened to rise up and overwhelm her. ''It wouldn't even matter that I was sleeping with you. But . . . I *do* care, Carter. Don't you see? And I love

David and I don't know what happened to him. I have to find out, Carter. I need to know for sure if he's dead . . . or alive. I didn't betray you, Carter. I didn't.''

"I never said you did." Carter's voice was unsteady and his anguish clouded the air.

"I didn't know Dan until a few days ago. I'm not sleeping with him." She winced with Carter's reaction. "He really is trying to help you. Don't screw things up just because I hurt you. Dan's not part of that."

"I didn't ask you if you were sleeping with him." Carter looked away from her, all muddy and mixed up inside. "I'd like to trust Dan, but there are a lot of men and women living on this base. They're the ones who are going to pay if I make a mistake. How well do *you* know Dan Greely, Nita?"

"He's on your side. Carter, he *is*."

"I'll keep it in mind," he said, and looked back at the gate, giving in to his need to escape her. "I've got to get back. I'm sorry." His eyes avoided hers. "About the misunderstanding."

"Carter?" She closed her lips tightly, because there was nothing to say. He wasn't really *hearing* her. He was trapped by his responsibilities, just as Dan was trapped by her father's ghost. He was walking away from her, back to his gate and the crushing weight of his burden.

She could call him back. She could tell him how she knew that Dan wasn't an enemy.

Rachel started to cry, and she turned her back on the gate. She was afraid—afraid of what she would feel if he believed her. I'm trapped, too, Nita thought bitterly. In her sling, Rachel kicked and fussed. "You don't feel me." Nita scooped her into her arms as they walked back to the truck. "You're David's daughter, sweetheart. He'll get here sooner or later and it'll be all right. We'll leave, go somewhere else." Pretty words. They had the feel of a fairy tale.

They had almost reached the truck. Nita gasped as the dusty ground suddenly shimmered. Something was *wrong*. She clung to Rachel as colors brightened around her. Grass? Stunned, Nita stared at the vivid green blades beneath her feet. Tiny droplets of water glinted on their tips, and fuzzy yellow flowers swayed in the gentle wind. Spindly young trees scattered white petals across the grass and more yellow flowers swayed on long stems. Nita had seen pictures of flowers like that, tried to recall their name but couldn't. She clutched Rachel, frozen with terror and awe.

Beyond the grass and the yellow flowers, the river was full of water.

There wasn't that much water in the whole world. There *couldn't* be. Nita took a stumbling step toward it. It stretched away from her in a wrinkled gray sheet, streaked with white. The hills on the far side looked miles distant and the water foamed at the foot of the dam. There was no sign of the base.

"Carter!" Nita cried in sudden terror. They would be dead, all of them, buried under that gray water, *drowned*, for God's sake. She tried to run, but the access road had inexplicably moved and the ground wasn't where her eyes told her it was. Unseen humps and hollows jarred her. She stumbled, fell, twisting desperately to protect Rachel, ground slamming the breath from her body, bruising her hip. Her face was full of invisible dust and Rachel was screaming, her terror a beating wing in Nita's head. Breathless, Nita hid her face against her daughter's struggling body, surrounded by grass and flowers, wondering if she was going crazy, wondering if the world was going crazy.

Footsteps thudded on the hard ground. "Hey, are you all right?"

Someone's worry pricked her and hands touched her shoulders.

"Are you hurt?" The hands had shifted to Rachel, as if to take her from Nita's arms.

"I'm okay." Nita forced her eyes open, then shuddered at the sight of green grass. "No, I've got her." She clutched Rachel to her.

A man was bending over her. A tail of blond hair hung down over his shoulder and his vivid blue eyes reflected his concern. Nita shook her head, not trusting her voice, wishing he would go away and leave her alone. She stretched out her hand. The grass stems didn't bend or flatten and she felt only dust and sharp gravel beneath her palm. She clenched her trembling fingers into a fist.

"Oh, shit," the man said softly.

Slowly the green landscape faded, thinning away like smoke from a smothered fire. Nita clutched the hiccoughing Rachel to her, watching the buildings of the riverbed base reappear. She looked up at the blond man. "You did it," she said numbly.

"Listen, I'm sorry." He squatted beside her, radiating anxiety. "It's just . . . a fancy holo projector. I was testing it. I didn't mean to scare you."

"You're *lying*." Nita scrambled to her feet, hearing hysteria in her voice. "*You* did this. You made me see *water* in the river."

"No." His distress flowered in Nita's head. "It's a holo. I'll show you how it works." He held out a small gray box.

"That's all right," she said quickly. He was afraid, and his fear had the effect of calming her. "I . . . won't tell anyone," she answered his anxiety. "It's all right. Really. How did you *do* that?"

He opened his mouth to protest, then shrugged. "I'm . . . not sure." His eyes were sharp and wary on her face. "I think . . . it's a vision of the past. I just see it. Sometimes other people see it, too."

"It was so real," Nita whispered.

"You saw that much?" His eyes narrowed. "Most people just catch a glimpse, and that's if I'm standing right beside them. I was clear over near the culvert when you started running." He gave her a wary, measuring smile. "I'm Jeremy Barlow."

"I'm Nita Montoya and this is Rachel." His wariness rubbed at her. Remembering Seth, she nodded, understanding suddenly. "It really *is* all right. I don't think you're a freak or a demon or whatever people guess when you scare them. And I really won't tell anyone."

"I'm relieved," he said wryly.

He didn't particularly believe her. "How can you see the past?" she asked softly. "How can that be?"

"I don't know. Here." He held out a hand to help her up.

His hand was crippled, the joints thick and ugly. She noticed the stick he had dropped on the ground. His knees hurt him; now that her fear had faded, she could feel it. He was looking at her thoughtfully, deciding whether or not she was a serious threat.

"I could always make things appear," he said, probably deciding that it was too late to matter. "Like this." He held out his palm and a brilliant green insect blinked into life above it, settling delicately onto his fingers. "The . . . visions came later." He shrugged. "I do magic shows at local markets."

"Were you in Tygh Valley?" Nita's eyes widened. "This farmer told me about someone who did magic. He said it was fake."

"Tygh Valley." The wariness had come back, stronger than before. "Yeah, I went through there. They weren't a very good crowd."

"They hate anything strange." Nita shivered with the memory of Seth's thin, molten ugliness. Rachel whimpered and she hugged her close. "They hate anything they don't understand, like the boy they stoned. You're right to be scared of them." She jumped as Jeremy's hand closed on her wrist.

"You *know* I'm scared of them, don't you?" His voice was hushed, but excitement blazed behind his eyes. "You're reading my thoughts. That's how you knew I was lying about the projector. That's why you saw the river so well. You're a telepath!"

"No! I don't know." His intensity frightened her, and his fingers were bruising her arm. "I-I know what you're feeling," she faltered. "Scared, or angry, or whatever. I don't know what you're thinking."

"An empath. That's what you are." He looked down at his hand and let go of her abruptly. "Sorry. It just surprised me . . . meeting someone else who's different."

Nita rubbed the marks his fingers had left. He wasn't dark inside the way the trader had been dark. His excitement had a desperate feel, like someone lost in the Dry who had finally sighted a house. A feel like thirst and hope balled up in a knot.

"I didn't hear any gossip about empaths at the market." He was watching her face. "You don't tell people, either, do you?"

"No." Nita shook her head, trying to banish Carter from her thoughts. "I don't. Doesn't it bother you?" she asked bitterly. "That I knew you were afraid? That I know you're excited now?"

"No." He tugged thoughtfully at his tail of hair. "It doesn't. But it would probably bother most people."

"It . . . does."

"I'm sorry. I didn't mean to corner you . . . oh, hell, yes I did." He tossed his hair back over his shoulder with an impatient jerk of his head. "I've heard all kinds of stories about the kids who get born in the Dry, but you're the first person I've met . . ." He frowned, groping for a word. "Who's like me," he finished at last. "More like me than most people, anyway. Don't you ever wonder . . . why we are? Don't you want to *know*?"

"I wasn't born in the Dry." Nita shrugged the sling higher on her shoulder, looking away from his intensity. She wanted to flee this strange man, and wanted to stay at the same time. "I'm not sure I know *who* I am," she said in a low voice. "I haven't gotten to the *why* yet. I've got to go." She opened the truck door, still hesitating. "Do you need a ride somewhere?"

"No, thanks. I've been camping in that culvert. Some of the

highway kids told me it was a good place. I've been doing the market in town.''

"I haven't been down there for a while. When you were on the road, did you ever meet a David Ascher, by any chance?'' Nita asked him because she had to ask. "In his forties, curly gray hair? He's about a head taller than you and lanky.''

Jeremy shook his head.

"Oh, well.'' She pulled the door open and boosted Rachel onto the patched seat.

"I figured it was time to move on—when you guessed.'' Jeremy leaned on the open door. "But I think I'll stick around. I want to talk to you some more. About what we are. And maybe why.'' Hunger flickered in his eyes, like distant heat lightning. "Will you come down to the market and look me up?''

"I . . . I'll try,'' Nita said, trapped by that heat-lightning hunger. "But I don't understand. What are you trying to find out?''

"Why we are.'' His eyes held hers, dry and blue as the sky. "I want it to matter,'' he said softly. "All our loneliness, everything we lose by being the way we are. I want it to *count*. Don't you?''

"Yes,'' she whispered. For herself. For Rachel. It was his hunger, but it seized her suddenly, shook her to the center of her being. "I'll look for you,'' she said. "I promise. And I won't tell anyone about your magic.''

"Thanks.'' His brief smile lit his eyes like a shaft of sunlight and he stepped back to close the truck's door.

She had seen water in the river. Nita remembered the pictures on Dan's wall as she backed the truck around in the narrow road. Yes, she had seen *that* river. That yesterday. Jeremy lifted a hand as she drove past him: a small figure limping back up the dusty road. *I want it to matter,* he had said. She had wanted it, too, and the intensity of that wanting scared her.

Nita drove back to Dan's farm, not sure if she wanted to see this man again or not.

CHAPTER THIRTEEN ☆

"Glad I could pry you away from The Dalles." Johnny lifted his glass of wine in a toast. "I don't think I dare take a uniform out to lunch up there. I could get lynched."

"It's not funny." Carter sipped at his own wine, then set it down. "I've had to declare the town off-limits to all Corps personnel." He poked at the slices of cooling meat on his plate. This Bonneville restaurant was as good as any in Portland. He hadn't eaten real meat in weeks. He set his fork down.

"It's that bad?" Johnny asked quietly.

"You're my boss. You see the reports." He picked up his wineglass and glowered into its ruby depths. "You tell me."

"By the reports, you're doing a great job. I came out here to find out what wasn't included."

"I'm sorry." Carter dredged up a smile. Even in the dim light of the restaurant, Johnny's face looked thin and strained. "I'm growling at you like you're Water Policy incarnate. There's not much to tell." He sighed. "Corps people hate locals; locals hate the Corps. It can blow, any time. Any more cuts coming down?" he asked bitterly.

"Of course. But not soon." Johnny speared a leaf of blanched endive.

Of course. Of course there would be more water cuts, unless the rain came back. He watched Johnny finish his salad. People around The Dalles ate mostly hi-pro soybeans. That's what they grew, and they were cheap. If they didn't take vitamin supplements, they ended up with chronic vitamin deficiencies. The battalion's surgeon had told him it was endemic out in the Dry. It caused a lot of birth defects, she had said. "So how are *you* doing?" he asked Johnny.

"Everybody loves us since Mexico backed down." Johnny

grinned, but his eyes were serious. "Your water-cut blues weren't in vain. Listen, I didn't come out here just to visit," he said slowly. "I heard a little . . . tidbit from my senator buddy, Paul Targass." He wiped his mouth and tossed his napkin onto his empty plate. "There's a rumor going around that Pacific Bio's in bed with the Corps."

Carter opened his mouth to protest, but closed it without speaking. He remembered the hungry look in Gwynn's eyes, remembered Morissy. Water was power, and power was always for sale. "Who?" he asked softly. "Someone at the top?"

"Don't know." Johnny shrugged. "But Pacific Bio's concentrating on their West Coast operations—so keep your ears open." He finished his wine and emptied the bottle into his glass.

"I'm not sure I'd catch it, unless someone yelled in my ear." Carter grimaced. "You're good at the rumor game. I'm not."

"Yes, I *am* good at it. That's partly how I ended up where I am, and we both know it."

That hungry glitter was back in his eyes. Hunger for power? Johnny had always been on top—no one had ever doubted that he belonged there. "What does Morissy have on you?" Carter asked abruptly.

"What kind of crack is that?" Johnny flushed. "Whatever you thought you picked up at that party, you didn't." He leaned forward across the table. "Let me tell you something; Pacific Bio may think it can own me, but they're going to find out otherwise."

"I didn't mean it that way." Carter leaned back, his uneasiness deepening. Johnny was drunk. He'd had most of that bottle of wine. "Take it easy," he said gently. "I'm on your side, remember?"

"Yeah, that's right. Good old Carter, always there to back me up—until you decided that the damn Corps was more important."

"I wouldn't have been much good to you in politics." Carter sighed. "Moral support I can give you from inside a uniform."

"You'd have been there." Johnny drained his glass. "I used to bug you, didn't I? Make fun of how you hated to break the rules."

Carter couldn't afford to break the rules back then. His mother had known how it worked—without a pricey education you went exactly nowhere. She knew it well enough to pay for it on her back for years, putting up with Warrington and her own guilts. I never told her that I understood, Carter thought bitterly. There had been no way to say it in words—so he had busted his ass in school instead. Johnny's father had had the money and clout to get his son out of any mess, but Carter was another story. So

Carter had worked hard to keep both their asses out of the fire. Sometimes it had been tough.

In the end, it had been Johnny who had saved *his* ass.

"I'm on top, Carter." The naked hunger in Johnny's eyes made Carter look away. "No one's bigger than Water Policy. And no one is going to fuck that up for me. *No* one."

"I don't see how they can." Carter looked up as a waiter appeared at his side.

"Colonel Voltaire?" He held out a compact phone. "Call for you, sir."

The little food he'd eaten turned to stone in his belly. "Voltaire here," he said.

"Colonel?" The voice on the phone sounded tinny and distant. "This is Captain Moreno, in Communications. I've got Chief of Police Durer on the line. He says it's an emergency and he won't talk to anyone but you, sir." The captain sounded nervous. "I'm sorry to interrupt you, sir, but you said—"

"It's all right." Carter sat on his irritation. God, what now? "Patch him through."

"Hello?" A new voice boomed in Carter's ear. "This is Chief of Police Durer calling from The Dalles. It seems that I have a couple of your boys locked up down here."

Great. "On what charges?" Carter growled. "And why didn't you talk to Major Delgado?"

"The charge is assault. And we both know that there's no point in a local talking to Robert Delgado. We picked up your boys on the interstate, Colonel. They busted some kid's head with a tire iron. I think you'd better send a batch of MPs down here to collect these guys and do it quick. Before word gets around."

A kid. Great. Carter clenched his teeth. If the soldiers had committed a crime in town, they were Durer's meat. If he wanted them out of his jail, the situation was bad. "I'll send some people down right away," he snapped.

"You do that, son." Durer hung up.

Shit. Carter called Security and ordered a detail of MPs out to pick up the soldiers. By the time he got off the phone, the table had been cleared. "You *do* sound good when you're giving orders." Johnny grinned. "Very official." There was a needling edge to his tone.

"I'm sorry," Carter said. "I've got to get back." Durer didn't like uniforms much. It might be a good idea for him to talk to the police chief in person.

"So go be an officer." Johnny flashed him a mock salute and rose. "I'll call you next time I'm in town."

Carter looked after him as he left. Johnny was pissed. Whatever he wanted from Carter, Carter wasn't providing it. He sighed and looked down at the table. The restaurant had kept their water glasses filled during the meal—a touch of old-days custom that had doubtless been reflected in the bill. Carter touched the rim of Johnny's full glass. That small amount of water would matter to a lot of people. Carter wondered what the waiter would do with it.

From Durer's tone, Carter had half expected a mob at City Hall, but it was quiet. Carter saw to the transfer of the two bruised and sullen NCOs. They claimed that the kids had started it—that it was the bunch who hung out near the truck plaza. They'd had baseball bats, the men claimed, and they looked battered enough for it to be true.

Carter could believe it. He sent them back with Security and went inside to do his talking.

"The kid's thirteen." Durer hunched his thick shoulders, elbows planted firmly on his desk. "Look, Colonel, I'll level with you—he's one of those highway kids. Anyone else could probably shoot him in broad daylight, and only a few of our upstanding citizens would give a damn. But a uniform did it. Do you get my drift?"

Durer didn't like uniforms much, but he liked the prospect of facing a lynch mob even less. "Is the kid going to live?" Carter asked.

"He got a concussion." Durer shrugged. "I don't think the doc's too worried. You keep your tough-guys out of town, Colonel. We don't need this."

"We have to use the highway," Carter snapped. "Caught any of those rock-throwers who've been busting our windshields yet?"

"I'm doing my best." Durer shoved a handful of papers into a battered metal filing cabinet. "I'm real short-handed."

"Yeah." Like hell. Carter turned on his heel and left the stifling office, remembering the blond kid's feral eyes in that culvert.

Had the kid in the van had eyes like that? There was blame enough to go around here. More than enough. Carter paused outside, breathing deeply, struggling with anger. By tonight, everyone in The Dalles would know that uniforms had tried to kill a kid. And when he had the company CO Article 15 the

NCOs for the tire iron, his own people would bitch because he was being soft on the locals. And Johnny was pissed at him.

He was fucking tired of being everyone's enemy. Carter yanked the Chevy's door open.

"Hello, Carter." Greely sat in the passenger seat. "How come you won't see me?"

Carter hesitated for a moment, anger still hot in his chest, half tempted to tell Greely to get the hell out of his car and drive away. With a jerky shrug, he dropped onto the seat. "Hastings ordered me to break off all relations with the Coalition."

"Crap on that." Dan let his breath out in a rush. "We need to talk, orders or no orders. It's getting bad, Carter."

"Tell me about it." Carter stared through the windshield, seeing Nita's face in the reflection of the sun on the glass. *Is Nita Montoya your lover?* Five words. He couldn't say them. He could only listen to them play over and over inside his skull, remind himself that they had nothing to do with him, or with his job here. "I don't think I can talk to you," he said out loud. "Even if I was willing to disobey Hastings's direct order. I keep wondering about that protest. Nice, that it all happened in one place. Convenient for the media. It was convenient for whoever holed the Pipe while it was going on. We were all busy, and that leak cost me an official reprimand."

"You think I set you up?" Dan sighed. "*Why*, Carter?"

"Let's just say that I don't *know* that you didn't." Carter clenched his fist, pounding very gently on the steering wheel. "I can't stick my neck out for you any more."

"You're not sticking it out for *me*, damn it." Dan was angry now, too. "I thought *we* were doing it to keep people from dying around here—uniforms *and* locals."

"Did you ever find out the name of that redhaired agitator?" Carter changed the subject abruptly.

"Bill, with no last name." Dan frowned. "He disappeared after the Shunt and no one's seen him since. I never did catch up with him."

"I want to believe you," Carter said softly. "But too many people depend on me to make the right decisions."

"Corps people." Dan's voice was bitter.

"Yes. And locals." Carter twisted the key and pumped the gas as the engine stuttered and caught. "I'm keeping an open mind. That's all I can do right now."

Dan looked at him for a long moment, then climbed stiffly out of the car. "You're shooting yourself in the foot," he said quietly. "We need to work together more than ever. If you change your mind, leave a message with Bob, at the government store."

Carter slammed the car door and gunned the engine. Part of him agreed with Dan—it would be a hell of a lot easier if he had some kind of local cooperation. Nita might not even be up there anymore. She might have moved on. What the hell did it matter, anyway? She'd told him it was over between them, so drop it. Teeth clenched, Carter took the corner onto the street too fast. A middle-age woman carrying a plastic pail had to jump for the curb and the pail tilted, spilling dark-red beet roots across the street. Carter saw her raised fist and shouting mouth in his rearview as he turned onto Second. Guiltily he slowed the car. At the next intersection, he braked to let a teenage kid push a rusty wheelbarrow across the intersection. It was full of firewood—salvaged bits of weathered lumber from some ruined building or other.

The kid looked at Carter, scowled, and spat. Carter's lips tightened and he stepped on the gas as the kid bounced the barrow up onto the sidewalk. The engine stuttered again, hesitated, then roared. Carter frowned, uneasy. The car had been fine on the trip down to Bonneville and back. He drove down two more blocks, past empty storefronts and the bar that still did business. A block farther north, the street ended in warehouses and the railroad tracks. Three blocks to his right, the weekday market filled the parking lot of the boarded-up supermarket. As Carter turned the corner, the engine coughed and died. Cursing, he reached for the phone to call Security back. The phone was gone from its cradle. It had been there when he had parked at City Hall. Swearing softly, Carter climbed out of the car and lifted the hood. This was *not* a good place for a breakdown.

"Hey, look who's here. One of the uniforms."

Carter let the hood fall closed with a bang. He hadn't noticed the half-dozen men lounging in the shade beneath the star-spangled marquee of the town's one theater. They were young, all of them, their expressions eager and ugly. The skin tightened between Carter's shoulder blades.

"He's brass, looks like. A hotshot."

"You in town for a little action, hotshot?"

"I seen him at the Shunt last week," one of them said excitedly. "He was the guy givin' the orders. The head honcho." The man was younger than the rest and his voice squeaked.

"Yeah, he's the boss, the fucker who cut our water."

As if some unspoken cue had been given, they started toward him, moving easily, hands loose at their sides. They had pack faces, hungry and grinning. Carter looked up and down the block. The market was too far away. No help there anyway—not for a uniform. "Don't buy yourself trouble," he said, knowing he was wasting his breath. "You'll just end up in jail."

"Baby, no one's gonna touch us. We're gonna kick the shit out of you and it's gonna be fun." The round-faced man grinned, eyes bright. "Beckers got a foreclosure yesterday. You Army assholes want to run us off, don't you? Take our land for yourselves?"

"We don't have any use for your land." Carter took a step backward. He was Goddamned *sick* of running. "There isn't any more water than what you've got," he snarled. "Can't you get that through your heads?" He was sick of being rational, of trying to talk sense into these stubborn hicks.

"There's water for the damn valleys."

"But not for us."

"Valleys counts more than we do, huh? Fucker. We'll teach you to try and run us out." The round-faced man lunged forward, the others on his heels.

If he had come armed . . . Rage blossomed in Carter's head, but he hadn't come armed. So he ran. Again. His feet pounded on the concrete as he dodged around the corner. They were shouting behind him . . . couldn't tell how close . . . couldn't stop to see. His salt-burned lungs already blazed with fire and his pulse thundered in his ears. They were going to catch him. To his left, the ruins of an ancient wooden building had sagged onto the street. Carter leaped a splintered beam, looking frantically for a hiding place. Maybe in that warehouse at the end of the block . . . OREGON CHERRY GROWERS, the faded letters proclaimed. No cherries anymore. Carter raced across the tracks, his feet sliding in the roadbed gravel. They were right behind him. Gasping for breath, he flung himself around the corner of the warehouse, dodging between a rusty forklift and the peeling wall.

"This way," a voice hissed. "In here."

Carter caught a glimpse of denim blue and a man's face in a crack of darkness. He slithered between two warped sheets of metal siding. No time to worry about a trap. A hand closed on his wrist, guiding him into darkness. Momentarily blind, Carter bumped into something that felt like a pile of stacked cardboard. He leaned against it, his knees shaky, trying to smother the labored rasp of his breathing. Footsteps thudded outside.

"He went this way."

"I bet he went through that hole in the fence there. Check those doors."

Metal rattled close by and Carter stiffened.

"Door's locked," the shadowy figure whispered. "The crack's hard to see."

He knew that voice. The sounds of pursuit were fading; he squinted at the man standing beside him, blinking as his eyes adjusted to the dim light. "Jeremy?"

"I told you I might see you around." Jeremy gave him a lopsided grin. "I'm glad I did. You can't run for shit."

"I'm glad you did, too." Carter sat down hard as his knees threatened to give out. "I can't run. I worked in the Michigan lakebed." He was getting his breath back at last. "The dust screws up your lungs. I owe you for my ass."

"Yeah, I think you do." Jeremy sat down beside him. "This is kind of a bad neighborhood if you're wearing a uniform, you know."

"Do tell." Carter grinned. "Bad luck that my car died where it did. If it *was* luck." Someone had swiped his phone—so that he couldn't call for help? And Dan Greely had been sitting in his car. Waiting to talk? Or had Carter surprised him doing something else? He sighed, looking around at the shadowy interior of the old warehouse. Wooden fruit crates and bales of flattened cardboard boxes towered in haphazard piles, coated with cobwebs and a thick layer of brown dust. "You're living here?" A sleeping bag, a water jug, and a scatter of cooking utensils lay on a freshly swept spot on the concrete floor.

"It's free."

Nita had said that, out by the culvert. Nita and Dan . . . "I think I'm a fool," Carter said bitterly.

"I doubt it," Jeremy said, his voice dry. "I'm an outsider, remember? I've got nothing riding on this crazy horse race. From what *I've* seen and heard, you're doing pretty well with a pretty shitty situation."

A glowing insect popped into the air in front of Carter, who flinched in spite of himself. "A dragonfly?" He'd seen a picture somewhere. Fascinated, he passed his fingers through the iridescent green wings. "That's incredible," he breathed. "Could I take a look at your projector?"

"Sure." Jeremy reached into his pocket, hesitated. "I guess I'm going to be rude and say no," he said. "Professional secret."

The pocket was empty. Carter could see the bulge of Jeremy's misshapen fist through the worn fabric. It clicked suddenly—he'd known it, really, but it was easier to believe in some kind of fancy projector. "My God, *you're* doing it. There *is* no technology that can project a holo that well!"

"Sooner or later I always blow it. I guess it's some kind of . . . shared hallucination or something."

He was watching Carter from the corners of his eyes. He'd been like that in the car, Carter remembered. Wary. Back when they'd first met, when Carter had given him a ride . . . "That waterfall I saw." He whistled softly. "That was you, too, wasn't it? You were right there. Tell me about this stuff, will you? I've never run into anything like it."

"Yeah, it was me . . ." Jeremy dragged the words out reluctantly.

His body was wire-tight, drawn into itself, as if he were ready to jump in any direction. It reminded Carter suddenly and sharply of the kid in the culvert. "Hey, take it easy." He held out a hand, palm up, watched Jeremy's eyes follow it as the boy's eyes had followed the bat. "What's wrong?"

"Nothing." Jeremy's eyes shifted back to Carter's face and his posture relaxed fractionally. "I'm never sure . . . how people are going to react. Do you understand why it's dry, Carter? Really *understand* it?"

Carter opened his mouth, closed it again. He knew the words: global warming, precipitate glaciation . . . Hell, he knew the mechanics of water distribution better than most people in the world. "No," he said softly. "I'm not sure that I understand it. Not like you mean. It's too damn big to understand."

"I don't understand this, either." Jeremy held out his hand and the dragonfly reappeared, fanning its glowing wings delicately as it perched on his palm. "I can make the little things happen. The visions of the past come on their own. I don't know how, or why. People don't understand the drought, and it terrifies them. They don't understand the things I do, either. Sometimes . . . they get a little crazy."

"What do they do?" Carter asked softly. "Blame you? Make you some kind of scapegoat?"

"Sometimes." Jeremy shrugged. "I've heard stories about other kids being born with . . . weird powers. People usually kill them." He paused. "My father used to beat me every time he caught me making. It was this drifter who gave me the magic-show idea. He thought what I did was wonderful. So I tried it, after I left home." He gave a short laugh. "I damn near got myself killed."

"Shit."

"It eats at you," Jeremy said in a thin, cold voice. "It tempts you. People want to give you power. They want to worship you. It makes you want to go ahead and be that god or devil or whatever the hell they see. And then, when they find out that you've fooled them, that it's all an illusion . . . they want to punish you."

His tone made Carter shiver.

Jeremy laughed softly. "I'm really confusing you with all this, right? Your fault for figuring out my scam. Maybe it's because I met this woman the other day. She's kind of like me. Different. She's an empath—she hears your emotions and your feelings. All of a sudden, I needed to tell her this stuff. I guess it's been building up for a long time—needing to *tell* someone. But I haven't seen her since, so you get to hear it, like it or not."

He sounded better, and some of his tension seemed to have eased. "Why'd your dad beat you?" Carter asked.

"Maybe because he was scared." Jeremy shrugged. "Maybe because I was his son, and what I was might be his fault. Maybe because he didn't understand it any more than he understood the drought. He was afraid of the drought, too. He should have been. It finally killed him."

"He plowed his soul into your land?" Carter asked softly. "And died with it?"

"You were listening, at that party."

"Yeah, I was listening." Carter watched the gathering shadows turn the stacked crates into shapeless towers of darkness. "Is it worse, seeing how the world used to be?"

Jeremy was silent for a long time. "Sometimes," he said at last. "I keep wondering if we could have stopped the drought somehow."

Carter got stiffly to his feet and went to one of the front windows. It was getting dark. He rubbed dust from a windowpane, wondering how many kids were hanging out at the truck plaza.

"I'm going to walk back to the dam with you." Jeremy fumbled in his pack, then straightened with a small pistol in his hand. He held it comfortably and Carter noticed that the trigger guard of the compact automatic had been partially removed to accommodate Jeremy's thickened fingers.

Carter looked at it. "I shot a kid once," he said slowly. "During a riot. I pulled the trigger because I was scared and mad—mostly because I was scared. I thought I'd never do anything like that again. But if I'd had a gun this afternoon, I would've shot one of those men. Maybe there's no way to keep this mess from turning into a war. Maybe fighting is the only way we know."

"You're kind of hard on yourself, aren't you?" Jeremy looked down at the gun in his hand. "When people want something from you and you can't give it to them—sometimes they hate you for it. Let's go." He slipped the gun into the waistband of his jeans. "I know a route that should be safe."

Carter slipped out the crack after Jeremy, shadows crowding his heels. The scabby towers of the old grain elevators filled the alleys between the warehouses with darkness. Carter and Jeremy followed the rusted railway tracks along the bank of the riverbed. Semi rigs slept in the truck plaza lot. Lights gleamed behind barred windows in the old motel, but Carter didn't see any kids.

They went slowly, at Jeremy's limping pace. "Your knees hurt you, don't they?" Carter said. "I could get you some painkillers from the pharmacy at the base."

"No, thanks," Jeremy said, and the smile was back in his voice. "I tried booze and drugs once or twice when I was a kid. Things . . . get out of hand. Visually, I mean. You wouldn't want to be anywhere near me."

The wind whispered dryly and Carter welcomed the yellow wash of light from the big halides above the lower gate. He returned the guards' surprised salutes briskly. "Thanks for the convoy," he said, turning back to Jeremy.

"No problem." Jeremy's faded shirt hung open, unbuttoned. The light gleamed on irregular patches of shiny white scar tissue. They blotched his chest and flat stomach, ugly and visible against his tawny skin. Burn scars?

Jeremy noticed Carter's glance. "This old guy was pretty good at picking up my visions." He touched one of the scars. "He thought that if I could see water, I could find it, maybe make him rich. He figured if he tortured me long enough, I'd do it for him. After that I made up the projector," Jeremy said softly.

"If you need to get onto the base, come to either gate," Carter said. "I'll leave orders to let me know, any time."

"Thanks." Jeremy gave him a short, sharp nod. "Don't forget," he said. "People around here want something from you, and *you* can't give it to them, either." He turned abruptly and vanished into the darkness without a backward glance.

CHAPTER FOURTEEN ☆

The beans at the west end of the field were ripening too early. Nita's feet stirred up the brown dust of the path as she carried the yoked pails of freshly picked soybean pods back to the house. Dan thought it was because they weren't getting enough water, that a feeder line must be plugged. The beans were too immature to dry, Dan had said, so they'd have to go fresh to the local market.

"So we pick beans, right, love?" Nita murmured to her daughter. "It beats chopping bushes."

Rachel grinned and gurgled, waving her fists.

"Glad you agree." Nita smiled, but it turned into a sigh.

Carter wouldn't talk to Dan. The town was so full of anger that it made her sick to her stomach when she went in to market. The smart thing to do was leave before things got worse. She shifted the pole across her shoulders, wishing suddenly and intensely that she could step back across time to the hills and David and the bees. She had been safe there. Nita reached the edge of the field and walked on out to the rim of the gorge. Far below, she could see the rocky ledges that had once been Celilo Falls.

The picture was there, on Dan's bedroom wall. Nita could believe in the river, looking at Jesse's painting of cascading water. Jesse had been *remembering*; it came through in the soft colors with a feeling of past. The paintings reminded Nita of the man she had met by the culvert—Jeremy—and her vision of the river. She had had that same sense of past.

Thinking of river water, Nita rounded the corner of the house and stopped in surprise. A battered car stood in front of the porch. She hadn't heard it come down the road, and didn't recognize it. One of the Coalition people, probably. They came and went all the time. Nita thumped the bean pails down on the porch, lifted Rachel out of her sling, and opened the door.

"I wondered who the hell was sleeping in my bedroom." A small, wiry woman looked up from the table. She had short-cropped, graying hair and the tattooed left forearm of a convoy trucker. Gold chains glinted at her throat and half a dozen bright gemstones winked from the rim of her right ear. "So Danny's finally gotten tired of sleeping alone, huh? He went for a young one this time." She looked Nita up and down as if she were a goat for sale in the market.

"I work for Dan." Nita flushed. "He told me I could use your room."

"Relax, honey. *I* don't sleep here." The woman stood, stretched like a cat, and gave Nita a thin smile. "I'm Renny Warren," she said. "I own this farm, in case Danny forgot to mention it."

"Oh." Nita blinked. "You're Jesse's daughter."

"Yes." Renny said the word casually, but the whip-flick of her resentment made Nita wince. Closed subject.

"Where is Danny, anyway? Off meddling, as usual?"

"He's out picking beans." Nita heard the stiffness in her voice and tried to hide it by settling Rachel on her quilt.

"The kid doesn't look like him."

"She's not his daughter." Nita straightened, staring down at the compact woman. "I'm not sleeping with him."

"A wee bit defensive, aren't you?" Renny patted Nita's cheek lightly.

She was enjoying this, Nita realized suddenly. She was trying hard to make Nita lose her temper. "Of course I'm defensive." Nita let go of her anger and laughed. "Everybody in town thinks I'm in bed with Dan." She smiled at the older woman. "I should wear a sign: 'I am not Dan Greely's lover.' "

"They wouldn't believe you." Renny arched one eyebrow.

"That's why I don't bother." Nita returned the trucker's smile, felt the woman's twinge of disappointment. I won that round, she thought, and wondered what the contest was all about. "Can I get you water? We've got beans left from last night, if you're hungry. And fresh tomatoes."

"I'll take the water. I eat a lot better than beans." Renny leaned against the table, her eyes on Nita. "I hear The Dalles is taking on the Army."

"I guess so." Nita frowned as she filled a mug. "I'm staying out of it, thank you."

"You think Danny's going to let you stay out of anything political? I guess I'll sell this place, buy some land in the Willamette Valley." Renny sipped at her water, her expression casual. "They're irrigating a lot of new acreage down there. Bushes are a hot crop and they don't take as much labor as beans. I wouldn't need anyone year round. I could contract for seasonal crews."

Nita kept the smile on her face as she knelt to dangle the wooden beads for her daughter. She felt the needling edge beneath Renny's words and knew she was being baited again. Was Renny trying to get a reaction out of her, get her to protest the proposed sale as a threat to Dan? Probably. Nita chirped at her daughter, feeling Renny's exasperated shrug without having to look. "Do you want me to go tell Dan you're here?" she asked sweetly.

"No." Renny laughed suddenly and set down the empty mug. "Tell him I'm in town, staying down at the truck plaza. I'll be around." She reached out to cup Nita's chin in her hand. "You're too good for either Danny or this dead town. If you get tired of digging dirt, let me know. You might make a good trucker. We could find out."

Absently tickling her daughter, Nita watched Renny stride across the yard and climb into the car. She wasn't quite sure what Renny had just offered.

She told Dan about Renny's visit as they drove down to the market.

"You never know when Renny's going to drop by," Dan said neutrally. "How did you get along?"

"All right, I think," Nita said. "I'm not sure why."

Dan gave her a thoughtful, sideways look. "Renny's touchy," he said slowly. "We've never really liked each other much. Sometimes I think the only reason she keeps the farm is that she owns it and I work for her and she likes that. I don't see much of her." He shook his head. "Have you seen my tool folder? The one that I keep in the glove box? It's missing."

"I haven't seen it," Nita said. He felt sad. About Renny? He felt a little angry, too. I'm tired of knowing, Nita thought sullenly. She looked out the window at the concrete wall of the dam stretching across the riverbed. She could feel the town even before they reached the main street: tension hummed in the air like the buzz of a kicked beehive. Nita shivered and held Rachel tighter as her daughter began to squirm.

"It's early for fresh beans." Dan parked at the edge of the market lot. "We should do pretty well."

Nita settled Rachel in her sling and lifted two pails of the green bean pods from the back of the truck. Dan picked up the other two pails and they walked down the block to the market. The noise made her fingers twitch.

" 'Lo, Dan," a chunky man called out. "Hi, Nita. I've been lookin' forward to meeting you. There's space here." He waved at the asphalt beside the pile of soap he was selling.

"How're you doing, Pete?" Dan set his pails down.

Nita smiled grimly at the soap vendor as she put down her pails. His lust felt like sweaty fingers on her skin. She spread out a towel with an angry snap so that Dan could pile the bean pods onto it. If Pete didn't knock it off, she'd kick his damn soap right into his lap. That should wilt him.

"Hi, Carl." Dan straightened as the chief of police marched up. "You look a little grim this morning. Anything wrong?"

"Maybe." Durer cast a quick, hard look at the obviously listening Pete. "Want to come along for a little ride with me? I've got something to show you."

"Like what?" Dan's voice had gone flat in anticipation. He expected trouble.

He was right. Durer was upset. Angry. Rachel kicked, her face screwing up to cry as Nita bounced her.

"I'll be back in a little while, okay?" Dan was getting to his feet, brushing dust from his jeans. "You don't mind staying here by yourself?"

"I know how to sell beans, Dan." Nita smiled for him. He didn't do a half-bad job of reading Durer himself, but what was to read? she thought bitterly. What would there *be* besides trouble? Pete was seething with curiosity and lust in about equal proportions. Nita turned her back on him and began to arrange the beans.

"See you in a little while," Dan called as he walked back toward Durer's car.

Not soon enough, Nita thought, but didn't say anything. He was tired. It wasn't a physical tiredness, although it had taken him a long time to heal from the beating. This weariness hummed beneath his every word. He didn't want to be doing this. He didn't want to stand in the middle again, between the Corps and the people of The Dalles. He was trapped, Nita thought as she tucked Rachel into her lap. Trapped by her fa-

ther's ghost. "I think it's time we moved on," she whispered to
Rachel, and pretended that she didn't feel a pang at the thought.

The beans sold faster than she had hoped. Dan had been
right—most crops weren't quite ripe yet, and green soybeans
made good eating. Dan had given Nita a list of the goods they
needed and she was able to trade for most of them before noon.
The three rough blocks of soap that Pete swapped her for a
bowlful of beans smelled like rancid vegetable oil. They smelled
like his constant, irritating lust. Nita wrinkled her nose at the
bars as she tucked them into the pack. Too bad no one else had
soap to trade today.

A tall, fair-haired man stopped in front of her blanket. "I'm
looking for Dan Greely. Do you know where he is?"

Everyone in the whole damn riverbed knew she was living
with Dan! Nita eyed the man. He was dressed very city. "He's
off with Chief Durer," she said. "He'll come back here eventually. If it's important, you should probably wait."

"Chief Durer?" The man smiled, but his eyes were evaluating her. "Is there a problem?"

Nita blinked at the sudden clutch of satisfaction in the man.
As if he were *glad* that there was trouble? As if she had answered
a question for him? Wariness tightened her stomach. "I don't
know—" she began.

"Hell, yeah, there's trouble." Pete clucked his tongue from
behind his soap pile. "Any time Durer comes looking for Dan,
you can bet your ass it's no social call. The uniforms are probably cutting up rough again. They beat up some kid last week,"
he announced with relish. "You hear about that?"

Nita squashed a fierce desire to kick the jerk. "I'll tell him
you were looking," she said, ignoring Pete. "What was your
name?" She smiled at him, hoping that she looked dumb and
sweetly innocent. "Can he find you somewhere?"

"My name's John Seldon. I'll catch him later." He wasn't
smiling, but he was still pleased inside.

Nita watched him walk away, trying to place the name. John—
Johnny. It clicked suddenly. This was Carter's friend; the one
he cared about, or owed a debt to—she wasn't sure which it was,
and maybe Carter didn't know, either. He worked for the government, she remembered. So why did he want to see Dan?

She definitely didn't like him.

The sun rose higher, driving what little shade there was into
hiding. Nita spread a sunscarf over her head and shoulders and
leaned forward as she nursed Rachel, so that her shadow would

shade her daughter. A knot of people had gathered on the far side of the lot. Nita heard laughter and applause and felt distant ripples of excited pleasure. Pete tucked a dirty cloth over his pile of soap and wandered down the street to watch. Nita craned her neck, curious, but unwilling to disturb Rachel's sleep. Some kind of entertainment?

The crowd broke up after a while, scattering among the stalls, still full of laughter and good feelings. It was a nice change after the tensions that had filled the air. Nita stretched cautiously and winced. Her right foot was asleep and her shirt was soggy with sweat beneath Rachel's sleeping warmth.

"Hi. I'd about given up on you."

Nita looked up. "Jeremy." She smiled, pleased to see him again, a little apprehensive at the same time. "Was that you, down the block? Making people laugh?"

"Uh-huh." He sat down beside her, his sky-colored eyes on her face. "I thought I scared you away, on the riverbank."

"You almost did." Rachel was hungry, and Nita lifted her shirt, glad that Pete hadn't returned yet. "I haven't been hiding from you. I was at the market last week, but I didn't see you. I . . . don't like coming into town."

"I bet." His smile touched his eyes like sunlight. "Even I can feel the tension. It must be hell for you."

"It's . . . kind of wearing." It made her feel funny, talking about it like this. Sometimes David had asked her what she heard in the bees' song, but that was all. He didn't ask her about what she heard from people, or how it felt to hear it, and that silence had become hers, too. She had never really put it into words before. "You made people feel better with your show. I appreciated it," she said wryly.

Jeremy's smile was crooked. "I'm good for something, I guess."

Nita sucked in her breath. At the end of the block, where the street ran up into the hillside, the ground had gone suddenly green with grass. Tree branches, heavy with leaves, swayed above the roof of the supermarket. Tiny white flowers bloomed beside her, poking up through the cracks in the parking lot's surface. "It's beautiful," Nita murmured. She tried to touch one of the blossoms, but felt only gritty asphalt beneath her fingertips. Jeremy was staring at it, bitter inside. Sad. "I'm glad I can share this," she told him as the green vision vanished. "Now I know how it used to be. I can tell Rachel, when she's older. She needs to know."

Jeremy's slow smile lighted his pale eyes and eased some of the bitterness inside him.

"It's like you've pulled a moment out of the past, spread it out for us to see," Nita said.

"For you, maybe."

"Excuse me?" A stocky woman with a pack slung over one shoulder had paused in front of the quilt. "Do you have any beans left at all?" She frowned into one of the empty pails. "I meant to stop by earlier, but I got busy talking."

"I have a few left." Nita reached for the pail beside her and tilted it to show the woman the pound or so of pods remaining in the bottom.

"That'll do." The woman gave her a broad smile. "I can even give you scrip."

Nita wrapped the beans in the faded piece of cloth that the woman had handed her. As she started to put them into the woman's pack, she froze, hand poised in midair, heart contracting.

"Something wrong?" the woman asked.

"Where did you get that pack?" Nita asked.

"I bought it." The woman eyed her warily. "Julio has a little secondhand store in Mosier. He comes into town for the weekend market. Is it yours? Was it stolen?"

The weight of the heavy blue cloth made Nita's fingers tremble. She turned the flap over slowly. The letters *D A* had been embroidered on it. Nita touched the slightly crooked curve of the D, tears burning her eyes, threatening to spill over.

"What is it?" Jeremy touched her shoulder. "Nita?"

"David Ascher," Nita whispered. "This is David's pack." They were both staring at her uncomprehending. "I've been looking for him," Nita said through the lump in her throat. "My husband. He was supposed to meet me here."

"I'm sorry." The woman covered her mouth with her hand.

"What about the man who sold this to you?" Jeremy asked her. "What's he like?"

"Julio Moreno?" The woman sounded surprised. "He's honest, if that's what you're asking. His family has lived in Mosier forever. They grow sugar beets. Julio could tell you where he got it. I don't think the man ever forgets anything."

Nita stacked the empty pails together, gathered up Rachel, and scrambled to her feet. "I've got to go talk to him." Rachel squirmed and fussed as Nita tucked her into the sling.

"Why don't you keep the pack?" The woman cleared her throat, her pity warm in the air. "If you'll swap me for yours."

"Thank you." Nita emptied her pack onto the ground and handed it to the woman. "Thank you very much." She rubbed the worn fabric gently.

David had bought the cloth at the local market. He had taught her how to sew with that pack. It had been a hard job and she had made a lot of mistakes. There was the seam that she had resewn four times. She had thrown it out the door of their tent after the third time and David had laughed at her temper. Nita's throat closed on tears as she tucked Rachel's quilt, the water bottle, and a spare diaper into the familiar folds.

Rachel cried in a constant, irritable complaint as Nita walked back to the truck. Dan wasn't back yet, but she couldn't wait for him, couldn't wait any longer . . . Jeremy had followed her, not saying anything as she tossed the empty pails into the truckbed. She opened the door and felt for the keys beneath the seat. It was only ten miles to Mosier—they could be back in an hour. Dan would understand, Nita told herself, but she didn't care if he did or not. She stared at the keys in her hand. *You should know how to drive,* David had said when she had turned sixteen. He had traded precious honey for the use of a clunky old station wagon and he had taught her how to drive. Nita climbed onto the seat.

She had to go to Mosier. Right now.

"I think I'll come with you." Without waiting for her reply, Jeremy pulled open the passenger door and climbed in.

"No, thanks." Nita glared at him, needing to be angry at him—at someone.

"I'm just asking for a ride." He made no move to get out.

"Fine. I don't care." Nita started the engine. She was afraid. She was terrified.

Rachel started crying hard, her face red and angry as Nita backed the truck out of the lot. Not because I'm upset, David, Nita thought fiercely. That's not why she's crying. She drove west, past the empty car lots and abandoned shopping centers that clustered at the edge of town. Rachel finally stopped crying. Nita looked sideways to discover that Jeremy had her daughter on his lap and was making a bright-green insect hover above her face. Rachel reached for it, smiling tentatively, her face still swollen with weeping. Nita felt a stir of gratitude for Jeremy's presence, but a cold stone of fear sat in her chest, squashing the words down inside her.

West of The Dalles, one of the stark cliffs had crumbled into the riverbed. It had taken a section of the interstate with it and traffic had to turn off onto the old highway. Nita took the two-lane winding road fast. The land rose on their left, barren slopes patched with tough weeds and clumps of sunscorched grass, pierced by rocks like broken teeth. You could see the stumps left from the orchards that had died and been cut for firewood. Cherries, Dan had told her. She had never eaten a real cherry. They were too expensive. Cherries came out of the vats, fed by the bushes that had killed the Valley and hadn't needed David's bees. A few tall poplars remained from the old windbreaks, like posts in a vanished fence. Nita forced herself to slow down, afraid of what might happen if the land went suddenly green.

It didn't go green. Jeremy made glittering butterflies and tiny green frogs for Rachel and the hills remained dead and brown.

It took less than half an hour to reach Mosier. Nita parked in front of an empty auto-body shop. Across the street, a tall white house stood up on a bank above the level of the road. Clothes hung on the wide porch, swinging in the wind, and Nita caught sight of cluttered chairs, saw the glint of glass on tables. Julio's secondhand store.

Jeremy handed Rachel to Nita without a word. Clutching her daughter, Nita climbed the steep steps that had been cut into the bank. The wide porch was crammed with clothes, old tools, china plates and cups painted in vivid colors, plastic dishes, and furniture. Some of the clothes looked as if they had been hanging on the porch for years, faded into drab pastels by the sun. Others looked new and fresh, as if they had come from a store.

"You wish some help?" A lanky man wearing a too-large denim overall stepped from the house. His left arm was scarred and twisted, but his eyes looked young, in spite of his gray hair. "You are looking for clothes, *señora*?" He smiled at Rachel. "For the *niña*?"

"No. Thank you." The words stuck in Nita's throat. Slowly she held out the pack. "This belongs to my . . . husband." Her voice trembled in spite of herself. "A woman said she bought it from you."

The man's face took on a wary expression.

"I don't mean . . . I'm not accusing you of stealing it." Nita flushed.

"I did not think you were." Julio Moreno shook his head slowly and Nita cringed at the texture of his reluctance.

"Tell me," she said.

He spread his hands. "I . . . found the pack." He looked beyond her, at the barren, brown hills. "It was away from the road, in some rocks, you know. It was empty." Moreno coughed a little. "There were bones," he said. "It is easy to die in this land."

Bones. Nita stared at the pack in her hands, blue cloth, bought with the honey she and David had gathered, sewn in their evenings together. "Was there anything to . . . show who he was?" *He?* Why he? she thought in terror. The bones could have belonged to a woman.

"He wore jeans, *señora.* A shirt, blue or green, who can be sure? His hair was dark, I think." He shrugged, his brown eyes full of sympathy. "I put the bones in the churchyard." He pointed up the street. "That is where bones belong. Even now, when it is so easy to die."

"Will you show me?" Nita whispered. She didn't dare look at him, didn't dare look at Rachel who would have David's blue eyes and his face. Instead, she kept her eyes fixed on the pack in her hands, a wad of blue cloth that had smelled like honey and David's sweat once, smelled like a stranger now.

"Lo siento mucho, señora," Moreno said softly. "I will show you."

The stone he had used to mark the grave was a stone from the hillside, gray lava rock, dusty and squarish. Nita touched it with her fingertips, feeling its coolness and its weight. It was heavy, like death. *It is easy to die in this land.* Nita wondered how the man whose bones lay beneath the stone had died. Had he fallen, hurt himself, or gotten sick? Had someone killed him for what was in David's pack? He had died so close to a town, so close to a road and people.

So easy to die, in this dry land.

"It wasn't David," she said out loud.

Julio Moreno, head bowed, twisted arm hanging at his side, said nothing.

Nita turned away from him, angry at his silence.

Jeremy was waiting at the overgrown fence around the tiny graveyard. "I'll drive back," he said, and lifted Rachel from Nita's arms.

At the truck, she climbed into the passenger side without speaking. Rachel had fallen blessedly asleep and didn't wake as Jeremy tucked her onto the seat beside Nita. In spite of his hands, Jeremy handled the wheel easily. Nita stared out at the brown land as they followed the road's twists and turns through the dust. "I don't want him to be dead," she whispered, but a tiny part of her—a small place deep inside—was relieved. Oh, God. Nita leaned her head against the door, wanting to cry, wanting to weep for him. Her eyes remained as dry as the soil in the dead orchards.

Dead, it was all dead. The road circled around the head of a deep, rocky canyon. An old house sat down in the bottom, huge and dilapidated. A hint of majesty still clung to it in spite of its sagging roof and gaping, glassless windows. Green was visible down there—the stingy, irrigated green of the present. Carefully watered rows of beans filled the floor of the canyon. As the pickup labored around a bend, Nita lost sight of the house. She wondered dully who had built it, out here in this lonely canyon.

Up on the rim again, Jeremy pulled over onto the shoulder of the road and shut off the engine. "Come for a walk," he said, and it was a command, in spite of his gentle tone.

She had no strength to refuse. When Jeremy scooped up Rachel and held out his hand to her, she climbed out of the truck. They were up above the narrow little canyon. The wind whipped at her hair, trying to tug it loose from her braid. A promontory jutted out from the wall of the gorge like a round island of rock, connected to the land by a narrow neck. Nita followed him out onto it. The center of the promontory looked hollow, like a bowl, and the broken skeletons of old trees jutted up from the rocky ground.

Jeremy sat down with Rachel on his lap and pulled Nita gently down beside him. "I found this place years ago," he said softly. "I come back every so often."

The dry clifftop wavered to life around them. The hollow became a pond, ringed by trees whose branches were tipped with young leaves. Stiff green blades poked up through the still water and tiny flowers carpeted the green grass, white, pink and purple. Silently Jeremy pointed. Nita turned her head and caught her breath. Beyond the rocky edge lay the river. It stretched between the carved walls of the gorge, vanishing eastward and westward into an opalescent haze. The wrinkled sheet of gray-green water shimmered, shading into browns along the shore. She could see the highway down below her. Dozens of trees dotted the ground, and the hills were . . . green.

"The river is so big," Jeremy said softly. "How could anyone who lived with this ever imagine that it could be empty?" He shook his head. "How much of it was our own fault, the Dry?

Did we let it happen, because we couldn't believe in it, because we had so many rivers, so much water?''

He loved this lost world, in spite of how much it hurt him. His sadness blended with the sweeping curve of the river, wove itself into the green hills that would really be dry and dusty if you walked on them. Nita looked down at the ground in front of her. Flowers glowed among the lush grass stems, smaller than her little fingernail. There were pink and white stars and fringed blue cups with white throats. A bird fluttered soundlessly in the bushes and the branches swayed, their new leaves bright green or bronzy red. There was so much *life* around her. She was drowning in life. It filled her up in an aching rush, overflowed to spill down her cheeks as tears, dissolving the stony numbness that filled her.

''He's not dead.'' Nita clenched her fists, squeezing invisible dust between her fingers. ''I don't want him to be dead. Those aren't his bones, do you hear me? I love him. I love him so much.''

''It's all right, Nita.'' Jeremy's thickened fingers were gentle as he stroked her back. ''If he died, he didn't desert you. Don't punish yourself for how you feel.''

''Bastard! I didn't ask you!''

Rachel began to scream. Jeremy caught Nita's wrist as she started to scramble to her feet. Teeth clenched, she tried to jerk free, but he was strong, for all his crooked fingers. She slipped, gasped as she went down onto her knees. The pain cracked her anger and the first sob shook her. Jeremy put his arms around her and gathered her against him, murmuring meaningless sounds of comfort as she wept against his shoulder. The sobs hurt her, tearing their way out of her flesh, making her shake with their force. After a long time they finally slowed, fading into hiccoughs.

Jeremy was holding her tightly, his cheek against her hair, the warmth of his comfort gentle in her mind. Slowly she straightened. ''You're wet.'' She touched his tear-soaked shirt and drew a shuddering breath. ''You're right,'' she whispered. ''Part of me wants to believe that he's there, under that rock—that he didn't run away. He was so afraid.'' Nita choked on fresh tears. ''He was afraid of the Dry, because it was eating the land. He was afraid . . . of me, because I knew about his fear and that kept it alive. He told himself that he didn't mind that I knew what he felt, but down deep . . . I made the fear worse. He couldn't hide from it if I knew it was there.''

"I'm sorry," Jeremy murmured. He pulled a bandana from his pocket and gently wiped her face.

Rachel had stopped crying. Jeremy had tucked her onto his lap and she was sucking on her fist, staring intently at his face.

"She likes you." Nita giggled, heard the shrillness in her voice, and stopped. She touched Rachel's cheek with a gentle finger, seeing David in their daughter's face. "What if she *is* like me?"

"What if she is?" His eyes were on hers, pale and intent. "Is that why you think he left you?"

She looks like you, David had said. "Maybe," Nita whispered. "I don't know."

"You'll teach Rachel that who she is, and what she is, matters. You'll teach her to be proud of herself and her gift," he said fiercely.

Need. She met his eyes, feeling it, not sure what it was that he wanted from her. "Gift?" Anger came back to her suddenly. "It's not a gift to eavesdrop on pain and lust and anger. I don't want to hear. I don't want to know." Rachel wailed as Nita snatched her from Jeremy's lap. She ran back to the truck, stumbling on the dusty ground that she couldn't see. Jeremy limped slowly after her.

"Don't be angry," he said when he caught up with her. "I know it's hard for you. It's hard for me—what I am—and my makings don't have any real value. Your ability *means* something. People are so far apart, even when we try damned hard to be close. You narrow that gap for us, Nita."

"I can't," she whispered. She looked around at the flowers and the distant pond, losing herself in the sweep of the river and gorge. She could feel peace in this place, like moisture in the air.

"It's spring," Jeremy told her softly. "That's why it's so green. I've seen it in summer, too, but it's dry then. It looks more like . . . now. I thought you needed spring."

"Thank you." Nita touched his face, hearing loneliness in his voice, thick as layered dust. "Thank you for doing this for me. Don't ever think it doesn't have value. Please."

He took her hand between his, kissed it gently, and climbed into the truck. The land didn't turn dry and brown again until they were well below the crest.

CHAPTER FIFTEEN ☆

"I told Voltaire to keep his tough guys in line." Durer scowled over the rim of the steering wheel. "If he wants to start a war around here, he's sure doing it right."

"Take it easy, Carl." Dan grabbed for the dash as the chief of police slammed the four-wheeler through an old wash. "You do that again and we're going to have to walk back. What exactly did Sandy tell you, anyway?"

"Just that she'd found a body. The Wilmer girl." He slowed a little as they bounced down into the next wash. "She was pretty upset."

"Then how do you know a soldier's involved?" Dan asked patiently.

"Sandy said so." Durer grunted. "I hope she's wrong."

He didn't think she was. Dan scowled up at the rocky wall of the gorge above them, a sinking feeling in the pit of his stomach. Sandy didn't jump to conclusions easily. "Don't lay all the blame on Voltaire. I think he's trying to do the best he can, but he can't do it on his own. He's young." Dan sighed. "He's got a lot to learn."

"He's not that young," Durer growled. "He doesn't give a shit about anybody who doesn't wear a uniform."

Dan made a noncommittal sound. There was no point in arguing with him. Carl didn't like the Corps' presence on his turf and never had. Dan wished again that the Shunt fiasco hadn't happened. If wishes were horses . . . Carter had been willing to cooperate with the Coalition up until that point. Well, Dan could understand his suspicions—and Carter had the feel of a man who didn't trust easily. Maybe Nita knew how to reach him. There was something between them—or there had been. She wasn't talking about it, anyway, so maybe he'd better let it alone.

Dan fingered the fading lump on the back of his head. No, it

155

wouldn't be hard to interpret that Shunt riot as a setup. Especially since the saboteurs had chosen that afternoon to hole the Pipe again. He leaned his head briefly back against the seat, back aching from picking beans. My fault, he thought bitterly. I should have read the crowd better.

He was losing his touch—getting old. The redhaired bastard hadn't helped the situation, either. Where the hell had he come from?''

"There's Sandy." Durer hit the brakes and eased the car off the road. "She found the body while she was out looking for that damn goat of hers."

"Hi, Dan." Sandy Corbett smiled, but her face looked haggard. "I'm glad Carl dragged you along. This is a little much for me."

"Show us, Sandy," Durer said heavily.

Dan tried to catch Sandy's eye, but she wouldn't look at him. She was carrying a blanket folded over one arm.

"Over here." She led them down a gentle slope toward a clump of spindly firs.

He could see where a car or truck had pulled off the road, then driven down to the trees. The tracks were just visible in the dust; sharp enough to be fresh.

"Don't step on 'em," Durer growled. "I'll get Kelly to photograph 'em for a match. He went out to the Welsh place to pick up the doc."

The girl lay on the ground beneath the thin branches of the young firs. Dan looked away from her bare breasts and the dark blood that streaked her pale skin. Candy Wilmer. She'd turned seventeen last spring. The air was still in this hollow, protected from the wind. Dust motes glinted in a sunbeam, and a trick of the light blurred the girl's face. Her hair was dark, long. It took him back thirty years, and in a moment of vision he saw his sister Amy, lying in the dust beneath the broken face of Celilo Falls. She had climbed up onto a sheer ridge of rock one bright, hot morning, and jumped.

"Can I cover her, Carl?" Sandy was staring down at the girl, her face pale, jaw set. "The knife's over there." She jerked her head. "Just tossed away. It's an Army knife." Her lips twitched, then thinned. "That damn fool colonel. Why the hell did he let this *happen*?" She shook out the blanket with a snap and draped it gently over the girl.

Dan recognized the faded flowers on the fabric. It was the spread from Sandy's bed. He put his arm around her shoulders, feeling the fine tremors that shook her as he pulled her close.

"I taught her piano. She was so *good.*" Sandy's voice cracked. "God damn him," she whispered. "Whoever did this. And Voltaire, too. I hope they blow the Pipe out from under them."

It was grief talking, but she was wounded, and wounds like this never really healed. She'd had her share of wounds—they all had. How many could you carry before you quit trying? Dan held Sandy close, stroking her hair, hurting for Candy and for eighteen-year-old Amy who had jumped from the top of Celilo Falls so many years ago. For one, life had been way too short. For the other, it had been too long.

Behind them, the sound of an engine broke the quiet. "Kelly's here with Doc," Durer said briskly. He had picked the knife up carefully with a plastic bag: a big lock-blade with the Corps' turreted castle on the handle. "I'd like to keep this kind of quiet." He stared bleakly at the knife. "This is all we need right now."

"What are you going to do, Carl?" Sandy's voice shook. "Just let it go? Pretend it didn't happen, that Candy's not dead?"

"Hell no, woman." Durer flushed. "I'm going to ram this down Voltaire's throat—in private. Word'll get around soon enough," he said grimly. "And when it does, some folks are gonna want to settle the score."

"Stupid, to throw the murder weapon away like that," Dan said softly. "Unless you particularly wanted it found."

"I thought of that," Durer said heavily. "I haven't passed sentence yet."

No, he wouldn't. Whatever his personal feelings were, Durer was a fair and honest man. Kelly had driven up with the doctor, and Dan watched Durer surreptitiously pocket the bagged knife. He needed to talk to Carter. Kelly had the biggest mouth in town. Knife or no knife, folks were going to draw their own conclusions once word of this got around. He might have to try the back way onto the base. It was a big risk, with tensions as high as they were. Getting shot wouldn't help anyone.

"Can you drop me back at the market?" he asked.

"Sure." Durer nodded, giving Dan a sideways glance. "Someone's got to go tell the Wilmers." He cleared his throat.

Dan had done this kind of thing too many times already. He wondered suddenly who they would tell first, if he got shot. Sandy?

"I'll do it, Dan." Sandy touched his arm, her face calm again, in control. "I know Anne pretty well. Dan? What I said before . . ."

"I know." He touched her lips to silence her, kissed her gently on the forehead. "Thank you," he murmured. "For doing this."

He and Durer didn't talk much during the ride back to the
market. From Durer's expression, he was as pessimistic as Dan
about the future situation. Someone outside was trying to set
Army against locals; Dan was more sure of it than ever. And
they were doing a damn good job. The only question was who.
If he had that answer, Carter would listen to him. He'd *have* to
listen. "You haven't heard any news of that Bill guy?" he asked
as Durer turned down the main street. "You know—the redheaded trader I was asking about?"

"Yeah, I know who you mean. No, no one's seen him that I
know of." Durer pulled over against the curb. "Looks like
someone borrowed your truck." He nodded.

It was just pulling up down the block. Dan walked over. It
was Nita, but someone else was driving—a blond stranger. Nita
looked as if she'd been crying.

"What's up, Nita?" He eyed the stranger, who was still in
the cab. "Are you all right?"

"I sold all the beans. I had to go . . . check on something."
She slid down from the seat, not meeting his eyes.

Something was wrong.

She looked up quickly, as if he'd spoken his worries out loud.
"Can I tell you later?" she asked, and her voice was unsteady.

"Sure," he said gently. "Or not at all." The blond man had
come around to their side of the truck. He was leaning on a
stick—had some kind of joint disease from the look of his hands
and knees.

He remembered a boy with joints like those. Dan felt a cold
breath on the back of his neck. A kid, out in the Dry. A kid who
had had . . . magic in his crippled hands. He had been twelve,
which would make him thirty-two now. Dan met the stranger's
eyes, his flesh contracting into goosebumps. "Jeremy?" he
asked softly. It was as if something had waked the past today,
drawn it out of the dry soil like smoke rising from a buried fire.
"Your name isn't Jeremy, is it?"

" 'Lo, Dan." An insect popped into the air between them,
glowing like pale fire in the sunlight.

He'd called it a firefly, all those years ago. He'd asked Dan if
that was what a firefly looked like. "My God." Dan stared at
it. "It *is* you. I heard someone was doing a magic routine in
town, but people are saying it's some kind of light show."

"I always wondered how you made out. I wondered if I'd run
into you again." Jeremy didn't hold out his hand, but just stood
there. If he was angry, if he was glad to see Dan, it didn't show.

Nothing showed. Dan became aware of Nita, still and silent, watching them intently. "After I left, I thought maybe they'd hung you," he said awkwardly. It was hard to meet those cool blue eyes. He wanted to look away, to hide from the rising memories with movement and distraction. "I almost went back for you," he said. "But I didn't. I just kept on running—I wasn't looking back, in those days. I'm sorry."

"Don't be," Jeremy said. "They didn't hang me. You didn't run out on me. *I* decided to stay, remember?" He reached into the bed of the pickup and retrieved a battered pack.

"Do you need a place to stay? I've got room." The words were coming too fast, stiff and full of awkwardness. Artificial. From the expression on Jeremy's face, he heard that awkwardness and interpreted it for the reluctance that it was.

"I'm fine, thanks." He slung his pack over his shoulder. "Take care of yourself, Nita."

"Jeremy?" Dan asked softly. "Did your dad ever accept your makings?"

Jeremy stared out into the riverbed without answering. For an instant, Dan caught a flash of green from the corner of his eye—an afterimage of grass and gray water, like one of Jesse's paintings.

"No," Jeremy said at last. "I scared him. Listen." He frowned, threw Nita a quick glance, then turned back to Dan. "Not everyone thinks that what I do is wonderful. Don't tell people it isn't a light show, okay? She'll tell you." He touched Nita's arm, and his face softened suddenly. "Take it easy."

"I will," she said, and took his hand.

Bemused, drowned and surrounded by ghosts and the past, Dan watched him limp down the street and disappear around the corner. "Where did you meet Jeremy?" he asked absently.

"Right here, in The Dalles." Nita was looking at him, her forehead creased thoughtfully. "I didn't realize you knew him."

"It was a long time ago." Dan shook himself, wanting to brush the nagging past away as if it were a cloud of springtime gnats. "You look beat," he said. "Which is how I feel. Let's go home."

"Sounds good," Nita said, and sighed.

The town looked ugly in the level beams of the setting sun, dry and dusty. Empty. A scrap of paper skidded down the middle of the street, pushed along by the wind. Dust eddied in a doorway. But the town wasn't empty; it was full of invisible murmurs. I don't want to hear them, Nita thought. Jeremy wanted her to listen, to *be* something. And she couldn't. She didn't *want* to. She leaned back against the seat as the truck climbed up to the rim of the gorge, missing the dry folds of the mountains with a terrible intensity. Their tent had smelled like honey. David had laughed when she tickled him awake in the dawn coolness. He had put his arms around her, kissed her face and neck, made love with her on the rumpled blankets. His love had the feel of beesong, soft and gentle.

But the bees had begun to die. She had traded the tent for the food she had needed for the trip. Nita stared down at the angled line of the dam as they drove up along the wall of the gorge. The gray concrete wall looked forbidding, like a fortress built on the stony dryness of the riverbed, closed and unfriendly. Nita held her restless daughter tightly in her arms as the truck bumped along the narrow road. Dan was quiet, full of his own shadows, small darknesses flecked with razored bits of pain and guilt. Because of Jeremy. He had hurt him, or thought he had. Jeremy thought so, too. He had been angry—closed up and resentful.

I don't want to know this, Nita thought sullenly. Whatever you and Dan did or didn't do, it's over. Done with. I can't change it, Jeremy, and I have enough sorrow of my own. I can't make anything better. What is it that you *want* from me?

Something. The memory of his *needing* nagged at her, making her angry and uneasy by turns.

When they reached the house, Nita busied herself with Rachel, nursing her, cleaning her with the oil that she'd bought at the market. For once Rachel was all too willing to fall asleep. Nita pinned a diaper on her daughter and tucked her into the bed. Rachel's eyes were blue, like David's eyes. Pain moved inside her, squeezing a lump up into her throat.

Whose bones were under that rock? David's? Do I *want* them to be his? she asked herself in anguish.

She went out onto the narrow porch and leaned against a splintery post. She could look clear down into the riverbed from up here. The rocks of the old falls looked dark in the twilight shadows. Nita closed her eyes, remembering David's face, how he felt when he bent over a hive, all full of peace. But the fear had grown until it had filled him up, like an invisible cancer.

A tear spilled over to slide down Nita's cheek. She sighed and wiped her face as she felt Dan's quiet approach. He held the blue pack in his hands, the flap folded over to show the crooked letters. He didn't say anything, just looked at her, his eyes full of questions.

Nita nodded, then turned back to the riverbed. "Someone found it," she whispered. "He could still turn up."

"I'm sorry." Dan's sadness fell around her like the twilight shadows. He came to stand beside her, and as he looked down at the rocky falls far below, his sadness deepened. "It was strange, running into Jeremy again," Dan said after a while. "I thought he was dead."

Guilt?

"I was drifting back then, conning people for food. My luck ran out in this little town out beyond La Grande. The folk there decided to hang me. I don't know." His laugh was short and tinged with bitterness. "I guess maybe I deserved it. Anyway, Jeremy helped me get away. He was twelve—just a kid. He was going to come with me, but he changed his mind at the last minute." Dan let his breath out in a slow sigh. "The townfolk were going to know that he was the one who let me out, but I walked away anyway. I let him stay behind. They might have hung him in my place. I knew that, but I still walked away.

"It scared me, what Jeremy could do. It was magic and it was real. I . . . didn't want it to be real. I didn't want to believe in something like that, so I left him behind."

It scared me . . . The echoes were still there, mixed with the guilt. Fear, like David's.

Dan was staring down at the falls again. The sadness had deepened into grief.

"Who died down there?" Nita asked softly.

"My sister, Amy." Dan looked at her sideways, a little startled. "Is it that obvious?"

"You seemed so . . . sad." Nita bit her lip, because Jeremy had scared him, and she would scare him, too. "I didn't know you had a sister," she said quickly. "I'm sorry."

"So am I." Dan sighed. "Amy took care of me when I was a kid, after our folks died. We didn't do too well. Maybe she blamed herself for that, or maybe she just got tired. One day she climbed up the rocks and jumped off. She broke her neck. I thought about her today, and I haven't thought about her in a long time." He frowned down at the shadowed falls. "One afternoon I asked Jeremy to make her face for me. For a minute, out there on that dusty mountainside, she was alive again. I guess that's what scared me. It wasn't just a picture, it was *Amy*, like he'd brought her back to life."

"It's the past. Jeremy touches it," Nita said. "He makes you see it."

"I didn't want to remember the past."

Maybe he still didn't. The dry falls had vanished into shadow, and it was getting cold. Nita shivered and Dan put his arm around her. For a long time they looked down into the riverbed. The sky had deepened to a royal blue and the first stars winked like dry eyes, low on the horizon. There was no water in that rocky ditch, just ghosts, shadows of the past. Nita leaned closer against Dan's warmth. His arm tightened around her shoulder and Nita felt the warm stir of his desire.

The fierce ache between her own legs took her by surprise. She closed her eyes, breathing faster. If she tilted her head, he would lean down and kiss her. Once their lips touched, there would be no turning back. They would go into his room and make love on the narrow bed, beneath the paintings of Jeremy's river. When she woke in darkness tonight, she would feel his warmth beside her, smell his sweat and his skin, hear the sound of his breathing. She wouldn't be alone. She could burrow against him and he would murmur in his sleep, put his arm around her as David used to do.

And that, of course, was it. Dan reminded her of David. Nita sighed. Because they were about the same age? Or was it Dan's quiet patience on the surface, hiding doubt beneath . . .

Dan wasn't David.

Nita took a small step away from him, her body aching to move closer, lean against him, and take the comfort he would offer, fill the empty space inside her with passion. She stifled a pang of regret as he read the small rejection accurately and lifted his arm from her shoulders. Silently, without touching, they went back into the dark house.

"You need to be careful," Dan told her as he switched on the solar lantern and hung it over the table. "We had a rape-murder last night. Out near Sandy's place."

Nita listened in growing horror as he told her about Candy Wilmer and her death. "Maybe it wasn't one of the soldiers," she said hesitantly. "Maybe someone just wanted it to look that way."

"That occurred to Durer and me." Dan set the pot of leftover beans on the table, his expression grim. "But a lot of people aren't going to look beyond that knife. They don't want to look. The only hope we have is to find out who's behind the sabotage. It's not someone local, or we'd know who was in on it by now. I can see someone busting the Pipe for revenge, but what about the rest of this stuff? Someone wants to start a war between the Corps and The Dalles. Why?" Dan leaned his elbows on the tabletop, staring moodily at the bean pot. "Carter asked me that question and I can't answer him. Who wins? No one. There's only so much water and there's only so much land under hoses. Carter's right. The equation only comes out one way, no matter what." He sighed and spooned cold beans onto his plate. "I'm losing my touch. People want to listen to the Ransoms, not to me."

"It's my father, isn't it?" Nita asked harshly. "That's what keeps you here. His ghost. Why don't you let it go?"

"Sam's part of it." Dan put his fork down. "I feel like they're right there in the shadows, watching me: Amy. Jesse. And Sam. Maybe you're right. Maybe it's time I quit."

He was thinking defeat, not release. He was thinking death. Something tickled the back of Nita's mind. It had something to do with what Dan had just said, but she couldn't put her finger on it. She spooned beans onto her plate, not really hungry, but not wanting to face the darkness of her bedroom. At least Rachel was there. She would have that much.

"I'm going to bed." Dan stretched, his fatigue filling the room like a haze of dust. "Are you sure you're all right?" he asked gently.

"Yes." She met his eyes, stifling a last twinge of regret. "Thanks."

"If you need anything, call me," he said as he disappeared into his bedroom.

Nita sighed, feeling her own weariness. She scrubbed her plate clean in the pan of sand that stood on the counter. It was getting dirty; she'd need to get a fresh panful tomorrow. Renny's unexpected visit this morning had made her forget. Renny! The trucker's name jogged her memory, shaking the elusive tickle free. Frowning, Nita hesitated, wondering if it was really important. Right now, tonight, she didn't want to knock on Dan's door.

But a girl had been raped and murdered. Who would die next—Carter? Nita grabbed the lantern, walked resolutely across the floor, and tapped lightly on the warped panels of Dan's bedroom door.

"Come in." He was sitting in bed, the sheet across his lap, eyebrows arched with his wondering. The yellow light made his tanned shoulders gleam like polished wood, outlined his wiry muscles with shadow.

"Renny told me something odd." Nita licked her dry lips, didn't look at his erection prodding the sheet. "She said that they were putting new land under soaker hoses down in the Valley. To grow more bushes."

"What?" Dan sat up straighter. "Carter told me that the reduction was intended to keep the Valley's share constant, that there would be crop losses down there if they cut the flow at all."

He wasn't thinking about sex anymore.

"If Renny's right, someone is handing out a line of bullshit. You don't get a federal permit for new fields if water's tight. I wonder who's shitting whom," he said softly.

"It's not Carter." Nita bit her lip as Dan looked at her.

"I think he was telling me the truth—or what he thought was the truth," Dan said slowly. "Remember I said that no one stood to win?" He frowned, his face lined and full of shadow. "This changes things. I'm not so sure that's true anymore. Somebody may be pulling strings to get new fields in." His frown deepened. "If so, it has to be someone who's big enough to *pull* those kind of strings. If Carter isn't behind it, he needs to know what's going on. He should have the sources to check it out. If he believes me. I guess this is where I throw the dice and find out how my luck is running."

"I'm coming, too," Nita said.

Dan shook his head, giving her a crooked grin. "I can add two and two and come up with four. Do you think Carter is going to listen to either of us if we're standing side by side? I'm sorry if I messed things up between you."

"You didn't." Nita flushed and looked away.

"He'll listen to me if I can give him something concrete. He doesn't want a war here any more than we do."

"They won't let any civilians on base, so you're going to sneak in, aren't you?"

Dan smiled for her. "The worst he can do is jail me for trespass."

Her father had trapped this man, on that dusty afternoon when the men had come. The blood that had stained her had hardened into a chain around Dan Greely's throat. "That's not the worst that can happen to you," Nita said bitterly. "You can get yourself shot."

"I said the same thing to your father once."

"And he didn't listen, either. Well, he should be proud of you." Nita turned on her heel and fled to the sanctuary of Rachel's dreams.

CHAPTER SIXTEEN ☆

It was late. Carter looked up and felt a mild sense of shock at the flood-lit darkness beyond his office window. It had been late afternoon when he had finally made it back to his deskful of flow reports. He stretched, wincing at the crackle of vertebrae in his neck. It had been a relief to bury himself in solid, comprehensible numbers. He understood turbulence and flow dynamics. The numbers always meant the same thing—they didn't change, didn't twist into something else.

Private First Class Carolyn Allison had been shot today while out on patrol. Someone had hidden in the rocks along the riverbed, had shot her in the chest with a 30.06. An old hunting rifle, probably—possibly the same gun that had killed Delgado's brother. Carter stared at his reflection on the window glass. It was a stranger's face—flat and unfamiliar, the mouth set in hard lines, the eyes unreadable. He had spent part of the afternoon in the infirmary. Carolyn Allison would live, but it had been close.

How much of this is my fault? Carter wondered. The face in the window stared back at him, eyes accusing. If he had come down hard on the Shunt demonstration, would it be better now or worse? Carter shook his head in a short, negative arc. He had lost any sense of perspective or control; he was groping now, feeling his way. Fucking up?

A flood of transfer requests cluttered Carter's desk. He had denied them all—although he couldn't blame people for wanting to bail out. Hastings had told him that he couldn't expect any new people for at least another week, and perhaps not even then. Even before the shooting, sick calls had been escalating. The accident rate had soared. Tired people made mistakes, and the doubled patrols he'd had to put out were wearing them all ragged. Morale sucked. And now Durer was on his case, claiming that a Corps member had committed a rape and murder in The Dalles. He'd undoubtedly announced his bloody verdict to everyone in town—which had probably resulted in the shooting, Goddamn it. Carter had ordered an armed fast-reaction team to be kept on five-minute alert status. Things were that bad.

A knock at the door made him jump. "Come in." He turned away from the window.

It was Delgado, carrying a manila envelope. He saluted, his posture stiff and straight. "I'm afraid that I've exceeded my authority, sir, but I've come up with something that I have to show you."

"How exactly did you exceed your authority, Major?" Carter reined in his temper with an effort. Since the beating incident and his subsequent discipline of the major, relations had been strained, to say the least. Damn Hastings, anyway. "You're walking a thin line with me," he said coldly.

"I understand, sir." Delgado stared at a spot on the wall above Carter's head. "I had one of my men keep an eye on Greely."

"The Dalles is off-limits. By my direct order."

"Yes, sir, but I sent him out before you gave the order, sir. He was discreet." Delgado opened the envelope and placed two glossy photographs down on the desk in front of Carter. "He took these, sir."

Carter stared at the two photos. Each picture showed the same two men. In the first shot, they stood together in front of the government store, apparently deep in conversation. In the second, they walked down a street, side by side. Dan Greely and the redhaired agitator. Greely had said that he didn't know the man's name, that he'd only seen him around. "Who took these?" Carter asked heavily.

"Sergeant Roth, sir, from Support. He's good with a camera."

"I want to talk to him. Right now."

"Right away, sir." Delgado gave him a brisk salute and departed.

Carter pushed the incriminating photos a few inches away with his thumb. They could be innocent. He *had* asked Greely to check out this man. Oh, *sure*, they were innocent. Carter let his breath out in a bitter sigh. He had liked Dan Greely, and he had resisted the evidence that was all around him—dismissed it as circumstantial in a foolish desire for an ally in this mess. No more. He swallowed, tasting bile in the back of his throat. What about Nita? Where did she fit in? He still dreamed about the kidnap; he saw blurry faces bending over him, asking questions. Would they come clear one night? Would one of those faces turn out to be Nita's?

By the time he finished interviewing Roth, it was very late. Carter tucked the photos into his pocket, locked his office, and walked down the echoing corridor. There would be coffee in the mess. He should go get a sandwich, he told himself, but he wasn't hungry. A private was coming in as he reached the main doors.

"Sir?" She saluted. "I just escorted Chief of Police Durer off the base. I called your office, but you'd left."

"Oh, yeah." Carter ran a hand across his face, realizing just how tired he was. "He stuck around this long?" That meant he hadn't found anything very useful. Carter swallowed his anger and looked more closely at the woman. "You kicked that local off me at the Shunt," he said, recognizing her. "Wasson, right?"

"Yessir." She grinned. "I was glad to be of service, sir."

"Did Durer find anything?" Carter asked as they walked to the door.

"He copied all the gate logs." Her face was carefully neutral. "And he took prints from tires down at the motor pool. I don't think he was satisfied, sir."

"He thinks we're covering up for someone, never mind that we've given him full cooperation." Carter's lips tightened. "He wants to pin this on the Corps so bad he can taste it. Damn local."

"Sir."

Carter looked at Wasson. Her face had gone tight, closed. "Something wrong, Private?"

She shook her head, eyes averted.

"Hold it a minute." He put out a hand as she started to open the door. "I'd like to know. It's not an order, Wasson. I'm asking."

She looked at him, looked away, obviously angry. She had something to say, but he was a colonel. "I . . . grew up in Hood River, sir." Twin spots of color glowed on her cheeks and she stared stiffly at the wall. "It's hard for us, sir. We're locals. Our families are 'hicks.' " She gave him a hard, bright look from the corner of her eye.

Expecting a reprimand? Carter sighed. "I haven't given much

thought to that, and I should have," he said wearily. "Tell me about it, Private."

"We're . . . caught in the middle," she said tightly. "We're *Corps*. They were our friends, the ones who got killed. I knew Sonny and Tom real well. Sonny and I were . . . close." Her lips twitched. "My family used to grow cherries in Hood River, but the trees were old and they died off when it started to dry up. Mom's still there, living with my brother. I don't know how they're going to make out with this water cut. I mean—" She stared at the doors in front of her, struggling for words. "I know we don't make the rules, but I feel like the Goddamn enemy sometimes. Excuse me, sir."

What he should tell her, of course, was that she was Corps, first and foremost. But she knew that, or she wouldn't be hurting. Carter sighed. "It's tough, isn't it? You catch shit from your buddies for siding with the locals and you feel like a traitor to your family at the same time. You're damned either way." There weren't too many locals on base, but there were some. He'd better find out who, first thing in the morning. He should have found out at the beginning.

"I was stationed in Chicago when the big riot started," he said. "We got sent out to break down the barricades afterward and help pick up the bodies. I . . . recognized one. We used to play ball together, after school." Domino had been one of the few people in Johnny's crowd who had accepted Carter. Carter wondered how he had ended up on the lakeshore, ragged and dirty and dead. "I felt like shit."

"If you'd had to shoot at him, would you have done it?"

Carter met Wasson's eyes, seeing the fear in them. Did she lie awake nights, staring into an ugly future where she looked through a rifle sight and recognized her brother? "I won't let Chicago happen here," he said softly.

"Yes, sir. Thank you, sir." She snapped him a brisk salute.

Carter watched her march down the corridor. That salute was the first one he'd seen in days that had really been meant. He pushed through the doors, leaning against their weight and the heaviness in his chest. He'd made one hell of a promise to Private Wasson, he thought morosely. He hoped he could keep it.

Outside, he shivered in the nighttime chill. The wind was picking up. Grit rasped on concrete and Carter blinked, his eyes tearing as they filled with dust. His goggles were on his desk, but he was too tired to go back for them. All he wanted to do was fall onto his bed and go to sleep. Even a shower could wait.

He cut through the alley, seeing nothing—hearing no door open behind him. Who had grabbed him, and why? In the glow of his porch light, Carter fumbled with the lock, swung the door open . . . and froze. Dan Greely was sitting on his sofa.

"We need to talk," Dan said.

"You're right. We do." The pictures felt like a lead weight in his pocket. Carter stepped inside and closed the door very softly behind him. "I have something to show you. Just stay there a minute." He walked past Dan, into the bedroom.

His anger was a cold weight inside him. He opened the drawer of his nightstand, every motion controlled and deliberate, and took out his Beretta. Dan hadn't moved from the sofa. He went very still as Carter reentered the room.

"I'm not armed, not even with a knife." His eyes fixed themselves on the gun in Carter's hand. "What's gotten into you, Carter?"

"You tell me. Keep your hands on your knees. Where I can see them." He lifted the phone, called Security.

"Carter, will you wait one minute?" Dan said urgently. "What the hell is going on here? I snuck in because what I have to say is important. If you really give a damn about what's happening on the riverbed, listen to me. For God's sake, man, at least tell me why this gun bit?"

"Did you ever find that agitator?" Carter asked tightly. Even now, a part of him wanted Dan to explain the pictures.

"No." Dan shrugged. "He split, as far as I can find out. I never did catch up to him."

Fuck you, Greely. The cold anger was spreading through his body, turning him to stone. If he had not been so credulous, so damn ready to listen to this man's golden tongue . . .

"You need to hear this." Dan spoke rapidly. "Someone is getting permits to irrigate new acreage down in the Willamette Valley."

"Bullshit." Carter had wanted help—wanted to believe that that was what Dan had been offering. "They're already irrigating to capacity down there. That's why we have to absorb the flow cut."

"That's what you told us." Dan's eyes were intent on Carter's face. "Do you know that for sure?"

"General Hastings gave me the numbers himself."

"How good are his sources?"

"Tight," Carter said. "And you have proof, right?" Like hell.

"I don't." Dan looked troubled. "I was hoping that you could check this out. That's why I came here—to ask you to do that. I think maybe we're all being set up."

"You talk very slick," Carter said bitterly. "How dumb do you think I am?" Dumb enough, so far. He should have listened to Hastings on day one.

"Carter? What happened?" Greely clenched his fists on his knees. "The Shunt was a mess, but that's all it was—a bad judgment call on my part. What the hell got you thinking that I've set you up?"

Carter reached into his pocket, pulled out the photos, and tossed them facedown into Greely's lap. "After I talked to you at City Hall, my car broke down. And someone had swiped the phone." He smiled grimly. "I had—shall we say—a little bit of trouble with some locals on my way out of town. Turns out that someone had played games with my engine. We found a wrench down in the engine compartment. It had the initials DG on it." He stared at Greely. "If Judge Lindstrom and Durer weren't in your pocket, you'd be in jail right now."

"They're not in my pocket, but they're fair men. Can I look at these?" At Carter's nod, Greely picked up a photo, turned it over. For the space of three heartbeats he went very still. "Someone faked these," he said at last.

"One of my people took them. I talked to him."

"He's lying to you." Dan laid the photo down and sighed. "I wondered who swiped my tools. It's a frame, Carter. A good one."

"I don't think it is. And don't tell me about any three days for trespassing. This time, we hold you for the U.S. Marshal. We're charging you with kidnap, tampering with government property, and water-flow obstruction. *And* trespass."

"I don't think you can make any of that stick—except the trespassing."

"Maybe not, but it will be at least two weeks before the marshal even gets around to collecting you. I can't spare anyone to transport you, and he's down in Medford right now. If you *are* innocent, you'll have a great alibi for anything that happens."

"Carter, you're making a mistake." Dan's eyes were bleak. "Sandy Corbett and I have been working our asses off to keep a lid on things. You need our help a lot more than you realize."

"If that turns out to be true, I'll apologize."

"It'll be too damn late for apologies by then."

Security knocked on the door and Carter let the MPs in, glad for the interruption. Dan stood quietly as they cuffed him, his face expressionless. He looked over his shoulder as the MPs led him out of the room. "You're wrong," he said to Carter. "About a lot of things."

Yeah, he'd been wrong, all right. Carter went to put the Beretta away. He had never thumbed off the safety; it was as if his subconscious had decided that Greely wasn't really a threat. "Hell," he said out loud, and slammed the drawer closed.

And what if Dan had been telling the truth? a small voice nagged at the back of his brain. About the new Valley fields?

He was lying, Carter told himself. Feeding Carter a new line of bull. But that small voice wouldn't let it drop. If Greely was right, then the Corps was cutting water that didn't need to be cut—and someone was getting acreage at the expense of the Columbia farmers. Carter remembered Private Wasson's face when she talked about her family down in Hood River.

Pacific BioSystems? They were the prime suspect, of course. Carter shrugged as he stripped off his coverall. It would be easy enough to check. They couldn't keep that kind of thing secret; the permit application for any new irrigation line had to go on record, and the records were accessible. Just to be sure, just for Wasson's sake, he'd check again.

He threw his dirty coverall into the corner, feeling more alone, less sure of himself than he had since his first day here.

CHAPTER SEVENTEEN ☆

The wind picked up during the night. It blew down the gorge in fierce gusts, shaking the old house, tugging at the dried-out shingles, sifting dust and grit between the cracks in the walls. Awake in the darkness, Nita listened to the wind, listened for the sound of Dan's truck. Rachel whimpered and struggled in her sleep and Nita held her close.

"It's me, isn't it?" Nita murmured. "I'm giving you bad dreams, worrying about Dan." She touched her daughter's dark hair, fine as wisps of silk. What will I tell her when she asks me why she hurts? Nita stared into the darkness. I'll have to tell her that I did this to her, that I gave her all the world's pain.

The windows rattled, closed against the blowing dust. Nita slipped out of bed and tiptoed across the room to peer through the glass. The sky was dark and starless, and Nita shivered in her thin shirt. Maybe Carter would listen. Maybe he would believe Dan.

Carter didn't trust anyone. Not really. He wasn't going to believe Dan.

The wind rose to a booming crescendo just before dawn, but by the time the sun was well up, it had dropped to fitful gusts. Nita fed Rachel, wanting to start for town *right now*. It wasn't to be. Outside, the dust storm had bowed the plants to the ground. If she didn't do something about it, Dan would lose his crop. She had been hired to take care of them. Chafing at the delay, Nita spread Rachel's blanket in the shade of the box that housed the water meter and set her daughter down. Rachel grabbed for her toes, drooling and grinning. "You *are* teething, aren't you?'' Nita peered into her daughter's mouth, then tickled her round belly until Rachel laughed.

Draping her sunscarf over her head, she started down the bean rows, propping up the wilting stems, shaking dust from wind-shredded leaves. The powdery dust stuck to her skin as the morning crawled by, turned muddy by her sweat. Nita wiped her face, back aching, unwilling to take a break. Only a few more rows. The water would come on soon and soak the field. Maybe it would help.

Finished, at last. She scooped up Rachel, started for the porch. She had stopped listening for the truck, so the figure limping up the track to the house caught her by surprise. Jeremy. In spite of her worries, she smiled as the riverbed shimmered and filled briefly with green and brown water. ''Did you walk all the way from town?'' she asked as they both reached the porch. ''Would you like a drink?''

''Yes and yes, thank you. People used to say 'Hello, how are you?' a generation ago.'' He grinned at her. ''Now, we say 'Hello, would you like a drink?' I guess thirst is more important than someone's state of health and well-being these days.''

''I never thought of it that way. Sit,'' she said, because his knees were hurting. ''I'll bring it out here.'' The pain had a worn feeling to it, like a piece of stone that had been polished by wind and sand until the sharp edges had worn away. They had hurt him all his life, she guessed.

She carried two mugs out onto the porch, handed him one. ''Is there anything I can do? For the pain.''

''You feel it, too?'' He looked down to touch the lumpy bulge of his kneecap. ''That must be rough sometimes.''

''Yes.'' Nita drank half of her water, her eyes on the dry gash of the riverbed below. ''My father used to sit here,'' she said softly. ''I wonder if he could remember it—water in the river-bed. Maybe that's why he worked so hard to save this town.'' Because he had remembered how it was, believed that it might be like that again, some day? ''Or maybe he was like me,'' she whispered. ''Maybe it trapped him—all those needs and hopes and fears around him. Maybe he couldn't say no. Jeremy, she's going to blame me.'' Nita poked her finger into Rachel's palm, swallowed tears as Rachel clutched it. ''I did this to her.''

''She's only going to blame you if you deny what you are.'' Jeremy tilted his head and the ground around the house went green with short, tough-looking grass.

''How can I deny it?'' Nita asked bitterly. She reached out a hand, passed her finger through a stalk of white flowers. "It still surprises me," she murmured. "Are you doing it on purpose?"

"I can't really control the visions. They just happen." Jeremy crossed his arms on his raised knees, moody suddenly, full of shadows. "I came up here to . . . apologize to Dan. For yesterday. I was . . . rude."

"He felt guilty," Nita said. "That he left you behind."

"Did he?" Jeremy looked surprised. "I wasn't angry about that. What he told me, back then, was that my makings mattered—that they were something wonderful. I stayed behind because I believed him, but they never did matter. Not the way he meant. I got—hurt finding that out." He touched his chest lightly, eyes dark with remembered pain, "I needed somebody to blame for that, and I guess he was convenient. I never really expected to see him again."

The hurting inside him was worse than his knees. Nita reached for Jeremy's hand and his fingers tightened around hers.

"What you are *matters*," he murmured.

"The past matters, too, Jeremy."

"No, it doesn't." He stared down into the river. "It just makes the dust seem worse. It makes people crazy. Where *is* Dan?"

"I don't know." Nita lifted her head, her worry coming back in a rush. "He went down to the base last night, and he didn't come back. I was just about to go down there." She picked up Rachel, went to get her sling, and twisted it over her shoulder.

"The base is closed to civilians."

"Maybe Carter will talk to me. I hope so."

"I've met Carter Voltaire," Jeremy said thoughtfully. "I like him. I get the feeling that he's caught in the middle of this water stuff and it scares him shitless."

"He doesn't trust Dan." Nita tucked Rachel into the sling. "He thinks that Dan's behind the sabotage, and he *isn't*."

"So go tell him that. Tell him how you know."

"Just like that?" She looked away, clawed once more by that sense of need. "He won't believe me."

"Won't he?" Jeremy followed her into the house as she went to get a water jug. "I think he will. Is that what you're afraid of, Nita?"

Need. "Cut it out." Rachel started to fuss and Nita scooped her out of the sling. "What do you want from me, Jeremy?"

"I want you to use your talent." Jeremy lifted Rachel out of her arms. "Would you fill this one, too?" He held out his own jug. "I think I can get us onto the base."

She was about to refuse—to say that she didn't want any company—but the sound of an engine interrupted her. Dan. It wasn't—she knew the sound of his truck—but she ran outside anyway, wanting to hope, to believe that someone else had given him a ride home for some reason. The car was just pulling up beside the porch—a new electric, covered with dust. Nita halted at the top step as the driver got out. It was Carter's friend.

"Hello." He smiled at her, but he wasn't pleased to see her. "Is Dan Greely around?"

"No, he's not," Nita said quickly. "He's in town. Could you give us a ride, on your way back?"

"I'm sorry." His expression of polite regret covered a stab of irritation that made Nita wince. "I'm going straight back to Bonneville. I'm on a tight schedule." He glanced pointedly at his watch.

"Which means you have to drive right into The Dalles to pick up eighty-four." Jeremy had come out onto the porch behind Nita. "Out here folks don't say no when someone asks for a ride. Walking in the sun is grim."

Nita watched Johnny notice Jeremy's hands. His revulsion showed briefly on his face—clearly enough for Jeremy to catch it. "Maybe I'll just wait around for Dan for a while." His smile was wearing thin. "I'll look for you on the way down, pick you up if I see you."

"If we've got to walk, we'd better get moving." Jeremy shoved his hands into his pockets. "Coming?"

Nita hesitated. This man wanted them to leave. Why? What did Dan have that was worth stealing? Nothing this man couldn't buy with the money in his pockets, from the look of his clothes. "I'm going to stick around, too." She sat down on the top step, ignoring Jeremy's surprise. This man didn't know Dan. Dan would have said so. And last night Dan had said that maybe the stakes here were higher than he had guessed. She lifted Rachel from the sling and sat her on her lap.

"Oh, forget it. I'll give you a ride." His smile was more in keeping with his sour mood now. "No point in sticking around here for nothing."

He knows, Nita thought, and felt a sudden chill. He knows that Dan isn't coming back. A fist closed tight in her chest, making it hard to breathe.

"I think I'm lost." Jeremy was puzzled. "Are we getting a ride, or staying here?"

"Let's go." Nita stood quickly. "We appreciate the lift," she said, giving Johnny a sweet smile.

He didn't speak to them as they climbed into the car. Cool air whispered from the vents, making Rachel chuckle with delight. He didn't say one word as he eased the car down the rutted road into The Dalles. He was pissed that they'd been at Dan's house—what had he been after? Was he doing something for Carter? She almost asked him, but something made her decide not to. He pulled over at the interstate ramp and stopped the car with a jerk. "I hope this is okay."

And to hell with you if it isn't? "It's fine," Nita said as they got out of the air-conditioned car. Carter owed this man. She wondered what the debt was—and who had named it a debt in the first place. She jumped as Jeremy put his hand on her arm.

"Want to tell me what was going on?"

"I don't know." She frowned at him. "He doesn't know Dan, and he wanted something in the house."

"Maybe one of us should have stayed," Jeremy said thoughtfully. "Maybe he has some kind of connection to this Pipeline mess?"

"He does," Nita said reluctantly. "He's Carter's friend." Full of nagging dread, she followed Jeremy to the gate.

The guard scowled at them, but Jeremy wasn't worried. He smiled at her and gave her a thumbs-up. The dread thickened in her belly, growing heavier as the minutes ticked by. Carter finally appeared, walking fast. She didn't need to see his face to feel him frown as he spotted her.

"Jeremy?" He looked at Nita, avoiding her eyes. "Don't ask me to let Dan go. I assume that's why you're here."

"He's here?" Until this moment, she hadn't realized how much she had feared that he was dead. Like her father. "You arrested him?"

"Yes." His face tightened. "With cause. I'm sorry."

He was hurting inside. He hadn't listened to Dan, didn't want to listen to her. In a moment, he would turn around and walk back through that glittering metal gate. And I'll go back to the beans? Nita thought. Her father had died because he hadn't done that. Dan was following in his footsteps. "Carter, you need to hear me," she said. "Because you care about what's happening here."

"Call it payment," Jeremy said to Carter. "For the other day."

Carter frowned, looked at Jeremy and away. "I can spare you a few minutes. That's all." He sighed, not wanting this at all. "It's not going to change anything," he said.

"We'll take what we can get," Jeremy said cheerfully.

Afraid, Nita walked through the ugly gate. The uniformed guard saluted Carter and his eyes slid to Nita. He leered at her openly behind Carter's back and his hot lust raked her. She lifted her chin as she marched past him. A moment later a strangled squawk made her look back over her shoulder. The guard was slapping frantically at his back, neck craned to stare over his shoulder. Nita sneaked a look at Jeremy.

He walked serenely beside her. His face was calm, but she felt his amusement. She touched his arm lightly, smiling in spite of her apprehension. The moment of humor helped. She kept her hand on his arm as they walked down the dusty street between the sterile blocks of buildings. Carter wasn't taking them to his apartment. She looked up at the looming cliff-face of the dam, hoping they wouldn't go any closer. The air was full of anger, fear, and tension. It pressed around her, smothering as a heavy blanket, making Rachel cry. The dam seemed to lean over her, ready to fall. Carter turned aside and held open the door to a long, low building.

It was cool inside, as cool as the car had been. The sweat on Nita's skin chilled instantly, and Rachel cooed. They were walking down a pastel-walled hallway lined with doors. Two uniformed men passed them, their bland faces masking hostility. Nita nearly stumbled into Carter as he stopped to open a door.

He stepped aside quickly, not wanting to touch her, and ushered them into his cramped office. "Dan Greely trespassed on Corps property last night." Carter closed the door with a small bang. "He's safely locked up, waiting for the U.S. Marshal. I can't let him go, and that's the bottom line. Is there anything else?"

Rachel began to cry again, fretful and shrill. Without a word, Jeremy stepped forward and lifted Rachel from Nita's arms. "We'll wait for you outside," he said, and walked out of the office.

Nita felt a flash of panic as the door closed behind them, cutting off the sound of Rachel's fretting, shutting her in with Carter. "Dan came here to tell you something important," Nita faltered.

"He didn't have anything important to say to me."

He was *hurt*. "Damn it, Carter." Nita groped for anger, seizing it like a lifeline. "Didn't you even *listen* to him? About the new fields in the Valley?"

"It's not happening." Carter lifted his shoulders in an exaggerated shrug. "I'm busy, Nita."

"It *is* happening." Words, words, she needed words. Nita took a deep breath, feeling as if the cooled air was too thin to breathe. "Renny Warren—a trucker—told me about them, and I told Dan. He thought it was important—important enough to risk getting arrested or shot to tell you. Doesn't that matter to you? Or are you in on this? Is that it?" She felt a sudden chill. "Your friend Johnny gave us a ride this afternoon. He was snooping around Dan's house. Are you both in on it? Are you getting some kind of cut for giving water to the Valley?"

"No," Carter said softly. "I'm not, and neither is Johnny."

His anger stung, but it filled her with relief. He wasn't in on it. "Okay, I apologize. But Renny Warren was telling the truth. Dan said you had to cut the gorge because the Valley crops would die—but that's not true, is it?"

"It is true. I can't help but think you're saying this so I'll let Dan go. Johnny's in San Francisco, by the way." Carter turned his back on her and bent over his terminal. "I have a lot of reports to catch up on."

"He's not in San Francisco. He was at the market yesterday." Nita walked around the desk and leaned on his terminal so that Carter had to look into her face. "You still think I've made some kind of choice between you and Dan," she said bitterly. "The choice is not between you and it never was. I didn't walk away from you. I *ran* away because I care about you too much, and I don't know if David's alive or dead. I don't want to love you when I don't know . . ." Her voice broke and she looked away from him, fighting tears.

"Nita?" Carter wanted to put his arms around her, but crossed them tightly instead. "This Renny was either lying or wrong," he said gently. "As for Greely, I have proof that he was involved with the people who dumped me in the desert. He also sabotaged my car last time I was in town. I'm sorry, Nita, but the proof is real. He did it."

"What kind of proof can you have?" Nita clenched her fists. "It didn't happen."

"I have photos and an eyewitness."

Now! This was the time to say it—to tell him that Dan couldn't lie to her, that no one could really lie to her. "They're wrong. Fakes. I'll bring you proof," she gasped, failing, afraid, despising herself in that instant, for her fear and her failure. "I'll bring you proof that those fields are real. If I do that, will you let Dan go?"

"If you can get me solid proof, it'll make a difference." Carter looked at her, looked away—doubting himself, doubting her. "I can't promise you any more than that. Dan might be safer here, Nita."

"I'm not just worried about Dan." The words caught in her throat. "I'm worried about you, too, Carter. Who betrayed you in the past? Who hurt you?"

He stood up suddenly, and she stepped into his arms. Their kiss was a hard and bruising sharing this time, full of anger, doubt, love, and pain . . . hers and his, all mixed and twisted together. She thrust herself suddenly away from him, tasting blood on her lip, trembling, wanting to scream at him or cry. He made no move to touch her again, but stood stiff and still beside his desk, eyes dark with his anguish.

Someone tapped cautiously at the door and they both jumped.

"Come in," Carter said shortly.

Nita remembered the uniformed man who pushed the door open. He was the one who had found Carter that night up on the gorge rim. His familiar, ugly darkness filled the office like a sour smell.

"What is it, Major?" Carter sat down stiffly behind his desk, frowning.

"We got a report from the team at the Shunt." He turned deliberately to stare at Nita.

"Say it," Carter snapped.

The major hesitated just long enough to make his point. "Corporal Roscoe reported in, sir. He and his team spotted some suspicious activity in the hills above the riverbed. A hick fired a couple of shots at them and took off. The corporal is asking for permission to pursue, sir."

"They can't leave the Shunt valve unguarded."

"By the time another team gets out there, the bastards'll have vanished." The cold eyes flicked toward Nita, away. "I could have another detail at the Shunt inside of a half hour, sir. The hicks'll never know there's no one there." Hot eagerness flared like lust in the man. "We could catch them, sir."

"No." Carter stood. "Tell the corporal to go after them, but one soldier stays at the Shunt. Get the alert team out there, pronto, and put a squad on alert in case there's trouble. Armed, Major."

The officer snapped a brisk, pleased salute and strode out of the office. Nita stared after him, her skin dotted with goosebumps. He was so full of hatred. Was it her imagination, or had some of that hard, ugly hostility been directed toward Carter?

"You'd better go." Carter was staring at the map on the wall. "If . . . you turn up anything concrete, come to the lower gate. The guard there will contact me."

He wanted her out of here. "Who was that man?" she asked. "The one who was just here?"

"Major Delgado. Why?"

"He . . . doesn't like locals."

"His brother was one of the people who got killed last spring. Nita." Carter wouldn't meet her eyes. "You have to leave, right now."

Yes, she knew. She hurt, too. "I'll bring you your proof," she said, and fled.

CHAPTER EIGHTEEN ☆

Carter half rose as Nita left, then sank down into his seat again. No point in calling her back—there was nothing more to be said between them. Nothing. He stared at the riverbed map on the wall, not really seeing it.

Who betrayed you? she had asked. Why had she asked *that*? He leaned his face in his hands, remembering the single spot of blood on the bathroom rug. She had been so neat, Mom, so careful not to make a mess. Why this memory? He shook his head to banish the image. Could you call suicide a betrayal? No, but then why had he thought of it? He let his breath out in an angry rush. They were putting in new fields down in the Valley. A trucker had told Nita and she, *she*, had told Dan. Obviously she was trying to save Dan's ass.

He wanted to believe her—oh, God, how he'd like to be able to do that. His phone line beeped. Swearing softly under his breath, Carter reached for it.

"Hey, Carter." Johnny's voice came cheerfully over the line. It wasn't a video connection—just voice. Public phone booth? "I'm tearing through town," he said. "Got time for a quick lunch?"

He *was* here. "I thought you were down in San Francisco," Carter said cautiously.

"I had some official business with the general. Carter . . ." He hesitated. "I need to talk to you."

"Can you come here? I can't get away."

"Damn. I'm on a tight schedule." Johnny sounded harried. "This is important. Remember what we were talking about over lunch? Paul's little theory?"

"Yes," Carter said slowly. "About a Corps link to Pacific BioSystems."

181

"I'm on a public line, so I can't say much more—but it seems to be in your backyard," Johnny said.

Delgado? Hastings? "Who?" Carter asked softly.

"Like I just said . . ." Johnny cleared his throat. "Listen, we don't have concrete proof yet, but we're working on it." His tone was guarded. "Watch your back, okay? I'll let you know as soon as something breaks. It's big, Carter. Keep it in mind, okay?"

Oh, yes, he'd keep it in mind. "Thanks," Carter said. "Oh, yeah—were you up at Dan Greely's house this morning?"

"Yeah." There was a short silence. "Who told you?"

"Nita." So she had been telling him the truth about that; it gave the rest of her story weight. "She said you gave her a ride."

"So that was Nita?" Johnny was trying to sound casual. "She was . . . up at the Greely place. Is she . . . staying there?"

"Yes, she's living there," Carter growled. "It's a free country."

"Hey, I'm sorry," Johnny said awkwardly. "I didn't know."

"Forget it." He didn't want to get into it right now. "What were you doing up there, anyway?"

"I thought I'd meet this local agitator face to face. It's . . . part of what I was telling you about. I needed to . . . check some things out."

"Check some things? What are you doing, Johnny?" Carter swallowed sudden anger. "Playing amateur detective? People are getting fucking *shot* around here."

"What do think it means to be a regional director for Water Policy?" Johnny's tone was cold. "We're supposed to be *out* here, in our districts. This isn't supposed to be a desk job, Colonel Voltaire. This is my responsibility more than yours, remember?"

"I'm sorry." Carter flushed, embarrassed. He *had* thought of Johnny as sitting at a terminal reviewing other people's reports. "I apologize," he said. "But let me deal with Greely. He's locked up right here, as a matter of fact."

"He is? Well, I guess I can stop looking for him, then." The harried tone was back in his voice. "I've got to take off pretty soon. Watch yourself, okay?"

"I always watch myself," Carter said. "Thanks, Johnny." He put the phone down slowly.

Hastings? He was big enough to make it worth Pacific Bio's time, and he had access to every patrol schedule. Through Delgado? Maybe his dislike of Carter hadn't been due to his unexpected promotion. Maybe Hastings had been worried that Carter was a plant, sent to spy. Had he been worried enough to shoot him full of drugs and ask? Whoever had grabbed him from the base had learned the schedules and routes to a T. Or had been wearing a uniform.

And Greely could be the local connection. That fit, too, no matter what Nita wanted to believe. Cold inside, Carter touched numbers on his phone. This connection *was* a video link. His neutral smile felt stiff as a clay mask on his face.

The general scowled from Carter's screen. "Colonel? Anything wrong?"

"I don't know, sir." Carter frowned, watching Hastings's expression. "I have some news that I thought you should hear. A trucker claims that new fields are going in down in the Willamette Valley."

"They're not." Hastings frowned. "The farms are hurting for enough water to keep the crops up off the ground as it is. You know how truckers talk. Is that all?"

"I didn't believe it either," Carter said quickly. "Not at first. But the woman involved says that she can give me proof. If she can, then there's a cover-up going on. A big one, and we're being had. I think it's worth looking into, sir."

"Proof changes things." Hastings grunted. "What kind of proof did she have, and who is it?"

He seemed genuinely surprised, but that could be an act. "The trucker is a woman named Warren, sir. She . . . didn't have the proof with her."

"Renny Warren?" Hastings snorted dismissively. "She owns the land Greely works and she's one of the biggest black-market operators in the Northwest. Renny Warren is slick enough to keep her ass out of jail, but I wouldn't call her trustworthy. Not by a long shot."

"I see." Carter frowned. Another link to Dan Greely.

"I guess I can't blame you for being taken in." Hastings reached for something out of range of the video pickup. "You didn't know the connection. Did she tell you what she had?"

"No, sir. She's supposed to bring it to me," Carter said briskly. "I'll call you when I get it."

"If it checks out, call me. Don't bother me otherwise." He scowled, his expression faintly contemptuous. "I don't need to waste my time on a wild-goose chase. I didn't think you had the time to waste, either. I'm glad you have everything under control out there."

Fuck you, too. "With the general's indulgence, I am respectfully requesting permission to pursue this matter," Carter said through clenched teeth. It would be very easy to believe that Hastings was pulling the strings. Did you sell us out, General? "I think it matters, sir."

"Do what you want." Hastings made a chopping gesture with one hand. "Just don't let any of those damn locals hole that Pipe. You got it?"

"Yes, sir." Carter broke the connection. So Nita's source of information had a direct connection to Greely. Carter leaned his chin on his hands and stared moodily at the blank screen. All threads in this tangled web led smack to Dan Greely. Either he was the center of all this . . . or Nita was telling the truth and Dan had been solidly and carefully framed.

By whom? Hastings? Doubt nagged at Carter. If he was behind this, wouldn't he act friendlier—try to allay any suspicions Carter might have? He was almost asking Carter to suspect him.

Maybe he was just a bastard.

It occurred to Carter that he wouldn't shed many tears if Hastings ended up in a court-martial.

CHAPTER NINETEEN ☆

Nita walked down the hall from Carter's office, her shoulders drooping. Jeremy was sitting on the floor near the main door, with Rachel asleep on his shoulder. "I don't need your gift to know that we locals aren't very popular here." He got to his feet, careful not to disturb Rachel.

His unspoken question hummed in the air. "I didn't tell him," she snapped. "So just drop it, okay?"

"I didn't say anything," Jeremy said mildly.

Nita pressed her lips together, took Rachel from him, and tucked her into her sling. He wouldn't have believed me! she wanted to yell at him. It wouldn't have made any difference!

He might have believed. And then he would have known that Dan was innocent.

And he would know about her.

Jeremy was disappointed. Nita stalked toward the gate, furious: at Jeremy, at Carter for his damn doubts, at herself for being afraid. She almost welcomed the hostility of the uniformed men and women around them. It reinforced her anger, made it burn brighter and hotter. The guard took their passes, his eyes cold, and waved them through.

"Now what?" Jeremy leaned on his stick, struggling to keep up with her fast pace. "What next?"

"He wants proof that Dan's not involved." She didn't slow down, didn't look back at him. "I have to prove that the new fields exist. I have to go talk to Renny Warren."

"The trucker? I've heard of her. She'll be at the plaza, if she's in town."

"She won't help me," Nita said bitterly. Jeremy's knees were hurting him and she finally slowed down, teeth on edge from his pain. "She doesn't like Dan."

185

"You can figure out how to persuade her."

"What do you *want* from me?" Nita swung to face him. "Why can't you just lay off?"

Rachel woke up with a jerk and began to cry, kicking her feet and squirming in the sling.

"No!" Nita shook her. "Not you, too. No, do you hear me, I can't stand it!" She turned and ran. The stony ground jarred her feet and sweat stung her eyes, muddy with dust, salty as tears. Rachel screamed and struggled in her sling. Sobbing for breath, Nita finally staggered into the shade of the culvert. "I'm sorry, honey." She scooped her shrieking daughter into her arms. "I'm so sorry—I love you," she gasped, burying her face against her daughter's rigid body. "I do. Rachel, honey, stop crying. It's all right." Only it wasn't all right, and it would never be all right, not as long as she lived.

A green dragonfly popped into the air above Rachel's angry face.

"Go away," Nita whispered.

"No." Jeremy leaned against the wall beside her, sad. "I remember when our milk goat had a crippled kid. From the water or the dust, my dad said. That kind of thing happens a lot out in the Dry. Deformities and . . . strangeness. The doctor in La Grande had a name for it: water deprivation–induced zoonoses."

Slowly Rachel's angry wails subsided into hiccoughing sobs. She reached for the dragonfly, batting at it irritably at first, then grabbing for it with a tentative smile.

"I don't want to believe that it's the Dry that causes people like you or me to be born," Jeremy said softly. "I don't want us to be a bunch of dust-induced mutations. What if we're the first sign of change? What if the whole human race is . . . adapting somehow? So that we can live with what's happening, instead of killing ourselves and the land trying to fight it?"

"What does it matter, *why*?" Nita said bitterly. "What difference does it make?"

Jeremy sighed and laid a gentle hand on her shoulder. "Dad said that crippled goat kid wasn't worth the water it would drink. It would never get around very well—never be much use. So he took it out to the garden. He cut its throat with the big knife from the kitchen. He held it over a hill of beans, so that its blood watered the plants. I want us to be *hope*, Nita. Not mistakes."

Nita looked sideways at the thick, gentle fingers on her shoulder. His swollen, twisted knees hurt—they hurt all the time. How much farm work had he been able to do? His father had thought about that knife when he was born. Jeremy knew it, and that knowing resonated through his words. Nita closed her eyes, shivering. "I love Rachel," she whispered. "No matter what she is."

"Do you?" Jeremy turned her gently around to face him. "If you don't accept yourself, you'll never really be able to accept Rachel. *You'll* be afraid of *her*."

"That's not true!"

"Isn't it? Ask yourself, Nita, and listen to the answer." He sighed. "Are you going to go see Renny Warren now?"

"Am I going to try to manipulate her into helping Dan, do you mean?"

"Yes."

"I was afraid." Nita hugged her daughter close. "I wanted to tell Carter—it would help Dan. Carter would have listened, I should have done it, but . . . I couldn't."

"Do you love him?" Jeremy asked softly. "Is that it?"

"Yes," she whispered, and shuddered violently.

Jeremy put his arms around her, sad for her, sad for what would happen when she finally had to tell Carter.

"Let's go find Renny Warren." Nita straightened. "Right now." She pulled her sunscarf from her pack and draped it over her shoulder to shade her daughter's face. "I could never be afraid of you," she whispered fiercely. "Never."

Rachel yawned and Nita held her close, sweat soaking through her shirt like blood. The sun was still high overhead. Shadows were no more than slivers of darkness at the base of rocks, and the whitewashed walls of the Plaza Inn glared white in the harsh light as Nita approached. The faded red roof of the building had a scabby look. Fallen tiles littered the cracked asphalt beneath the eaves, and four semi rigs with triple and quadruple trailers baked in the asphalt lot.

"They look so shiny," Nita murmured. "As if they've just been polished."

"They probably have been." Jeremy eyed the glittering chrome and black of the nearest truck. "Truckers wash their rigs all the time. It's a symbol. You're doing pretty badly if you can't afford the water to keep your rig clean."

Nita looked at her distorted reflection in the gleaming door of the cab beside her. Washed with water. She remembered the precious minutes spent in Carter's shower and wrestled with outrage. How did they wash these monsters? Coiled hoses hung on the side of the building. There was a tap on the wall, too, safely caged away inside a locked metal-mesh enclosure. Did they uncoil the hoses and spray gallons and gallons of water across the trucks, then let it evaporate in the sun? Nita tried to guess how much it would take to wash a single truck. Enough to wash diapers for Rachel for a month? Enough to wash them every time, instead of putting them out in the sun to dry until the smell got too bad? A puddle had collected beneath one of the hoses inside the enclosure. Nita's toes twitched with the desire to walk through it, to feel the tickle of sun-warmed water splashing across her dusty skin.

"That's awful," she breathed. "How *can* they?"

"I wouldn't talk like that in front of Renny." Jeremy smiled faintly. "Truckers have their own values. They can be a little . . . touchy."

Jeremy was thirsty, Nita could feel it, but the wasted water and the spotless trucks didn't bother him. Nita frowned, shifting Rachel into a more comfortable position on her hip. Sometimes it seemed as if Jeremy had no real allegiances. He could be friends with Dan and Carter and the truckers with their wasted water, because none of it really affected him. And that was it— it *didn't* affect him. His green past was as real to him as this dusty present, and he was caught between them, trapped by his visions. Nita touched his hand lightly, pierced by sudden comprehension. He was *alone*.

"This way." Jeremy took her hand, his smile warming his pale eyes. "Only the cops use the front door." He pulled open a gray metal door with no markings. Cool air rushed out, chilly enough to make Nita gasp. "The rigs have good air-conditioning. Truckers like it cool." Jeremy ushered her into a dimly lit, windowless hallway. Doors opened in the dirty pastel walls every few feet. Metal or plastic numbers had been pried off the panels, leaving ghostly images behind. The magenta carpet underfoot was stained and the air smelled of dust and dirty clothes.

"You know a lot about truckers." Nita looked apprehensively down the hallway.

"I keep moving. Someone always figures out the projector scam sooner or later, so I don't stay long in any one place." Jeremy shrugged as he led her down the hallway. "I ride with truckers a lot. Some of them pair up, but you cut your profits that way, so they mostly drive solo. They're bored and lonely, so they'll trade miles for a little entertainment. They like my makings. I don't have too much trouble getting around."

"Truckers waste water."

"They drive through the Dry because it takes too much fuel

to go around it. Big convoys are usually pretty safe, but sometimes they cross with just a couple of rigs or even alone, if the
pay is big enough. Hijackers get some. Breakdowns get some.''

"Okay.'' Nita let her breath out. "I'll stop bitching. Maybe
Renny'll let me sit on the hood of her truck next time she washes
it.''

"Don't even ask.''

A door opened suddenly and a man stuck his bearded head out
into the hallway. "You lookin' for someone?'' he asked casually.

It wasn't a casual question. "Renny,'' Nita blurted out quickly.
"Renny Warren. She said she was staying here.''

"Did she?'' The man's deepset eyes moved slowly from Nita
to Jeremy and back again. "You friends o' hers?''

"Nita is.'' Jeremy nodded at her. "You're Wasser, aren't you?
You gave me a ride from 'Frisco up to Portland a few months
back.''

The man's face went still for a moment; then his thick lips
smiled in the carefully trimmed nest of his reddish beard. "I
remember you,'' he said. "The guy with the butterflies. How
ya takin' it?''

"As it comes.'' Jeremy shrugged. "You?''

"Same.'' The man jerked his head down the hall. "Renny's
on this floor. Second from the end. Take it easy.'' His maned
head disappeared and the door closed softly.

"I think he had a gun. In his hand, where we couldn't see
it.'' Nita looked at the closed door and shivered.

"Probably. Truckers don't kid around. You don't wander
through here unless you're invited. Come on.''

Second door from the end. Nita took a deep breath and tapped
softly. Renny hadn't scared her at the house. Down here, in this
dim, dirty corridor, her pulse fluttered.

"Yeah?'' The gemstones winked in Renny's ear as she peered
through the partly opened door. "Change your mind about digging dirt, babe? And who's this?'' Her eyes roved over Jeremy,
dismissed him.

"He's a friend of mine. Jeremy Barlow.'' Nita made no move
to touch the door. "Can I talk to you, Renny? It's important.''

"Why not? I'm awake and I've got nothing better to do.''
Renny opened the door wide with a single, tight swing.

Nita walked past the muzzle of the small automatic in Renny's
hand. For some reason, Renny's gun wasn't as frightening as
the gun in the hand of the bearded trucker. If Renny shot her,
she would kill her, Nita guessed, but Renny wouldn't pull the

trigger unless she was certain that she needed to. Nita looked around. She had expected more of the corridor's grime. Instead, the room was light and clean. An expensive holo-video combination stood on a chest of drawers made of what looked like real wood. A luxurious bed took up most of the floor space. A couple of upholstered chairs and a small, round table crowded between a heavily draped window and the bed. Yellow light from the ceiling fixture warmed the rich colors of bedspread, rug and walls. After the corridor, the luxury took Nita's breath away.

"So tell me, babe. Why the visit?"

Nita sat down in the chair Renny indicated, trying to gather her thoughts. Jeremy had seated himself on the far corner of the bed, obviously staying out of the way. "I wanted to know more about the new fields down in the Valley," she said. "The ones you mentioned at the house."

"Why?" Renny was suddenly wary.

Nita frowned, thinking fast as she bounced a chuckling Rachel in her lap. "The Corps cut the water flow in the gorge. They said they had to do it to keep Valley crops from dying." She looked at the trucker from beneath her lashes. Renny was leaning against the dresser, arms crossed, frowning a little. She wasn't angry or even very curious. The yellow light struck sparks from the chains around her neck and a trace of sleepy lust hung in the air. "I think someone's running a scam," Nita ventured.

"So? Danny's got you playing politics after all, huh?" Renny's eyes flicked Nita like a whip. "Danny likes power games."

Now what? "Dan's out of the picture," Nita said in the mildest tone of regret. "He got himself arrested."

"Did he?" Hot emotion flashed and faded behind Renny's benign look of surprise. "So why the interest in the irrigation water?" She raised one eyebrow.

This time it was a serious question. "Leverage comes in handy sometimes." Nita smiled at the wiry trucker. "I thought *I* might try a career in local politics. The time seems right."

"While Danny's in jail, you mean? You're a sharp little bitch, aren't you?" Renny's laugh filled the room, too large for the small woman. "So good-hearted Danny took an operator under his wing, did he?" She grinned at Nita. "By the time he gets his ass out of jail, you'll have his perch on top of this shit pile all sewed up?"

Approval. Renny understood this kind of move. Nita gave her a small, sleek smile. "I need to know who's getting a cut from those new fields," she said softly.

"That *would* be worth something. You'll own someone's ass. Myself, I can't see why you want to bother with this dumpy town, but that's your business." Renny crossed her ankles and leaned back, sure of herself, sure of Nita now. "What's my cut?" she asked.

Nothing for free. Not from this woman. Nita made a show of considering.

"How about Danny?" Renny said softly.

Nita shrugged, listening hard to the resonances behind the trucker's words. Careful . . . "Sure." She made her voice casual, put *casual* into the slant of her shoulders and the curve of her spine. "Tell me how and when." She felt Jeremy's twitch of reaction. You wanted me to play this game, she thought sullenly. Shut up.

Renny was watching her, debating, trying to decide if Nita was acting or not. Nita wiped a thread of drool from the corner of Rachel's mouth, then wiped her finger on her pants.

"Hell." Renny snapped her fingers dismissively. "Danny'll dig his own grave. He's been working at it for years. No, I don't think I'll let you off the hook that easily."

Nita felt the slow heat of Renny's smile and her skin prickled. That lust hadn't been directed at Jeremy.

"We'll make it an IOU, babe. Deal?"

"That's too vague."

"Take it or leave it."

"I want to be able to say no when you turn it in." Nita winced at the bite of Renny's irritation.

"Forget it, babe." Renny yawned.

She'd fucked up once today already. If she didn't get the proof . . . "All right. An IOU." Nita drew a shaky breath, skin tingling with Renny's interest. "But you have to deliver something I can use. Concrete proof."

"No problem, babe." Renny gripped Nita's hand. She was smiling, full of creamy satisfaction, ready to be generous. "So what do you need? Names? Title transfers? All the sneaky little back-door connections?"

"Everything." Nita let her breath out in a rush. "In hardcopy."

"Like I said, no problem." Renny shrugged, made a flicking motion with her fingers. "I know a lady in Portland who's hot on a terminal. She'll dig up everything you need. No one hides *shit* from Lydia."

"Great." Nita stood, settling Rachel on her hip. "When can you get it for me?"

"*We'll* leave right now." The wiry trucker grinned at her. "I've got half a load for the city already. That's enough to pay expenses. Why wait?"

We? "How do I get back here?" Nita fished for Rachel's beads, trying to hide her unease.

"Babe, you can hop a ride anywhere you want. Even with the kid." Renny sounded dryly amused. "But I might pick up an eastbound load, and if I don't, I'll find you someone who owes me a favor." She grinned. "That way you don't have to pay on your back. A little gift from me. You're bringing the kid, right? With those boobs, you got to be nursing." Renny eyed Rachel. "She's not going to scream the whole way, is she?"

Nita shook her head, then looked at Jeremy. "Would you stay up at the house for me?" she asked him. "If the beans don't get watered tomorrow, they'll wilt."

"Sure." Jeremy nodded. "I've worked beans before."

"You got a half hour." Renny opened the door. "I've got to pick up my stuff and warm up the rig."

Jeremy walked past her, out into the grimy hall. Nita followed him outside and around to the front door of the inn, the entrance that only the cops used.

"You did good." Jeremy squatted in the meager shade.

"I did what you wanted me to, didn't I? I listened to her. I gave her what she wanted to hear." Nita stared out into the hot splash of sunlight on concrete, her skin still tight with Renny's hunger. "What happens if I say no to her IOU?"

"It wouldn't be a good idea," Jeremy said reluctantly. "Truckers back each other up."

Nita thought of the bearded trucker with his aura of violence and shivered. A big engine growled a bass note in the parking lot. Renny, already? Nita swallowed a knot of apprehension, gathered Rachel into her arms, and stood up. "I hope this satisfies Carter," she said bitterly. "I hope it satisfied you."

"I'll meet you at the house," Jeremy said as the snout of the black and chrome truck appeared around the corner. He squeezed her arm briefly. "Good luck."

At least he hadn't reminded her that she could have saved herself this by telling Carter up front about her ability. As Renny swung the door open, Nita swallowed her worry, tucked Rachel into her sling, and clambered up into the high cab.

Renny sat in a padded seat—the only seat. Embroidered cushions, a tiny kitchen unit, shelves, and cupboards turned the rest of the cab into a plush—if cramped—living space. Nita looked apprehensively at the gleaming bank of gauges and buttons on the dash as she settled herself gingerly on the carpeted floor beside Renny's seat.

"Relax, babe." Renny ran a blunt-nailed finger down Nita's arm, her eyes glinting with amusement. "You scared of me or the truck? I don't collect till I deliver your dirt, so you're safe till then."

Needling again. Nita lifted her chin and managed a smile. "I've never been in a truck, that's all. It's . . . amazing."

She didn't have to pretend awe. She could feel the power vibrating through the cab, but it was quiet inside, so cool that her skin had gone tight and bumpy. She brushed her palm across the thick crimson carpet. The dashboard was paneled in what looked like real wood. Nita touched the satiny finish, tracing the rich grain. Silver winked at her from knobs and the rims of gauges. Needles quivered and green numbers flashed.

"You got your mouth hanging open like a native, babe."

"I can't help it."

Renny tossed her head. "Take a good look—she's a sweet rig. I won't waste power specs on you, but it's one of the best on the road. Custom design. If the kid gets sleepy, you can put her on the futon back there. Don't let her piss on it."

"I've got diapers on her—" Nita gasped as the truck suddenly swerved. She fell against the door, grabbing for Rachel.

"What the hell?" Renny snarled. The truck swerved again. "What's that bastard trying to do? If he scrapes my fender, I'll run him flat."

Clutching the door, Nita peered through the windshield. A battered van was crowding the truck, forcing Renny to steer close to the rough shoulder of the highway.

"Duck," Renny yelled, and hunched down.

Bits of glass stung Nita's face and she heard a sound like a backfire as she crouched over Rachel.

"The fucker's shooting at us." Bent low, Renny clutched the wheel.

The truck shuddered and lurched. Renny was cursing in a continuous monotone, her voice barely audible over the roar of wind and engine noise. More glass stung Nita's neck and she gasped at a white explosion of shock. I'm hit, she thought, and then: It's Renny. Rachel began to scream as the truck swerved again. Nita caught a flicker of cold, focused hatred, lost it. That wasn't Renny. She recognized that hatred. The cab shuddered and metal crunched. A wreck? Renny gave a wordless cry as another impact shook the truck, but there was triumph in her tone.

It was over, whatever was going on. They weren't going to crash. Nita raised her head cautiously, trying to soothe her screaming daughter. Vibrations shook the cab, but they were still moving, still on the highway. Renny clutched the wheel with both hands, her face set and white, eyes squinted against the dust in the air. More holes pocked the window in Renny's door, and blood soaked her left sleeve.

"I ran the fuckers off the road," Renny said between clenched teeth. "Good thing they were so low. Door's bulletproof and you can't hit much anyway, shooting up. A 'jacker would've sprayed the windshield and we'd have gone off for sure."

"Stop," Nita said. "You're bleeding."

"I noticed, babe." Renny bared her teeth. "But I don't think they went off fast enough to do serious damage. We'll stop down the road."

Her arm was beginning to hurt with a hot, grinding pain. Nita clenched her teeth. Rachel was still screaming, squirming with Renny's pain. Nita soothed her daughter as best she could, and used her sunscarf to block the holes in the windshield so that Renny didn't get too much dust in her face. Renny didn't stop until they reached the Mosier detour. Once off the interstate, she pulled over onto the shoulder of the two-lane road, struggling one-handed with the wheel. The truck finally jolted to a halt and Renny leaned back against the seat, her face white.

"I want the medical kit from that top storage cupboard," she said. "There's a gun under the seat. Get that first."

Nita put the crying Rachel onto the futon and found a squat rifle in a concealed holster beside Renny's seat. She handed it to Renny, then took down the green plastic box of medical supplies.

"You handle the gun if I pass out. It's full auto." Renny opened one eye. "Nine millimeter; not much kick. Point it and pull the trigger. Don't swing it around—aim steady and you'll probably hit something. Safety's there."

"Let's hope they don't show." Nita carefully set the gun down on the floor and opened the box.

Renny carried a lot of medical supplies. Nita fumbled through bandages and surgical instruments, vials of antibiotics, painkillers and stimulants. This was all black-market stuff, worth a small fortune. This was where the antibiotics on Dan's shelf had come from. She looked nervously down the road, but saw no sign of the van. She reached for Renny's injured arm.

"I'll take care of it." Renny slapped her hand away. "Give me those scissors."

"Shut up and sit *still*." Nita clenched her teeth against Renny's pain. "I'm doing it." She began to cut away Renny's blood-soaked sleeve. "What pills do you need to take?"

"You're a gutsy little bitch. You'd better do a damn good job." Renny swallowed a groan as Nita swabbed the wound with disinfectant. "I'll need the white tablets for infection and two of those orange capsules for pain," she mumbled through tight lips. "They're loaded with meth, so I won't nod off. Custom mix."

"The bullet went through," Nita said over Rachel's cries. "It's bleeding pretty badly." She dug her fingers into Renny's armpit to compress the main artery. Out in the hills, you learned how to deal with injuries; David had taught her. Nita pressed a fresh gauze pad against the ugly exit wound, feeling relieved as the bleeding slowed.

The orange capsules worked fast to dull Renny's pain. Rachel finally stopped screaming and fell into instant, exhausted sleep. Feeling shaky herself, Nita finished cleaning the wound and bandaged Renny's arm. Blood had run down Nita's arm to her elbows, had dripped onto her worn jeans. She taped the bandage in place, wiped her hands, and began to put the supplies away. Renny looked better, not so pale.

"Nice job." Renny managed a faint grin. "I was right. You wouldn't make a half-bad trucker." She pushed her door open and slid awkwardly to the ground. "Look at my rig." She glared at the crumpled skin of the truck's gleaming fender. "I'd like to get my hands on the bastards. Do you know who they were?" Her good hand locked on Nita's wrist.

"I . . . think so." Now that it was over, Nita's hands wanted to tremble. "It was a Major Delgado in the van. From the base. It's because of the fields. He doesn't want me to get that proof. I'm sorry, Renny."

"You gave me his name. We're even." Renny's eyes were cold. "Don't worry. You'll get your proof, babe. You just make damn sure you twist someone good with it." She touched the bandage on her arm, flexed her fingers, and winced. "Let's go," she said as she swung herself into the cab. "I want to get to Portland before those caps wear off. There's some fiber tape in that cupboard. You can patch the windshield while we drive. Leave the gun where you can reach it."

CHAPTER TWENTY ☆

Carter left his office and went down to Operations, needing to be there in person. He had taken a risk, leaving the Shunt valves with a single guard, even for half an hour. The safe thing would have been to deny Corporal Roscoe's request, to have had him wait until the relief detail showed up, and only then gone after the sniper. But by then he would have vanished. It had happened a dozen times already.

So he had taken the risk. Carter paused outside the big double doors, wondering if he'd let himself get infected by Delgado's blood lust. Partly. He had to admit it. He wanted to get his hands on the people who had been twisting him and the Corps. And partly he wanted to get hold of someone who would know if Dan Greely was part of this or not. He'd *wring* it out of the bastard, if he had to.

Nita claimed Dan was innocent. Carter shook his head, remembering the ferocity of their kiss, tasting her on his lips.

He couldn't afford to believe her.

He couldn't afford to believe Dan Greely.

He couldn't afford to believe *anybody*. Except maybe Johnny.

The comm link at his belt beeped. The major's voice came over the link. "Delgado, here. The relief team was ambushed, just west of the Shunt. Roscoe called in for support. We've got casualties."

So the war had finally started. Carter felt cold. "I want that squad rolling now," he said harshly. "Major?"

"Sir?"

"*No* local people on this mission. Pass it on to the unit's CO."

"Yes, sir," Delgado said briskly. "We're rolling."

"You stay," Carter snapped. No way Delgado went out on this one. "I'm taking it."

"Sir?"

Carter slapped the link back onto his belt. Too late to weep now. Soldiers were down. Worry about blame later. He ducked into Operations, where Major Bybee gave him the all-clear. No problem with the flow—not yet. He left Operations almost at a run and burst out into the baking afternoon heat. The squad was riding two of the battalion's new AAVs—armored and able to take any dry terrain. The captain in charge saluted and Carter returned it as he scanned the troops. His eyes narrowed and he veered around to the rear of the nearer truck. "Private Wasson?"

"Sir." The private's sandy head jerked up as she snapped him a salute.

"You're off this assignment. Get out."

"Sir?" Her face flushed. "You can't do that. Captain Westerly . . ."

"You heard me," Carter snapped. He'd deal with Westerly later. "Move it, Private."

Face sullen, she climbed down. The first vehicle was already pulling out and the grunts on this one were looking carefully elsewhere. Wasson yanked her rifle out of the truck bed and stalked away, her shoulders rigid.

"Sir?" Westerly saluted, her face tight.

"Later." Carter cut her off. "Let's go, Captain." She hadn't expected him to come along, and looked for one instant as if she were going to protest. Her salute was razor sharp, but her eyes were almost as sullen as Wasson's. Carter swung himself up into a seat without returning it, angry at Westerly, angry at himself. He'd handled that badly, but hell, there hadn't been time to handle it any other way.

The grunts behind him were silent. Because he was there. "This is a hell of a situation," Carter said. "We're supposed to be running water, not shooting people." The AAV lurched forward and he grabbed for a handhold.

"I'm tired of getting shot at and taking it." The low voice was just audible.

Carter could feel the sudden stillness all around him. "You think I'm pretty soft on the hicks, don't you?" Carter looked back, picked out the dark-haired kid who'd spoken. A private— Carter read his name, Andy Stakowski. "They can shoot us a hell of a lot easier than we can shoot them. You think about that, Private." The kid looked angry. He was, what—nineteen? Twenty? "If that Pipe leaks, we have to go out and fix it. That makes us sitting ducks. If a war starts, we'll lose it. But we'll take out the bastards who are shooting at us. In spades.''

"You said it," someone whispered from farther back.

Carter watched the walls of the gorge slide past. They were all scared. *We're not combat troops*, he thought bitterly. People joined the Corps to design lifts, or watchdog flow turbulence, or run a dozer. It was easy to think *hick*—a faceless enemy you could shoot at. It would be something else to look through your sights out there and recognize the guy who sold your kids' shoes. The vehicle rocked as it hit a stretch of bad pavement, throwing him back against someone's shins. "Sorry." Carter glanced over his shoulder to find himself looking into the young private's face.

"It's a rough ride, sir." He hesitated, blushing red again. "I'm sorry, sir. About what I said."

"It's okay," Carter said. "We got people down out there. Let's get to them." The kid's eyes were bright with excitement, and Carter wondered if he'd even heard what Carter had been saying. He was ready to be a hero. *It's not like the videos,* Carter wanted to tell him. *People scream when they get shot. They shit when they die.* He would never forget the stink of blood and bowel as they'd picked up the bodies in Chicago. Dead bodies bloated fast in the heat.

The rattle of automatic weapons echoed back and forth between the walls of the gorge, coming from everywhere and nowhere. The AAV was slowing and Carter's stomach clenched. "Keep your heads down," he yelled as he leaped from the back of the still-rolling truck. "Scatter and get under cover. If they're up on the rim, we're easy targets."

He landed lightly as the rest of the troops piled out. The men and women hit the ground running, scrambling for whatever cover they could find. Roscoe was waving from a jumbled pile of rocks near the bottom of the riverbed.

"They're in the bunker," the corporal yelled. Another short burst of weapons fire rattled down the gorge. "They've got Uzis, sounds like."

Doing *what* in the bunker? "We've got to get some people close enough to lob in gas." Carter crouched beside Westerly. "Send one team around to the north, another along the Deschutes side of the bunker. If they can come up on it from behind, they can get in pretty close under cover. We'll keep the bastards busy up front."

"Yes, sir." Westerly scuttled away, crouched low.

It might already be too late. It wouldn't take much to wreck the automatic valves. Carter snatched his comm link from his belt.

"Operations. Major Bybee here."

"This is Colonel Voltaire. Any trouble?"

"Negative, sir. It's running fine."

"We've got intruders in the Shunt bunker. Put an override on all manual control." Worst-case scenarios unrolled like a bad movie in his brain. "Get ready to shut the flow down fast. Call me on my link if anything shows up on the boards." He thumbed off the link and scrambled down the slope toward Roscoe's rock. A Corps 4×4 lay on its side at the bottom of the bed; Carter thought he could see a body behind the wheel. Corporal Roscoe, a light-skinned black man with a long, bony face, reached for Carter as he got close and pulled him down behind the shelter of the dusty boulder.

"I'm sure glad to see you," he said fervently. "Our relief team walked straight into an ambush."

Carter looked past him. Another body lay in the sun—a dark-haired woman.

"The hicks were waiting for them, sir." Roscoe's eyelids flickered. "Lopez and I were up on the rim, sir. We couldn't do anything. Lopez got it when we tried for the truck. They were already in the bunker, sir. Amesworth was there." His shoulders jerked.

Ten to one Amesworth was dead, too. Carter put a hand on the corporal's arm. He slithered around the side of the boulder to peer up at the bunker. It's concrete walls gleamed white in the glare. If one of the teams he'd sent out could get gas in there, they'd have them. He'd have salvaged that much from this mess. Carter looked back up the bank. His people had spread out over the rocky slope of the riverbed. Sporadic bursts of gunfire rattled down the gorge—all Corps fire. They were keeping the bastards busy, as ordered. Carter's jaw tightened as two new vehicles pulled up along the highway. Media. Who the hell had called them? He reached for his link again. "Any trouble?" he asked Operations.

"Negative," the tiny electonic voice told him. "Thumbs up. We've locked out the manual controls."

Carter frowned as he replaced his link. "I haven't heard any more shots from the bunker. I wonder if they sneaked back into the Deschutes bed. They'd be out of sight from this angle. I don't like it." Carter was full of a growing uneasiness. "They had plenty of time to screw up the Shunt before we got here. What are they up to?''

"Colonel?" Roscoe cleared his throat. "They knew every move we were making out here. I think someone set us up, sir. Someone from the base . . ."

Yeah, and called in the media to come watch the action.

An explosion cut off their words, roaring through the gorge like a vast roll of thunder. A fist of concussion slammed Carter flat. Rocks and dirt showered down, some chunks big enough to hurt. Ears ringing, blinded by dust, Carter wondered why the thunder of the blast didn't stop. It went on and on and its low, hissing rumble shook the ground. Dazed, blinking, he lifted his head, caught a glimpse of brown movement, as if the riverbed itself had risen and was sliding toward them. With a flash of horror he realized what he was seeing.

Water.

They'd blown the Pipeline and a wall of water was rushing down the riverbed. Carter staggered to his feet. "Up to the road," he yelled hoarsely. "Move it!"

Captain Roscoe was already scrambling up the slope. Carter started after him and nearly tripped over a limp body. It was the private. The kid. His face was bloody, and he groaned as Carter hauled him to his feet. Carter slung the kid's arm across his shoulder and staggered as the first rush of water hit them. Debris rode a crest of dirty foam, tugging at him with incredible force. Why the hell didn't they shut down the flow? The flood washed higher, shoving the barely conscious private against him.

This water was no illusion. Carter went down on one knee under the weight of the boy's body and the water seized him, cold and chest deep. Something slammed into his side and pain blazed through him. He couldn't stand up . . . arm was numb. The flood sucked him backward and he stifled a cry as cold water closed over his head. Stand up, he told himself, but the kid's body twisted in his grip, dragging him deeper. Carter's foot scraped the bottom, then slipped off. They were rolling, tumbling down the riverbed. He slammed against a rock and a spear of new pain blasted the air from his lungs. His mouth filled with water and his lungs spasmed as he struggled not to cough, not to breathe.

Let go, his brain screamed at him. Let go and you can make it. But his fingers had turned to stone, locked into the fabric of the kid's coverall. The fire in his lungs was going to win in a minute, and he'd have to breathe. One more kick. His legs felt heavy and weak, but his toe caught a rock and shoved him a few inches forward.

A hand closed on his hair. Fingers dug into his armpit and Carter's head broke water. He sucked in a blessed, agonized breath, choked on water, and gagged. Sunlight dazzled him, turned the world to a blinding kaleidoscope of silver light. Someone was yelling. The hands locked under his armpits, dragging him higher, out of the cold clutch of the water and onto the welcome heat of the rocks. Carter took another breath and cried out as pain knifed through him.

"Keep working on him," someone said loudly. "Got a pulse yet?"

Of course I have a pulse, Carter wanted to say, but it hurt just to breathe. He coughed and the world went gray and fuzzy. Hurt. He coughed again and groaned, sucking in the searing, wonderful air.

A face moved into view, blocking out the glare of light. "You're the biggest fish I've ever caught." Johnny gave him a faint grin. "The only one, for that matter. Not bad for a beginner." Water dripped from his hair, running down his face.

"What the hell?" Carter whispered.

"I showed up with the cavalry. Or the media, as the case may be. Not too many people can drown in a dry riverbed, but you sure tried hard. They shut the flow off upstream, by the way." Johnny's face looked pale in spite of his flip tone. "It was something, seeing water in the river. Scared the shit out of me, if you want to know."

"Thanks." Carter forced the word out through the pain that clogged his chest.

"Any time." Johnny looked across Carter and his face got grave.

Carter heard the murmurs. The kid. The voice had been talking about his pulse. Carter tried to look, but when he moved, pain filled his vision with wavering black spots.

"Take it easy," Johnny soothed. "They're going to bring a stretcher down for you in a minute."

"Did he make it?" Carter didn't need Johnny's headshake. He had heard the answer in the hushed voices. Damn, damn, damn. He closed his eyes, tears of anger burning beneath his lids. He had held on to him. He hadn't let go and that should have counted. It should have fucking *mattered*.

It seemed to take a small eternity for a medical team to arrive from the base and struggle down the bank with their equipment.

Shaded from the sun by a makeshift awning rigged from a shirt, Carter watched the mud dry in the riverbed. The saboteurs had vanished, had probably set the charges and slipped up the Deschutes bed. The blast had shattered the multiple pipes where they entered the Shunt complex. The emergency system should have shut down the flow the moment the pressure dropped, but it hadn't. Something was wrong about that, but pain fogged Carter's brain and he couldn't think straight.

"How're you doing, Colonel?" One of the paramedics bent over Carter, settling a metal-framed stretcher beside him. "We're going to move you in a minute, okay?" His face looked grim. "Just lie still and let us do it all." He wrapped a blood-pressure cuff around Carter's arm, pumped it tight, frowned at the dial, then nodded. "All right." He slid his arms beneath Carter's hips and upper legs. "One, two . . ."

Carter felt more arms beneath his back, felt someone else supporting his head and neck.

"Three."

They slid him sideways onto the hot plastic padding of the stretcher. Carter had been prepared for pain, but something *moved* inside him. Bone grated across bone, and sickness welled up in his belly.

Oh, shit, I'm going to throw up, Carter thought, and passed out.

CHAPTER TWENTY-ONE ☆

It wasn't bad as jail cells went, Dan thought. He'd been in worse. Lying on his back on the narrow bed, he stared up at the ceiling and sighed. Someone had gone to a lot of trouble to fake those pictures. Carter would have dismissed that conveniently discovered wrench as the most blatant of planted clues—a nine-year-old could have seen through it—if it wasn't for those damn pictures. Dan rolled over onto his side, his leg muscles twitching with his desire to get up, pace the ten-by-ten space of his cell, do *something*.

Who had done the frame? And why? He kept coming back to those particular questions, hoping that something would shake loose. Nothing did. The people holing the Pipe and shooting at the uniforms weren't from The Dalles. He was pretty sure of that much, but someone was running a damned efficient operation. It could even be a uniform.

The most obvious candidate was Carter himself.

Except that this had started back when Watanabe had been CO. So Carter probably wasn't in on it—or at least he wasn't the central figure. He sure was swallowing the frame. It didn't help that he and Nita had something between them and he saw Dan as competition. Damn hormones, anyway. Sometimes they were more trouble than they were worth. Dan rolled off the bed, stood up, and stretched. Four bare walls, a bed, a toilet/sink, and a door with a sliding window and a slot for the meal trays. No clock, so he was measuring time by meals. Which made it evening—too early for him to be very sleepy. How many days until the U.S. Marshal collected him? He could get a lawyer then, might even make bail if it was set low enough. For now he was Corps property, which meant he sat here while Carter maybe made some major mistakes.

Carter might have listened if it hadn't been for those pictures. Dan balled his hand into a fist and pounded lightly on the bed-spread. The video eyes in the corners of the room watched him impassively. He scowled up at them, then let his breath out in a slow sigh. Time to pace again. Five steps to the wall, turn around, five steps back. Just do it for a while and tune out the brain. Only he couldn't tune it out—no matter that it didn't seem to be working too well these days.

The lock clicked and the door opened.

"Daniel Greely?" A round-faced man wearing a lieutenant's insignia jerked his head at Dan. "Out."

"Where are we going?"

The lieutenant shoved him against the wall without answering, jerked his arms behind his back, and handcuffed him roughly. The cuffs were too tight and Dan flexed his tingling fingers.

"Move."

A hand between his shoulder blades sent him stumbling forward. Halfway down the corridor, Dan stopped suddenly. Another corridor intersected the one they were in, and a uniformed body lay on the floor, facedown. Another uniformed man was just straightening up. Dan's eyes widened as he recognized the redhaired agitator. Yeah, this would complete the frame: bust him out of the Corps jail and it would be nailed tight. Carter wouldn't listen to a word he had to say.

Dan threw himself backward. The man behind him grunted and staggered as Dan's weight hit him. Dan twisted away, struggling for balance, started running back down the corridor. "Help," he yelled. "Someone help!" It was hard to run with his hands cuffed behind him. If he could make it back into the cell, maybe the video cameras would record the struggle, at least.

Footsteps pounded behind him. Five yards more . . . he wasn't going to make it . . . Dan grunted as a shoulder slammed into his back. He went down hard on his face, gasping as the floor slammed the breath from his lungs. His attacker was strad-dling him—a ton of weight on his back—pinning him to the floor. Dan tried to get his knees under him, but he couldn't do it. Hands clawed at his arm, pushing the sleeve of his shirt up. A sharp pain stabbed him—a needle. He tried to fight, but they were both holding him down.

The redhaired man grabbed a handful of Dan's hair, twisting his head back until he looked him in the face. "You're escaping, like it or not." He smiled down into Dan's eyes. "You and Hastings have been running quite a neat little scam. Voltaire will be impressed when he finds out."

"Help!" Dan croaked. Whatever they'd injected him with was kicking in. The corridor was going fuzzy around the edges, and warmth trickled through his veins, softening his muscles. A fog was rolling in, narrowing the corridor, blurring the man's face. Dan squinted, trying to bring him back into focus. "Bastard," he tried to say, but his tongue was thick and clumsy. He was going to end up like Sam, after all. A part of him had known for a long time now that it would happen this way. Dan felt a sudden sharp regret that he hadn't told Nita more about her father, because she needed to understand, because Sam had been a good man and a good friend. He struggled—one last fierce effort that levered his shoulders clear of the floor.

Then the fog closed in and floated him gently away.

CHAPTER TWENTY-TWO ☆

"Where exactly are we going?" Nita asked Renny. Bonneville was behind them. Up ahead the interstate curved away from the riverbed, veering west toward Portland.

"Lydia works for Pacific BioSystems—the big vat company." Renny concentrated on the road. "It's north of the city, out where the Willamette bed hits the Columbia."

"Oh." Nita shifted Rachel on her lap, dangling the beads for her daughter's clutch. Rachel batted at them, her face screwing up again, still cranky.

Because of Renny. Nita stared out the window, wishing she could deny it, wishing that it wasn't true. In places, the riverbed ran narrow and deep and steep cliffs leaned over the road, like curtains of stone. What did Jeremy see when he walked along this highway? Nita turned away from the window, cuddling her daughter who hurt with Renny's pain. Damn Jeremy, anyway. What did he want from her?

He wanted her ability to matter. Jeremy's dragonflies hadn't mattered to a father who had watered bean plants with blood. She wondered how close that knife had come to Jeremy's throat. Too close, she guessed. It had left a scar that would never heal. We sacrifice the unfit to the Dry, Nita thought: beans and beets to biomass bushes, goat kids to thirsty plants, a strangely talented child to the realities of dust and hunger. What was my father sacrificed to? she wondered bitterly. Water? Water is our god. No, drought is our god and we offer it water. And blood.

Jeremy and I aren't unfit. We are *different*.

She thought about the Robinson boy Seth had told her about, shivering at the memory of his hard, molten hatred as he had gently tried her door. They had thrown rocks at that child until he bled, until he ran crying out to die in the Dry. Nita shivered

206

as Rachel's hand closed over the beads, and she stroked her daughter's cheek lightly. What would she tell Rachel? What might Sam Montoya have told her, if he hadn't chosen to die for his town?

"This is our turn-off." Renny worked the wheel awkwardly, eased the rig off the wide asphalt lanes and onto a curving exit ramp.

There were a lot of cars on the road—more cars than Nita had ever seen at one time. They made her nervous as they whisked by. People could obviously afford fuel in the city. Nita had never been to Portland. The largest city she had visited had been Eugene. She hunched her shoulders, oppressed by the people. It was like a huge crowd murmuring, murmuring, all around her. The truck had exited onto a wide city street. Buildings, concrete, brick, or flaking metal, crowded the road. Up ahead, weathered machines crouched on an asphalt lot. Nita recognized a front-loader and tractors. Others were larger, their functions less comprehensible.

"This was an industrial district, years ago." Renny raised her voice to be heard over the engine noise admitted by the broken windows. "A couple of good mechanics still operate here, but the city bulldozed a lot of it for the camp."

The road curved sharply around a mound of rubble. The rubble had been shaped into a wall of gray, crumbled concrete, twisted metal, and debris. Orange electrified wire, strung on white plastic poles, topped it. Beyond the fence lay the camp. Originally it had been laid out as neat rows of barracks, spaced by wide streets. Now haphazard shacks, cobbled together from plastic, cardboard, and scraps of rusty siding, crowded the spaces between the buildings. Dark knots of humanity huddled in strips of shade, or the doorways of the shacks. A flock of naked children chased each other through the dust near the fence.

The government guaranteed water, housing, and basic medical care, if you needed it. You lived here if you had to take them up on it. Nita looked away. Despair drifted from the camp like the stench from a pit toilet. This was why Dan had driven down to the base to talk to Carter, Nita thought suddenly. People he knew—Sandy Corbett or Bob in the government store—might end up here. This camp had been here when her father was alive. Nita hoped suddenly and fervently that her restless, angry brother Ignacio wasn't in there.

That would have hurt her father more than anything else.

The rubble-and-wire fence ended and Renny shifted gears.

Nita was grateful when the dark echoes of the camp's occupants faded.

"This is the place." Renny braked, turned down a wide, new-looking street. "I'll park us behind the loading dock tonight, run on into town with the rest of my load tomorrow."

Nita looked out the window at an enormous building. "The roof looks like a tent," she said. It rose above stained concrete walls in white peaks and billows, shining in the sun.

"It's made out of cloth." Renny slowed as they approached a wide chain-link gate. "This used to be an old racetrack—horses or dogs, I forget which. Pacific Bio put one of those Israeli roofs on it. Cheaper than building something new." She pulled a plastic card out of an inside pocket and handed it to a uniformed security guard.

He ran it through a slot in the tiny gatehouse behind him, then handed it back. "Run into some trouble?" He eyed the truck's battered fender.

"Nothing I couldn't handle."

"Dock R." The gate began to rattle laboriously open. "Around to the right."

Renny put the rig into gear and the truck crept forward with a growl. "I usually make this stop." She looked at Nita from the corners of her eyes. "I've got some good customers here. Very inside folk."

Customers for what? Renny was waiting to see if she'd ask. Baiting her again? Nita leaned against the door, tired of the game, tired of Renny's pain.

"I get them some good deals on antibiotics. I've got a sound connection in Chi. I used to have a couple, but the other guy got his in the riot." She clucked her tongue. "Lost a lot of good contacts in that nasty little war."

Carter had been there. In the middle of that nasty little war. That was what *he* was afraid of—that it would happen in The Dalles. They were circling the huge building, passing loading dock after loading dock, concrete ledges that jutted out in front of wall-mounted valves and racked lengths of corrugated plastic pipe.

"This is where they unload the tankers," Renny said conversationally. "They digest the chopped-up biomass at local plants—use some pretty fancy bacteria to do it. Then they haul the digested sludge—syrup, they call it—to the plant here. Add a few chemicals and bingo, you can grow a ton or so of cherry or wheat cells."

"Do you carry the syrup?" Nita asked.

"Not me, babe." Renny's lip curled. "That's for the tanker jockeys. The stuff stinks and it's sugar, mostly; hell to get off the metalwork." She and Nita clenched their teeth as she used both hands to back the truck up to a wide platform. Rachel fussed.

"Everybody out." Renny killed the engine, leaned her head back against the seat. "End of the line."

Her face looked gray. Fresh blood had soaked through the bandage on her arm.

"Is there someone here who can look at that?" Nita gathered up Rachel.

"You did a good enough job." Renny's eyes snapped open. "I'll get unloaded and then we'll find Lydia." She shoved her door open and hopped down.

Nita wasn't fooled, but she stood silently below the concrete dock as a coveralled kid hurried up. He took the flimsy sheet of hardcopy that Renny handed him, nodded, and scurried away.

"I deliver custom office supplies," Renny said dryly.

Which were really antibiotics. Nita watched Renny open a hand-size panel on the side of the trailer to key in a long sequence of numbers.

"Some of the hotshots use palm locks. Techie toys." She sneered. "All a 'jacker needs is your hand to open the back. It doesn't have to be attached to you. Numbers they have to dig out of you, and sometimes that buys you a way out."

She sounded matter-of-fact.

The kid reappeared, followed by a rectangular platform on wheels. It had a rail along one side and its wheels squeaked as it trundled along the dock after him. The hair on the back of Nita's neck prickled. The kid wasn't touching the thing. It was following him like a dog, creaking along at his heels.

"Magic." The kid noticed her expression and leered at her. "I trained him myself. Stop, Max. Sit." The platform obediently halted. Slowly the bed sank between its wheels, until it rested on the dock.

"Stop trying to impress the natives and get the boxes, punk." Renny scowled up at him. "Those cargo trucks are voice activated with a three-chip brain," she said to Nita. "Pacific Bio likes gadgets. You got to stop gawking, babe."

Nita grimaced at Renny's mix of irritation and amusement. "So I'm a native," she said. "Whatever that means."

"Means you're no trucker and you don't know the city from

squat. Give me that.'' She snatched the hardcopy sheet that the
sulky kid was holding out and scribbled an ID number across
the bottom. ''Take care of that merchandise.'' She showed her
teeth briefly and tossed a folded leaf of scrip in his direction.

''Yessir.'' The kid grinned, caught the scrip deftly, and tucked
it into a pocket. ''I'll take real good care of it.'' He turned on
his heel and whistled two notes to the cargo truck.

It lifted itself obediently and trundled after him, four small
cartons stacked neatly on its bed. Renny slammed the trailer
doors. ''Let's find Lydia,'' she said. ''Then I want to sleep for
a while. Damn that bastard.'' She touched a raw scrape in the
truck's gleaming paint. ''I hope he went through the windshield.''

Nita shifted Rachel onto her hip and didn't offer her arm to
the trucker. Renny would bite her head off, no matter that she
was feeling shaky. An echo of the older woman's cold nausea
tightened Nita's stomach as she followed Renny up the flight of
concrete stairs that led to the loading dock itself.

''We'll take the back way.'' Renny fished the plastic card out
of her pocket and stuck it into a slot beside a green metal door
with no handle.

A bell chimed and the door slid sideways into the wall. Humid
air puffed into their faces and Nita wrinkled her nose at the
smell. A maze of gleaming pipes and round tanks surrounded
them, and a low, throbbing hum tickled Nita's ears, making her
feel as if her bones were vibrating inside her flesh. Rachel
squirmed on her hip, chuckling.

''Like it, child?'' Nita touched her daughter's nose, smiled at
her wide grin.

''You coming?''

Nita hurried after Renny, ducking beneath overhanging pipes.
Some of them were no thicker than her finger. Others were as
big as tree trunks. ''What are these for?'' she asked as she
caught up with the trucker.

''The big ones carry the raw syrup. The little ones carry all
kinds of stuff. Trace elements, chemicals, antibiotics.'' Renny
shrugged. ''Ask Lydia. She's the one who plays with all this
shit.''

They were skirting the main floor of the vast building now.
Sunshine filtered through the white fabric of the roof, filling the
space with soft light. Huge tanks stood in rows: round, silver,
domed with clear plastic. The humid air was dense with odors—
sweet, dank and heavy. Nita caught a whiff of citrus smell as

she climbed a metal stairway after Renny. From up here she could look down into the nearest tank. Thick yellow sludge filled the tank, scummed with an oily layer of clear liquid. Like fat on a pot of soup, Nita thought. She wondered what it was, feeling slightly revolted. She'd eat beans any day, thank you.

Renny was waiting for her on the narrow walkway that ringed the factory, radiating fatigue, pain, and irritable impatience. Without a word, she pushed open one of the doors that lined the walkway. It opened into a small office. The color struck Nita first: every square inch of wall space was covered with pictures of flowers, some old, some bright and new, holos and what looked like pages from old magazines. Rachel cooed with delight. The rainbow of colors overwhelmed Nita. She recognized a few of them from the dusty hills above the valley—yarrow, desert parsley, and fleabane. David had told her the names of the plants as they hunted bees together. There were even real flowers growing beneath a small, shaded light tube. Petals like the wings of a butterfly unfolded above crystal dishes of pale golden jelly.

"Well, well. And when did you wander in?" A small woman stood up from her seat in front of a large terminal complex. "Renny, you should have told me you were coming. My God, what happened to you this time? Hijackers?" She walked into Renny's embrace, careful of the trucker's bandaged arm.

She looked as if she were in her thirties, with a thick mane of short hair so blond that it was almost white. Her skin was paler than any skin Nita had ever seen, and her eyes were a vivid lavender as she turned to smile at Nita. "Hi," she said. "I'm Lydia."

Nita took her hand, surprised at the strength in the woman's long fingers. "I'm Nita." She felt awkward and out of place.

"Nita needs some answers, so I brought her to you. I think I'm going to go crawl into your bed and sleep," Renny said. "I'm feeling a little frayed."

"You look like hell." Concern flickered in Lydia's eyes, and she kept her arm around the trucker's waist. "You all right? You going to tell me what happened?"

"Later, and yes, I'll live. I'm just ready for some rest."

"So go rest," Lydia snapped. "I haven't changed my door code. Nita can tell me what she wants."

Renny laughed suddenly, disengaged herself from Lydia's arm with surprising gentleness. "I'm not arguing." She gave Nita a

lopsided smile. "She'll get you everything you need, babe."
The door closed softly behind her.

"Damn that woman." Lydia let her breath out sharply. "I
don't suppose you're her lover, are you?" She raised a pale
eyebrow at Nita.

"No. I'm . . . not." Nita felt herself blushing. Jealousy? No,
that wasn't what this woman was feeling.

"She's such a bloody loner." Lydia lifted her shoulders in a
jerky shrug. "So. What is it that you need from me?"

"Renny said that you were good with . . . information."

"Yes, yes, I can crack anybody's security. Spill it." Lydia
perched herself on the edge of her terminal console, one foot
flicking the air.

Worrying about Renny. "I need proof that someone is putting
in new fields in the Valley. I need to know who's doing it. Renny
thought you could find out for me."

"Is that all?" Lydia dropped into her chair. "Honey, that
should be no problem." Her long fingers danced across her
keypad and one of the screens in front of her flickered.

Rachel was kicking, fussing a little. She wanted to get down.
Nita shrugged her pack off her shoulder, took the quilt out, and
spread it on the floor. Rachel wanted the flower pictures. Her
frustration flared like heat lightning as she rocked onto her hands
and knees. One hand moved, then a knee. With a frustrated
screech, she flopped onto her face, but she was closer to the
bright wall.

"Kid, you just crawled." Nita laughed softly. "All you need
is practice now."

Rachel rocked to her knees again, made it two crawling steps
closer to a picture of a yellow trumpet-shaped blossom. Her chin
banged the bare floor this time and she started to cry, angry
more than hurt.

"It's all right, all right." Nita picked her up. Her daughter's
body felt tense, rigid with her effort. Hers was a hot, pure emotion, simple and direct. *I want!* Nita held Rachel close to the
wall, smiling at her gurgling pleasure. Were there any flowers
in the camp they had passed? "You won't grow up there," she
murmured to her daughter. "I won't let you."

"This is turning out to be more fun than I expected." Lydia
spoke up. "Someone has gone to a lot of trouble to misfile
permit applications in some very creative ways."

Lydia was pleased. Nita leaned over her shoulder, but the

jumble of letters and numbers on the screen made no sense to her at all.

"Apparently a new company is behind the applications. The interesting thing is that this particular company—AgriCo—is owned by a dummy corporation. The majority stockholders are keeping a low profile."

"Does that mean you can't get the information?"

"You've got to be kidding." Lydia sniffed. "What it means is that I have to sneak into some very tight stock exchange files and find out who really holds the reins here." She hummed to herself. "Whoever did the hiding was good," she said after a while. "I bet it was Rico. It's his style . . . although if it is Rico, he's getting just a wee bit careless in his old age." A second screen flickered.

"What do you do here?" Nita asked, fascinated.

"Record keeping, inventory, formula integrations, payroll, and so forth. Drudge work." Lydia grimaced. "But Pacific Bio has bucks, so I've got state-of-the-art equipment. Can't ask for more than that. Aha!" Her fingers pounced and the screen flashed a column of numbers. "It *was* Rico. Someday I'll tell him about the hole he always leaves in his security jobs. Maybe. Your permits are in the laser tray," she said absently. "They're all to AgriCo, but in a minute . . ." She hissed softly, tapped more keys. "In a minute you'll have the rest of what you need to link AgriCo to your mystery shareholders. There are only two real ones. The others are ghosts." She lifted her hands from her keypad and spun her wheeled stool around. "It's all yours, honey. Got anything else I can play with?"

"I don't think so." White sheets were sliding silently out of a slot in the front of the console, settling delicately into a wire tray. Nita lifted the top sheet.

"Your mystery duo went to a lot of trouble to hide. Smart of them to hire Rico, but they should have hired me." Lydia smiled, full of satisfaction. "It wasn't nearly as much of a challenge as I'd hoped. Rico must have been having a bad day."

"I'm not sure I understand this." Nita looked at the sheets. Some of them seemed to be copies of legal documents; others were lists of dates and dollar amounts.

"It's all there—records of stock transfers to the dummies, subcorporations, the whole messy electronic trail. Those are your men." She pointed. "The names on line one. I'm a little suprised. I know Pacific Bio's been trying to lever the general's ass for years, but I thought he was cold steel legal." She shrugged. "I guess they finally found the right lever. Everybody's got his price."

Nita stared at the paper, her skin flushing hot and cold. William Hastings. That was the first name. Carter's boss—which put him squarely in the middle. But it was the second name that shook her.

Dan Greely.

"You're wrong," Nita said, and flinched at the hot flash of Lydia's anger. "I didn't mean it like that. Renny said you're the best."

"I am, at that. Nice that she noticed." Lydia's anger eased. "I'm not wrong, honey. Sorry. What happened to Renny's arm, by the way? If I know her, she won't tell me."

"Someone shot at us. Because we were coming here to get this." Nita shook the papers gently, struggling to make sense of what Lydia was telling her. "Lydia . . . I *know* that Dan Greely isn't involved with this stuff." She looked at the woman's strange eyes. "Is there any way that this might have been . . . faked? To fool someone like you?"

"Honey, I trust my information a hell of a lot more than I trust your intuition." Lydia crossed her arms, her eyes hooded. "Yes, someone could have gone to a lot of trouble to fake this, but I doubt it."

She was worried about Renny and offended, too. "You're the best," Nita said desperately. "Maybe whoever did it wanted to make sure that they could fool even the best. Will you see if there's anything else?"

It wasn't enough. Lydia was about to refuse, to go look in on Renny.

"Someone's going to laugh if they fool you."

"Let them laugh." Lydia raised one eyebrow. "If they're able to fool me, they're entitled."

She didn't believe that she could be wrong.

Maybe she wasn't. Nita listened to the rush of her own pulse in her ears. Maybe Dan *had* been stringing her along. Maybe she didn't hear what she thought she heard when she talked to him.

No. She shook her head, hands clenching into fists. She was what she was. And Dan was . . . Dan. He hadn't lied to her, and she knew it. Which made this another piece of the frame. "This information is a trick." Nita drew a quick breath. "I know Dan Greely isn't in on it because I can sort of read minds and . . . I know he isn't." She ran out of words suddenly, light-headed with tension.

Lydia was staring at her, eyes thoughtful, her surprise well hidden behind the calm mask of her face. "How do you *sort of* read minds?"

Nita discovered that she wanted to start shaking. "I just hear . . . emotions. Not words or anything. I guess I'm an empath." Jeremy's word for her. "But I know . . . when someone's lying," she said desperately. "I *do*."

"*You* could be lying, but I think you'd do a better job of acting if you were. I don't think I'll ask you to prove it." Lydia tilted her head, considering. "I don't think I want to know . . . what people are thinking. I expect you don't like it much, either, most of the time."

She was thinking of Renny. She believed Nita. She had considered, doubted, and made her decision. Just like that. Nita swallowed the lump that clogged her throat. "Will you do it? Find out what's going on here?"

"Yeah, I will." Lydia frowned at her flowered wall. "I wish you *were* her lover," she said softly. "That's about what it would take to live with Renny. A mind reader. She won't tell you squat, she just snarls. And she . . . needs someone. She needs to care about someone enough to be careful. One of these days she's not going to come back."

Love? Yes, and anticipation of that day.

"She cares about you," Nita blurted.

"I know." Lydia's eyebrows rose above her strange eyes. "She does, but I'm no empath. She pisses me off, and I let it show, and we fight. I hate trucking, and Renny goes nuts cooped up here."

"I'm sorry," Nita said.

"Me, too. Sometimes." Lydia shrugged and went to stand in front of her light. "This is a cymbidium." She picked up the butterfly flower. "One of the techs cloned it for me. The original plant came from old-time Hawaii. This one is a ladyslipper, from a swamp that dried up years ago. The cells come from the national germ plasm bank down in Texas."

Lydia's flowers grew from frozen bits of the past. She would understand Jeremy. Nita watched Lydia replace the delicate blooms beneath the light. Renny didn't talk about the past. She only looked ahead, at the road in front of her. Nita touched Lydia's arm lightly. "Do you have a med kit or something?"

she asked. "Renny's arm is bleeding again, but her kit is locked in the truck."

"I'll get you what you need. If you can get Renny to let you do anything about it, you're ahead of me." Lydia sighed. "She's so damn macho."

They clattered down the stairs, past the vat of yellow sludge. "What is that?" Nita asked.

"Corn cells. They're engineered to produce large amounts of oil. The pressed cells go into that new fake meat."

"I see." She would definitely stick with beans.

Lydia took Nita to the company infirmary. The bright, clean rooms, crammed with cupboards and equipment, were empty. Lydia collected a roll of gauze, tape, and sterile pads from various drawers. "What antibiotic is she on?" she asked Nita.

"I don't know the name. They're white tablets."

"Like this?" Lydia picked up a bottle and tipped two tablets into her palm.

"I think so."

"You're probably right. This is the stuff she brings in with her 'office supplies.' Too bad I can't have the doc look at her, but company policy is very, very tight on that score."

"Won't you get in trouble for taking this stuff?" Nita looked up at the dark eye of one of the video cameras that hung in every corner. It made her feel nervous, as if cops might show up at any minute to arrest her.

"Relax." Lydia followed her gaze. "These are all digital pickups. I ran a handy little preedited segment before we came down here. We've got two more minutes before Security sees anything but an empty room." She ushered Nita into the corridor. "I'll check on this Greely guy for you. I thought Rico was a little careless—maybe he was careless on purpose." She smiled a little sadly, her lavender eyes on Nita's face. "I don't envy you, honey. I don't envy you at all. Go talk Renny into taking care of herself, will you? I need to get to work."

"I will," Nita said, and discovered that she wanted to cry. "Thank you."

"Thank me when I come up with some answers." Lydia touched Nita's cheek, turned, and walked quickly away.

CHAPTER TWENTY-THREE ☆

"You have fucked up in every possible way in this command." Hands clasped behind his back, General Hastings paced across Carter's small bedroom. "You had no business letting Roscoe leave the Shunt, and your negligence cost us the lives of six soldiers." He spun around, his finger stabbing at Carter, face as hard as carved stone. "I will personally see that you get busted for this, mister."

"Sir." Carter forced the word through tight lips. Whether or not Hastings had anything to do with this, he was right. Carter *had* fucked up. He remembered the feel of Andy's coverall as the flood slammed them down the riverbed. He clutched it in his dreams, woke up with bloody nailmarks on his palms.

No, damn it. He hadn't fucked up. Not completely. "Sir?" He pushed himself higher on the pillows, sucking in his breath as his broken ribs stabbed him. "I had a reason for what I did. With all due respect, sir—"

"Cut out the formal crap, Voltaire."

"All right, I will." Hell, he was screwed anyway. "We need to find out who's behind this." Or do you want to, General? "It's some kind of outside setup, sir. I'm sure of it." He struggled higher in bed, fighting the buzz of the doctor's painkillers, watching Hastings's face. "Someone is deliberately trying to start a shooting war between the Corps and the locals. And yes, the locals are playing right into it, but they're not *behind* it. If we could have caught those snipers yesterday, we'd have found our connection. Sir!" He clenched his teeth as the room wavered in front of his eyes. If Hastings was the guilty one, Carter couldn't read it—couldn't read *anything* in the man's face. "We're on the edge of major bloodshed here. I made a bad

217

judgment call yesterday, but damn it, I'm trying to stop a war from happening.''

"Are you?'' Hastings's tone was icy. "I think everyone realizes that someone is tipping off the terrorists about patrol schedules. Someone set up that ambush yesterday.''

"I agree, sir.'' Carter drew a shallow, careful breath. "I suspect that it's Major Delgado,'' he said, and waited for Hastings's reaction.

"The major has been reporting directly to me.'' Hastings's eyes pinned Carter. "On my orders. He's been here as long as I have, and I trust *him*.'' He stressed the word delicately. "I have my own theories about who is the leak around here. I've been keeping a close watch on your local connections. You and Greely are in on this together, Voltaire.''

"No.'' Carter stared at Hastings, stunned. "It's not me.'' Hastings could be the guilty one—could be saying this to cover his own ass—but the words shocked Carter anyway. Hastings could be innocent, and in that case . . . Carter licked his lips, struggling for an explanation. "I've dealt with Dan Greely, yes, because he is *the* liaison to the locals here, but I don't trust him. I never have. I have never betrayed the Corps. Sir.''

"We're going to look into that.'' Hastings's expression didn't soften. "You are confined to your quarters until further notice, do I make myself clear, Colonel?''

"Yes, sir,'' Carter said between his teeth.

"What action I decide to take will depend on my investigation here. Meanwhile, the situation calls for drastic measures, and I'm going to take them.'' His gray eyes glittered like bits of dirty ice. "These local troublemakers got away with it last time they acted up. Water Policy was soft and it wouldn't endorse emergency measures, but it's not so soft this time around. This time I put the bastards in their place. After this we'll get a hell of a lot more cooperation around here.''

Hastings was out for revenge. Out for blood. "What are you planning to do?'' Carter asked.

"I'm going to shut the Columbia down dry, from the Klamath Shunt to the Willamette Shunt. Not one drop beyond the federal minimum goes through the meters.''

Which meant cutting it down to Personal Maintenance Allowance, the minimum share of water guaranteed to each individual served by a federal water system. That wouldn't give people around here enough water to keep kitchen crops alive, or to do anything except survive. "You can't do that.'' Carter leaned forward, wincing as his ribs stabbed him. "General, that'll wipe the farmers out."

"I can and I will." His smiled was grimly triumphant. "I've been granted full emergency powers by Water Policy. They're scared shitless that a big water loss will short Mexico and give Canada a reason to kick over the traces. Ask your buddy." His lip curled. "I've been authorized to take whatever measures are needed to keep the southern share up to maximum. It comes right out of these bastards' meters—every drop. The break should be repaired by tomorrow, but the Willamette and Sacramento systems have lost over twenty-four hours of flow. If we divert everything over the calculated minimum down the Shunts, we can minimize crop losses in the valleys and keep Mexico's share constant. It'll teach these murderous bastards a lesson they won't forget for a long time."

"Sir?" Carter swallowed. "Only a handful of people are involved in the sabotage. A lot of innocent farmers are going to lose their crops and their land." Private Wasson's family, for one. Sandy Corbett.

"There are no innocent people along this riverbed." The general's eyes had gone hard. "I've asked for Rangers as backup, and my request has been granted. They're unloading now."

Rangers. Stunned, Carter sank back onto his pillow. Rangers were the elite, and they hated this kind of call. Rangers had been brought in to back up the 82nd Airborne in Chicago. That was when things had gotten out of hand, although that particular fact had never made it into the media.

"Voltaire?" Hastings paused in the doorway. "Tell me what you know about Greely's escape."

"What?" Carter stared, head full of buzzing, his thoughts a jumble. "What escape? What are you talking about?"

"Someone sprung him last night. Two men in uniforms. The guard saw that much before they hit him."

Carter eased himself back against the pillows, black spots dancing through his vision. "I don't know, sir." Did Hastings really think he had set this up, or was he guilty? "I've got an alibi," he said bitterly. "Ask the doc."

Hastings's expression was contemptuous. "I heard how you ended up out here, by the way. Seems this senator did a little string pulling for a particular posting. Targass is tight with Water Policy." Hastings's lips twitched as if he wanted to spit. "You and your buddy cooking something, Colonel? He might be Water Policy, but he can't save your ass."

Carter stared after him, barely registering the slam of the door. Someone *had* pulled strings to get him posted here. Senator Targass . . . he'd heard the name before, but the where and when wouldn't come.

Hastings thought he was a traitor, or claimed to. And maybe, in a sense, he was. Carter closed his eyes. How much had he let Nita and his liking for Dan Greely affect his judgment? Six people had died at the Shunt. Andy Stakowski had barely turned twenty. There had been nine Corps death in the last year. Carter let himself sink into the haze of pain and drugs. If Hastings shut down the Columbia flow, the land along the river would dry up and blow away. How long would it take? Two days? A week? He'd never farmed, and had no idea how quickly crops would wilt and die.

Whose fault?

"Sir?" A hesitant voice roused him. "Colonel Voltaire, sir?"

"In here."

"I'm sorry, sir. I knocked." Private Wasson appeared in the doorway to his bedroom, half hidden by the doorframe. "I'll pull cleanup for a month if my sergeant finds out about this." She glanced nervously over her shoulder. "But I heard you got hurt bad, sir."

"Just ribs." Carter pushed himself painfully up onto the pillows again. "Thanks, Private." She wanted to ask him something. What did she think he could do for her, anyway? He couldn't do shit for anyone, including himself. "What's up?" he asked her wearily.

"Sir, is it true that we're going to shut the water down along the riverbed?"

Rumors got around fast in this place. Carter wondered if she'd heard that Hastings was out to bust him yet. "Yes." Carter sighed. "It's true."

"*Sir.*"

The anguish and anger in that single tight syllable finally penetrated. Carter narrowed his eyes, seeing what she was trying to hide. "Private, come into the room. All the way in."

She marched stiffly to the foot of his bed and stood at attention. The bruises on her face were dark and new. Her mouth was swollen and Carter could see a raw, ugly scrape on her arm below the sleeve of her coverall.

"I was ready to go along yesterday," she said in a low, taut voice. "I got permission from Captain Westerly, and I was as ready to shoot as any of the others. Maybe my family does live along the riverbed, but I'm Corps, sir.''

The rumor about Roscoe's being set up from inside must have gone around, too. Carter sighed, rubbed his face. "You made a tough decision and I took it away from you. I didn't do it very well, either. I apologize, Private."

She lifted her chin. "This would have happened anyway, sir. Sooner or later. I left one of them in worse shape."

"Good for you. I'm sorry about your family," he said. "I'm sorry about all the people who are going to pay for this when it isn't their debt. I did my best to keep that promise I made to you."

The private was silent for a long moment, her eyes fixed on that wall above Carter's head. "Sir? Is it true that the guy we've been holding has escaped? The head honcho from The Dalles?"

"It's true."

"You weren't . . . moving him, sir? Like down to Bonneville?"

Carter shook his head, his eyes on her face. "He wasn't going anywhere until the U.S. Marshal showed up to claim him. Why?"

"I . . . saw something, while everyone was . . . at the Shunt." Wasson scowled down at the floor. "An officer and an NCO were taking this man out to a car—graying hair, kind of tall, wearing jeans—and he fell. I stopped to see if they needed any help. The guy was in cuffs, and the lieutenant said he was a prisoner, that they were moving him down to Bonneville. Sir, the man was out of it." She frowned. "He was either pretty sick or drugged."

Greely had been drugged? "Would you recognize them again if you saw them?" Carter sat forward gingerly.

"I . . . *did* recognize the corporal. He's down at Bonneville. I was there before I got transferred up here." Wasson looked at him, finally. "He's from Hood River. A local."

Which meant what? That the leak was in Bonneville—maybe out of Hastings's office? A cold anger was forming in his belly. "Thanks." He held out his hand to her. "You're Corps first. I won't forget it."

She clasped it, then released him abruptly. "If someone from the Corps is behind this, I'll find out."

There was a smoldering heat in her eyes that worried him. "We'll do it my way," he told her urgently. "I'll pull a personnel record for you, and you see if you can recognize this corporal's name. Don't discuss this with *anyone*, is that understood?''

"Yes, sir. I'll keep my mouth shut and my ears open."

"I'll call your CO and get you assigned to HQ platoon as my aide. We'll go over the list together.''

"Yes, sir." Wasson saluted him smartly, her eyes glittering. "I'll recognize that guy's name." She spun on her heel and marched out of the room, nearly colliding with Johnny as he came though the front door.

"What was that all about?" Johnny pulled off his goggles and tossed them onto the chest of drawers. "Man, it's dusty out there. You look a hell of a lot better than the last time I saw you, by the way.''

"What are you doing here?" Carter grimaced as he leaned forward. "How did you manage to show up in time to pull me out of the water?" He managed a grin for Johnny. "Talk about timing.''

"I tagged along with the media." He sat down on the foot of Carter's bed. "I've got an inside source on the payroll, and she tipped me off. I guess someone called them and told them about the fireworks. You didn't see the airtime, huh?''

"I heard about it." Carter clenched a fist. "The whole country thinks we're in a war, and in a day or two we will be.''

"Hey, the public's pissed at the locals, not at you guys." Johnny shrugged. "The media slanted it as water pirates after California's irrigation water. Since another food shortage is hitting the East Coast, you'll get applause for anything you want to do.''

"It's not the publicity angle, Johnny. It's what's going to happen *here* that I'm worried about.''

"That's the locals' problem." Johnny put a hand on his shoulder. "They've set this mess up. They've got to deal with the results, not you.''

"They haven't set it up." Carter groaned and lay back as the pain clutched him.

"Hey, you okay?" Johnny leaned forward, worried. "What did the doctor say, anyway? They wouldn't let *me* on base, yesterday. Hastings has this place nailed shut. I had to go through Washington to get past the old fart.''

"That must have pissed hell out of Hastings." Carter breathed shallowly, waiting for the spasm to pass. "I broke four ribs. They missed my lung but did some damage. Nothing that won't heal," he said bitterly. "Johnny, I'm under arrest, if you want to look at it like that. I'm confined to quarters. Hastings accused me of setting this up.''

Johnny leaned back, arms crossed, face thoughtful. "Can't say I'm surprised."

"You did mean him. On the phone."

"I couldn't say so. Not on an open line. We have absolutely no concrete proof." Johnny shook his head, his expression sober. "I think I almost got you killed."

There were lines of strain in his face and dark circles beneath his eyes. "It wasn't your fault." Carter put a hand on his arm. "I wish I'd known sooner, though."

"I just found out. My buddy Paul in DC has been snooping around for me, digging whatever dirt he can on the general. I thought you might need it."

Paul. The name clicked suddenly. Paul Targass. "You did it." He stared at Johnny. "You had Targass get me posted out here. *Goddamn* it, Johnny."

Johnny recoiled. "Hey, take it easy. Yes, I did that," he said harshly. "Why not? You're a damned good officer, and I . . . needed you out here. Pacific Bio's already on my back. If I fuck up, the rest of the Committee will be after me like sharks. I'm not . . . very popular." He met Carter's eyes. "You're the only person in the whole damn empty world that I can trust. I had a chance to get you stationed out here and, damn it, I took it. I did it for me, all right? Because I'm a selfish prick and I always will be. Is that what you wanted me to say? Okay, I've said it." His voice cracked, and he looked quickly away.

"I wish you hadn't done it." Carter sighed, his anger fading. Johnny could be like that—just do it, and ask later. Or never. "Well, I'm here, and I think you're right about it being Hastings." He scowled. "I think Delgado's in on it, too. That flood happened because of a fried board. The flow should have shut down in less than a minute, but it was ten minutes or more before Operations ran the override and closed the valves. That emergency system is checked weekly. The last recorded inspection was only two days before the break."

"You think Delgado sabotaged it?"

"I think Andy Stakowski died because of it," Carter said softly. "Someone gets to pay for that."

Tomorrow a truck would carry the six caskets to the dry plot of ground that was the base's cemetery. A flag would cover each casket. They would flutter in the dusty wind as a firing party fired three volleys. The chaplain would read a moving service, a bugler would play "Taps," the flags would be folded and presented to the next of kin. The river had covered that piece of ground once. Jeremy would see water if he looked at the graves. That's what those men and women had died to protect, Carter thought bitterly—water. Not freedom, not democracy. Just water.

Life.

"Wasson—the private you met on your way out—might hand us the key. She recognized the corporal who sprung Greely. He's from Bonneville, but she can't remember his name. I'm going to pull a personnel record for her."

"So it *is* Hastings." Johnny was nodding. "Wasson, you said?"

"Yeah." Carter swung his legs over the side of the bed, hissing between his teeth. "Hand me the phone, will you? I've got to call Personnel for that record."

"Wait a minute." Johnny's eyes gleamed. "When I went up to Greely's place yesterday, I meant to do some snooping. I didn't get the chance, but that might be a good place to go right now. Greely wouldn't dare go back there. We could look around. Greely's the local connection, I'm sure of it. There's got to be some shred of evidence in that house—something that will tie Hastings solidly into this. Let's go find it."

His eyes were glittering with the old, school-days fire, the let's-do-it look. What the hell difference did it make if he went AWOL or not? If he could get his hands on something solid . . .

"Get your car." Carter stood, wavering a little, clutching the wall for support. "Park right in front of the door. I don't know if they've got orders to stop me at the gate or not."

"You lie down on the floor and I'll toss some stuff over you." Johnny grinned. "No sweat."

It's not a game, Carter wanted to say, but maybe it would always be a little bit of a game for Johnny. He limped over to his closet and rooted out a jacket and folded bedspread to add to the camouflage. A cold anger was filling him, like water seeping into a dry pot. Someone was behind this. Someone had set up Carter, the Corps, and The Dalles. Nine Corps people had died so far. And how many locals? The Wilmer girl, at least. The person behind this owed for those lives. Carter opened his dresser drawer, took out the Beretta, and made sure it was loaded. He was going to make certain that they paid what they owed.

CHAPTER TWENTY-FOUR ☆

Crouched on the floor of Johnny's car, Carter held his breath as Johnny braked at the gate to surrender his pass.

"You better watch yourself out there." The guard's voice sounded as if she were in the backseat with Carter. "Something big is going on. The whole town's on its way out to the Shunt. I hope you're heading west—you're not going to get anywhere going east."

Another demonstration? Sweat stung Carter's eyes. Hastings had his Rangers out there. He closed his eyes, urging Johnny silently to step on it, get them the hell out of here. The car lurched forward, gathering speed.

"It's clear." Johnny glanced in the rearview as Carter emerged from the concealing clothes pile. "No sweat."

"Did you hear that? About the Shunt?" Carter eased himself onto the back seat. "The shit's going to hit the fan if *anyone* does *anything*."

"I heard." Johnny shook his head. "You can't do squat, Carter. Except get yourself killed out there. Possibly by Hastings, if he's your boy. Come on." He braked at the truck plaza, then swung left onto the state highway. "What counts is getting some kind of hard evidence on somebody. So that we can nail them. I'll bet you a hundred bucks we find something at Greely's house."

He was right, the logical part of Carter agreed. The only thing to do was to concentrate on getting some kind of concrete proof. Nita might turn up with something—or she might not. Carter didn't want to examine the whys of that "might not." If she wasn't part of this, she was still unwilling to see Greely as anything but a hero.

The afternoon sun streaked the gorge wall with stark black

shadows, giving the stony bones of the earth an austere beauty. Those rocks would still be here tomorrow, whether a hundred people died or none. They wouldn't care, one way or the other. The events of this day, of this past month, were nothing more than a flicker of light and darkness to the earth. Unimportant. Ghosts were following him, lurking just beyond the range of his vision. The kid in the van. Amesworth and Lopez. The Wilmer girl and Andy Stakowski. How many more to come? They topped the rim of the gorge and he clung to the door, breathing in quick, shallow gasps as the car bounced across the rocky track that led to Dan's house. He had to find something. Some kind of answer.

Maybe then he'd know whether he'd fucked up or not.

Greely's beans lay flat in the dust, yellowed and dying. No water. Johnny pulled up in front of the weathered little house and Carter climbed stiffly out. Last time he had been here, he had been bringing the beaten Dan Greely home. Things had looked so fucking hopeful. Slowly he climbed the warped steps. The main room looked as barren as he remembered it: table, chairs, woodstove, and sink. Dan's bedroom door was open, but the other was closed. Nita's room. She had walked through that door, flushed with sleep, pushing hair back from her face. The pain of the meeting smote him, fresh and sharp as if it had just happened.

The door handle turned and the door opened. For one dizzy instant, Carter thought it was Nita. Then the blond hair registered. "Jeremy? What are you doing here?"

"I *was* watering Dan's beans. Only there's no more water." Jeremy yawned and gave Carter a quizzical look. "What's up? How come you're out here?"

"Have you seen Dan?"

"I thought you had him locked up?"

"Who's this?" Johnny stepped through the doorway, a wary eye on Jeremy. "Oh, yeah. I remember you."

"Carter, what's wrong?" Jeremy ignored Johnny. "You look like shit."

"He got his ribs busted when the Pipe blew." Johnny walked over to the kitchen, began opening cupboards. "Wow. Whatever else this guy's into, he's got some good black-market connections." He held up a brown pill bottle and whistled. "*I* can't even get this stuff."

"You want to butt out?" Jeremy limped over and slammed the cupboard door. "What's all this about, anyway?"

"I need to search the house," Carter said wearily. The weight of the Beretta dragged at his belt, refusing to be ignored. "Right now."

"He's on your side."

"How do you know?" Carter clenched his fists. "How the hell do you *know*, Jeremy? You give me a solid reason, and we'll both believe it."

"Nita told me."

The quiet words hit him like a blow. "She could be wrong. She could be . . . biased."

"I don't think so." Jeremy's tone was mild. "Relax, Carter, I'm not going to make a fuss. If it makes you feel better to search, do it. I don't think Dan would mind. Where is he, if you don't have him?" He was frowning now. "He didn't come back here."

"He escaped. Or he was kidnapped. You tell me which." If he had been kidnapped, he might very well be dead. It would be a hell of a way to prove his innocence.

Carter turned his back on Jeremy and yanked a drawer open, sorting quickly through a handful of kitchen utensils. Johnny was going through the cupboards, looking into pots, lifting stacked plates. Jeremy sat down on the corner of the table, his foot flicking like a cat's tail, watching them rummage through Dan's things. Carter left the main room to Johnny and went into Dan's bedroom. Watercolors lined the walls. They had been painted on sheets of rough paper, and Carter wondered if Dan had done them. They all showed water in the river. Carter stared at a picture of gray-green water cascading over gray rocks. It looked . . . real. Like Jeremy's visions. A flat photo stood on the small table beside the bed. Carter picked it up. A gray-haired woman with a strong face looked out at him, smiling quizzically, a little warily. Carter put the picture down carefully, wondering who she was.

Dan's drawers yielded clothes, odds and ends, and a sheaf of papers that turned out to be old bills, receipts, and meter records. Carter peeked behind the watercolors, but nothing had been hidden there, either. Hand on Nita's door, he hesitated, afraid, angry at that twinge of fear. He shoved the door open, pretending that he hadn't said a tiny prayer in the depths of his chest. Her room smelled faintly of honey and piss—Rachel's contribution, no doubt. The bed was neatly made and Nita's pack stood against the wall. She had put her clothes into the top drawer of the dresser. She didn't have much—an extra pair of jeans and a couple of shirts. Carter turned the soft folds of cloth over, catching a faint whiff of her scent. She must never have had much—only what she had been able to carry with her. *I'm worried about you*, she had said in his office, and there had been tears in her voice. Carter's fingers were trembling. He clenched his hand into a brief fist, then opened the next drawer down.

It was there, under the pile of stiff, dry diapers, tucked beneath the yellowed newspaper that lined the drawer. Stock certificates. Pacific BioSystems stock, made out to Dan Greely. And a handwritten note, stuck between two of the certificates. *Here's the next installment. We've got a new CO coming in and I've got to talk to you about strategy. Same place, tomorrow night.*

It wasn't signed, but Carter recognized the handwriting. Hastings put those strange, jagged tails on his Ys.

Very carefully, he folded the certificates and tucked them into his pocket. Very carefully, he straightened the pile of diapers. Nita didn't know, he told himself, but it didn't really matter if she did or not. The cold anger was freezing him solid, turning him to ice. He felt no regret, no hurt, nothing but an icy purpose. Dan Greely and William Hastings had run this show together. They had done an incredibly neat job of pulling Carter's strings and making him dance.

The ghosts were crowding into the room. He could almost see them—faint outlines against the ancient wallpaper. They didn't say anything, just waited. The whole town was down at the Shunt, desperate because their fields and their futures were dying. Hastings was down there with his Rangers. It was going to happen: Chicago all over again. Because Carter had believed in Hastings, had been willing to trust Dan Greely.

Because he had fucked up.

This time it *would* be his fault.

Carter touched the butt of the Beretta lightly, feeling the paper crackle in his pocket. It might be enough to send Greely to prison and get Hastings in front of a court-martial. And it might not. Hastings was a general. Politics would come into it, and one or the other might get off.

"Carter?" Johnny stood in the doorway, his expression eager. "You find something?"

"No," Carter said. This wasn't Johnny's fight. "Maybe you ought to look. I'm getting fuzzy."

"Sure." Johnny stepped past him and yanked a drawer open.

Carter limped quickly through the house, his ribs hurting with every step. He thought he could make it, but Johnny caught up with him at the car.

"What the hell are you up to?" He put a hand on the car door.

Carter pushed him away, opened the door, and hit the electronic lock to lock the passenger side. He was in a hurry. Maybe, if he got down there in time, it wouldn't happen. The ghosts were waiting for him, crowding the backseat of the car. They were impatient, too. "Just stay here," he said to Johnny.

"Like hell." Johnny grabbed his good arm. "If you found something, I need it. We've got to use it and use it fast."

It wouldn't be fast enough. "I'm sorry," Carter said, and brought his fist up in a solid right hook.

The pain nearly buckled his knees, but he caught Johnny square on the jaw. He went down sprawling, and Carter slid behind the wheel, icy sweat sticking his shirt to his back. He could drive one-handed. He could manage that much. He backed the car around, breath whistling though his teeth, and stepped hard on the accelerator. As he roared back up the road, he glanced into the rearview mirror. Johnny was picking himself up out of the dust, yelling something after him.

He didn't get to die for Carter's mistakes. Carter turned his attention back to the broken track and concentrated on driving.

CHAPTER TWENTY-FIVE ☆

The countryside looked different from the seat of a truck. Kneeling on Renny's plush carpet, Nita watched the riverbed unreel beyond the highway. Your perspective changed up here; you saw the dust and rock and the pump stations from a different angle. Nita stroked the cab's carpet—not really carpet but acoustic skin, reinforced by an electronic noise-cancellation system. With the windows intact, you could barely hear the purr of the engine. The quiet and the cool dustless air made the wind-scoured land look even less real.

"We're so . . . removed," Nita said out loud.

"How so, babe?" Renny tossed her a quick glance, then turned her attention back to the interstate.

"They aren't real. The rocks, the riverbed." Nita squirmed. Renny's arm was hurting her again, but she wouldn't take any more of the orange painkillers. "I wish I could take a turn and give you a break," she said.

"I've been worse off. Quit clucking at me like a mother hen." Renny smiled faintly. "You're right. It's not real, all that dust out there. I don't particularly want it to be real, either. I don't want to look any farther than the road in front of me, babe. Give me a nice room in a plaza somewhere, a good dinner, and a sharp deal. That's real enough."

"You don't look behind you," Nita said. The past stepped on Renny's heels, as it had stepped on David's. "Lydia keeps it all around her, doesn't she? The past?" Preserved in the succulent leaves of long-dead plants.

"You say some strange things, babe." Renny gave her a sharp sideways look.

Past and present. A dusty barrier divided one from the other.

Only Jeremy really straddled it. Nita sighed, urging the truck to move faster, watching the rocky scar of the riverbed drift past.

"That stuff Lydia dug up is worrying you, isn't it?" Renny said.

Yes, someone planted that stuff, Lydia had told her. *Sorry, I can't give you names yet. Rico's getting better in his old age. It's going to take me a little while to pick up the loose ends for you. But don't worry—I'll find you some.*

"Yes. I guess it is," Nita said.

"She'll get you what you're after. No one hides shit from Lydia for very long."

"It . . . might not be in time." Nita pressed her lips together. A terrible sense of urgency nagged at her. "Something's happened," she said. "I know it."

"You were shitting me." Renny shot Nita a look. "You're no operator. You're in this as deep as Danny."

"I didn't mean to be." Nita looked at the trucker, trying to read the barbed tangle of Renny's emotions. "It was strange, coming here. People are nice to me because I'm Sam Montoya's daughter."

"So you're Sam's kid, huh? Yeah, Sam was another operator. Kind of a hero around here, too. That why you came here?"

"No." Nita twisted to look over the back of the seat, but Rachel was still asleep on the futon, sucking on her fist. "He was no hero to me. I think I hated him," she said softly. "Because he let those men kill him, Mama blamed me for it." His blood had spattered her and it had never washed off.

"You don't hate him anymore?"

"I don't know." Nita frowned. "I think I understand why he did what he did. He knew those men would come for him, sooner or later. He didn't want us—the whole town—to die, too. I hope—at the end—it still mattered to him."

Renny grunted. "I never gave a shit about Jesse. We scratched to live, and she would've done a lot better without a kid. I was an accident. If she'd had the guts, she would've left me out in the Dry when I was born. I chained her to that farm and we both knew it."

Hurt. Nita shivered. "Then Dan came along," she said with sudden comprehension.

"Yeah, then Danny came along. He's my age, did you know that? Almost exactly. I was twenty-three when he moved in with her. I heard about it from a friend of mine. I was working the east–west routes then, not getting back here much and not trying to.'' She gave a bitter laugh. ''I guess Danny had something to offer Jesse that I didn't.''

Nita closed her eyes. ''Papa died because he stopped to hide me behind the truck—so the men wouldn't kill me, too,'' she murmured. ''No, that's not really so. They probably would have killed him even if he *had* run. You could see for a mile around the house and I remember that they had rifles. But he didn't run, and he died.''

Corre! Mama had screamed. Run, Sam!

''How old were you, babe?''

''Five, I think. About that.''

''It's a damn dusty world to grow up in,'' Renny said. She shook her head and concentrated on wrestling the truck off onto the Mosier detour.

Up there, in the old graveyard, lay the bones Julio Moreno had found. Nita looked at the folded hills and the dead orchards—such an easy place to die. The truck growled a low note as it climbed up over the crest where Jeremy had showed her spring. ''This land is full of our ghosts,'' she said. ''It's crowded with ghosts.''

''Ghosts, huh?'' Renny shifted on her padded seat as she eased the truck back down to the freeway again. ''Jesse talked about ghosts, but I never tried very hard to see 'em. Could be that's what Dan did for her—saw her ghosts. Maybe they shared some.''

The bitter thorn of Renny's hurt had softened just a little bit. Nita reached out, met Renny's hand halfway. For a silent moment their hands clasped; then Renny winced and let go to wrestle the truck back onto the interstate.

''Come down to the plaza before I take off.'' She gave Nita a crooked grin. ''I'll teach you to drive this baby. Then you can take over next time I get shot.''

''I will,'' Nita said.

They passed the abandoned car dealerships and empty shopping centers that fringed the west end of The Dalles. ''We'll drop the rig at the plaza and pick up one of the loaner cars,'' Renny said as she eased the truck down the exit ramp. ''I don't drive this baby up that goat track to the farm.''

''I'm going to the base.'' Nita drew a slow breath. She had no proof to offer Carter yet, nothing that would save Dan. Except herself—what she was. ''I can walk from here,'' Nita said as they turned into the plaza.

Dust eddied across the plaza's asphalt lot. A single rig baked in the sun. ''It's too empty.'' Renny scowled. ''Stay put a minute. I want to find out what's up.''

The dust sifted into the truck as soon as Renny opened the door. She cursed and slammed it, ducking her head against the dusty wind as she ran across the parking lot to the door. Something was wrong. Nita played with Rachel as she waited, trying to ignore the clench of unease in her belly, trying to keep Rachel from noticing it. A waste of time: Rachel fussed and slapped at the dangled beads. There was no puddle beneath the caged hoses today. A dust devil twisted at the corner of the building, and Nita hugged her cranky daughter. Renny was coming back. Nita winced as she yanked the door open and swung into the cab. "What is it?"

"Bad news." Renny scowled at the distant wall of the dam. Curtained by blowing dust, it bulked like a cliff wall across the riverbed. "Somebody blew the Pipe while we were on our jaunt. A lot of uniforms got killed."

Carter? Nita sucked in her breath, afraid to ask, afraid to say his name out loud. "Do you know who?" she managed.

"No names, babe. A bunch of them got offed in an ambush and a couple more got drowned when the Pipe went. Drowned, can you believe it?" Renny's laugh carried no trace of humor. "Josie says it's war around here. Water's cut off and they aren't going to turn it back on. Uniforms blew away a truck last night. Turned out to be a family with a kid. The locals are crazy mad, on their way down to the Shunt to kill uniforms and turn the water back on. Josie's a good lady. She waited to tip me off, but she's out of here now." Renny gave Nita a sharp look. "She's right, babe. How 'bout if I give you that driving lesson in Boise?"

Nita shook her head, full of wordless fear. "Will you give me a ride up to the farmhouse?" she faltered. "Before you go?" Jeremy would know what was going on.

"You're as thick-headed as Danny," Renny growled. "But I figured that." She pulled a key from her pocket. "I got us a loaner. We'll have to go through town and cut over to the house by the back way. The Army shut down the highway between here and the Deschutes bed. Even the rigs have to wait for an escort before they can go through. Josie said everyone is pissed as hell. I don't know any more than that."

And Carter? What about Carter? His name kept sneaking into Nita's head as the battered little loaner car chugged its way along the winding road that followed the rim of the gorge. An ambush, Renny had said. Corps people had died. Carter was in charge, the leader. Had he been out in the riverbed? No, Nita told herself, but the word carried no comfort. He felt so damn responsible. Rachel squirmed and Nita bounced her, trying to distract her, trying to distract herself from her own fears.

Beyond the car window, rows of irrigated beans or beets swung past. Some of the plants were shriveling in the sun. The landscape still looked unreal, but this sense of unreality had the dull gloss of shock. They had been gone only twenty-four hours. Everything had looked so hopeful when she had left. Now The Dalles was dying.

Renny turned the car onto the narrow track that led to the farmhouse and braked to a halt. "Listen to me, babe. You got nothing to bargain with, right? People are about to start shooting." She studied Nita's face for a long moment, then started the car moving again. "I've already offered Boise, so I won't say it again. But you be careful, babe. Hear me?"

"I hear you," Nita said as the car pulled up behind the sagging, gray house. "I'll be careful, Renny." She climbed out, Rachel clutched awkwardly in her arms. "Take care of yourself."

"Hell, I'm not running off yet." Renny looked grim. "I'll stick around to see what's up. If it's bad enough, I might want to cross the bridge and head up to Goldendale and ninety-seven. That gets me back to the riverbed, and I can give this dog and pony show a miss." She got out and slammed the door.

Renny was worried. About her? "Thanks," Nita said softly, grateful for Renny's presence beside her. Out in the fields, the beans lay dying. What if Jeremy wasn't here? What if no one was here? What had happened to Carter?

Jeremy and Johnny Seldon were on the porch, sitting in the shade. Johnny had a damp towel pressed against his face. "Nita!" Jeremy's relief hummed in the air. "I didn't hear you drive up. Hello, Renny. Want some water?"

"Jeremy, what's going *on*?" Nita struggled with the fear that wanted to choke her. "Is . . . Carter all right? Was he at the Pipe?"

"He's all right, Nita. He was here just a few minutes ago," Jeremy said gently.

His words were comforting on the surface, but there was no comfort in them. Nita felt herself going pale. "What's wrong?" she whispered.

"He decked me." Johnny raised his head. "He knocked me flat and took off. I don't know what got into him."

He was pissed. Nita turned her back on him. "I don't understand," she said, hugging Rachel to her. "What's going on, Jeremy?"

"I'm not sure." Jeremy put an arm around her. "Come on inside, put Rachel down, and have a drink of water. I'll get you a glass, Renny." He urged Nita gently into the dim interior of the house. "I think he found something." He looked at her sideways. "They were searching the house, looking for proof that Dan's involved with the sabotage. And all of a sudden he bolted out of here. He acted . . . pretty upset."

"He found what we were after." Johnny followed them inside, pulled out out a chair, and dropped onto it. "He found proof that Greely's connected with Hastings. Where the hell did he go with it?" He banged his clenched fist down on the table. "Goddamned idiot."

Nita stared at him. "There is no proof," she said. "Not here."

"There had to be. A letter." Johnny took the wadded towel away from his swollen face, scowled at it. "Something."

He was so easy to read. "You *know* there was something here." Her eyes widened. "You put it here. That's why you came up here the other day—not to see Dan—I knew that. You wanted to hide stuff for Carter to find."

"You got a problem, lady?" Johnny refolded the towel. "I've never even met Dan Greely. Of course I didn't plant anything here."

He was lying. "You hid something about Dan and General Hastings," she said softly. "The same kind of thing Lydia found—stuff to tie them together and tie them to Pacific Bio-Systems. So everyone will believe that they've been making money from those fields Renny was talking about."

Rachel was squirming in her arms, protesting that Nita was holding her too tightly. They were all looking at her. Renny was perplexed. Jeremy was listening carefully. And Johnny—behind his cold, untroubled face—was afraid.

"*You're* behind it," she whispered. "*You* hired Rico to fix the records and make it obvious enough to find. You've done it all, haven't you? The sabotage—the shooting. How could you do this to Carter?" Her voice trembled and broke. "My God, he *loves* you."

Johnny lunged for her and gasped as the heel of Jeremy's hand caught him hard in the shoulder, jolting him back into his chair.

"Sit still," Jeremy said mildly. "I think that's about enough." This time, they all looked at the small automatic that had appeared in his hand. He didn't look very clumsy, holding the gun.

Johnny clutched the tabletop with both hands, breathing through his mouth. "She's making it up." He didn't take his eyes from the gun. "She's Greely's lover, sticking up for him. I want to see one single shred of proof."

She didn't have a shred. And she didn't give a damn. "I know where he is." She turned to Jeremy, pleading now. "He's at the Shunt. Josie said that everyone was going there, going to kill uniforms." She remembered the darkness in him when he'd talked about Chicago. "He'll try and stop it, and . . . I don't think he'll care if he gets killed. We've got to go find him."

"Nita, are you sure?" He frowned at Johnny. "The Shunt is probably the most dangerous place in the country right now."

Jeremy didn't want to go. "Never mind." Nita jerked her head, struggling to think. What could he do, anyway? What could anyone do?

She could tell Carter the truth. If she could find him. He would still blame himself, still try to stop it. He would blame her, for telling him about Johnny, but there was nothing else she had to offer. Nothing. "Renny?" she asked desperately. "Can I borrow your car?"

"You're *worse* than Danny, babe. At least he has some sense." The wiry trucker snorted, her eyes warily fixed on Jeremy's gun. "You got a tank up your sleeve? Heavy hardware? What the hell is the *point*?"

"I don't know." Nita met her eyes.

"Shit." Renny looked away, her scowl moving from Jeremy's face to Johnny's and finally back to Nita. "You and Danny. Load up, babe. You don't know these goat tracks for squat and I do. No point in your getting shot any sooner than you have to."

"Thanks, Renny," Nita said softly. "I owe you again."

"Yeah, you sure do. It goes on the account. Let's go." Renny turned her back on Jeremy's gun to push through the door and out into the glare of daylight.

"I'm coming." Jeremy got slowly to his feet. "I guess I'm in on this, too."

Nita held out her hand, because he was doing it for her and there were no words to thank him. He took it, squeezed hard, and let go. Renny already had the engine running by the time they reached the car.

"What about me?" Johnny followed them, wary and furious. "How the hell do I get out of here?"

"Walk," Jeremy suggested as he climbed into the backseat. "Better take a water jug. There's an extra one on the sink in there."

Renny growled something unintelligible and put the car into gear. She hadn't been kidding when she had talked about goat tracks. The car bounced like a ball on the rutted trails—you couldn't call them roads—that led back from the rim of the gorge and down into the Deschutes bed. Rachel alternately fussed and chuckled, liking the ride, reacting to Renny's throbbing arm and the emotions that filled the car. No one said anything. Only Jeremy looked serene, but he wasn't. Nita clenched her teeth and tried to keep Rachel's head from hitting the door. They didn't pass a single car—the countryside might as well have been empty.

The deep scar of the Deschutes bed opened out in front of them as they topped the rise. The narrow track dove straight down toward the bottom of the riverbed. Trucks and cars clogged the flat ground along the old bank, blocking the road that led down to the Columbia bed itself. Renny eased the car down the slope, rear wheels slithering in the loose gravel. "Busy place down here," she said dryly. She pulled the car over behind a battered blue pickup and turned off the ignition. It was quiet. A bird chirped somewhere, an incongruous sound that made Nita want to laugh or cry.

"Everybody out," Renny said. "You all do what you want, but I don't plan to die for any natives."

She was speaking to Nita. Jeremy climbed out silently, tense but calm. Nita scooped up Rachel and followed him. She could hear no gunfire, no screams, no shouts, no sounds of violence. A pump station gleamed in the sunshine.

It looked so peaceful, but even from this distance, Nita could feel the gathering violence, like a dust storm on the horizon. Had her father *known* when those men had driven up their road? Had he felt his death coming to him? Rachel squirmed in Nita's arms and she held her daughter tightly, acutely aware of Rachel's warmth and weight. *How can I take her down there?* Nita thought with sudden terror, and then: *If I die, who will take care of her?* She hadn't thought of dying before, but the possibility of death eddied up the riverbed like the stench from a rotting carcass. "Renny?" Nita swallowed the words that clogged her throat. Silently she held out Rachel.

Renny's eyes narrowed and Nita braced herself for refusal.

"Until you get back." The trucker reached suddenly and took Rachel from Nita's arms. "I'm no mother, babe. You come get her damn soon."

"I will," Nita said huskily. She walked away as Renny slammed the car door. *I'm never going to see Rachel again,* she thought.

Jeremy touched her arm lightly. "Bad?" he asked.

"Yes." Nita drew a shuddering breath. "I'm feeling them. It's never been like this before."

"You've never been in the middle of a riot before." Jeremy took her arm, his eyes dark with concern. "Are you sure you can handle this?"

"I don't know." Nita shook herself. "Carter's here. He thinks Dan did it. He doesn't know about Johnny."

"Dan's not in jail anymore." Jeremy shaded his eyes, staring down the riverbed. "Carter said that someone helped him escape. He didn't seem very sure that Dan was willing to go."

Which meant what? She didn't know, and couldn't make thoughts come together in her aching head. Maybe Dan was dead. Maybe he was safe. It didn't make any difference to here and now and the stinking violence that clawed at her. Nita held Jeremy's hand tightly as they threaded their way between the parked vehicles, grateful for his presence. He was calm, and she could focus on that calm, use it to fight the buzz of emotion that was glowing steadily stronger. Even here, Jeremy stood a little apart from this dusty riverbed, one foot in his green past. His detachment helped. There were people ahead. She stumbled, shuddering. So many people. And more cars. Trucks . . . They were so *angry*, and there was death in that anger. What difference did it make if you died now—maybe it would be better now than later, when you were starving, or watching your kids sell their asses in the camps . . .

"I was out on the rim when the Pipe blew," Jeremy said softly. "I saw the water come down the bed in a wave. It wasn't a river, it was a flood. Ugly. Destructive. It scared me. Can you find Carter in this?"

Yes, this was a flood, too. Individual emotions merged into a dark torrent of rage and fear and the need to hurt someone, anyone. "I . . . don't know," Nita gasped.

She could hear the sound of the crowd now, a murmur of angry voices that had been cut off by a trick of acoustics and the bulge of the riverbed wall. A rough barricade made up of vehicles and junk blocked the interstate. Most of the people milled behind it. A lot of them had guns. She was panting, suffocating, as if the anger and desperation had burned up the oxygen in the air.

"Nita!" Sandy Corbett separated from the crowd, haggard and dusty. "What are you doing here? Do you know where Dan is? We heard he'd been arrested."

"Dan's disappeared." Nita swallowed, her throat dry as dust. "Sandy, what's happening?"

"What does it look like?" Sandy said bitterly. "Everyone has their back to the wall. Not one of us is going to have a crop left, if the Army doesn't turn the water back on pretty soon. That bunch that hangs out at the theater started it, yelling all over town how they were going to come out here and turn it on themselves. We scraped together enough money to call in a law firm from Portland. They say they can get an injunction to force the Corps to turn the water back on, but it's already too late for a lot of crops. I don't know." Sandy spat into the dust, her face twisted with anger. "This time I'm about ready to listen to the hotheads. What do we have to lose?"

"Sandy, you have to stop it," Nita gasped. "Johnny Seldon's behind it all, and I've got proof. He *wants* this to happen."

"Seldon? The Water Policy guy? Well, I'm afraid he's going to get what he wants." Sandy looked away from Nita, shoulders drooping. "I can't stop this, honey. Dan couldn't stop it. It's too late."

"It can't be too late. You'll die, don't you understand? The uniforms'll shoot you." And Carter would die, too, because this was Chicago all over and it was his fault and he couldn't live with it. He would get himself killed and then he wouldn't have to live with it. "We've got to do *something*," she cried.

"Nita, easy." Jeremy grabbed her by the shoulders, gave her a single, hard shake. "Calm down," he said urgently. "You're reacting to all this. Come on, Nita."

Yes, reacting. Nita clutched Jeremy—Jeremy who knew *here* and a gentle green past—and realized that Sandy was staring at her, thinking *crazy*. "All right," she gasped. "I'm all right." Barely. Her nails had left bloody half moons on Jeremy's forearms. "It's so loud. I don't think I can hear Carter," she said in a small voice.

"Think, Nita." Jeremy scowled at the Shunt bunker and the Corps vehicles pulled up around it. "If he found Seldon's planted evidence, he'd think Hastings and Dan are behind this—right?"

"Yes." She shuddered. What would he do? "He'd go find the general," she said slowly. "To accuse him. I think."

"If Hastings isn't in on it, then the worst thing he has to worry about is getting himself arrested for insubordination." Jeremy gave her another, gentler shake. "If he's over there, he's as safe as he can be down here. I don't think we ought to go stomping up to the bunker just now."

Someone was yelling at the mob over a loudspeaker. An officer. Any second now the shooting would start. Any second. Any second. And Carter would die in it. She knew it as surely as if it had already happened. She shuddered, barely aware of Jeremy's hands clutching her arms, struggling for calm. The mob mind beat at her: rage/fear/anger . . . ''It's happening!'' she cried. ''Jeremy, stop it! We *have* to stop it.'' Whatever the Army man had said, it had been the wrong thing.

You've had your chance, Harold Ransom was bellowing through an electronic megaphone. *Let's do it!*

''The lady was right. No one can stop it, Nita. We're getting out of here,'' Jeremy said.

Too late. Too late. Toolatetoolatetoolate . . . A shot cracked out across the riverbed. Another. Someone screamed, but if there was pain behind that cry it was lost in the crowd roar. People were moving, running, firing their weapons. Rage and death pumped through their veins: *Kill them. Kill them, the way they've killed my crops, my family, my life* . . . Shots rattled, too fast to be anything except Army rifles. Another scream, close this time, and now Nita caught the faint shock of someone's wound. She screamed Carter's name, but her voice was lost in the roar, drowned.

''Goddamnit, Nita, *come on*!'' Jeremy yanked her into a run. Blinded, deafened by the bellow of the mob, Nita stumbled along in his grip.

The mob would sweep over the bunker as the water from the broken pipe had swept over Carter. Soldiers would kill locals, locals would kill soldiers, and the water wouldn't come back on. Everything that had mattered to her father, everything that had mattered to Dan would be gone, swept down the riverbed by this ugly flood . . .

''Jeremy, wait!'' Nita dug in her heels, clinging to him, dragging him to a halt. ''You saw it—the flood. Make it again— make it *big*. Like the river's really flooding.''

''I can't.'' He jerked her forward. ''I can't control the visions. Just the little stuff.''

''Yes, you *can*. You made spring for me, remember? You *do* it, Jeremy, it doesn't just happen.''

He shook his head, full of dust and denial, his face freezing into stone. He wasn't going to do it, wasn't going to listen to her. He was going to run away, was going to keep on running, the way he'd run all his life. ''You're scared,'' Nita screamed at him. ''You *know* you can do it. You just don't want to admit it, because then you'll have to face what you are. You'll have to *use* it. You want me to do that for you! So you don't have to!''

Jeremy slapped her across the face.

Stunned by the blow and the white-hot slash of his rage, Nita fell, sprawling facedown in the dust. He wouldn't do it and nothing could stop it now. Her father had finally lost. Dan had lost. Gunfire, screams, and shouts pierced her. Terror clawed at her, louder now than the rage. It was all over, all over, and nothing would be left that mattered. She lifted her head . . . and screamed.

A wall of water towered over her. It filled the upstream riverbed with foamy madness, stretching from wall to rocky gorge wall. It was bigger than the dam, a wall of darkness, ready to crash down on them, drown them all . . . Nita struggled with the overwhelming urge to run, escape, even as she told herself that it was only Jeremy, that he had *done* it. People around them were seeing it, but not everyone, not at first. The ones who did panicked, and their fear, their belief soaked through the mob mind, solidified the curling crest of water until everyone saw it as clearly as she did: an unimaginable ocean of water rushing down the riverbed toward them.

It's only Jeremy. That knowledge began to slip away from Nita, blasted by a thunderclap of terror as locals and soldiers dropped weapons, screamed, and fled, clawing their way up the stony riverbanks in blind panic. The muddy wave curled higher, closer, moving in nightmare slow motion, streaked with dirty foam. Nita clung to a rock, struggling for sanity. In a few moments that water would sweep over the bunker, thunder down on her head, smash her, choke her, drown her.

Jeremy, Jeremy, it's only Jeremy. A burly man in a Corps uniform stumbled by, his eyes white-ringed and wild. *It's only Jeremy.* Nita fought the wash of emotion that threatened to send her stumbling and scrambling along with the mob. She clung to the brown chunk of lava rock as if she were struggling in a real flood. Slowly . . . slowly, the crest of the terror passed as the riverbed emptied. Nita sobbed once as the world began to reshape itself. Jeremy's wave still curled in the riverbed, closer, but moving very slowly. Too slowly to be real.

Engines roared as cars and trucks pulled away. The few men and women who still milled in the riverbed looked dazed and bewildered. Jeremy knelt in the dust, fists clenched, eyes fixed on his hovering flood.

"Jeremy?" He didn't react as Nita knelt beside him. In a spurt of fear, she shook him. He resisted for an instant, his muscles rigid, then sighed and lowered his head.

The water vanished, leaving nothing but sunbaked riverbed behind.

"They're all running." Nita put her arms around him, trembling with the aftermath of the terror. "You stopped it, Jeremy."

"I did . . . didn't I?" He was trembling, too. He got unsteadily to his feet, leaning heavily on her, as if the terrible vision had sucked all the strength out of him.

"This way." Nita put her arm around him, guiding him toward an outcrop of rock. "I'm going to try for the bunker. I think . . . Carter will be there. He'll know it was you, Jeremy. I have to tell him it's not Dan and the general before—something happens." Now that the worst of the mob rage had ended, she could think again. Dan. Where was he? Dead, like her father? He had expected it. Nita swallowed a knot of tears and looked up and down the riverbed. It looked strange, unfamiliar, changed by the brief presence of the water.

"I'm coming with you." Jeremy pushed hair out of his eyes, taking a deep breath. "I'm all right. Can you listen for individuals again? I don't want to meet some terrified uniform with a rifle."

"I can do that, I think." Close individual emotions would stand out like bright sparks of light against the murky background of confusion and fear. "We're okay." She clutched his hand and they began to pick their way toward the Shunt.

There was so little sign of the flood and its effect. The baked clay of the bed didn't hold footprints. Someone had dropped a battered hunting rifle, and it lay wedged between two rocks. Nita and Jeremy worked their way around one of the long lava ridges that cut the riverbed. A body lay in the dust on the far side—a boy. Nita recoiled. He lay on his back, head twisted at a sickening angle, his wide-open eyes staring at the sky. He looked about fifteen.

Jeremy groaned softly.

"If you hadn't done it, he would have been shot by a uniform," Nita said fiercely. "Or he would have ended up in a camp. And how many more?" She clutched Jeremy's arm, aware suddenly of a familiar touch in the murk of distant confusion. "Carter," she breathed. "I think so, anyway."

Alive. Not dead.

"Wait." Jeremy held on tight to her arm. "Slow, Nita, or we'll both get shot. We're pretty close to the bunker."

Not slow, no. The feel of him terrified her. There was death there. She yanked free of Jeremy's restraining hand and broke into a run.

CHAPTER TWENTY-SIX ☆

Reason finally penetrated Carter's cold rage as he sped away from Dan's house on the gorge rim. He was wearing a Corps uniform. Which meant that he would be damn lucky to make it back to the base alive, never mind down to the Shunt. And he had to make it down to the Shunt. Hastings was there—with his Rangers. What was Hastings's plan? he wondered bitterly. Or was this simply the general's chance to kill as many of the locals as he could?

Carter braked, fighting the car one-handed onto the rough shoulder of the main road. Pain from his ribs was making him dizzy, but he fished in the backseat and found a shirt. It was a white dress shirt with a food stain on the front—part of Johnny's cleaning, no doubt. He slid his arms into the too-large sleeves. It would do. No pants, but with his coverall rolled down around his waist, he looked more local than uniform—as long as he stayed in the car.

He put the car into gear and headed down the hill, toward the highway bridge that crossed the riverbed. The few locals he passed—and the town might have been a ghost town, my God, everyone must be out at the damn Shunt—barely glanced at him. He would have to come up on the Shunt from the Washington side of the gorge. Hastings must have thrown roadblocks across 84, and he wasn't sure what orders concerning himself might have been issued. Probably none, since he wasn't officially under arrest, but he wasn't taking any chances. Purpose had contracted to a cold lump in his gut, a heavy presence that he carried carefully, like a bomb set to go off.

Justice or vengeance? Did it matter? Carter shook his head, lips tight. Killing Hastings wouldn't bring anyone back to life, but maybe it would balance the scales just a little. An eye for an

243

eye . . . He crossed the bridge and turned eastward on the Washington highway. Hastings would have thrown barricades across this road, too. He braked, stripped off the shirt that had camouflaged him through The Dalles, and pulled his coverall up over his shoulders. The Corps insignia gleamed on the collar. He had sworn an oath of office when he had been commissioned. The words came back to him suddenly and clearly, as if he had spoken them only this afternoon. *I do solemnly swear that I will support and defend the Constitution of the United States* . . . And the Corps, by its very existence, had shredded the Constitution. Water counted a hell of a lot more than individual rights. . . . *against all enemies, foreign and domestic* . . . Hastings was the enemy here. And Dan Greely. He drove fast, carrying death inside him, its cold weight like an unhatched egg, a bomb. He was a delivery system now, and nothing more. A guided missile.

The Shunt bunker came into view, across the riverbed on the Oregon side. A dark mass of humanity seethed at the mouth of the Deschutes bed. Carter shivered, seeing Lakeshore in those dark figures, remembering flames and gunfire and blood. A wooden barricade barred the access road that led down to the bunker from this side. Two guards lifted rifles, sighting on the windshield as a third man waved him to a halt. Carter stared impassively at the small black mouths of their weapons, waiting for them to recognize him.

"I'm sorry, sir." A corporal leaned in at the window. "The general said that no one was to come through here."

"He didn't mean me," Carter snapped.

"I'd better check, sir—"

Carter stepped on the accelerator, and because Hastings hadn't named him specifically, and he was, after all, a colonel, the corporal nervously waved him through. The Shunt was right ahead. Carter drove down into the riverbed and parked the car, his skin tightening. No one was working on the Pipe. They were all behind the parked trucks, crouching low, rifles in hand. Rangers, and regular Corps.

It was happening. Now. He was too fucking late.

As Carter flung the door open, gunshots cracked. The rear window of his car disintegrated and he dove for the ground, realizing belatedly that he was out in plain sight, well within range of local rifles. Locals were running into the riverbed, taking cover behind rocks, firing. One of the running figures fell. Another. Carter spotted Hastings near the bunker. Time.

Lifting the cold weight of death and justice inside him, he started running, bending low, zigzagging from rock to rock.

Someone screamed hoarsely. It was a shriek of fear, not pain. Carter glanced up, then tripped and fell, barely aware of the pain in his ribs. Water! The dark wall curled over their heads, streaked with foam, ready to break. Carter heard more screams, heard his own voice. *Run!* his brain screamed at him, but he couldn't run, couldn't look away. Memory seized him. In a moment the water would suck him up, tumble him down the stony riverbed in its cold, unbreakable grip.

Jeremy, a tiny voice whispered in his brain. *It's Jeremy.*

Yes, yes, the wave wasn't moving fast enough—not like the ugly brown flood from the Pipe. It wasn't real. Soldiers ran past him. A wide-eyed corporal dropped a rifle and it bounced, the barrel barely missing Carter's face. Blind with terror, people stumbled, fell, were pulled to their feet by friends and ran on. "It's all right," Carter shouted uselessly. "It's an illusion."

No one listened. He could feel their belief, their terror. Even knowing it was Jeremy, his own muscles twitched with the desire to run. It was so damn *real*.

For a seeming eternity it threatened, and then . . . it vanished. Carter found himself staring at baked clay and dusty rocks, his heart still pounding. "Damn," he whispered. "Goddamn." He drew a shaky breath and looked around.

The riverbed looked as if the wave had actually hit. The mob had scattered, and cars and trucks were pulling out on the Oregon side. The barricade was nearly deserted. Dust blew away on the dry wind, and a few sprawled bodies lay in the sun. Drowned by an imaginary flood? Carter wondered numbly. Killed by real bullets, by the Chicago that had almost happened. For the moment, it was over. God, what had Jeremy *done*?

Now, maybe, there was time to stop it. Carter touched the cold weight of his gun as he staggered to his feet. Hastings would be near the bunker; he wouldn't have run far. Carter started limping toward the bunker. Most of the Corps people and the Rangers had headed for the Washington side of the riverbed, up above the parked trucks. The Shunt bunker appeared to be deserted, although a small detachment of Rangers was already scrambling across the riverbed toward it. No Hastings.

"Carter? Carter, wait!"

Nita's voice? Carter turned, relief that she was all right leaping like a flame in his chest, turning sick as he remembered the stock certificates in the drawer beneath the diapers. And then she was running toward him, her black hair coming loose from its braid, whipping in the wind, her arms reaching for him. And his own arm went up—to hell with where the certificates had been—went around her tight, because people had been shot here today and one of those bodies might have been hers. Her embrace wrung a gasp from him and she stepped back suddenly, eyes brilliant with concern.

"You're hurt," she said. "You were there, weren't you? When they blew the Pipe?"

"Yes, I was there." He touched her face lightly, full of loss and longing. Nothing had changed, and everything had changed. Dan Greely was behind this and she wouldn't believe it. By the end of this day, it wouldn't matter what there was or might have been between them.

"You're wrong." Her eyes widened and she grabbed his hand. "Carter—whatever you found in Dan's house, it was planted. To make it look like he and General Hastings were getting paid by Pacific BioSystems. It's not true." She clung to his hand as he tried to pull away from her. "That's why I came down here. To tell you."

"I'm sorry, Nita." Maybe she had seen her dead father in Greely. Maybe that was why she wanted him to be some kind of hero. He'd taken over her father's job, after all.

"I'm not just wishing." She clung to his arm as he started for the bunker. "Carter, I know who did it. It's Johnny Seldon. Carter, I'm so sorry."

"Johnny?" Her accusation stopped him. "Nita, you're wrong. Let go," he said gently.

"He wanted you to find it—that 'proof' in Dan's house. He put it there, Carter. I *know* it."

Johnny *had* dragged him up there. "How do you *know* this?" He twisted savagely out of her grasp, angry because she was always standing up for Greely, because this couldn't possibly be true, no matter how much Johnny had been around this mess. "Tell me how the hell you're so sure?"

"Carter—what do you owe him?" Tears glittered in her eyes. "What did he do?"

What did he do? "He's my friend," Carter said softly. "And he kept me from going to prison. Because he was my friend." A shot boomed close by. Carter cursed and ducked, dragging Nita down beside him. Nice move—stand out in the open and wait to get shot. He looked around, but there was no one, no sign that anyone had shot at them.

"Dan!" Nita scrambled to her feet, her face white.

He grabbed for her, but she was running, scrambling over the rocks that stuck up out of the riverbed. They were down in an old channel here, out of sight of the Shunt bunker and the riverbanks. Carter swore and went after her, calling her crazy and an idiot, afraid for her. He rounded a spire of water-worn lava and halted in his tracks.

Hastings sprawled facedown in the dust between two ridges of rock. His face was turned toward Carter and his eyes stared sightlessly at the rocks. He looked pissed, angry at the death that had caught him at last. Dark blood stained the dust beneath his face.

Dan Greely leaned against the rock less than ten feet from Hastings's body, a large-caliber revolver in his hand. Carter looked at him, but felt no surprise. The numb sense of purpose had repossessed him.

"Carter?" Nita stepped between them, face white.

He ignored her, keeping his eyes on Greely, who was staring at the revolver as if the sight of it confused him. He opened his hand suddenly. The gun landed in the dust with a dull thud and the sound of metal on stone.

"Don't," Nita said softly.

Carter looked down, realized that he had drawn his own gun. This time the safety was off. "Move, Nita," he said gently. Hastings was dead. The scales were almost balanced. The stony purpose he had carried in his chest was unfolding—a cold flower unfurling steel petals. The ghosts were waiting for their blood. "You are some bastard, Greely," he said calmly.

"No." Greely's voice was thick and slow. "I didn't—"

"Carter, wait!" Nita stepped back toward Dan, her arms spread to shield him.

Carter edged closer. The gun was on the ground. He might be able to yank her out of the way and get in a shot before Greely could get his hands on the gun . . . Warrington had fallen backward, so *light*, as if his bones were full of air . . . the kid in the van had been twelve . . . Greely stood so fucking still, just watching, not making any move to reach for the gun. As if he were waiting for Carter to pull the trigger. As if he wanted it to happen.

"Stop!" Nita took a step toward him. "You hear me first." She swallowed, trembling in the face of his terrible coldness. He didn't want to hear, wasn't going to hear her. "Johnny did it," she cried. "Johnny Seldon, do you hear me, Carter?" He

heard that. With a surge of relief, she felt the twitch of his denial.
"He's behind the sabotage, not Hastings. Not Dan." He didn't
answer her, but she had his attention now. "He is. Do you
care?" She made her voice bitter. "Or do you just need a blood
sacrifice to pay for your guilt?"

His head jerked a little. That had gotten to him. That had
hurt, and, thank God, a little of the crazy coldness warmed to
anger.

"I've heard you out on the subject of Dan Greely." His eyes
never left Dan. "And I know Johnny isn't behind this."

"Oh, no, I'm not wrong." Nita lifted her shoulders against
the weight that wanted to drag her to the ground. "Johnny told
me he hadn't planted the things you found, but he was lying,
Carter. He told me he wasn't behind the sabotage, but he was
lying then, too. *No* one can lie to me." She kept her eyes on his
face, waiting for him to look at her. "I can hear your thoughts,
Carter. I know what everyone feels. Happy. Sad. Angry. When
you lie, you get watchful, a little tense. You can't hide it from
me."

Carter's hand tightened fractionally on the gun.

"And you don't believe me."

"No. I don't."

"I'm like Jeremy. A freak. A mutation. I felt my father die,"
Nita said softly. "It hurt him when they shot him. He wanted to
live—he wanted to live so much. I felt every minute of my mother's hatred for me, because my father had died instead of me
and she had loved him. I feel it all, Carter. Every bit of pain,
every bit of anger. I don't really want you to believe me, because
if you believe me, you'll be afraid of me. Like David was afraid
of me. And . . . I'll feel that, too."

He looked at her at last, a small muscle twitching at the corner
of his mouth.

"You don't really think it's Dan," she said, and her voice
wanted to crack with the pain she was handing him. "You need
someone to blame because you think it's your fault. You're scared
shitless that I'm right. You're scared that Johnny really *is* behind
this—you know he could be, and you're afraid that he betrayed
you."

His eyes blazed at her and the gun shook in his hand. For one
terrible second Nita thought he was going to shoot her. She sank
to her knees, tears overflowing finally, scalding their way down
her cheeks.

"Do you think I *like* it?" she cried. "Do you think I *want* to hear your pain? I love you, Carter, and now you know what I am, and you'll be afraid of me. Dan didn't shoot this man. He isn't behind this, do you hear me? Are you listening? Johnny Seldon is. Lydia will get me the proof, and if you kill Dan, you'll blame yourself forever for it. Don't *do* that to yourself, Carter. Please?''

Carter looked down at his hands. They were shaking. He thumbed on the safety, afraid of what might happen, afraid of what almost *had* happened. I wanted to shoot her, he thought in a moment of terrible revelation. Because she had looked at him, had *seen* him, had thrown that seeing in his face. Because he didn't want to hear her.

Because, deep down inside, a part of him knew that she could be right about Johnny.

Pacific BioSystems. That was the tie-in. *They think they can own me*, Johnny had said a lifetime ago. *They're going to find out otherwise.*

So Johnny had maybe used him. Johnny. The only person in his life he had been able to count on—who had always been there. The one person who took him for who he was and not what he wasn't. He didn't want to believe her—no one could read minds.

Half an hour ago, a man had filled a dry riverbed with an imaginary flood.

Carter shoved the Beretta back into its holster and raised his head slowly, forcing himself to look Dan Greely in the face. He still looked confused. Drugged? Carter sighed, exhausted suddenly, in pain, knees threatening to buckle under him. ''Maybe it is a frame,'' he said thickly. ''I don't fucking know. You better get out of here.''

Nita gave a small, choked cry, her face turning up to the rock crest above them, her body stiffening.

''You bastard.'' Delgado rose to his knees on the rock, a rifle in his hands, aiming straight at Carter's chest. ''You dumb asshole. Why didn't you just shoot him?''

He'd been there all the time. Carter stared up at him, seeing insanity in his white-rimmed eyes, seeing death there. For Dan? For him? Delgado could kill all three of them with that thing. ''Major, get down here.'' He threw all the authority he could manage into his voice, making it crack like a whip.

Delgado ignored him, watching Nita. ''You screwed everything up, you hick bitch.'' His eyes looked like black holes in his pale face. ''Proof, huh? I'll give you proof.''

"Nita, down! Now!"

Jeremy's voice, hoarse and urgent. Carter caught a glimpse of his blond hair and limping gait out of the corner of his eye, and thought he saw a gun in his hand. Delgado was aiming at Nita—he couldn't miss at this range. Dan was moving toward her, stumbling and clumsy, but he couldn't do anything. Carter yanked the Beretta from its holster, his heart pounding. Delgado saw him and the rifle barrel swung back in Carter's direction, moving so fucking *fast*.

"No!" Nita screamed.

The rifle in Delgado's hands wavered and swung back in her direction. Carter brought the Beretta up just as Delgado fired. The short burst of ugly sound crashed from rock to rock, deafening Carter as he pulled the trigger. The Beretta bucked in his hand and the bullet caught Delgado in the chest, spinning him sideways, toppling him backward off the ledge. He slithered down the side of the ridge in a shower of small stones and dirt, landing in the dust with a slack thud.

Behind him, Nita cried a hoarse note of anguish.

Carter turned slowly, not wanting to see. But it wasn't Nita—it was Jeremy. He lay sprawled on his back and she crouched beside him, her face twisted. Bright blood soaked the bottom of his shirt. A lot of blood. Dan went awkwardly to his knees beside her. He fumbled at his shirt, wadding it into a pad. Cold inside, Carter touched Jeremy's throat. There was a pulse; thready and uneven, but there.

"He's dying," Nita said.

Her matter-of-fact tone and her wild eyes scared the hell out of Carter. She *felt* this—Jeremy's wound, his dying. If she was what she said she was.

He looked at her face and his last doubt vanished.

"See if you can stop the bleeding," he snapped at Dan. "I'll get the paramedics down here." He touched Nita's shoulder, but she didn't look at him, gave no sign that she even knew he was there. What was it like to feel someone die? What did it do to you? Carter scrambled to his feet, ribs screaming.

"Hurry," Dan said.

Carter started for the bunker and the trucks. He was white and shaking by the time he reached the bunker, clammy with icy sweat. Medical teams were just arriving from the base. He grabbed the first team he saw and sent them scrambling down to Jeremy, wanting to follow them, to see if Jeremy was still alive, to see how Nita was.

Not yet. He had to find the Rangers' CO, pronto. He needed to sort out the confusion, assess injuries, Shunt security, and the needs of the moment. The water, the ghost flood, was on every pair of lips. Eyes twitched upstream every few minutes, as if people expected another rush of water to come thundering down the riverbed. Ghost flood. That was as good an explanation as any, Carter decided grimly. He soothed nervous officers, told them that it was over, and then got one of the medical people to give him painkillers for his ribs and a little Ritalin to keep him on his feet.

The stretcher team hurried past him with Jeremy, faces intent, IV bag swinging. ''How is he?'' Carter asked, and got a head-shake in reply. Alive, at least. There was that much hope. Carter saw no sign of Nita or Dan. They had disappeared. Worried, he issued strict orders forbidding retaliation against locals, saying a silent prayer that it would keep Nita and Dan safe.

He sent out details to search for any injured people who might still be in the riverbed. Soldiers and locals both, and don't miss any locals, he told them. It was time to start healing the breach, but it was going to be a damned tough breach to heal. The bodies were coming in. Six locals, so far. Two Corps people, not including Delgado and Hastings. For the moment, he was letting them remain victims of the riot, so that made four. Slowly he sorted through the mess.

The painkillers didn't help much, and after a while Carter had to stop. He leaned against the side of one of the trucks, realizing with vague surprise that the sun was going down. He was aware of his heart pumping blood through his veins, the ache of his abused ribs.

He could see a stretch of the east bank of the Deschutes bed from here. Once there had been some kind of park up there. The dusty ground was divided into little rectangles by the remains of asphalt paths and parking strips. People had probably parked their RVs or pitched their tents there in the old days. Now dust drifted along the curbs, and only stumps were left of the trees that must have shaded the campground.

What would Jeremy call up out of that dusty square of ground? Grass? The ghosts of kids running and playing, maybe swimming in the river? Carter wondered if any of those kids had lived to see that park go dusty and dry. There was only so much water, and there were so many people who needed it. If Jeremy died, Carter would never know what that damn park had looked like. He swallowed, exhausted in spite of the Ritalin, too tired to deal with this anymore. He had been keeping thoughts of Johnny at bay, building a fence of activity to hide behind.

Carter closed his eyes briefly, seeing the dusty landscape of the apartment he had shared with his mother. There had been an empty sound to the bang of the door when he'd gotten home from school that afternoon. He had called her name because he always did, even though she was sometimes out of it already, if she'd finished with the big house early. He wasn't sure why he had looked into the bathroom. He didn't know why she had cut her wrists—she had so many fucking pills. Maybe that was why: after all the years of pills, death had to be something different. Not just more pills. She had been so careful not to get blood on the floor.

He had called 911 because that's what he was supposed to do. And then . . . Warrington had come in. The old bastard. How many nights had Carter lain awake, listening to them through the wall? Sometimes she had cried afterward. Carter had tried to go comfort her one night. The door had been locked, and she wouldn't open it. Not even when he knocked. That afternoon the old bastard had looked at her—had looked at Carter sitting there, holding her hand.

And he had started crying.

Carter didn't remember much after that—just blurry images of Warrington on the floor—paramedics—cops cuffing his hands behind him. The images were like someone else's photos, found in a drawer. He had been just too old for juvenile court. And the charge had been murder. Johnny's dad had paid for the lawyer and the expensive experts who had testified that Mr. Warrington had died of an aneurysm that would have undoubtedly happened anyway, and not because Carter had hit him.

So he had ended up with an assault conviction and a suspended sentence. Because of Johnny.

Carter wiped his face, feeling sweat and mud beneath his fingers. Time to finish up—before the drugs wore off. Time enough, later, for Johnny. He turned away from the dusty park with its ghosts of playing children. The riot was over, but it wasn't an ending. Even if they got the water back on tonight, some people were going to lose their crops. When would the next flow cut come down? The struggle along this riverbed would never end. Carter took another painkiller and went to check on the status of the repairs.

* * *

It was dark by the time an NCO drove Carter back to the base. He had sent a couple of people to look for Nita and Dan, but they'd had no luck. Carter hoped that they'd made it back to the farm, but this was not the time for soldiers to be wandering through The Dalles. He had one hell of a load of reports to attend to.

Screw the reports.

Carter ordered the driver to let him off at the infirmary. Hospitals smelled alike—miltary or civilian. Carter tried to decipher that odor as he waited for the doctor. Disinfectant, urine, hope, and fear? He looked up as the doctor walked into the sterile little waiting room. She was dressed in blood-spotted surgical greens and she looked tired, too. "Your civilian's stable," she told him. "He's in Recovery, so you can't see him. We got him right into surgery, but there's some spinal damage that is going to be a bitch to fix." She sighed, looking at visions on the pastel-green wall behind Carter. "How good is this guy's medical insurance?"

Medical insurance? Carter didn't laugh. "What kind of damage are you talking about?"

"Too soon to tell." The tired eyes got more tired. "Maybe paralysis from the hips down, if there's no intervention. Maybe only partial loss of use. Can you give me some ID and any kind of history on this guy?" She was eyeing him, frowning. "Then I think you'd better get some rest, sir. Consider it an official prescription. Do you need something for pain?"

So Jeremy might end up paralyzed. That was a bitter reward for what he'd done. "I've already had too many pills," Carter said curtly. "Call me if you hear anything on Mr. Barlow's condition."

Fuzzy, struggling to think, Carter gave an orderly Jeremy's full name. That was about all he knew about Jeremy—except that he had stopped another Chicago this afternoon, had saved a lot of lives. Except that he could summon the green past that none of them would ever see, could give them hope for the future—that maybe it would be green again some day and it was worth hanging on for. The orderly didn't want to hear about that.

Sleep, he thought as he left the infirmary. I need to sleep. The short walk to his apartment seemed to take at least an hour, but that was all right. It felt good to let go at last and give in to the chemical fog that kept trying to seep into his skull. The Ritalin was wearing off, leaving a trembling exhaustion in its wake. Carter pushed his door open. For a moment, the darkness moved, pregnant with echoes of his night with Nita. Wishing suddenly, fiercely, that she was waiting here for him, Carter groped for the switch and flicked on the lights.

Dan was sitting on the sofa.

"You do this a lot, don't you?" Carter closed the door and leaned against it, thinking that if he moved, he'd fall down. "Why don't you try the gate?"

"The base is still officially closed." Dan's eyes narrowed. "You look like shit."

"You're the second person to tell me that in the last ten minutes. I guess it's true." Carter tried for a chair, just made it. He leaned his head back, not sure he was ever going to be able to lift it again. "Where's Nita?"

"At the plaza with Renny. Worrying about Jeremy," Dan said. "Worrying about you, too. How is Jeremy?"

"In Recovery." He decided not to mention the doctor's prognosis. "The doc will call me if anything changes. I'll call the store. Tell me what happened." Carter managed to sit up straight, realizing that he had stopped doubting Dan. "I'm too beat to be judgmental, so I'll listen."

"Our redheaded friend and someone else showed up at my cell in uniform," Dan said slowly. "The idea was to make it look like I'd shot Hastings. I think Delgado was supposed to kill me afterward. Anyway, they shot me full of something, and after that everything is kind of blurry. They kept me tied up in a basement for a while, then I got another shot. We missed Jeremy's show." He frowned. "I think we were driving down into the riverbed when the flood happened. I remember someone shouting and the car bouncing hard enough to shake me out of the fog. Nita says he scared hell out of everyone."

"He sure did." Carter rubbed his aching eyes. "He stopped it, Dan."

"I . . . don't understand what he does." Dan sounded hesitant. "But it's really something." He shook his head. "I guess the guys who had me were far enough from the effect that they didn't bolt. Anyway, things got fuzzy again. When they cleared up, I was looking at Hastings with a gun in my hand. I expect it was the gun that killed him."

"I forgot about that damn gun." Carter's eyes snapped open. "It killed Hastings, and it's got your prints on it."

"No problem." Dan looked at him sideways. "I made it disappear."

"You don't take chances, do you?"

"Sometimes I do," Dan said softly. "Do you think we can start over?"

"I think we have to." Carter sighed. "I've got to trust you, Dan, because I . . . can't do this by myself. I'm a uniform." He met Dan's eyes. "I'm sorry. That I got taken in by that frame."

Dan grimaced. "It was a damn good frame."

Yeah, it had been that: precise and carefully put together. The kind of neat, complicated construct that Johnny could do so well . . . Carter leaned his face into his hands. "We'll have water back in the local lines by morning. I'll give you the final numbers tomorrow. For the interim, I have the authority to increase the flow. The numbers still aren't going to be good."

"No, they won't be." Dan didn't smile. "Seldon did a lot of damage. It's going to be tough around here, and people aren't going to want to hear reasons."

"If it *was* Johnny." Carter looked away. "I'm not sure about that yet." *Why,* Johnny? Carter jerked his head, hurting, and not wanting to hurt any more tonight, damn it. "We'll just have to do our best on this." He looked at Dan, noticing the fresh bruises on his face and the red weals on his wrists where he'd been tied or cuffed. "You don't look so good yourself," he said. "Do you need a ride home?"

Dan shook his head. "I'm staying at the plaza tonight. Thanks. Nita really is worried about you. She cares a lot." Something flickered in his eyes. "I didn't know . . . about what she could do."

I love you, she had cried. *Now you know what I am and you'll be afraid of me.* "I didn't know, either," Carter said. She scared Dan; it showed in his face. Not a lot, but a little. Carter let his breath out in a long sigh, hazed with drugs and pain and exhaustion. What would someone know about you if they could read every nuance of your fear or doubt or joy? A lot. Am I afraid? he asked himself. He couldn't answer that question—not yet. Not tonight. But he would have to answer it for himself, and for Nita. "I'll get you an escort," he said to Dan. "You can go out the gate." He pushed himself up onto leaden legs, amazed at how incredibly heavy his body had become in the last few minutes. "Dan? How the hell do you get in here?"

Dan gave him a crooked smile. "There's a low spot on the riverbed side of the fence, out behind the kitchen compost bins. This kid was stationed here about two years ago. He was a Corps electrician, and he was Sandy's nephew. He diddled the fence a little, just enough so that you could slide under without getting zapped or setting off the alarm. Sandy and I know about it, no one else.''

"Thanks," Carter said.

He made sure Dan got out the gate safely. Black fog was creeping into the edges of his vision, lying in wait for him when he turned his head. It was rolling in fast and it tasted bitter, like defeat, like failure. There were no real beginnings and no clear endings here. The wind blew down the gorge, whirling dust into the air, wilting the waterless crops. It would be dry tomorrow. Dry next week. How many more water cuts? How much more bloodshed? Carter leaned his forehead against the window, staring out at a twisting column of dust in the street. A lot of people had to eat. A lot of people had to drink. The numbers had the last word, they sent the water here or there. The good guys didn't always win. Sometimes the bad guys did. Sometimes no one did. Carter reached for the phone, tired beyond belief. "I need a car and a driver," he said to the sergeant on duty. "I have to go down to Bonneville."

CHAPTER TWENTY-SEVEN ☆

Johnny's motel was still lighted—all of Bonneville was lighted.
Carter stared in confusion, realizing belatedly nearly a half hour
still remained until the power curfew, never mind that it felt like
3:00 A.M. Carter had the driver park the car by the motel office. He
got out, stifling a groan, to discover that every muscle in his body
had stiffened during the ride down from The Dalles. His ribs
speared him as he pushed open the office door. A string of metal
bells jangled and Carter jumped. Nita would know it—that he
was afraid to go knock on Johnny's door.

"Can I help you?" A heavy woman with a strong face and
wiry gray hair stuck her head into the room. "You need a
room?"

"I'm here to see a friend of mine. John Seldon. What room
is he in?"

"Just a moment and I'll ring him." Smiling a professional
and noncommittal smile for him, she picked up a cracked plastic
handset from behind the counter, punched numbers. "Hello?
This is the front desk. There's a man here to see you."

"Tell him it's Carter."

"A Carter? Okay." She smiled at Carter, a genuine smile this
time. "Fourteen," she said. "Third from the end."

"Thanks." He pushed through the door, out into the dry
night.

It was already getting cold. As he started across the parking
lot, the city lights winked off suddenly, leaving only a scattered
few gleams of exempted illumination. The sudden darkness
pressed down on him, heavy as the darkness inside a grave.
Carter hesitated, groping for an excuse to turn around, knowing
that there was none, could be none. A door opened, spilling light
across the dusty asphalt. The motel paid an exemption fee, then.

257

"Carter?" Johnny stood in the rectangle of light, a lanky, familiar silhouette. "Come on in, man. Shit, I'm glad to see you. Where the hell did you go this afternoon? Is what I'm seeing on the news true?"

"I don't know. I haven't had time to watch it." Carter walked into the room as Johnny stepped aside. It was a nice room, carpeted and freshly papered, with free water. A rumpled double bed faced the color TV. The remains of a sandwich lay atop a sheet of crumpled deli paper on the table and a bottle of beer stood on the nightstand.

"I was worried about you." Johnny peered into his face.

"Don't tell me I look like shit, okay?"

"You do, but I won't. You want a beer?" Johnny picked up the bottle on the nightstand. "I tried calling you at the base. Tell me about this crazy happening out at the Shunt—the media had something totally unreal about mass hysteria or something. Wobbly pictures of the Shunt, and people running, and a lot of confused locals claiming they'd seen water in the riverbed. *Water*, and the riverbed was dry as a bone. What's going on? Never mind. He shoved a chair at Carter. "Sit down. You look like you're going to fall down, for crying out loud. Where's the stuff you found? The stuff from Greely's house?"

Carter sat because his legs wouldn't hold him up any longer. It was damned easy to doubt what he knew—to fall into the old, comfortable patterns of friendship. Of trust. Johnny looked anxious. Because he'd been worried about Carter? Or because things hadn't worked out? Carter straightened his shoulders with an effort. "Tell me about Pacific BioSystems, Johnny."

"What about it?" Johnny's eyelids flickered—barely enough to notice. "Sure. What do you want to know?" He pulled up the other chair, turned it around, and straddled it.

"I want to know what you were trying to do." The words came out leaden, without expression. "Why frame Dan Greely and Hastings with Pacific Bio? Why ruin the farmers along the Columbia? What does it gain you?"

"What the fuck are you talking about?" Anger flashed across Johnny's face, turned into sudden comprehension. "Nita Montoya." He snapped his fingers. "She's been giving you an earful, hasn't she? Carter, I know how you feel about her." He shrugged, his face full of sympathy. "I think you're going to have to face the fact that she's in bed with Greely. She'll say anything to clear that guy."

No one can lie to me, Nita had cried, so full of anguish.

"You planted the information that ties Greely and Hastings to Pacific Bio. Proof exists that you did it," Carter said. "Hastings is dead. So is Delgado, so you're in the clear there, if he was working for you. But you can't slip out of this one clean." They hurt, those leaden words. Oh, God, they hurt. "You've been my best friend for a long time," Carter said softly. "But you've hurt a lot of people here. You've *killed* people, Johnny."

Time slowed to a crawl as they stared at each other. Carter remembered the crowded desert of the school halls and the faces that never really looked at him, or looked at him only with contempt. He remembered the alibis he'd given Johnny so that Johnny didn't catch shit for joyriding in the cars he swiped, or screwing around when he was supposed to be studying. He remembered the sticky feel of blood on his fingers and the cold reality of cell bars.

"I won't cover for you," he said unsteadily.

"I didn't kill anybody. You think you can save the whole fucking world, don't you?" Johnny looked away from him, his face twitching. "The world doesn't give a shit, Carter. You'd do better to save yourself and your friends."

"Delgado said something like that."

"Why couldn't you just leave it *alone*?" Johnny lurched to his feet. "You wouldn't have gotten hurt."

He had wanted Johnny to deny the whole thing, had been ready to believe him—as ready to believe that denial as he had been ready to believe in Dan Greely's guilt. Carter lowered his head. "Why?" he asked numbly. "Why did you do this, Johnny? You've got it all."

"Yeah, I have it all," Johnny whispered. "Do you know how fast I could lose it? After Amber and I split, I got a little crazy. You were busy with your fucking Army games, and I . . . was on my own." He stared down at Carter, haggard in the yellow light from the overhead fixture. "I was drinking, screwing around a lot. This little bitch I'd been seeing tried to shake me down one night. Blackmail! Yes, she was underage, but *she* solicited *me*. I—I didn't mean to kill her. Morissy showed up two days later. With pictures. She'd set the thing up with the girl, planning to lever me with the threat of a sex charge. And I'd handed her my ass on a platter." His face had gone white. "Morissy thought she *owned* me. No one owns me, Carter. No one. And this was the way out. Do you know what would happen if it came out that Pacific BioSystems had bribed a Corps general to give them extra water, that they had started a local water war? The media would crucify them with joy, and we'd have an excuse to really bring them to heel. Someone needs to yank the bastards into line, and if they leaned on me then, I could claim it was a frame. Revenge for exposing them. Carter?'' His lips trembled. ''The girl—it was an accident.''

An accident. ''Meanwhile, The Dalles ends up another Chicago,'' Carter said softly.

''I told you, you wouldn't have gotten hurt.'' Johnny made a chopping gesture with his hand. ''I made sure of that. Hastings and Greely would have taken the heat and you would have been a hero for finding out about it. I'd never have let you get stuck in the middle. Your ass has been covered the whole time. Everything would have worked out fine,'' he said bitterly. ''Those farmers ought to be planting bushes along the Columbia, anyway.''

''I fried out in the Dry. Did you have your hired help dump me out there just to turn me against the locals?'' Carter looked at Johnny, wondering what Nita would hear right now, wondering if he wanted to know. ''Who raped and murdered Candy Wilmer, Johnny? How much did he get paid for that? Ten people died down in that riverbed today. *Ten.* Delgado almost shot me. Did I mention that?''

''Sometimes things got out of hand.'' Johnny looked away. ''Delgado wouldn't have shot you. He was supposed to—''

''To shoot Dan? My God, I don't believe you're saying this stuff.'' Carter leaned his head in his hands, wanting to wake up, to sit up in bed and realize it was all a crazy nightmare. ''Does it matter so much, Johnny?'' he mumbled. ''A fucking seat on Water Policy?''

''Yes, it matters.''

The hissing intensity of Johnny's voice brought Carter's head up, raised the hairs on the back of his neck.

''My father's one of the top economists in the world. He's a fucking icon, and I'm Trevor Seldon's son. Not Johnny Seldon. All my life I've been *Trevor Seldon's son.*'' Johnny's eyes glittered. ''But now I'm Water Policy. *I* control his water. I control his fucking *life*. He's never had this much power, Carter. He never will.''

Carter looked away, hollow inside, full of pain. ''I told you that Private Wasson could identify the men who sprung Greely.

They were working for you, weren't they? Were you planning to kill her, too? How about me? You could kill me. Maybe no one else has any idea that you're behind this.''

"Stop it, Carter." Johnny's voice was low and hoarse. "I didn't shoot anyone, and no one can pin those deaths on me. I didn't murder that girl. Goddamn it. If you'd been around—if you hadn't gone into the fucking Army—this wouldn't have happened.''

"No, Johnny." Carter drew a slow, deep breath, and got stiffly to his feet. "It's not my fault. I should turn it over to the media—your connection to all this. Everything I know and guess." He stared at the flowered paper on the wall. "That's the only just thing to do—let the people who have been hurt know who really did the hurting." It would exonerate the Corps and Hastings. It would exonerate Carter. "If you resign from Water Policy . . . I won't," he said softly. "Because . . . once upon a time, you were my friend.''

"I can't just *resign*. Listen! Wait a minute!" Johnny's voice had gone high and tight. "I think we can cut a deal. You brought a civilian into the infirmary—yeah, I still have my sources, Carter—is he a friend of yours?" Johnny's eyes were desperate. "I also hear he's in bad shape. I'll pay for his treatment—whatever it takes to put him back together—if you'll dump anything incriminating—just forget we ever had this conversation. Do we have a deal?''

His hand on the door, Carter hesitated. What had Hastings said—that there were no innocent people along the riverbed? He'd been wrong. There was at least one innocent person in all this: Jeremy. He had never really been part of this war, but he had saved a lot of people. And he was going to pay a damn high price for doing so.

Carter closed his eyes briefly, seeing Johnny, really *seeing* him, for the first time. He would always come first. Not the numbers, not the thirsty men and women who lived or died by Water Policy's decisions; it was Johnny Seldon, first and foremost. "No," he whispered. What had Jeremy said about the Dry?—that sometimes you have to make ugly choices. "I want to hear on the news tomorrow that you've resigned.''

Nita would know. She would know that he had done this to Jeremy. He yanked the door open and stepped out into the cold, dusty night. Johnny called his name, but he didn't look back. The wind that never stopped blowing filled his eyes with grit and tears as he stumbled to the waiting car.

CHAPTER TWENTY-EIGHT ☆

The hospital corridor oppressed Nita. It was white and sterile, filled with echoes of pain and sickness. She tiptoed down it, her skin tight with gooseflesh even though it wasn't particularly cool, half expecting someone to stop her and demand to know what she was doing here. She'd come all the way to Portland to see Jeremy, who had been transferred from the base infirmary. The receptionist downstairs had told her his room number, but the numbers didn't want to behave rationally up here. Nita closed her eyes briefly, her head buzzing with the fog of discomfort-fear-despair that filled this place.

A chunky young woman in green pants and a loose green shirt paused on her way down the corridor. "Are you lost?" she asked with a smile.

"I'm looking for Jeremy Barlow. In room 421," Nita said. The woman's pleasant feel eased some of her tension. "I think I *am* lost."

"Not really. He's down here." The woman nodded at the right-hand corridor. "I'll take you." She fell in beside Nita, her curiosity like the smell of flowers in the air. "He has quite a talent, Jeremy. We moved him so that he could look out at the Willamette. Has he showed you the city? It was so *beautiful*." Her eyes had gone dreamy. "Pictures just don't do it, do they? You know, when I see it—really *see* it—I can believe it'll be like that again some day."

"He shows you?" Nita's surprise brought her to an abrupt halt.

"You bet." The woman raised a quizzical eyebrow at Nita's reaction, but decided to let it pass. "The more I do it, the better I can see it. I just caught a few glimpses at first, but some people see everything the first time. Clara, one of the surgical nurses, is good at it."

262

"That's wonderful," Nita said softly. He was showing people? Here? Where he couldn't escape?

"This is the place." The woman lifted a hand, smiling. "I'm Amelia Cary, by the way. A lowly resident. Say hi to Jeremy for me, will you? I'm supposed to be elsewhere right now."

"I will," Nita said, and pushed the oversize door open as the woman hurried away.

Jeremy was asleep. His face looked pale and fragile on the white pillow, haloed by his fair hair. Tubes trailed across the bed, IVs and a catheter, dripping fluid into his veins, carrying away the excess, as if Jeremy himself was nothing more than some kind of living filter removing a few nutrients from the slow, steady trickle of liquid. It frightened her. She shivered suddenly, wanting to shake him, wake him up so that she could be sure he was still Jeremy.

As if he had felt her anxiety, Jeremy's eyelids fluttered. "Hi." He turned his head on the pillow to look at her, and his smile was his own. "When did you get here?"

"A little while ago. They wouldn't let anyone in to see you before." She reached for his hand, closing her fingers tightly around his. "Jeremy, it's my fault. I should have heard Delgado. If I'd listened, I'd have known he was there. But Carter was going to kill Dan, and I just didn't listen . . ."

"Hey, stop." He squeezed her hand. "It's *not* your fault. Any of us could have ended up dead, any way it worked out. I'm not going to die, okay?" He squeezed her hand again, then grimaced and fingered the tubing taped to the back of his other hand. "It itches," he said. "I think they're through with all the surgery. That's what Dr. Cary told me this morning, anyway."

He wasn't sad. "Jeremy?" Nita framed the question she wanted to ask, but the words wouldn't come. *Spinal damage*, Dan had told her. *Maybe he'll walk and maybe he won't. They don't know yet.*

"Dr. Imenez was in this morning." Jeremy's eyes were on her face and he smiled now, reaching up to touch her cheek. "He's the one who's been doing the fancy stuff—something with fetal cells. He stuck me with a needle this morning. Up and down my legs. I couldn't feel anything when he did it before, but this time . . . I did. Not all the sticks, but some of them. He was pleased, Nita." He pushed her braid back over her shoulder. "I guess it looks good."

"Jeremy, I'm so glad!" She held his hands, smiling with the bright glow of his hope. He wouldn't have to spend the rest of his life in a bed in Dan's house. Surely. "I met Dr. Cary," she said, remembering the message suddenly. "She said to say hi. She said you were showing people your visions."

"I . . . am." He smiled, a little more tentatively this time. "It scares me—you can feel it, right? But I'm doing it. They're even running some tests—doing EEGs while I'm making stuff. They don't have a clue." He shrugged, uneasy, but not scared. "A lot of people don't see the visions very clearly at first. I still don't know why everyone saw the flood in the riverbed."

"It was because of the mob," Nita said. "I *knew* it was you, and it still terrified me. All the emotions ran together, sort of overlapped. Enough people saw the flood that they infected the others." She grimaced. "Or something like that."

"I guess it worked." Jeremy closed his eyes. "Carter said that a lot more people would have died if the flood hadn't shaken things up."

"A lot more," Nita said softly. His face looked thin, shadowed with recent pain. "Dan would have died. And Carter."

"You were right, Nita. About my not wanting to face the visions." He looked away from her. "The butterflies, the little stuff—they were okay, because they didn't really matter. They were just tricks. Fluff. The visions were . . . different. Maybe I blamed myself. Because they couldn't save my dad. I wanted them to save him, but they hurt him instead. He saw what the land had been like once, and . . . something broke inside him. I think . . . maybe he died sooner, because of it."

"No." Nita clutched his hand. "That's not true."

"Not even you can know that for sure, Nita." Jeremy smiled at her—a sad smile. "Whether it hurt him or not, they're *me*, the visions. My gift. I have to face it. I have to use it. You're right."

"Dr. Cary said it gave her hope." Nita swallowed tears. "That the world could be like that again some day."

Jeremy's smile warmed her. "It's still going to scare some people, make some people crazy, but I guess there's a price for everything, right?"

"Yes." Nita felt the smile tremble on her lips, made it stronger.

"What's wrong?" Jeremy's fingers tightened around hers. "What's troubling you, Nita? Carter?"

"So who reads minds now?" She laughed, but it caught in her throat.

"I don't need to try very hard. He was here this morning." Jeremy wouldn't let go of her hand. "I asked him about you. He said he hadn't seen you."

He was sad for her. Maybe that was just the way it had to be. *Her* price. "He hasn't been around The Dalles much." Nita looked away. "I haven't been to the base, either. Lydia gave Renny the connection that proves Johnny framed Hastings and Dan. I gave it to Dan, and he took it to Carter. Johnny's already resigned from the Water Policy Committee." She shrugged, making her voice light. "I've been . . . busy. Dan, Sandy, and I have all been busy. We've been trying to smooth things out between The Dalles and the Corps." *We.* "You know, I'm doing what Dan wanted, after all. I'm following in my father's footsteps."

"You're doing what you need to do," Jeremy said softly.

"I think so."

He sighed and frowned up at the ceiling. "Did you know that Johnny Seldon paid for my treatment? I couldn't have afforded it otherwise."

"Him?" Her eyes widened. "Why?"

"I don't know." Jeremy touched his abdomen lightly. "He came to see me. He's a strange man." He fell silent for a moment, frowning. "He said to tell Carter that this was a gift. Then he left."

"What did Carter say?"

"Nothing. He got kind of quiet when I told him, so I didn't ask. I'll take it," Jeremy said lightly. "I don't care where it comes from."

He had been terrified that he would be paralyzed. She could still hear the echoes of that fear. "It's all right now." Nita brushed a wisp of blond hair back from his face. His eyes were so blue—the color of the sky above the riverbed on a windless day. David's eyes had been almost that color. "I've got to go," she said. "Renny's got Rachel. She gave me a ride over here."

"Renny?" He laughed. "She doesn't strike me as the motherly type."

Nita smiled. "She says Rachel's not bad for a kid, told me she'd take her on as an apprentice in a few years."

"Rachel could do worse."

Through the window, she could see the river, and the city center on the far bank. Green grass fringed the sparkling sweep

of river, glowing in the sun. Trees bloomed along the sidewalks,
their bare branches clouded with pink blossoms. "It was so
beautiful," Nita breathed. "Thank you, Jeremy." She leaned
forward to kiss him gently on the lips. "I'll be back when I
can."

"Nita?" Jeremy's eyes were full of sympathy. "When I get
out of here . . . I'm going down to Tygh Valley. To see if that
kid they stoned might still be alive somewhere. He's like us,
Nita. There are other kids out there like us—other adults. I'm
going to start looking for them. Maybe we're some kind of answer and maybe we aren't, but we need to know about each
other. If you want to come along, I'd like the company."

If Carter is afraid of you, he meant. If you need to get away.
Dan was afraid of her, as David had been. "I might take you
up on it." Nita smiled for him. "I'll let you know." She left
the room before he could see her tears.

"You took your time." Renny sat in the strip of shade cast
by her battered loaner. Rachel was standing between her knees,
wobbly and delighted. "The kid's ready to start running," Renny
said. "She gets pissed when it doesn't work. I like her attitude."
She laughed and handed the drooling Rachel up to Nita. "Let's
go, babe. Feed her in the car if you've got to. I'm due on the
road."

"Can we make one stop?" Nita asked her as she climbed into
the car's baking interior. "Just for a couple of minutes?"

"Where and why?"

"In Mosier." Nita looked away from the comprehension in
Renny's eyes.

"Sure, babe," she said, and there was a trace of sadness
beneath her words.

It was one of those rare windless days in the riverbed. Nita
left Renny at the car with the sleeping Rachel and walked up the
steep little street, past the sagging white house where Julio Moreno sold his secondhand clothes and furniture. He was out on
his cluttered porch and he raised his good hand in a gesture that
was almost a salute. Nita nodded and smiled, but didn't stop.

Dust puffed up from beneath her feet to hang in the still air.
The heat stifled Nita, baking her flesh on her bones. The single
tree in the tiny cemetery cast a thin shade across the dust. The
newer stones were just pieces of lava or river rock; names and
dates had been scrawled across them in black, or blue, or silver

paint. Leaf shadows dappled the grave where Julio had buried the bones. Nita knelt in the dust beside the stone. She hadn't been able to find any flowers this late in the year, but she laid the small bunch of greenery that she had gathered on the grave: desert parsley and wheatgrass, a sprig of yarrow. At least the leaves were green and alive, even if they were already wilting. The stone was rectangular, reddish brown, smooth enough to have been shaped by hand instead of by nature. Nita touched the surface with her forefinger, feeling the tiny grains of sand beneath her fingertip. A few feet away another rough stone marked a grave. LUIS HANSEN read the fading blue letters. There were no dates on the stone, just the name.

Child? Nita wondered. Old man? She sighed and pulled the nail from her pocket. D. She scratched the letter into the surface, wavery white lines as crooked as the embroidered letters on the pack. A. David, I loved you. I still love you. V I D. You gave me space to grow up. You kept me safe. A S. I don't think I need anyone to keep me safe anymore. C H E R. She put the nail back into her pocket and put the bunch of greens on the stone. "I have to let you go," she whispered.

" 'David Ascher,' " Renny said from behind her. "You've made up your mind, huh?"

"Yes, I have." Nita stood up and took Rachel from the trucker's arms. "I loved him." She looked up at the dry folded hills above her. "If he's still alive, I hope he finds happiness."

"Come on, babe." Renny touched her shoulder. "I've got a schedule to keep."

Nita looked down at the stone for a last minute. An ending and a beginning. She would have to ask Dan where her father was buried. Julio had disappeared from his porch and the little town looked deserted as people waited out the afternoon heat. Water was running in the soaker hoses again—for now. When it got cooler, men, women and children would go out to work the fields until it got too dark to see, shaping their lives to fit the harsh rhythms of sun and water. This is what matters, Nita thought. We can look at Jeremy's green visions and hope for that future, but right now, this is what has to matter.

"Thanks for the ride," Nita said.

"I had nothing better to do." Renny slid into the front seat, reaching for Rachel who yawned and blinked. "You know, when we made our little bargain, I was planning to call you into my bed for a couple of nights." She chuckled softly. "I could tell it had crossed your mind and that you didn't like the idea much.

I thought you were sleeping with Dan, so I figured I could wing two birds with one stone.''

"I still owe you," Nita said. "You took Rachel, in the riverbed.''

"She'll make a good trucker, that kid." Renny handed Rachel to Nita and pulled her door closed. "We're even, babe. You make me think about things." She reached inside her denim shirt and pulled out a brown envelope. "This is for you."

Nita opened the envelope, removed the folded sheets. It was a copy of a land title, made out to her. "Your farm," she said.

"Jesse's farm, not mine." Renny pulled onto the old highway. "It was never mine. You can give it to Dan if you want. Or you can keep it and make your own deals." She shrugged, looking sideways at Nita. "Lydia told me a weird thing. She said you can hear what people think. Is there anything in that, babe?"

"I hear a little bit," Nita said softly.

"Too bad you didn't come along earlier." Renny turned her attention back to the road, but not before Nita caught the glint of tears in her eyes. They were climbing up over the crest now, the engine growling a protest as Renny shifted down. Up ahead was the promontory where Jeremy had called up a long-ago spring to comfort her. He was going to go looking for others like them. Not freaks. Not misfits. Different, Nita thought. That's all we are.

"Could you let me off here?" she asked suddenly.

"I can't wait, and it's a long walk to town. You sure, babe?"

"I'm sure."

Renny pulled the car into the crumbling circular drive. People might have come here just to look down on the riverbed—no, the river—in the old days. Nita looked at the dry rocky gash, remembering shimmering water and the soft tints of green life that Jeremy had showed her. Yes, it would have been worth coming up here, just to look.

"See you next trip," Renny said. "Take care of yourself."

Regretful? "I will." Nita leaned down for Rachel. "You take care of yourself, too. Can't you let Lydia help?" she asked softly.

"We tried that once. Hell, who knows? We might give it another shot sometime." Renny pulled the door closed, then lifted a hand to Nita.

The engine roared and the car leaped forward, down to The Dalles, where Renny would pick up her rig and head eastward; toward Boise, the next plaza, and the next deal. Always heading down the road, never looking back. Holding carefully to Rachel, Nita climbed the tangled ruin of old fence and walked out onto the promontory. There was no pool here today, just dust and stones and a view of the riverbed. For a moment Nita regretted her decision to come here. Veins of rock marched across the far side of the gorge, streaked brown and gray, carrying her eye farther and farther east, to where the walls of the gorge and the rocky bed of the river blurred into opalescent haze. Nita spread Rachel's quilt in the strip of shade cast by a dead tree trunk and sat with her back against the dry wood.

"This is our world." Nita propped her daughter against her raised knees. "There's beauty in it, if you look for it. We'd better look for it, because that's all we're going to get."

Rachel cooed and drooled, reaching for Nita's hair.

The sound of a car cut through the quiet, and Nita looked over her shoulder as the engine throbbed and died. A Corps pickup had parked by the ruined fence. She knew who was in it before he had even opened the door—she would probably have recognized him even in the middle of Portland.

Carter stepped gingerly across the old wire and walked toward her, a little hesitant. "I ran into Renny at the highway ramp," he said. "She told me you were up here."

"Did she?" Nita slid over and Carter sat on the quilt beside her, close enough that their bodies touched, arm against arm, leg against leg.

"I'm sorry. That I haven't come by." He looked out over the gorge, frowning, shy inside, unsure. "Johnny quit Water Policy," he said. "Renny's friend vanished the fake evidence against Dan and Hastings. I don't know who actually did the shooting around here, or killed Candy Wilmer. Probably the people who were working for Johnny. If Durer catches them, they might implicate Johnny, but so far they seem to have disappeared." Carter drew a slow breath. "I'm going to let it go at that. Dan's pissed at me, and he has reason to be, but he's going along with it."

"Because Johnny paid for Jeremy?" Nita asked softly.

"No." Pain lay beneath Carter's brief laugh. "He did that on his own. I don't know why."

"Because he was your friend once," Nita said softly.

"Do you *know* that?" His voice quivered, just a hair.

"I know that." She looked down at her daughter and stroked a wisp of dark hair back from her face, hurting with his hurt.

"I'm going to stay on here," he said slowly. "With the Corps or without it. People need to stand in the middle around here. They need to stick their necks out—like Dan. And your father.''

''And you,'' Nita said, because that was what he had done. ''And you'll always blame yourself a little for letting Johnny off. You'll always feel a little guilty, and I'll always know it. Carter? Will that keep it alive for you? Make it worse?''

He looked at her at last. ''I . . . didn't come looking for you,'' he said. ''Because I had to know how I felt about you . . . about what you are.''

Nita waited, her heart pounding suddenly, wanting to cover her ears, wanting to get up and run.

''Sometimes it's going to drive me nuts that you know how I feel. And sometimes it's going to be wonderful.'' He drew a slow breath, his eyes as dark as the rocks beneath the dust. ''I'm not afraid of you, Nita. I'm not afraid of what you are.''

No. He wasn't afraid. Nita took his face between her palms and kissed him. This time, there was no anger in their kiss— only love, apology, and a leisurely anticipation of what would come next.

Rachel's delighted crowing finally broke them apart. ''Child, you are going to get educated early,'' Nita said breathlessly.

''It's going to be tough around here.'' Carter put his arm around her. ''A lot of people have already gotten foreclosure notices from the Federal Credit Bureau. Full irrigation flow isn't going to be restored for another two weeks.''

''There aren't any good answers, are there?'' Nita looked into his eyes. ''Maybe all we can do is choose the best of bad choices. Sending Johnny to jail wouldn't help the people in the riverbed, would it?''

''I guess not. Dan said about the same thing. He's not too pissed.'' Carter shrugged, but some of his bitterness had eased. ''I guess we'll do the best we can.'' He pulled her lightly against him and kissed her again.

Nita closed her eyes, breathing his scent, tasting his skin, remembering, anticipating.

Rachel fussed.

''She's hungry.'' Nita sighed. ''See what happens when you get involved with nursing women?''

''I see,'' Carter said soberly, and then he laughed.

It was a happy sound; she couldn't remember ever hearing him laugh like that. He stretched out on the quilt and Nita pillowed her head on his shoulder, careful of his injured ribs. Tucked between them, Rachel nursed contentedly.

"Will you move in with me?" Carter asked.

"Not . . . right away." Nita stared down at the riverbed, listening to the slow, steady beat of her pulse, like a clock ticking away the seconds of her life. "I've hidden from the world . . . and what I am . . . all my life. I love you, and I could hide in that, too. I'm through hiding. I need to find out who I am and what I can do."

"Like Jeremy?"

"Like Jeremy. I have to do it on my own, Carter. But I love you and I'll be your lover. Enthusiastically."

"I'll buy that." He grimaced. "I guess I have to buy that. Oh, well. At least you won't have to sneak in under the fence." He rolled onto his side to look down into her face. "You know how I feel," he said softly.

"I do." Nita reached up, tracing the curve of his lips. "I feel the same way, and it scares me."

"Good," he said. "That makes two of us."

About the Author

Mary Rosenblum is a graduate of the 1988 Clarion West writers' workshop whose short stories have appeared in *Isaac Asimov's Science Fiction Magazine*, *Fantasy and Science Fiction*, and various anthologies. She currently resides in Oregon with her husband, two sons, and an eclectic assortment of livestock. *The Drylands* is her first novel.

DEL REY DISCOVERY

Experience the wonder of discovery
with Del Rey's newest authors!

. . . Because something new is
always worth the risk!

TURN THE PAGE FOR AN
EXCERPT FROM THE
NEXT *DEL REY DISCOVERY*:

McLendon's Syndrome
by Robert Frezza

A few tables away, Dinky the piano player was trying to learn "As Time Goes By." He was making a hash of it.

I whipped a Brazil nut out of a bowl and whacked it open with a sap borrowed for the occasion. The bowl was marked with the Prancing Pony Bar and Grill logo on one side and had "Squirrel Food" printed on the other.

A glass of limewater slid across the table, spun around twice, and stopped artistically beside my right hand. " 'Lo, Harry," I said without looking.

Harry, the Prancing Pony's proprietor, leaned across the table, which trembled slightly. He grinned. "Hello, Admiral." Clad from head to toe in Lincoln green, Harry could have passed for the bottom half of a very large tree. Portions of his green suit were covered with leaflike tendrils, which enhanced the effect only slightly.

I pitched the nut at him. "It's Journeyman MacKay to you, O fat innkeeper who only remembers his name because people shout it at him all day."

For some reason, Harry loves this line and encourages me to use it. His face broke out in various interesting directions. "Roger that, Ken." He eased himself into a chair. "How're they cooking?"

I sighed. "They're cooking, Harry. They're still cooking." In three trips to Schuyler's World, I'd spent a fair amount of time in Harry's bar and figured out most of his more obvious peculiarities. I pointed my thumb toward the ceiling. "You know, Harry. About this 'Admiral' bit—the itinerant ship I have the misfortune to crew is far more likely to be mistaken for orbiting junk than a Navy vessel, and since neither my civilian career as a journeyman spacer nor my military career as a reservist seems to be sprouting jets . . .''

Harry waited expectantly.

I figuratively threw up my hands. "Oh, skip it."

Deep disappointment welled up in Harry's eyes. Harry knows I'm an ensign in the inactive Navy reserve, which probably gives me more social cachet than most of Harry's clientele. Harry likes all things military and enjoys bumping people he likes up a grade or so—in my case from ensign to admiral.

I softened the blow for him. "Tell you what, Harry, I'll roll you double or nothing."

We used his dice, so two limewaters went on my tab. "You shouldn't be so hard on the *The Scupper*. She's not so bad," Harry said complacently.

"She's a cut above space debris," I conceded.

He shrugged. "I'm surprised to see you tonight. I thought you said you were heading out."

I waved my hands expressively. "Davie Lloyd Ironsides changed his mind for about the fourth time this week. Davie Lloyd the Iron-Ass is getting on my nerves a bit more than usual. I keep hoping he'll jam his pipe in the wrong orifice or something to break the monotony."

"I'm glad you decided to drop by. I figured it was going to be a dull night. Nice of you," he said, staring at one patron who suddenly decided that he didn't need a drink right that minute.

"The way I roll, you ought to pay me to stop in," I told him. "By choice, I'd have been in Callahan's Place, swilling your competitor's brew, but Elaine O'Day preempted that watering hole by virtue of seniority, intending to cuddle anything that could walk, fly or crawl."

"You know, Ken, I always thought torchship crews were supposed to cling like sand in cement," Harry observed.

I shuddered. "You must not remember Elaine. In any case, my shipmates avoid laying eyes on each other dirtside, and O'Day is not necessarily my first choice as a shift partner."

"Yeah, you mentioned that. She may not even be your second choice," Harry said, apparently recalling some of my pithier comments. "I brewed up a fresh batch of stew. Want some?"

"Uh, no thanks." Harry's son-of-a-bitch stew is made from the parts of a bull the bull can least do without. "How's business?"

Harry shook his head. "Not even fair. None of the farmers

are in town, and there's only one ship in orbit besides yours, one of the Rodents'."

"Rodents?"

"Two lights over. It's listed as Dennison's World. They have a few ships that touch here on their way out." Harry pointed to two dark, fuzzy bowling pins sitting on the other side of the room. "The big one there is a wheel over at the consulate."

It seemed natural to have large furry things sitting around Harry's bar. His hole in the wall looks more like a hole in the ground—he has fake tree roots dangling from the ceiling and mushrooms growing in hanging baskets. "He likes the place?" I commented.

Harry leaned over. "He gets buzzed on honey," he whispered.

"And you charge him double when he does," I replied, and bounced a nut off his chest.

Harry winked and grinned. Harry is an even-tempered guy who wouldn't hurt a fly—unless the fly really deserved it.

"How're things with you?" he asked, but his attention began to wander when a minor disturbance commenced involving a couple of barstools and a good-time girl on the other side of the room.

As Dinky switched to something a little up-tempo, Harry pushed back his chair and reclaimed the sap I'd been using to crack nuts. "Ken, I'm my own bouncer tonight, I've got to run. Oh, there's a woman, good-looking if you like them thin. She's been asking about you. You must be popular."

"Oh? That's news to me."

"Over there in the dark glasses," he said. He scurried off, pausing on the way to gently swat one enterprising citizen who had absently begun playing mumblety-peg on the table.

Harry keeps the place dark enough for the good-time girls to make a living, so it took me a few seconds to spot her. She was in the corner with a glass a few tables down from the two Rodents. Her hair was ash blond, shoulder-length. She was wearing a large silver butterfly pinned on a black bodysuit and large oval sunglasses, which looked strange even for the Prancing Pony. She was slim and wore black very well—her skin was fair and then some, pure alabaster. A long scar on her left hand made it look whiter by contrast.

The shades were definitely out of place. She must have noticed me staring, because she grinned—lots of teeth, but better proportioned than Harry's.

I knocked back half my limewater and made a wide circuit around the riot, dropping coins in Dinky's jar along the way. When I got to her table, I asked politely, "Hello, bright eyes. Is this seat taken?"

She looked up. "Not at all, spacer."

"Ken," said I, hoping to keep things on a first-name basis. As I parked, Dinky shifted to something slow and romantic.

"Catarina." She had a solitaire layout spread on the table in front of her, and I noticed her butterfly was sprinkled with blue stones.

I'm not real good with snappy pickup lines. She must have seen me hesitate, because she smiled. "Yes, I know I can put the black jack on the red queen, and no, please don't tell me how dangerous it is to fly your ship into a black hole."

Black holes aren't holes, nobody ever flies "into" one, and the procedure is about as dangerous as hopping the shuttle. The line is primarily known for its remarkable effect on vapid young things.

I must have looked hurt, because her smile widened.

"Let me buy you another drink."

"Uh, thanks. No." I consider myself a friend of Harry's, and his liquor is strictly for customers—Harry being perennially short of friends and unwilling to place the ones he has at risk.

"Business, then. You're Kenneth MacKay, off *Rustam's Slipper*."

I coughed.

"Occasionally known as *The Rusty Scupper*," she conceded. "You hit Schuyler's World four days ago. Your middle name is Andrew. You have ten months' seniority on a journeyman's rate, a reserve Naval commission, and an identifying mark on your left knee."

I looked down at my knees and then over at the cheatsheet she had spread across hers. "Are my eyes really brown?"

"You've seen *Casablanca*?"

"All four versions, including the one set on the moons of Jupiter. I've seen several versions more than once, *not* including the one set on the moons of Jupiter."

She chuckled again, sweeping up her cards and tucking them away into a little belt purse.

"Looking for a ship?"

"Curiously, I am." She was looking at me from behind those thick sunshades.

"Oh, a ship. That lets out *The Scupper*."

She actually thought that was funny. Just then a body came hurtling by our table, closely followed by a flying bowl of stew for emphasis. "Is it like this all the time here?" she asked.

I looked over to where Harry was escorting one citizen to the door and slightly beyond. "I understand around midnight the place gets lively," I said, and added, "Please don't feed me lines like that."

She clinked her glass against mine. "It's a deal."

"What do you plan on shipping?" I asked. The dark glasses and the way the conversation was becoming unhinged were both bothering me.

"How long do you plan on staying with the ship?" she asked, ignoring my question.

"At least another two months, eleven days, and four hours, but who's counting." I lowered my voice. "I'm sure you'd look spectacular without the sunglasses."

I saw her hesitate. She started to say something, but I shook my head. She peeled them back and blinked her eyes. She wasn't blind, she wasn't albino, but I sure bring home weird ones. Still, she had a great deal more about her than any other patron of Harry's, and I was about to cast my line when something struck me wrong.

It took a few seconds for me to puzzle it out. I wouldn't buy a suit in the light Harry keeps in his place, but I could see that the pupils of her eyes weren't even dilated.

I notice things like that. "Grandmother, what big eyes you have," I said. Something was clicking, but I couldn't put it together.

"They're very sensitive to light," she said with care.

"Grandmother, what fine, white, delicate skin you have."

She smiled wide. "Beauty cream and lots of sleep," she said with utter insincerity.

"Grandmother, what big teeth you have," I said waiting for the thought to decrypt before I made too much of an ass of myself.

She looked at me levelly for a long minute. "They're still growing a little."

It all come together. "I get it. You're a vampire!"

Science Fiction

at its best
from
Tara K. Harper